THE GIRLS IN THE CABIN

An absolutely unputdownable psychological thriller
packed with heart-stopping twists

CALEB STEPHENS

Joffe Books, London
www.joffebooks.com

First published in Great Britain in 2023

Cover art by Nick Castle

ISBN: 978-1-80405-918-0

CHAPTER ONE

CLARA
1984

Clara Carver never much liked the Black Place. Even at age nine, a big girl now, she'd never grown used to its rancid smell and the things that would brush across her skin like fallen eyelashes in the dark. She would leap to her feet and smack at her neck or her leg, and sometimes her hand would come away wet with an insect's insides. Sometimes, and more often than not, she would leave the Black Place covered in welts from the ants and blister beetles that lived there, anxious for Mother's calamine lotion to calm her sores.

Father told her the length of time she spent in the Black Place was up to her. If she were to mind her manners and do what he said, she could leave as quickly as a few short hours. If she were to cry and bang and cause a ruckus, time would pass much slower. Father said the things he did to her — the things that made her insides churn and left her whimpering with her arms wrapped around her knees — were a sign of his love for her.

"Clara, never forget how much I love you."

It seemed that his love changed with his moods. When the corn came in thick and sweet, and money was flush, Father would take Clara for ice cream at the malt shop in Meeker, along with Mother. He would

1

laugh and tell stories of the harvest, and how hard the men worked to bring it in. Mother would lace her fingers together and smile at him, and to anyone who passed, they seemed a normal enough family.

There were other times, though, when Father came home smelling of liquor and dragged Clara from whatever she was doing, out through the backyard and into the fields toward the Black Place. Sometimes, Father would force Mother to join him. She never resisted, but she didn't seem to enjoy it much, and Clara guessed she did what he wanted because she preferred those things to a belt or his fists in her stomach.

Clara only resisted once at age six. She'd been playing in her room with her favorite doll, Mabel, who had a head full of lemon yarn hair, when Father told her to come. She said no. It was late, and she couldn't bear the thought of leaving Mabel all alone for the night. When Father grabbed her, Clara clawed and scratched and kicked and bit. As a result, Father left her in the Black Place for two days. When Clara returned to her room, it was to Mabel lying torn in half with her cotton insides strewn over the pink comforter. Clara cried for a week, and, after that, she decided she would cry no more.

She learned to endure the Black Place. She forced herself to find comfort in the small places Father couldn't touch. She imagined a park with bright green grass and other children who would chase her up and down slides and push her on blue bucket swings. She pictured places other than the dust-caked farm with its rusted buildings and abandoned tractor equipment, places she'd seen in magazines and read about in books. Places like France with its gleaming metal cities and sun-speckled beaches, the sand as white as snow. She told herself, someday, she would escape the farm and go there.

But not today. Today was worse than most. Her stomach hurt, and sharp cramps tore through her abdomen like shards of glass. She craved light and air. She needed to escape the sweltering dark and reeking stench of the Black Place. It was as if something were swelling within her, a creature inside she could no longer control. It burst up her throat, and she climbed the steps to the hatch door and clawed and scraped and screamed for someone — for anyone — to free her. She smashed her fists against the iron hatch until her knuckles bled. Clara didn't care if her shouts brought the wrath of Father. She only wanted out.

2

But no one came, and she was about to return to her cot when she heard something click. She cupped a hand against a seam of light as the hatch squealed open, half-expecting to see the familiar outline of Mother's cruel scowl or Father's hard, brown eyes. Instead, she saw a girl not much older than herself with soft, white skin and a waterfall of raven-black hair. She wore a warm smile and a dress the color of the summer sky.

"Hello," the girl said. "I heard you knocking. Would you like to come out?"

Clara nodded and knew she had finally found a friend.

CHAPTER TWO

KAYLA
2022
DAY ONE

I climb a jutting slab of rock and hold Dad's phone skyward, tap it and hope for a signal or a text, anything to prove the outside world still exists. After three days of backpacking through nowhere, Colorado, I'm not sure it does.

I'm so *pissed* at Dad for dragging us out here. Camping somewhere new every night sucks, Dad snoring away in the tent like a broken tractor engine on one side and Emma kicking me on the other. If I had my phone, maybe I could distract myself. But no, Dad made me leave it in the car, even when I begged and begged. "*Sorry, kiddo, but we need to spend some time together as a family.*" What a load of crap. We stopped being a family the minute Mom died. Now we're just three strangers who live together.

Besides, camping was Mom's thing. Not his. He's only doing it because he thinks he has to — because Mom always talked about backpacking in Colorado someday. He's driving me crazy, asking me all these questions about boys and school and volleyball like he cares, which he doesn't. Not really. All he's ever cared about is his work because it gets him away from me and Emma and all of our drama. Or it used to, anyway. Now, with Mom gone, he's stuck with us.

But whatever; it's not like I can do anything about it. And, I have to admit, Colorado *is* pretty. There are lakes everywhere, stamped in perfect blue circles in between all the fir and pine. And the aspen trees, *wow*, are the leaves amazing — all these oranges and reds sparkling for as far as you can see. When we hike above the tree line, I can almost lose myself in the scenery. I say "almost" because the moment I do, I can practically feel Mom standing next to me, whispering in my ear.

Isn't it so beautiful, Kit Kat?

Everything has been so shitty since she died. I can't remember the last time I felt happy. About anything, really. It would help if I could talk to someone, but Dad is oblivious, and Mimi is never around anymore. Even if she were, she doesn't get me the way Mom did. I can't tell her about the stuff with Ethan and what a dick he was to ditch me right after we hooked up. It was my first time, and it couldn't have been worse. He won't even look at me now. Mom always told me to wait, that my first time should be special, but that if I did go through with it, I should tell her. And I *would* have. I totally would have. She wanted to be there to support me. Now there's no one to do that except Dad.

Dad. Ugh, he thinks everything is just fine because I hang out with Bree and Abby from time to time and get decent grades. He has no idea how much I hate my pasty white legs and skeleton arms, or that my chest belongs to someone in middle school, not that anyone notices. I'm pretty much invisible at Brookline High School. Or I was before Mom died, anyway. Now everyone looks at me like I'm damaged goods:

She's the one whose mom died, right?

God, she looks so sad all the time . . .

Oh, poor thing, that must be so hard on her. Cancer, I hear.

At first, I thought Mom would beat it. She'd sit there and tell me so — *"I'm going to beat this, Kayla. I promise."* — and I was dumb enough to believe her because she seemed so strong. What a joke. She never stood a chance.

I settle onto the rock and stare at Dad's phone, the dumb thing, then click on the photo icon. A picture appears, one of Bernie mid-bark, chasing Emma around the backyard with her sundress flared behind her like a cape. It's easy to tell the picture is B.C. (Before Cancer) because she's got this big smile splashed on her face. A real one, with the corners of her eyes crinkled. In the A.C. pictures, Emma's smiles are gone, or if they're there, they're totally fake.

My finger hovers over the screen, and I tell myself not to do it, not to swipe because I know what comes next. I do it anyway. It's a selfie of me and Mom at Canobie Lake, Mom in her swimsuit right after her diagnosis, looking happy, normal even, with her face still full and round. (*I can beat this!*) I swipe again, fall now, the leaves changing, Public Park alive with color. Mom's hair is gone in this one, her head wrapped in a cherry silk scarf. I hated it when she lost her hair. It felt so mean. Like, how could God take something so beautiful after all he'd put her through, the very thing she loved the most?

I keep scrolling, and my throat swells when I reach the hospital pictures. The first is of Emma nestled next to Mom on the bed, Mom giving the camera a cheery, fake thumbs-up. (*Maybe I'll beat this?*) Then one of me plopped in a chair beside her, crying. She has her hand to my chin, both of us staring at each other and being honest for once: there is no beating this, not this time. I remember looking at her and thinking, *Don't you do it. Don't you dare leave me. I can't handle it.* But I knew she would, and there was nothing — absolutely *nothing* — I could do about it.

"That's one of my favorites."

I nearly drop the phone. Dad stands behind me with his arms crossed and his face flushed red from the climb. For a second, I think he's about to blow up on me for leaving

Emma by herself back at camp, but instead, he settles onto the rock and pats my leg.

"She's so beautiful in that picture, don't you think?"

I glance at it, annoyed. Mom wasn't the only one he thought was beautiful.

"You look just like her, you know."

"That's what you always say." And he does. All the time. It drives me nuts. It's why I avoid mirrors. Every time I pass one, I see Mom staring back. Her auburn hair. Her lake-green eyes. The lips that are, in my opinion, a little too thin, set above a neck that's definitely a little too long.

"You know I said no phones on this trip, Kit Kat."

"Yeah, and I left mine in the car." *Kit Kat.* Mom's nickname for me since I was five. I used to love it. Now I can't stand it, especially when he says it.

"Hand it over," he says.

I toss it into his lap. "Fine. It's not like it works up here, anyway."

"Look, just hang in there one more day. You can call all your friends tomorrow when we're back in the car, okay?"

"Whatever," I mumble.

He falls silent, and we sit there for an awkward moment, watching the clouds blow off the mountains. I know what he's thinking, because I'm thinking it, too: I wish we could go back. Back to when cancer wasn't a thing and Mom was still alive. We all wish it. Especially Emma. She thinks if she just doesn't talk, doesn't say *anything*, it will somehow change things and bring Mom back. But it won't. Nothing will. She's gone, and no matter how quiet Emma is, or how badly Dad wants to fix everything, or how angry I get, things will never be the same.

He squeezes my knee. "We'd better get back before Emma jumps in the lake."

She won't. She doesn't do anything these days but sit around, looking sad while she colors.

"Besides," he says, pointing at the clouds, "rain's on the way. We need to set up the tent."

I move to stand, but he keeps his hand on my knee a moment longer, his eyes serious like he's about to have one of his "Dad" talks.

"What?" I ask, hoping to get it over with. I can't handle his lies, how he says he cares and how sorry he is for everything. *Blah, blah, blah.*

I groan, and he shuts his mouth, suddenly looking angry. My eyes heat up again, but I won't cry. Not here. Not anywhere. *Especially* in front of him. After the last year, I'm all cried out.

With a sigh, I stand and head for the trail before he can stop me.

CHAPTER THREE

CHRIS

We set back toward camp with leaves sprinkled around us in scatters of scarlet and gold. Ancient strands of blue spruce rise toward a gray sky, marbled and thick with the promise of rain. I can already smell the ozone dissolving in the air, blending with the sweet tang of pine sap and earth.

Kayla leads, flattening the dense mountain grass as she threads her way down the slope. She slows and steps gingerly over a fallen log, and I think for the thousandth time that she moves like Lexi. The way she centers her weight on the balls of her feet with each step, the way she swings her arms . . . it's almost enough to convince me I'm walking behind my dead wife and not my daughter. It's so damn frustrating. Kayla talks like her, smiles like her, does everything *just like her*, this living echo of Lexi; just enough proof to convince me that, *yes Chris*, she was here and, *yes Chris*, you did have that perfect life once.

That *other* life . . .

And Kayla is so damn frustrating. She shut me out the minute Lexi died, and no matter what I do, she won't let me back in. Not that I've ever fully understood what makes her tick, or what, exactly, it is she's thinking when she looks at me with her mother's eyes. I could at least figure out Lexi from time to time. Not Kayla. She was born beautifully pissed off — this red-faced, fist-balled infant ready to grab life by the throat. I never knew what might set her off. I still don't. Only Lexi did. She was the key to Kayla's puzzle, the one who cooled her flame, and now, with Lexi gone, I'm locked out.

"Never have a girl, Christopher. Do it, and you're in for a world of hurt." My father's words after my sister got knocked up at sixteen. *A world of hurt.* The Suicide Blog. I found it sand-wiched in Kayla's browser history. Detailed instructions printed in cheerful, blue font. I sat there, sick, eyes glazed, as I scanned it: when, exactly, to step in front of a moving train to prevent the engineer from braking; the exact number of painkillers to swallow, listed by milligram according to body type; how to jump, just so, when hanging yourself to ensure the rope properly snaps your neck. I imagined Kayla, clear as day, floating in a tub of cool, pink water with her skin turned as white as the porcelain around her. It made my stomach clench, that image. It made me sick.

She bit my head off when I confronted her about it: *"God, Dad, it's for a school paper. Don't I get any privacy?"* Then I was staring at the backside of her door, thinking, *Jesus, only fifteen years old, and my little girl already wants to kill herself. I have to do something.*

"Something" turned into backpacking Colorado's Flat Tops Wilderness. Lexi had begged me to take this very trip a year before her diagnosis. I'd groaned and bitched about it, too consumed with an upcoming board presentation to care. We were in the middle of a deadline — the lead bank in a huge corporate divestiture from which Gorman & Gorman would profit nicely. I was running the deal. It was my ticket, our ticket, Lexi and I, to a better life. Then Lexi stumbled out of the shower with her hair wet and dripping and smashed my hand to her breast.

"Do you feel it? Do you?"

I did. A lump that sucked the moisture from my mouth. I remember tracing my fingertip over the mound, thinking, *surely not, right?* Cancer happened to other people. Not us. Cancer was a threat on par with global warming and plastic oceans. Always there, but *out there* somewhere else. Terrible, but not our problem. We were good. We were right where we needed to be. Fine, even. We'd always been just that — fine.

She was gone in six months.

I swallow hard and curse myself for the memory and the instant hot ache of it. A piece of the past I can never recover, only relive over and over without changing a goddamn thing. And there are *so* many things I would change. But right now isn't the time for indulging my grief. No, I need to focus on breaking the move to the girls. I have to stay clear-headed.

It won't be easy. I can picture how Kayla will melt down when I tell her about Denver. She'll complain about leaving her friends and Lexi's parents. Tears will spill. She'll whine about how much she hates me, and how her mother would have never, ever, done something like this to her, even though it was Lexi who'd spurred our move from New York to Boston, who'd done this *exact* thing to Kayla when she was nine. But Kayla will get over it, and it's not Kayla who worries me most. It's Emma.

Boston is all she's ever known. To her, Boston *is* Lexi. It's why we have to move. She needs space to heal, space to speak again. Jesus, I still can't believe it. Nine months without hearing a single word from my little girl. God, how I miss the sound of her voice, of her laugh. I need that laugh right now. We all do.

The thought pushes me forward a little faster, and I catch up with Kayla and loop an arm around her shoulders as we break from the trees. She stiffens and squirms from my grip, and I wonder, briefly, why I even try anymore.

"Hey, why don't you cook us dinner tonight?" I say.

"You mean heat up the soup?"

"Well, sure, but after, we can have s'mores."

She rolls her eyes. "God, Dad, I'm not ten. And it's going to rain."

"We'll have time if we hurry. Emma would like some s'mores, don't you think?" I look for her as I say it, something tugging at me, a blank space by the packs where I left her coloring a few minutes earlier. "Kayla . . . where's your sister?"

Her eyes narrow and she scans the lake, the water turned to slate and rippling with the wind. Her lips tighten, and right then, in that exact moment, I know my daughter is gone.

CHAPTER FOUR

CLARA
1984–1986

Her name was Sydney. She lived down the road on the MacArthur cantaloupe farm, with fruit that grew fat and sweet on the banks of the White River. She'd moved from Alaska to Colorado in June, and she told Clara stories of wolves with neon-yellow eyes and grizzly bears who snatched salmon mid-air as they flung themselves upriver to spawn. There were tales of endless summer days and nights that lasted for months with stars so bright, they seemed lit by heaven itself. It was all so exciting for Clara, hearing these things, talking to a girl her age — a friend at last!

Clara had never had a friend before. Mother wouldn't allow it; she told Clara other children were prone to mischief and that the outside world had a way of corrupting one's soul and turning it over to the devil. Clara didn't know if she believed this or not, but she'd long since stopped asking her parents to go to the public school in Meeker or to the town park where she might find someone her age to play with. The last time she had, Father turned on the oven range and held her hand over the red-hot coils until her palm blistered. He said no meant no, and if she were to ask again, he would burn that evil urge right out of her.

So Clara knew better than to tell Mother and Father about Sydney. Instead, she rose early and finished her chores before noon, disappearing into the woods that skirted the Carver ranch to find Sydney where she found her most days, at an age-worn cabin they'd discovered nestled deep in a thick cluster of aspen. Clara's heart leaped every time she spotted the weathered wood siding, knowing Sydney would be waiting inside in a dress that matched her mood. Red for adventurous, blue for calm. Today she wore yellow, which meant fun, and she and Clara chased each other through strands of lodgepole pine for hours.

It's how they spent the summer — running through the woods around the cabin, climbing trees and exploring the land all the way up to the rim of the Flat Tops Wilderness. They often picked wildflowers — Indian paintbrush and grosbeak and wood nymphs — and wound them into crowns, which they placed upon their heads, both of them queens of the forest. When they grew tired, they would return to the cabin and lie upon its pine needle porch and make shapes of the clouds floating above them in soft, cotton clumps — pirate ships and tractors and butterflies with sky-spotted wings. Evenings came in pink and slow with the sun dipping orange on the horizon, and they played until the dinner bell rang.

How Clara hated that sound. She'd slip back to the ranch with the lightning bugs coming to life around her, looking like a thousand bits of gold floating among the branches. She'd catch her breath near the back door, her cheeks coated in dust, and prepare herself for Mother's questions. They were always the same: "Where have you been? Why are you so dirty?" As were Clara's answers: "Just playing." and a shrug of her shoulders. "Mm-hmm," Mother would respond, as if she knew there was more to the story than that. Still, she never pressed Clara too hard, and for that Clara was thankful.

Winters passed in much the same manner, with the two of them in the forest. They spent their days with tongues outstretched in search of snowflakes or sledding down the steep woodland slope near the shack. Sydney, Clara thought, had a laugh like a bell — high and clear — as they wound through the trees on Clara's toboggan and made snow angels at the base of the hill. They decorated them with pinecones and rich, green boughs of fir until their skin purpled over and their lips grew bright with frost. Those years were the best of Clara's life.

14

* * *

One summer day in early June, Clara's eleventh, a rabid bobcat attacked her near the pond that bordered Mr. Oatman's property. She and Sydney had been playing hide-and-seek, flitting silently through the towering cottonwoods that hemmed the water on the far end of the Carver property, when it happened. It was Clara's turn to hide, and she ran in a giggle as Sydney counted, her voice filtering warm through the leaves.

"One . . . two . . . three . . ."

Clara had found Sydney twice now, once ducking behind the tall, moss-covered boulder near the old cedar fence Mr. Oatman built when she was five, and another time crouched in a tall clump of field grass bordering the pond. Sydney had been silly to hide there. Her glittery pink top made her easy to see among all the green. But to be fair, Sydney had found Clara as well, sneaking up and tickling her from behind with a "Gotcha!" that made Clara jump every time.

This round was for all the marbles, hide-and-seek champion, so Clara knew she had to find the perfect spot. Sydney was on "eight" when Clara saw the hollow carved into the bark of an old cottonwood large enough for her to squirm into backward. She blinked cotton from her eyelashes as she did, watching it sugar down outside like a summer snowstorm. The way it collected on the pond's surface reminded her of the flakes of sea salt Mother dashed into pots of water before setting it to boil. Clara was still thinking about that, about how those thin, white flakes sat on top of the water and how sometimes she would put one on her tongue to see which one dissolved first, when the cry rose shrill and terrible behind her.

The pain was immediate, a slash to the back that sent her tumbling from the trunk. She rolled down the pond's bank and into a reeking blanket of pluff mud which sucked at her legs. The bobcat clung to her the entire way, slicing with a set of curved claws that dug into her arms and chest. Its eyes were an electric yellow, and Clara wailed and thrashed, certain the mouth full of sharp teeth would sink into her neck at any moment. But they didn't, and with a sudden jerk, she was free.

The cat hung suspended in mid-air above her, Sydney clutching it by the neck as it yowled and screeched and snapped. It was small, not yet fully grown, Clara realized, and something was wrong with it. Foam

15

dripped from its jaw, and its eyes spun in wild circles as it hissed and went for Sydney's face. She only squeezed harder in response, taking two determined steps through the stinking mud to thrust the animal's head underwater. There it struggled, the water boiling up in a mess of paws and fur and teeth while Sydney pressed down harder, deeper, her arms turning crimson with the effort.

"Don't kill it," Clara yelled, suddenly aware that was exactly what Sydney intended to do.

Sydney glanced back at her with a look fiercer than any bobcat's. "I have to. It hurt you. It might do it again."

Clara said nothing, and Sydney went back to her work, the brackish water bubbling less now, the cat's tufted ears calming, settling into a slow death twitch. First one flicked, then the other, and soon they stopped moving entirely. Sydney held the animal there for a long time, breathing hard and muttering, "You stupid thing. You stupid, stupid thing." She shook as she said it, "You stupid thing," and the bubbles finally stopped rising to the surface. She turned and walked back to Clara with the bobcat floating motionless in her wake.

"You killed it," Clara mumbled, in a daze.

Sydney took her hand with a sad smile. "To keep you safe. I'll always protect you."

And Clara knew she meant it.

CHAPTER FIVE

CHRIS

A crow caws and bursts for the sky, followed by another. They bank and beat against the air with black wings as my gaze drifts toward the blanket of pine pressed below the lake. It spreads out for miles in a dark, blue-green blanket peppered with clumps of blazing aspen that look like they've been lit on fire. I barely register their beauty as I cup my hands to my mouth.

"Emma! Emma, can you hear me? Emma!"

A gust of wind rips through the branches and swallows my voice, setting loose a storm of pine needles that buffet my face and neck. I raise a hand against them as Kayla skids to a stop next to me holding my pack. I take it and rip out my red shell jacket and put it on. Kayla is already shivering in hers — a light-green North Face windbreaker — hugging herself and rubbing her arms, blowing in her hands.

"She's got to be close," she says, scanning the woods.

"Did you get her coat?"

Kayla nods and holds up the purple jacket. My heart drops. It's already too cold out, the temperature dipping lower by the second. Emma must be freezing. I try to picture

what she was wearing when I left her to chase after Kayla —
a peach, long-sleeved Patagonia and a pair of blue leggings
because even earlier she was begging me to change out of her
shorts. I remember the moment, Emma tugging on my jeans
as we descended from Trapper's Peak, folding her arms across
her chest in a mock shiver. Her new language — pantomime.

I take the coat from Kayla. "Good, let's go find her."

* * *

We skirt the woods around the lake first, calling out for her
like she'll answer. She won't. I've tried everything to coax her
to speak: counselors and doctors and play therapy sessions
with other damaged kids. Weekend retreats spent kneeling in
front of her for hours on end with a puppet in hand, pleading
for her to speak, begging her, please, baby girl, please just
say something, anything. Nothing worked; the moment Lexi
died, my daughter became a stranger. It was as if someone
had swapped her with an identical version of herself, only one
without a voice, and with eyes that looked upon me as if they
didn't recognize my face.

Because she knows what you did.

No. Not now. I bury the thought and focus on the terrain in front of me, my eyes hungry for any sign of Emma's
passing: a footprint, a freshly broken twig with a lock of her
fine, brown hair twined around it. A trail of crayons. There's
nothing but the heavy scent of pine and my thudding pulse.
The sun leaks through the trees in weak, gray streams. I shout
for Emma in a voice that doesn't sound like my own — one
that is harsh and desperate and laced with panic. "Emma!"

Kayla parrots the call to my left. She's not far from me,
maybe fifteen feet, but her cry is a whisper in the rising wind.
I shudder to think what mine sounds like, or if it carries farther. I glance at my watch: five-thirty, then blink up through
the branches at the sky. We have another forty-five minutes
before the light dies entirely, probably less based on the wind

gusts that have set the forest to creaking around us, groaning like it knows a storm is coming.

Find her.

We push farther into the woods. Deeper. The trees watch us, silent and ominous, as we pass. The terrain grows heavy with pockets of scrub and piles of bracken and under-growth that make progress damn near impossible. We reach a deep wall of brush, and I re-route us south over a wide expanse of forest floor spongy with pine needles and fallen branches. My pulse crashes harder with each step, sticky ribbons of dread spreading through my stomach as the first few raindrops explode off my skin like bombs.

"Dad! Over here!"

I spin toward Kayla, and my heart leaps. A piece of fabric flaps off the bark of a gnarled white pine, a scrap of Emma's shirt, the same pink-peach color I remember from earlier. I draw closer and realize it's only a stray length of faded logging tape. *Where are you, Emma?* Kayla looks at me with wide eyes and gulps down a few breaths. I take her by the shoulders and squeeze.

"Listen to me, Kayla: You have to focus. I need your eyes right now. We have to find her before the sun sets."

She blinks and nods, streams of rain dripping through her hair, running down over her face. "Okay . . ." she says. "Okay, let's go."

We continue downslope, and the light dims further. I retrieve the flashlight from the pack. The ground falls away in front of me like a funnel, earthen berms rising on either side, everything already slick with drizzle. Kayla cuts in and out of the trees ahead of me, running now, her voice shrill as she cries for Emma. I'm close to running myself, struggling to keep up with her as she bounds over rotten logs, bursting this way and that, tripping and scrambling to her feet again.

The forest collapses into a pool of shadow. The rain grows harder, meaner, a cold spray that hammers my face and bleeds into my eyes. Spots swarm my vision. I shake them off and realize I've lost sight of Kayla. Bile hits the back of my throat. I shout for her, the trees creaking around me, the rain slashing sideways, pelting my ears and neck. I bellow again and spot her waving wildly at me from atop a sharp spine of rock to my left. She waves again, her arms cutting back and forth like she's drowning. A snatch of her voice bleeds through the storm.

". . . here!"

She rolls her shoulders back and yells again, but I'm no longer watching or trying to understand the words. Instead, I'm sprinting, my feet cracking through saplings and leaping over buried logs and stray piles of deadfall. I know I should slow down, that if I snap an ankle out here, we're all doomed, but I don't, because I know what Kayla's trying to tell me.

She's found something . . .

CHAPTER SIX

EMMA

I wrap my arms around my chest as tight as I can. It's raining all over me, *drip, drip, drip,* with these big drops splashing right in my face, and I'm so, so cold.

Stupid rabbit, why did you do this to me?

I feel bad the second I think it. He had a hurt leg like mine, and he was just a baby. So cute. The cutest. He didn't mean to do it. Maybe if his momma had been there, she could have helped him, but I didn't see her anywhere. A mountain lion or a bear probably ate her. Dad says there's lots of them in the mountains, and we have to be really careful if we spot one. But he didn't say not to help an injured bunny. Plus, his long ears reminded me of Hops' ears. (Hops is my stuffed rabbit, by the way.) Momma gave him to me right before the cancer took her. I remember exactly what she said: "*If you ever get lonely or scared, lovebug, kiss Mr. Hops, and I'll be right there beside you.*" Then she cried a lot and gave me a huge hug.

I hope she meant it, because, right now, I'm in huge trouble . . . and I don't even have Hops! He's back at the lake where I can't reach him. I'm stuck. Beyond stuck. I should

21

have stayed put, like Kayla said, but instead, I ran after the bunny to help him, only he was too fast for me, even with his bad leg. I got close a couple times, but then he disappeared into this thorn bush, and just like that — *flash!* — he was gone. I knew I was in trouble when I looked up. There were so many trees, I had no clue where to go!

Before the trip, Dad said not to move if we got lost. But that didn't make sense to me, just sitting around, waiting for him to show up. That's when I saw the hill, and the idea hit. I'm a really good climber. I climb the big tree in our backyard all the time. Dad calls me a monkey. Even Kayla won't go as high as me, the scaredy-cat. I figured I could climb that hill and Dad and Kayla would see me and get me back no problem. Plus, it looked super easy.

Wrong. There were all these boulders in the way I had to crawl over, and I got stuck on one. Then it started raining, and everything got really slippery really fast. I don't know what it was, the branch I grabbed or the rock, that gave out first, but before I knew it, I was falling down the hill. When I hit the ground, I couldn't breathe. I just lay there, and before I knew it, I heard this *boom, boom, boom* coming from above. When I looked up, it was too late — the rock was already landing on my foot. It's still there. I can't get it off, no matter how hard I push. And I've pushed and pushed and pushed!

Here's the problem: every time I do, my ankle burns like crazy. It's like it's on fire. The last time I tried, I actually passed out. The rain woke me up right away, though. Then my ankle was back to burning. Even worse than the time I grabbed Mimi's curling iron. Ouch, did that hurt. This feels like Mimi's curling iron times ten. Times a bazillion!

I even tried to yell. I tried and tried and tried, but my stupid voice *still* won't work. All I can do is cry and think about Momma and if she really is by my side like she said. I've looked everywhere. There's just lots of rocks and trees and mud. And dark. That's the scariest part. I'm worried Dad and Kayla won't find me before the sun sets.

I say a quick prayer, but it's not to God. It's to Momma, because, deep down, I know she's listening. I tell her to hurry, to please send Dad and Kayla before a mountain lion eats me just like it did the bunny's mom. The thought frightens me, so I sit up and push on the rock as hard as I can, and, *whoa*, it wobbles a little bit. A bunch of lightning bolts shoot through my leg, and just like that my voice comes out in a scream. A big one. That's when the lights go out.

I don't know how much time passes. All I know is my leg is hurting worse than ever when I wake up again. For a second, I think I'm dreaming or maybe that my brain is playing tricks on me. But nope, it's no trick, nuh-uh, because standing right over me, like a foot away, are Kayla and Dad.

CHAPTER SEVEN

CLARA
1987

It was a cool September afternoon when Mother caught Clara by the arm as she attempted to slip through the screen door and into the backyard.

"Where do you think you're going?"

"To the forest to play."

"Not today. There's too much to do, and you're getting too old for such things."

"Let go!"

It wasn't what Clara said that earned her the slap but how she said it, angrily, jerking free of her mother's grip with a quick twist. How she stared at Clara in that moment, with her cold, watery eyes narrowing, before bringing a hand hard across Clara's cheek. She told Clara never to speak to her in that manner and that Father would hear about this just as soon as he got home. That night, he took Clara to the Black Place and did with her what he always did before telling her there was to be no more play in the forest.

"You're done with all that."

Clara broke, the thought of abandoning Sydney too much to bear, and she thrashed against him until he lashed her wrists to the gunny-covered cot in the corner. He retrieved a small plastic container from his pocket along with a clear glass dropper bottle and set them near her feet.

"I don't want to do this, Clara, but you've given me no choice."

Clara watched as he squeezed the dropper bulb and spilled several droplets of water in the shape of tears across her forearm. He smeared the liquid into a wet circle with his thumb, then grabbed the plastic bottle and unscrewed the lid. Holding it with care, he tapped it until a few of the white flakes within spilled and settled across the shining circle on her arm.

"Do you know what this is, Clara?"

A bloom of heat enveloped her skin. She shook her head no.

"This is something called lye. When an animal dies, it becomes worthless. It no longer has any value. It must be destroyed. Lye is what I use to destroy them. Do you understand?"

Clara shook her head again, the heat in her arm rising, reminding her of a hot bath or the glass doors of a freshly lit fireplace.

"When a girl disrespects her mother or her father, she loses value."

She whimpered then, the heat no longer heat but a fire taking root in her arm, spreading through her muscle and sinking all the way to the bone. She yanked her hand, desperate to extinguish the flame, but the rope corded around her wrist only tightened in response.

"A girl who loses her value must be punished."

Clara's skin was turning pink now, the white flakes melting, and in her mind, it was as if Father had scooped up a handful of the sun and set it upon her flesh. She screeched then, a shrill cry born of something closer to the pain of a mortally wounded rabbit or a pig who'd lost its leg to a butcher's knife. It didn't sound human, her cry, and although Father kept talking, Clara heard none of it, her focus only on the white-hot blaze enveloping her arm, burning hotter and hotter with each passing second.

She shrieked and bucked until Father finally took up the dropper bottle and emptied its contents on her arm, wiping away the lye with his handkerchief along with a quarter-sized patch of her flesh. The sight of that oozing, bloody wound set Clara to spinning, and it wasn't long until she lost consciousness.

The pain brought her back.

All through the night, Clara heard Sydney scratching at the hasp, trying to work the bolt free, but Father had secured it with a heavy lock from which there was no release. He didn't return for her until late the next afternoon and dragged her out into the sweltering heat with her pants soiled. He spat a long, brown rope of tobacco and said, "Stay out of the woods or next time will be worse."

Clara nodded.

She went into the forest that night and found Sydney still at the cabin, surrounded by trees washed white as bone beneath a full fall moon. She was silent at first, unable to speak, afraid to tell Sydney the truth about Father, afraid that if Sydney knew about the things he did to her, Sydney would run home, disgusted with Clara, and never return. So, she said nothing, and Sydney sat there and waited until, after a time, she took Clara's hand with a small smile.

"You can tell me anything, you know."

It was hard at first, the words coming out in a slow dribble, but Clara managed to start, and they soon became a stream and then a river waterfalling off her lips. She told Sydney about what Father did to her in the Black Place and how Mother sometimes joined in. How Mother had once pressed the tip of a hot clothes iron beneath the hem of Clara's dress in the shape of little red triangles that blistered and burst a few days after Clara ate a package of Mother's shortbread cookies without asking.

It was like a weight lifting, the words had weight, and Clara felt lighter as she choked them out. It was like someone reaching deep down within her and scooping out all of the bad and hurt and sick she'd soaked up since the day she was pushed into this hateful world, unwanted and alone.

Clara had never spoken to anyone about this, Father had forbidden it, and now that she had, she didn't think she could stop. And she didn't want to stop, but when she looked up to see Sydney sitting wide-eyed, with clear liquid streaming down her cheeks, clutching one arm and rubbing away like Clara's words were made of sharp things, that they were razor blades, Clara knew she'd gone too far.

Suddenly, she wanted nothing more than to take the words back, to suck the hurt in again and keep it there. Tears stung her eyes, and she collapsed onto the floor in a blubbering heap, apologizing to Sydney

26

for everything, for all of it, begging her, "Please, will you please still be my friend?"

When Sydney stood and left, Clara buried her face in her hands with a sob, never more alone in her entire life than in that moment. Not in the Black Place. Not as she scrubbed toilets with Mother telling her how stupid she was, or how lazy and worthless. She was alone. Completely and utterly alone.

Except she wasn't.

Fingertips brushed her ear. A thumb wiped away her tears. Clara opened her eyes, and there she was, Sydney, staring right back at her with those bright blue eyes shining and as wet as hers. She pulled Clara into a hug and said her parents were mean to her, too, that they'd wanted a boy and had never really loved her, either. She said she hated the cantaloupe farm and wanted to move back to Alaska, but her parents would never let her. They were here to stay, and Clara was her only friend. That she was all Sydney had, too. Something about that touched Clara. In a way, Sydney was just like her — alone — and thinking that made their friendship feel special. More special than if Sydney had a bunch of other friends she played with when Clara wasn't around.

"Please don't let him take you away from me," she said to Clara. "I wouldn't survive."

"Never," Clara promised. "No matter what."

CHAPTER EIGHT

KAYLA

Even with his pack on, Dad moves fast. So fast, I have a hard time keeping track of him. He scrambles across the valley and bursts from the wall of trees in front of me, bending over to catch his breath. When he looks up, his voice is wound so tight, it sounds like it's about to snap.

"What did you see? Where is she?"

"Down there."

I stab my finger downhill, over a steep stretch of rock, toward where Emma is lying broken at the bottom. God, I can barely stand to look at her. She's all crumpled up on her side with this big boulder jammed on her foot. I'm lucky I saw her at all, and I wouldn't have if she hadn't cried out. It froze me for a second. I thought it was an animal screeching or something. But then I spotted her shirt and shouted for Dad. She hasn't moved once since.

He snatches my arm. "Show me. Quick, Kayla."

* * *

We head lower. I move as fast as I can. The ground is steep and uneven, the grass slick, with a near-vertical drop-off to my right. I can't see anything in the rain, all of it one big gray smudge through my stupid tears. I wipe at them angrily and go faster. Dad shouts for me to slow down, but I won't. I have to help Emma. *We* have to help her. I make it a few feet before a branch catches my foot. I pitch forward and nearly tumble over the edge before Dad snags my arm.

"Careful!" he says, pulling me to him. "Here, let me lead. Hold on to my shoulder."

I do as he says, and we start again, but it feels way too slow, Dad testing his steps and easing down sideways at times as he guides us lower. My heart is beating like a drum, and in my mind, I'm screaming at him to *Go! Go! Go!* All I can think about is reaching Emma, and how this is all my fault. I shouldn't have run off with Dad's phone like that. He told me to watch her for a few minutes while he fished. But as usual, I was too busy being selfish. And for what? To see whatever dumb picture Bree and Abby posted on Instagram? To catch up on my Twitter feed?

"I'm sorry, Emma," I whisper into the rain.

We reach the bottom of the hill, and I race for Emma. She looks even worse up close. Her hair is soaked along with the rest of her, her clothes drenched and sopping up the rain. Her face is so pale it reminds me of a sheet, and she's got her arms flung to the sides like she was making a snow angel and gave up midway through. And the boulder — *Jesus* — it's about the size of the mini-fridge Dad put in the basement back home. There's no way we can possibly get it off. *No way.* The thought freezes me in place, and I stand there with a hard knot twisting into my stomach until I realize Dad is shouting at me.

"—stand there!"

"What?"

"I *said*, don't just stand there. Get over here and help me!"

29

It clicks, and I rush to his side. He kneels next to Emma and cups her head, says something I can't make out through all the crashing rain. Branches creak and twist all around us, the whole forest whooshing and rippling like we're standing in the middle of a river. Dad gives Emma's head a shake and whispers in her ear. This time, whatever he says reaches her. She blinks and glances up with a pair of dizzy, unfocused eyes.

"We need to get this off of her right away!" Dad yells. "Here, help me." He stands and circles the boulder to where it lies pressed against a huge pine stump, then plays the flashlight over Emma's leg. I catch a glimpse of her shoe, a flash of purple cranked in the wrong direction. Everything turns to syrup.

"Kayla! Focus!"

I look at him. His eyes are wide, his eyebrows stretched so high on his forehead, they look like they're about to leap off his face. "I need your help!"

I scurry next to him and plant my hands on the rock. Its surface is slick with moss, and several leeches glisten from its base. Stars spit through my vision, the dizziness back.

Dad sinks his fingers into my arm. "Listen to me. On three, we push with everything we have. Got it?"

I nod.

"Kayla, we cannot let this thing come back down on her foot once we get it moving." His fingers dig harder. "Do you understand me?"

I feel myself nod again. It's like I'm stuck in a dream, or more like a nightmare. One I can't wake up from.

He braces his foot against the trunk, and I do the same, wedging my heel against its base.

"Okay, ready? One . . . two . . . three!"

I shove with all my weight. Everything comes back into focus: the trees and wind and rain stinging my cheeks, my arms. My shoulders burn and my legs shake. My knees pop and buckle. Dad roars and pushes, and, for a terrible moment, I don't think we'll be able to move the thing. But then the boulder teeters forward an inch, tipping up, up, up, until, with a wet sucking sound, it lurches from the mud and topples over.

Emma screams.

I stare at her foot. It's twisted in the wrong direction. Blood oozes from her ankle to mix with the rain. I go numb at the sight, my skin buzzing as I try to steady myself, but it's too late. I'm already falling . . .

CHAPTER NINE

CHRIS

Kayla's pupils roll beneath her eyelids, and I know she's going to faint before she does. I leap for her and manage to grab her arm as she crumples, then lower her gently to the turf and rush back to Emma. The break is vicious, beyond bad. Her fibula, most likely, based on the sick, sidelong tilt of her foot. I rip her leggings wide, and a sour wave of stomach acid drenches my tongue. I stand and pull my phone from my pocket, desperate for a signal. There's none, and I don't have time to search for one. I kneel and trace my fingers over the break, which sets Emma to shrieking.

I jerk my gaze up. "Shh. It's okay, baby girl. Shh. Daddy's here now. I'm going to take care of you."

I look back to the wound and hope the pounding rain hides the fear flooding my eyes. I have no clue where to begin; I haven't thought of basic survival in years, not since my Eagle Scout days, which are now long distant memories buried beneath decades of dust.

Think, I tell myself, *remember*.

From some distant recess of my mind, a command rises: *Find branches. Make a splint.*

Emma screams again, and I reach up and take her hands in mine. For a moment, I lose track of time, my heart thumping in time with the rain as Kayla appears at my side. Her eyes are woozy — two bleary circles stamped beneath a damp curtain of hair.

"Oh my God, what . . . what do we do?"

"Get me the pack."

She runs a hand over her face and shakes her head, blinks.

I snap my fingers. "Hey, hey, you with me?"

"Huh?"

"The pack, Kayla. Over there." I wave toward the base of the juniper where I left it a moment ago. "I need Emma's coat."

She hands it to me, and I reach in and tear out Emma's coat and spread it over her chest. Kayla kneels and pulls Emma's head into her lap, her breath coming fast, too fast, her chest pumping up and down in quick, little jerks. Her mouth flops open and closed a few times before her jaw tightens. That's when the convulsions hit.

She's going into shock . . .

I reach up and grasp her head, try to hold her still as a rope of foam bubbles over her lips. "Emma, Emma, baby, stay with me, okay?"

A hard blink. Another, her eyes coming back into focus.

There you are . . .

She's trembling, her entire body vibrating like she's about to come apart. I tip forward and press my forehead to hers, her eyes dizzy with pain, her skin clammy cold. "Emma, listen to me. You have to be brave, okay? I'm going to do something to help your leg, but it's going to hurt a lot. You can't move it, no matter what, or I'll have to start again. Do you think you can do that?"

She nods, a slight, barely there movement.

I stare at Kayla. "Hold her down."

* * *

33

I tear through my pack and rip out the Boston Bruins T-shirt Lexi gave me for my thirty-second birthday and wind it around Emma's shin, along with a pair of conifer branches, to stabilize the break before securing everything with my belt. The splint is sloppy work, a long way off from what she really needs right now, but it should hold as long as she doesn't put any weight on it.

I grab the flashlight and stand.

Kayla glances up, her eyes bulging. "Where are you going?"

"I have to find a place we can ride this out."

She shakes her head. "No, you can't leave us."

I crouch next to her and cup her face. "I'm not leaving you. But we can't stay here, and we can't move Emma until we find a safe place to take her. You have to trust me, okay? I'll be right back."

Kayla nods, her nose flaring. "Please hurry."

* * *

I struggle through the hardening rain toward the dark slash of granite I remember spotting as we descended the slope to reach Emma. It's impossible to see more than five feet with the storm drumming harder, the drops turning to sleet that batter and sting my face like bits of fiberglass. The flashlight is little help as I play it over the rain-slick scree field in front of me, moving faster than I should, forcing my feet forward and trusting them to find purchase. All the while, the images burn. Emma's forehead and frost-colored lips. The way her shin moved in my hand with that elastic feel as I set the bone. Her shrill cry and the way her eyes flashed.

Hang in there, Emma, I'm—

A rock tilts under my foot, and I slam down. Something sharp slices into my ribs. I groan and thread my fingers beneath my jacket. Pain slashes instant and hot down my side, but I'm not seeing stars, not fighting for consciousness,

34

so it can't be critical. I get back to my feet and reach for the flashlight . . .

. . . *which is gone.*

I drop to my knees, and the howling black of the storm fills my ears, rain leaching into my eyes, my mouth, moisture soaking my neck and back. I whip my gaze left to the blurry outline of trees, right toward more rock and stone. Time loses all meaning. My fingers go numb as they work outward in a circle, prodding desperately for the cylindrical shape I know is there somewhere. It's all that matters, finding it, because if I lose the flashlight, we're screwed. And then I catch a glimpse of something silver. A metallic reflection that I snatch and bring up, with my blood thrashing against my eardrums. I click the button. Nothing happens, the light dead. Gone. I jab it again, harder, then slap the base and screw it tighter against the battery with a prayer.

Please . . .

I press the button, and a puddle of cold light splashes across the stone. I raise the flashlight and push on, hope I'm moving in the right direction, that my memory hasn't failed me as miserably as I've failed Emma. It hasn't. A sheer cliff face materializes through the dark in snatches, sheets of water rushing down the pitted surface in thirsty tongues. I move quicker, the heartbeat in my ribs pulsing hotter as my eyes scour the cliff, hungry for what I hope is there . . . *has* to be there.

I spray the light over a scarred, horizontal ridge and then guide it higher up the cliff. A vertical sheet of stone peers back at me through the rain. I swing the flashlight lower and left, toward a thick tangle of bracken stretching along the base, then right, to more smooth, impenetrable granite. There's no shelter, no overhang or depression in the rock we can use to escape the downpour. A wave of despair hits, and I roar in frustration before spotting the black crevice hidden behind a thin bank of scrub oak.

We still have a chance.

CHAPTER TEN

CLARA
1988

Most nights, they met at the shack after dusk when Father was drunk in his chair and Mother had turned in for the night. Clara was careful about it, listening for the creak of Father's old leather recliner before stuffing two pillows beneath her comforter and slipping out the window.

They played card games by lantern light. Speed and Go Fish and Slap Jack. Sydney won most of the time, but Clara sometimes beat her, squealing with laughter when she shouted, "Speed!" After they grew tired of cards, they would lie out on the splintered shack deck and look up through the pine boughs at the stars, wondering if there were aliens somewhere up there looking right back at them. Yes, they thought. Definitely, yes. Sometimes, they would talk about what they wanted to be when they grew up. Clara thought a nurse; Sydney said a musician, even though she couldn't play an instrument, but she loved the sound of piano and had plenty of time to learn.

When it grew late, and the moon drew halfway across the sky, Clara would creep back home and into her room, but not before Sydney took her by the hand and said what she always said before Clara left.

"Run away with me."

*Clara wanted to; oh, how she wanted to. She could imagine it —
how they'd find a place somewhere deep in the woods all their own where
they could do whatever they wanted, whenever they wanted. They'd steal
cantaloupe and tomatoes and corn during the summer and hitch a ride
to Denver with a semi-driver before winter hit. Sydney said she had an
aunt there who could help them start a new life. They could trust her.*

*But no matter what Sydney said, Clara knew Father would find
them wherever they went. He would, and that would be the end of
everything.*

*So she told Sydney no, even though she didn't want to, and Sydney
stomped back home with tears in her eyes, saying Clara didn't really
care about her as much as she cared about Clara. It hurt Clara, but
still she said no, and, after a while, Sydney quit asking. That's when
Mr. Oatman's cat died.*

* * *

*It was late one Saturday afternoon when Mr. Oatman came knocking.
Mother answered the door while Clara busied herself in the kitchen
washing dishes.*

"Why hello, Arthur, what brings you by?"

"Hello, Mrs. Carver, have you seen Patches? He's gone missing."

"Why no, I'm afraid I haven't, but I'll keep an eye out for him."

*Mr. Oatman had a lot of cats on his farm, but Patches was his
favorite, and ever since his wife had passed the year before, he could be
seen most mornings out on the porch with a mug of steaming coffee
and the friendly orange tabby purring in his lap. Sometimes, Patches
would stroll across the Carver property chasing after birds, and Clara
would feed him a bowl of cow's milk. He had cream stripes and green
eyes, and Clara loved the way he nuzzled close when she scratched him
behind his ears.*

"Yes, please do, and let me know if you find him."

"We will, Arthur."

*Clara heard the worry in Mr. Oatman's voice, and she watched
him slink back to his truck looking just about as sad as she'd ever
seen him. He was a nice man with a ring of salt-and-pepper hair and*

a friendly smile, and Clara promised herself she'd keep an eye out for Patches, too; it was the least she could do.

She found him that night at the shack.

She'd slipped a few of Mother's chocolate chip cookies into her pocket at dinner, excited to share them with Sydney because they were that good, but found Sydney sitting in the corner of the cabin with her head bowed and didn't offer her one.

"What's the matter?" Clara asked.

"I-I don't know what's wrong with me," Sydney replied with her shoulders heaving. "I didn't mean to do it. I was petting him and rubbing his belly, and . . . and he just scratched me and . . ."

That's when Clara spotted the motionless ball of orange fur in Sydney's lap, and her heart gave out. Patches lay with his head twisted roughly to the side. A pink strip of tongue hung from his mouth, and Clara knew he was dead. She knelt and ran her fingers over the cat's cold, stiff stomach, wondering why Sydney would ever do such an awful thing.

"Something's wrong with me," Sydney said.

Clara thought maybe something was. But she didn't say it. How could she? Sydney was the only friend she had. And she'd been a good one. The best. And after all the things Clara had told her, how could she get mad at Sydney for something like this, even if it was really, really bad? Even if seeing Patches like that, lying broken in Sydney's lap, was enough to make Clara want to cry. But she took a deep breath instead and said, "Nothing's wrong with you."

"But there is. It's just . . . I get so mad sometimes," Sydney said, wiping angrily at her eyes. "I didn't mean to do it, but when I did, it made me feel . . ." She buried her face in her hands and shook her head, crying harder now. "No, I can't say it. Oh, God, I'm so awful, horrible."

"What is it, Sydney?" Clara asked. "You can tell me."

Sydney looked up with swollen eyelids and stared at Clara for a long moment. She hiccupped a few more sobs and then dropped her gaze back to her lap and mumbled, "I don't know why, but something about it made me feel a little better."

38

Clara didn't know what to say to that, so she fell silent until Sydney shook her head and looked away. "You must think I'm a terrible person. I hate myself!" And then she was sobbing again.

"No," Clara said, reaching out to squeeze her leg. "I get mad sometimes, too."

Sydney sniffed and gave her a hopeful look. "So, you don't think I'm a monster?"

"No, it was just a mistake. C'mon, I know where we can take him."

They buried the cat by moonlight beneath the large bur oak next to the cabin. They held hands as Clara said a prayer and Sydney cried. Then Clara made Sydney promise she'd never do something like that again.

CHAPTER ELEVEN

CHRIS

Kayla leads, guiding the flashlight into the jagged crack that's more of a gorge than a cave. A crumbling granite shelf blocks most of the rain as we work our way over a pile of rubble at the entrance and toward the cramped, stubborn space in the back. It's musty, with several layers of sediment and dust. Stone walls rise around us on all sides, the ground peppered with bone fragments scattered between piles of animal droppings. They look to be smaller than those of a bear's, maybe a mountain lion's or coyote's. Whatever they belong to, I pray it doesn't return tonight.

I crouch and lay Emma on a mostly dry patch of dirt and check her pulse. It's weak, a birdlike flutter that turns my blood to ice. I rub my hands together and attempt to warm them, then unzip her coat and run my fingers over her shirt and down her leggings. Everything is soaked, her skin waxy and rippled with gooseflesh. Shaking, I unsling the pack and rip free my GORE-TEX sleeping bag and spread it over the hard-packed clay. It's rated for temperatures much colder than these, stuffed with several layers of lifesaving down filling that I'm worried Emma's body won't have enough warmth to heat.

"H-how can I help?" Kayla asks, kneeling next to me. Her hair is glistening, several strands matted to her cheeks. She's freezing. I can tell by the way she speaks in rapid bursts, her breath forming long crystal plumes that dissolve into the dark beyond the flashlight. She's at risk for hypothermia. We all are. It doesn't take much to kick in, especially in temperatures like these.

"Strip," I say.

She blinks hard, her gaze muddy. "Wh-What?"

"Take off your clothes. I need your body heat." I glance at Emma. "You're getting in the bag with her."

She nods and stands, pulling off her coat as I work to undress Emma. It takes far too long, in reality only a few minutes, but my fingers are numb with cold, and each second that drags past feels like an hour. She moans as I guide her into the bag next to Kayla, cradling her splint so that it doesn't catch before zipping them both into the heat-reflecting fabric. I lie down next to Emma and sandwich her body against mine.

"D-dad, you need to get w-warm, too," Kayla stammers. She's a pale outline in the flashlight's shine, trembling so hard I can feel it through the sleeping bag. It's true, I'm beyond chilled, my entire body clenching, trying to hold onto what little warmth is left in my muscles, but I can't move. Right now, Emma needs my heat more than I do.

"I'll b-be fine," I stammer.

"Is she g-going to make it?"

It's the question I'm trying like hell not to ask myself. I reach over and trace my thumb over Kayla's ear. "D-don't speak, okay? Save your energy. You warming up?"

She nods and falls silent. The flashlight paints the rock behind her an eerie white. Shadows climb the walls and flicker with the rain. Emma's eyes dance beneath her eyelids, and I curse myself for leaving her alone to chase after Kayla. *You should have brought her, Chris. Lexi would have.* The thought sparks a memory: Emma as a baby the first time I held her, her weight so perfect in my arms. How my heart seemed to expand when I looked down upon her pink, shrunken face. I remember telling myself I'd do things differently this time around; I'd really try.

With Kayla, it had been different. I wasn't ready to be a father at twenty-five; I didn't possess the patience. Holding her felt different, a squirming human ball with bleary eyes blinking up against the harsh hospital light, me thinking, *I'm not ready for this. I want to put her back.*

The thought became a hot coal of shame I buried in a dizzying sea of firsts — first smiles, first laughs, first diapers, and toys, and nights spent sleepless in wait of that next grating cry. A first birthday party with Lexi's friends oohing and ahhing over Kayla as she ground her doll-sized fists into the cake and dragged it over her cheeks in little pink-and-yellow pastel streaks.

I'd watch all of these things like an actor, like I was a robot stuffed into a suit of skin. I'd smile and laugh when I should. Do and say the right things. *"Yes, she's beautiful when she sleeps,"* and, *"Yes, she's the best thing that's ever happened to us,"* or *"I am bonding, I swear."*

I wasn't. I'd escape to work whenever I could. The office provided me with the sense of order and control I craved. I still mattered there. At home, I was nothing more than an extra set of hands for Lexi to dump Kayla into the second I walked through the door. *"Feed her, I'm going to take a shower."*

We lost each other in those early months, Lexi and me. I remember sitting in the driveway, looking up at the house with grainy, sleepless eyes, wondering what was preventing me from running, from starting the car like my father had, and driving until I ran out of gas.

It was never that way with Emma. She just felt . . . right. Kayla was seven by then, and I knew I'd missed too many years, that time had gone too fast. This time around, I was determined to be a better father, and not just to Emma. To Kayla as well.

And now you might lose them both . . .

I straighten with a groan and stand, my bones cracking with cold as I grab the pack. My fingers are useless, so numb I can barely work the zipper. Thoughts clog in my head, thick and slow: get warm . . . find water . . . some food . . . call for help. I pull out a pair of fleece-lined jeans along with my spare sweater and strip, the air so cold I nearly topple. Kayla watches, her eyes bright pinpricks in the low light. I grab my phone and bring it to life. *No signal.*

I stuff it back in my pocket and snag a sack of trail mix from the pack, along with a packet of ibuprofen and my water bottle. I pass Kayla the mix, then kneel and press the pills to Emma's lips. Her eyes flicker as she gums them. I tilt her head and force a weak gulp of water into her mouth before laying a hand over her forehead. My chest constricts. She's too hot, but at least lying next to Kayla in the sleeping bag, she won't freeze to death.

I curl in next to them and realize Kayla is still staring at me.

"Why?" she asks, her voice so weak I barely hear it. "Why did you drag us out here?"

"Kayla, we're going to be okay. We'll make it out of—"

"Just stop. I don't . . . why can't you ever tell the truth?"

"Look, there are things you don't understand."

"You should have told her, Dad. She deserved to know."

A lump fills my throat, one I can't swallow or dislodge. Instead, I lie there and let it swell until her breathing slows. My father's voice burns through my head. *"Sometimes a man can't live for others anymore, Chris. Sometimes he has to live for himself."* His last words to me before he betrayed my mother and abandoned us for another woman. The last words I ever heard him speak. I hated him for that. I swore I'd never turn out like him, never damage the people I love like he damaged me. It's amazing how easy it is to lie to yourself.

I click off the flashlight and shut my eyes.

When I wake, Emma is shrieking.

CHAPTER TWELVE

KAYLA

I open my eyes, soaked in sweat, and it takes me a second to realize it's not mine. It's Emma's. She's burning up next to me, her breath forming a hot circle on my neck. She issues a pathetic whimper, and my heart cracks. Even if I won't admit it, I miss the sound of her voice and how her laugh made the house sparkle. It reminded me of an open can of soda with all the bubbles spilling out.

Sure, she annoyed me sometimes. She'd whine to Mom about pretty much anything if it meant getting her way. *Momma* this and *Momma* that. She'd say it like a baby, drag the syllables out like she was still three instead of seven — *Mah-ma, Kayla's being mean to me! Mah-ma.* God, it drove me so crazy.

There was this one summer day in particular, right before Mom got sick, when Emma was whining like always right in the middle of a show I was trying to watch, begging me to braid her hair or whatever. I couldn't handle it. I told her to shut up, and she started bawling like I'd bitten her head off, which I guess I had. Mom pulled me aside with a look like she was about to bite mine off, too, but then she sighed and said, "Why don't you go surprise your dad at the office and take him out to lunch? He'd like that."

I knew it would probably annoy Dad, me showing up unannounced and all, but escaping the house for a while seemed like a great idea, so I did it.

I took the bus downtown and hopped off in front of his building. As soon as I saw it, I couldn't help but get excited. Me and Dad used to go out for lunch all the time when I was younger, but then Emma came along, and he got a promotion, and all of that stopped. It was like his new job came with a chain. He never left the office. If it came down to work or making one of my swim meets or volleyball games, work won every time. Mom said it wouldn't last, that it was just a phase and things would slow down eventually, but they never did. Not really. I think that's why I was so excited that day; it had been so long since it had just been me and him together.

Anyway, I went up to his floor, and the lady at the front desk, whose name I've never been able to remember, smiled her big, red lipstick smile the second she saw me. "Well, hello, Kayla. What brings you in?"

"Hi, I'm going to take my dad to lunch."

"Oh, he'll love that. He's back in his office. Why don't you go surprise him."

I wandered past her, thinking the place looked pretty empty, which was weird because it was never that empty, but then I remembered Dad saying something the night before at dinner about a conference everyone was going to, and it made more sense. He had some reason he couldn't go, something about a big project he needed to finish. I wasn't really listening, because he was always in the middle of some big project. I only remembered the comment later, after what happened next.

I tried to open his door, but it was locked, which was strange; like, why would he lock it with no one around? It didn't make sense. So, I went to knock, but as soon as my knuckles hit the door, it swung open a crack because it hadn't latched right. And there he was: Dad sitting in his chair with this pretty brunette kneeling right in front of him. He had his pants down and his head tipped back with his eyes closed. He must have heard the door open because he jerked up suddenly, looking like he was about to have a heart attack. Then he saw me, and his mouth dropped open and my name fell out of it.

All I could think was *run*, which I did, faster than I ever had before. I ran right past the lipstick woman and out of that stupid building with my eyes burning. I walked around downtown bawling for an hour. I had no clue what to do or where to go. I didn't care, either. All I could think about was that girl with her head between Dad's legs.

At some point, a man who looked like Papa — that's my grandfather — stopped me and asked if I was okay. I told him I was fine, and then I took the bus home and went right up to my room. When Mom knocked and asked what was wrong, I shouted for her to go away. I didn't come out of my room all night, not even for dinner. I heard Mom and Dad arguing about it through the walls later. She wanted to know what had happened. I don't know what he told her, but I knew it wasn't the truth, because she never got mad enough . . . or quiet enough, which was usually what happened when she got really angry.

He woke me early the next morning and said things hadn't been going that well between them for a while — like that somehow made what he did okay. He told me I'd under-stand someday when I was older and that, sometimes, people make mistakes, even good people. He said he loved Mom and would tell her soon, that he needed to find the "right time," and for me to please keep it a secret until he did.

But then she got sick, and he never said a word. I didn't either. How could I? There was no way I was going to hurt her, not with how sick she was and how much she loved Dad. Something like that would have ripped her apart. Still, I hate myself for not doing it, just like I hate myself for leaving Emma alone at the lake. She's all that's left of Mom. This special piece of her she left behind for me to protect . . . and I broke her.

She whines, like she knows I'm thinking about her.

"Ems," I say. "Ems, you ok—"

She stiffens and jerks her leg. Her splint bangs against my shin and her eyes shoot open. Then she's screaming.

"Hey, hey, I'm right here." I try to stroke her hair, but she bats my hand away with another shriek. Dad reaches over with the water bottle, and she knocks that away too, then grabs it and gulps like she's never tasted water before.

"Not so fast, Emma. Go slow," he says.

But she's already done and back to crying, howling and shrieking right in my ear. I whisper for her to breathe and talk to me, that I've got her, even though I don't. I have no clue what she needs right now or how to help her. All I can do is keep telling her she's going to be okay.

The night slides by like that, in snatches: rain and wind. Emma screeching and flailing against me with her splint until the branches rub my skin raw. Dad doing all he can to calm her down. *Emma, you have to stay still. Moving will just make it hurt more.*

He feeds her more ibuprofen and rubs her shoulders, gives her sips of water. Finally, she falls asleep. At some point, I have no clue when, I do the same. When my eyes snap open again, the sun is up and it's snowing outside.

47

CHAPTER THIRTEEN

CLARA
1992

Clara decided, at the age of seventeen, she'd never seen a better-looking man than John Gibson. She often watched him through the clear patch of glass on her bedroom window as he tended to the rich black soil of the farm, tilling the earth into vertical berms for as far as the eye could see. He would arrive last most mornings, after the other ranch hands had already gone into the fields, dressed in a pair of patched overalls with a Chicago Cubs ball cap worn slightly askew on his head. He'd gather his tools from the bed of his truck and wind down the irrigation lines, checking them for leaks, until he became a small, dark speck upon the horizon.

Clara marked the hours until his return in the chores Mother assigned to her: 9 a.m., prepare the sweet tea, and milk the cow. 10 a.m., gather and fold the laundry and clean the bathrooms. 11 a.m., make lunch for Father and take it to him on the porch, a plate of beans and ham and toast with two pats of butter left to melt in the middle. 1 p.m., weed the vegetable garden and prune the tomato vines. 3 p.m., muck out the stables and walk the dogs.

The list felt endless, but it didn't matter. It gave her more time to imagine what John would taste like when she kissed him. Salt and sweat mixed with a hint of sunscreen, she thought, not that she'd ever have the courage to do such a thing. That would be ridiculous — she'd never even said so much as a word to him! But sometimes when she looked at him, he'd stare right back with his coffee-colored eyes and a smile that sent her to the stars.

Most evenings, it wasn't until the sun drew near the mountains that she spotted him, his skin darkened and his knuckles lined with dirt as he trudged toward the farmhouse. Every day she swore the same thing. She would finally speak to him. Today would be the day. And every day, rather than saying something, anything (Hello! Hi, there, I'm Clara!) her tongue remained stuck to the roof of her mouth, too swollen with nerves to function.

But she had time, she told herself, months yet until the combines wound through the stalks to bring in the corn. Father dismissed the ranch hands in mid-September, so she would need to do it before then, or it would be another long winter spent wishing she had. Her insides churned at the thought; outside of her time with Sydney, the winter months were bleak and endless, spent trapped inside with Mother and Father, whose moods soured with the lack of sunlight. But the harvest was still far off, she thought. Only June. No sense in worrying yet. So, it was with great alarm early one morning that Clara overheard Father laying into John through the open kitchen window in a tone he usually reserved for her.

"I won't have you showing up late again. It sets a bad example for the others. You're done here, John. Get your shit and go."

Those words sent Clara rushing outside onto the porch without a second thought, her voice leaping off her tongue in a squeak.

"Give him another chance, Father. Please."

He startled and turned toward her with his eyes swimming in whites the color of egg yolk. Clara thought he'd bat her away like a fly; that's how important she was to him, an annoying buzz at best. Instead, he looked at her for a long moment before a slow, queasy smile broke over his chin. "Fine. One chance, Clara. But it'll be your burden to carry if anything happens."

Clara knew what those words meant — "your burden" — and somehow, so did John, because he showed up bright and early the next morning, and the next, morning after morning, until even Father begrudged him a certain amount of respect. And, to her delight, Clara found it wasn't so hard for her to speak to John after that.

CHAPTER FOURTEEN

CHRIS
DAY TWO

I rub my arms and stare out at a frozen landscape that shouldn't exist, one bleached of all color but white. Milk-colored flakes spit sideways and pepper my cheeks, my ears. Aspen branches wilt beneath thick clumps of snow, their leaves iced over in showers of gold and orange that cling to the trees like fragile, frost-covered jewels. Threads of grass jut skyward through the arctic crust, brittle shards of glass rooted in place. The air feels heavy and wet, like the storm is ready to rip loose again at any moment. *How?* I checked the forecast for weeks, monitored it religiously until we hit the trail: a few overcast afternoons with the possibility — the *possibility* — of a few scattered rain showers. Not *this* . . .

"*You have to see the colors, Chris. They're remarkable.*" My boss's words as he stood hunched over my shoulder, staring at the computer screen with his coffee mug in hand. "*It's the perfect time of year out there. Not too hot. Not too cold.*" His definition of September in Colorado, nothing but powder-blue skies and crisp mountain air. Greg had done it the year before with his boys. He talked me through the route, what to pack and where to camp along the way. He'd analyzed the trip with the ferocity of an acquisition target. I'd never known someone so thorough, never seen a single sheet of paper out of place on his desk. So, if it was good enough for him, it was good enough for me. And just the thought of vanishing with the kids for a while, of escaping Boston and the memories of what we lost . . . I made the decision and never looked back.

God, how I wish I'd looked back.

Fix it, Chris.

But how?

Look at it like numbers. Find the solution.

A five-mile hike to the trailhead from Taylor Lake. It's what we were supposed to do today: reach the car and head north to Vail for the night. Then back to Denver and a non-stop flight to Boston in the morning. But where, exactly, is the lake? The campsite? A couple of miles? More? I realize I have no clue where to start or how far we hiked last night. There are no tracks to follow. Nothing but snow-covered ground and a complete sense of disorientation. And with the wind whipping down the cliff face outside, swirling and cutting across the slope in howling drifts, I'm not so sure I can get us safely back to camp. Or anywhere, for that matter.

Think. Break it down into pieces.

Work back to the lake, to the girls' packs and the camping stove. Get the girls warm. Feed them a hot meal and push the pace. Reach the car by mid-afternoon, and, with any luck, find a hospital for Emma nearby. Then leave this nightmare behind.

A story flashes to mind, an article I read on the plane on the way out here about a woman from South Dakota who'd strayed off the path on a day-hike with her husband. They hadn't been that far from here, somewhere near Breckenridge, the woman a wildflower photographer in search of columbines and larkspur. There was a picture of her, a mother of two, brunette, with a kind smile stretching a pair of rosacea-laden cheeks. They found her body in a washout a week later, three miles from the parking lot. It might as well have been ten. A quote from a park ranger said she got turned around and walked herself in circles for days. And it wasn't even snowing . . .

Kayla eases next to me and blows into her hands. Her hood is up, but her chin is the same color as my fingertips, the capillaries an angry red, the skin beneath her eyes lined in black circles. She's exhausted. We all are. The night was like a minefield, with Emma thrashing and rolling. Bawling. Me waking with a start to comfort her. Trying and failing to keep her hydrated and warm, soothing her back to sleep before passing out again, then waking in a lurch to her broken-throat cry once more.

"What are we going to do?" Kayla asks. Her voice is brittle, a glass chipping.

"I'm not sure yet."

"The lake can't be far, can it?"

"I don't remember the way. Do you?"

Her answer comes in silence.

Try the phone again.

I retrieve it from my pocket and tap the screen. The pixels glow blue with a still of Lexi, her arms draped over Kayla and Emma, all of them smiling. Another life. I hold it up and spin in a circle, raise the phone above my head. All I need is one bar. A single goddamn bar. *C'mon! C'mon!*

"It won't work," Kayla says. "Not down here. Maybe higher?"

She's right. I need to climb.

"Watch Emma, okay? Holler if you need me."

She nods.

Joints stiff and creaking, I work my way from the cave and toward a rock outcropping that looks high enough to see the valley below. My breath smokes white as I climb, my boots slipping on rocks and buried tangles of roots. Frostbite nips at my nose in needles, a prayer whispering off my lips as I reach the crest and raise the phone.

Please . . .

The signal icon blinks and spins in an endless loop. No bars materialize, no text message chirps, and a crawling desperation floods my lungs. I'm left staring out at miles of white and green forest pinned to a grizzled mountain backdrop. And something else . . .

I squint and tilt my head at what I'm convinced is an illusion. My heart quickens. Beyond the valley, past a dense line of trees, the earth flattens into a perfectly square patch of land I'm familiar with. One I've seen before, the backdrop of countless road trips. I know instantly I'm looking at a ranch or a farm. And planted at its center is a single, solitary glow. A bright, shining pinprick in the early morning gloom. A cabin or a house. *Light.*

I slide from my perch and race back to the cave.

CHAPTER FIFTEEN

CHRIS

We ease down the steep, forested slope. Emma hangs limp
from my arms, still wrapped in the sleeping bag. Every time I
jostle her or take a sudden step she moans, her face bloodless,
her lips cracked and flaking. I search for the light and spot
it hanging across the valley like a lifeline. It's all I care about
right now, reaching it, finding help for Emma and warmth
for Kayla. Her complexion has taken on a bluish tinge I
don't like. It's too cold out, breathtakingly cold, each pull
of oxygen forcing her to cough when she inhales too deeply,
my lungs protesting in the same manner, feeling as though
they're about to crack with each inhalation.

Snow blankets the terrain in a smooth, gray-white quilt,
smoothing the dangerously sharp contours of the slate and
shale I know lie piled beneath. I move slowly, testing my
weight with each step, easing downhill with my knees bent
at an angle to absorb the shock. I judge there to be maybe
six inches of dry crystal powder on the ground, with more
billowing down around us from the trees in light swirls, weak
for now, but not for long. The storm churns above us in a

dark, heaving mass as if taking a deep breath before expelling another lungful of snow.

An hour passes. The slope edges lower, angling across a thin stretch of granite that threatens to steal my footing. The going is treacherous, rocks slicing into my ankles, sticks and branches tearing at my calves. Streams of snow press wet and cold into my socks until I can no longer feel my feet. Kayla complains of the same before stumbling near a clump of aspen. She comes up sucking a button of blood from her palm and waves me off. "I'm fine," she says. "I'm okay."

She's not. None of us are.

We press on. The air is laced with the scent of iron and pine. My biceps burn and throb, the weight of Emma growing until I feel like I'm carrying a wet bag of sand. The pace is tedious, a brutal sidetrack down the mountain spent sidestepping logs and testing footholds for traction. I clutch Emma tighter despite the pain, for fear she'll slip free at any moment . . . that if I drop her, she'll shatter into a thousand pieces I can never put back together again.

After a time, the forest thickens, and we stumble across what appears to be a deer trail winding into a pocket of blue spruce. We take it. Towering stands of lodgepole pine interspersed with layers of oak and juniper watch us pass in silence, their branches creaking with the wind. Thick, white clumps of snow thump down around us, the leaves drifting overhead in muted patches of color — olive greens and butter yellows and flame reds that smear past beneath a sky the color of tar. Crystalline flakes filter down silent and still, the only sounds those of our breath and the crunch of our boots.

Lower. Farther. Deeper.

A branch snaps to my right. I flinch as a twelve-point buck explodes from behind a blue spruce in a blur of muscle and antlers. Emma swings wide in my arms, and her skull connects with the bridge of my nose. Light crashes through my vision as I totter and crash to the snow, doing my best to break her fall with my arms. She bucks hard in my lap, and I tell her to breathe, that we're almost there. The lie boils in my stomach, because I have no idea where "there" is or if we're anywhere close to it. She cries out again, her mouth slashing into a black hole cry that rips the blood from my heart. Kayla circles back with the water bottle and the last pack of ibuprofen. I tear it open and press the pills to Emma's mouth. She lips them and curls deeper into the sleeping bag, shivering so hard it vibrates my arms.

"How much farther do you think?" Kayla asks, staring at Emma.

"I don't know."

"We need to get her out of the cold soon."

"Yeah. Same with you. Let's go."

* * *

We reach the valley floor sometime around mid-morning. I scour the tree line on the other side of the meadow, my eyes desperate to find the light I spotted above. Kayla does the same before turning to me with her eyes dripping panic. "Where is it?"

"It's there. We just can't see it this low. Come on." I start forward and hope she didn't notice the tremor sliding through my voice.

We stay close, trudging side-by-side, Kayla raising an arm against the lashing wind and snow. It's driving harder now, whipping sideways with frigid blasts of air that tear at my neck and cut through my coat like it's not even there. I pull Emma's hood lower and tighten the strings so only her eyes are visible.

"Hang in there, baby," I say.

She peers up at me with pupils that are groggy and unfocused. And I quicken my pace.

A formless mass of earth rises ahead, fringed by a dense bank of willow whose stalks are bent stiff against the breeze. They rattle and churn as the wind rips through them, whirling clouds of snow stinging their leaves, strands of cattail interspersed in mustard-brown chunks throughout. I hesitate. Reeds mean ice, but there's no other way, and we're running out of time. Backtracking now would be even more dangerous than whatever lies ahead. I make the decision, and we press in.

Kayla shoves ahead in a brittle shower of snow and ice. I follow, leaves turned to blades by the frost slicing at my knuckles and hands. The wind tears at my face and teases water from my eyes that becomes ice as soon as it hits my cheeks. All I can focus on is moving my feet and holding onto Emma. It's all that matters, keeping her safe in my arms and taking the next step. And the next. It's what I do, focus on the steps, with the stalks cracking and snapping all around me, the earth turning to a boggy, frozen slush beneath my feet. Right, left, right, left. *Focus on that, Chris, the steps, and nothing else.*

Kayla stops suddenly and looks back. It's then I notice we're through and staring at a long, black sheet of ice, running from one bank to the other for as far as I can see. A thin, transparent layer that I know has no chance of holding our weight.

"Oh, m-my God," Kayla says, in a chatter. "We'll n-never get across."

"What about that?" I ask, nodding at a wooden smudge upstream.

"Is it . . ."

"Yes," I answer. *Yes.*

We make for the bridge together, the snow swirling harder, the structure coming into focus one foot at a time. It's rickety-looking, a footbridge with no handrails and nothing to stop us from crashing through the ice if we fall. But it's the first sign of humanity I've seen in days, and I can't help but feel a measure of relief. We're close. We *have* to be close.

Kayla crosses first, her arms spread wide as though she's standing on a balance beam. I follow, cradling Emma close. The grain rises up slick and dark through her boot prints. It's what I'm looking at, her boot prints, when a sudden blast of snow shrieks from the far bank and hammers into my eyes. I don't realize I've slipped until I'm falling.

I come down hard. One leg sheers off the bridge with a sharp crack, the other scrambling for purchase. Heat shreds my calf. White veins of light explode behind my eyelids as my skull cracks down. I'm vaguely aware of Emma crying somewhere, of Kayla shouting. Bits of snow pelt my face and batter my ears. I try to open my eyes and can't. There's a dark web of cotton leaking through my head, preventing me from doing so, a voice yelling for me to get back to my feet. Fingers prod my chest, grab at my waist.

"Dad! Dad, are you okay? Please be okay. Can you hear me? Dad!"

And then I'm fading again, the world spinning away no matter how hard I try to hold on to it.

CHAPTER SIXTEEN

CLARA
1992

Their first date was dinner and a movie in Meeker. Clara had to beg Father and promise she would be home no later than nine. He finally conceded, and John picked her up in his dented Chevy Silverado that Friday evening. He bought them a big tub of popcorn, which they shared, their buttered fingers sliding past each other until John took hold of her hand and set it in his lap. The feel of his palm resting against hers set Clara's skin on fire.

There were more dates. Checkered-table dinners at Ellison's Fried Chicken Stand and evening strolls down Main Street in search of butterscotch ice cream. Sunset drives became a favorite of hers. They would wind through the countryside and stop at the Wilsons' trout pond five miles down from the ranch. He kissed Clara there for the first time, in the truck cab, the air swimming with the smell of exhaust and his sandalwood cologne. She flinched back at first, John was no small man, his features clouding with those of Father's, but he traced his thumb across her ear and pressed his lips to hers, and Clara finally knew what it meant to be touched in a way that didn't make her skin crawl.

John didn't want much out of life, only to someday have a place of his own with some land to spread out. A farm like Father's, maybe, but one not nearly as large, and with goats instead of horses and cattle. Working outside felt like home to him, he said, and he could think of nothing better. When he asked Clara what she wanted, she couldn't answer, because she'd never really thought about it until now, and the answer was him.

Summer slid by quickly. Father allowed her to see John once a week, on Fridays, so long as she never came home past nine. John made sure to obey. He respected Father, referring to him as Mr. Carver, and the two men grew closer with each passing month. Clara often found them sipping iced tea on the back porch while discussing which crops needed tending and how to best bring in the hay. So, when Clara asked him to stay out late one Friday evening in August, she wasn't surprised when he said, "No, Clara. Your daddy will have my hide." And she knew it was true.

Mother only spoke about John once. Clara was sitting in the kitchen, enjoying the cool morning air blowing through the screen door, when Mother slid up behind her.

"Beat the eggs for breakfast."

Clara didn't hear her, lost in thought, remembering the feel of John's scruff against her cheek, and Mother wrenched her wrist so hard, she nearly toppled from the stool.

"That boy is no good. Listen to me. If you let him put a baby inside you, I'll make sure it never takes a single breath."

Clara nodded, her mouth working in a mumble. "Yes, ma'am."

When she told Sydney about it, later that night, at the cabin that felt more like a home than the farmhouse, Sydney crossed her arms and frowned.

"She's right, you know. Not about the baby, but about men. They're all the same, Clara. He'll hurt you like your daddy if you let him."

Clara hadn't expected that. It shook her. She told Sydney he wouldn't. She swore John would never do the things Father had done. John was kind and supportive and a gentleman. He had a blue heeler named Rosco he called his kid. She'd never seen John angry with him once, even when Rosco snatched a half-done steak from the grill in John's backyard a few weekends back. He'd only laughed and said the dog wanted to live a little and that Clara should do the same. She told

Sydney it was time she met John to see for herself, but Sydney twisted the sole of her white Converse into the dusty shack floorboards and shook her head.

"He'll turn on you at some point," she said, "once you give him what he wants. You'll see."

A fountain of anger bubbled up, and Clara argued with Sydney for the first time in her life. How dare she ruin this after all Clara had been through, after everything she'd suffered and endured. Why did she want to take this away from her? No true friend would.

"I just . . . miss you," Sydney said. "You don't spend as much time with me anymore."

It suddenly all made sense, and Clara shot forward with her finger out. "You're jealous, aren't you?"

Sydney blinked her big blue eyes until they filled with tears and said nothing in return. Then she balled her hands into fists and left, and she and Clara didn't see as much of each other after that.

CHAPTER SEVENTEEN

EMMA

I try hard to focus, but I can't. I'm covered in sweat and my eyes aren't working right. Every time I blink, the picture changes.

Blink. Branches and trees.

Blink. Snow and sky.

Blink. Kayla and Dad.

It feels like a bad dream, only it's not. I know because my leg is *killing* me. It won't stop aching. Whenever Kayla takes a step, I feel like I'm going to pass out. I wish Dad was still carrying me, but he's hurt now, too. I think he got cut or something when we fell, because he keeps leaving all these bright-red footprints in the snow.

I'm not sure how long we've been walking. It feels like hours. Hours and hours. One thing I've learned about being in this much pain is that it makes time work differently. Like last night when my leg wouldn't stop aching, and I kept having all these crazy weird dreams. Well, not dreams so much as pictures of myself tumbling down the hill over and over with the rock rolling right after. Then I'd wake up and really be crying. And screaming. It's all I could do — cry and scream.

Dad gave me some medicine to help with the pain, which it did some. At least for a while anyway, but not anymore, especially after he fell. When my leg hit the bridge, it hurt even worse than when the rock landed on it. It felt like a bunch of fireworks shooting off under my skin. It still does. I'm not sure how much longer I can stand it. But I'm trying to be strong. I'm trying, *really, really,* hard. And to be brave because Dad and Kayla keep telling me it's what I need to do. Also, it helps knowing Mom is watching out for me, even if I can't see her.

This is how I know: the day before she died, she put her hand on my heart and said, "*Sweet girl, I'll never leave you. I'll be right here with you forever.*" I loved when she called me that — her sweet girl — because I knew she meant it. I really *was* her sweet girl. I still am. Sometimes, I can even feel her looking down on me from heaven, just like when she sent Kayla and Dad to find me last night, which is why I'm pretty sure she'll get us out of this, too.

Just as I think it, Kayla stops.

"Is that . . . is that a house?"

"Yes," Dad says, limping up to us. "Oh my God, yes."

Then Kayla is running, and my leg is exploding as it bangs against hers.

"Emma, look," she says, slowing down. "Do you see that?"

At first, I can't. The snow is all over the place — sticking to my eyelashes and getting in my mouth. It makes me think of the snow globe Mimi and Papa gave me last Christmas with the pretty, white farmhouse in the middle. When you shake it, the house disappears, but not for long, because it only takes a minute before all the glitter settles on the roof again. It's what I'm looking at right now — a roof covered in white glitter.

Warmth fills my chest. I knew Mom would save us. I *knew* it. Still, it takes forever to reach the house. There's this yard we have to cross, the biggest I've ever seen, surrounded by a huge, black fence. Kayla almost drops me a few times

63

along the way. She's definitely not as strong as Dad. But she doesn't, and soon Dad is limping up the porch to knock on the door.

"Help! We need help!"

Something about his voice scares me. He doesn't usually sound like that, all screechy and tight, like he thinks a bear is chasing us or something. He knocks again, harder.

Bang! Bang! Bang!

"Please, is anyone home?"

Right when I'm thinking that maybe no one is, there's a bunch of clicks and snaps, and the door cracks open.

"Yes?"

Dad waves my way, talking super fast. "Please, ma'am, we need shelter. You have to let us in. My little girl is injured. We got trapped in the storm and—"

"Oh, Lord . . ." The door shuts, and I hear a chain slide free. When it opens again, I let out this little whimper. I'm so confused because standing right there in the doorway . . . is Mom.

CHAPTER EIGHTEEN

CLARA
1994–1996

John proposed to Clara on July fourth. The ring was small — a thin, gold band with a speck of diamond pressed into the center that glittered beneath the fireworks. Clara gasped when she saw it and flapped her hands as she said, "Yes, yes, yes." When John kissed her, Clara knew her life had finally begun.

The wedding was intimate, just the two of them at the county courthouse. John wore a button-down shirt with slacks. Clara wore a corded lace gown. They rented a home on the outskirts of Meeker, surrounded by willow trees with branches that swept the grass in soft, green curtains. John took a job as an electrician and worked odd hours while Clara studied to become a nurse. She wanted nothing to do with farming and spent as little time with Mother and Father as possible. John insisted they eat dinner with the Carvers on Sundays; he'd lost his parents to a car wreck when he was five, and he didn't understand Clara's reluctance when it came to her family. He'd asked a few times, but Clara refused to talk about it. Besides, Clara knew John adored Father, and she felt some things were better left buried.

They spent summer evenings on the back porch listening to the wind tease the willows and winters tucked inside the small living room watching old movies near the fireplace. Their bedroom was small, and Clara sometimes woke in the middle of the night in a panic thinking she was back in the Black Place, only to fall into John's waiting arms. His touch always calmed her, but there were some nights that took longer than others for her to stop crying. It was on one of those nights, with the rain pattering down softly outside, that he whispered something that set her heart on fire.

"Let's make a baby."

She hadn't seriously considered it until that very moment; she feared there was something of Mother in her, and Clara couldn't bear the thought of harming her child as she'd been harmed. She wouldn't, she decided. She was nothing like Mother, and John deserved a son with eyes as brown as his. It was all he'd ever wanted — a chance to be the father he'd never had. He talked about it constantly. He planned future camping trips, the three of them on a road trip to Yellowstone, or day trips spent driving through the Flat Tops to see the fall colors. They would save enough money to go to Disney World someday, and if things went according to plan, possibly even Hawaii. It all sounded so wonderful to Clara. A family all her own, one Mother and Father couldn't touch.

She found out she was pregnant three months later, and surprised John with a coffee mug she'd purchased at the antique shop in Meeker. "Good morning, Daddy!" it read in looping black letters that disappeared beneath his palm a moment before he dropped it with a shout. A boy, they both thought. They would name him Daniel.

She lost the baby in February with the snow filtering down gray and lifeless beyond their bedroom window. When she told John, he held her close and ran his fingers through her hair. This was normal, he said. It happened. They would try again. And they did, that fall, and Clara knew she was pregnant because her breasts ached, and her underwear came away spotted a light pink. This one lasted longer, nine weeks, before the baby's heartbeat failed. Clara had to have her uterus scraped to remove what was left of her dead child's cells.

John said all the right things, comforting Clara as he had before, but his gaze had dimmed, and he talked less. It was as if someone had reached behind his eyes and turned out the lights. They didn't speak of children after that, and John grew distant, spending long hours at work and even longer hours out with his friends, whom Clara never much liked; they drank and smoked and cursed in ways that reminded her of Father.

When John bothered to speak, it was to complain about his job and how much he hated it. He wanted nothing more than to breathe fresh air and work the land like he used to on the Carver farm. He drank and smoked and cursed in ways that reminded her of Father, and there were times she caught him glancing at her with a crease in his brow and a slight curl of his upper lip. It was the same way Father had looked at her growing up — with disgust. She'd become a burden to John, something he'd used up.

She grew lonely and poured her pain into her studies. She commuted to the community college in Rangely for a time, but it didn't make her happy. When John asked if she would get a job at the new medical facility in Rifle, Clara told him she would try, but she didn't; she'd already dropped out of school. She couldn't focus on anything other than the fact that she'd failed John in a way no woman should.

Her depression deepened. She spent her days in bed, rising most afternoons to pick at a piece of overripe fruit or nibble on a few crackers before lying down again. She kept the windows closed, and the house grew stale with the smell of spoiled food and musty air. John complained about it, and when that didn't work, he put his fist through the wall.

"Enough is enough, Clara. It's time to move on."

He stormed out then, shoving past her so hard, she fell and chipped her tooth on the oak floor. He didn't turn at her cry, didn't look back once, and she slept in the guest room that night and wept until her eyes ached. She wondered for the first time if John would hurt her like Father had if she made him angry enough. He'd grown hard and cold, and Clara questioned if she really knew the man she'd married.

But it was John, not Father, and he brought her flowers the next morning and forced her outside for some clean air. He told her he was sorry for the way he'd been acting, and that he loved her.

"I'll stop drinking so much. I know I haven't been good to you lately."

Clara smiled and nodded, but the hollow space in her chest carved by the children she'd lost ached with such an intensity, it was as if it had a heartbeat of its own, one she didn't think she'd ever get back.

And, despite his promises, John continued to drink and smoke and sometimes came home smelling of perfume or freshly scrubbed skin. It picked at her, those scents, but she let them go. John wasn't the cheating type. He'd never leered after women the way Father had, even when they were attractive or paid him attention, and Clara convinced herself she was being silly. She remembered the promises he'd made to Father all those years ago and how he'd never once broken them, never once been late to work or missed Clara's curfew. He'd promised Clara there would be no one else other than her for as long as he lived, and Clara believed him. John was a man of his word.

But even those thoughts didn't help much, and it wasn't until an unseasonably hot fall afternoon in late September that Clara's mood improved substantially. It was a good day; she'd been in the kitchen preparing a lemon chicken casserole, one of John's favorites, when the doorbell rang. It had been years since she'd last seen her friend, but Clara recognized her right away, slightly older now with her raven hair cut short above a lavender strapless maxi dress that fell to her ankles.

"Hello, Clara," Sydney said, and Clara invited her in.

CHAPTER NINETEEN

CHRIS

My brain goes slack, my lungs caught in a slow exhale. I'm breathless, frozen, because, for the briefest of moments, my wife is standing in the doorframe. She has the same rust-colored hair. The same pale-green eyes.

She speaks, and the illusion is broken.

"Oh my God, yes, please bring her inside."

She swings the door wide, and I take Emma from Kayla and limp after the woman and into a dark-hued foyer. Fire spits through my calf as she leads me past a sweeping staircase toward a living room whose details I barely register, only that it's cavernous and dim with furniture flung haphazardly throughout: a worn cherry breakfront pressed next to a pale-blue love seat. An office desk lying on its side surrounded by a slew of cardboard boxes. The woman sweeps a pile of books from a red-checkered sofa near the far wall and pats the cushion. "Lay her here."

Emma moans as I kneel and ease her onto the couch. I unzip the sleeping bag to a ring of pink skin crusted in sweat and pine bark. My fingertips hover over her calf before tracing across it, a series of white marks rising in their wake. The skin is tight and swollen with fluid.

"My God. What happened to her?" the woman asks.

"Hiking accident. A rock crushed her leg. I need to get this swelling down. Do you have any Advil or Tylenol? Anything like that?"

"In the kitchen. Yes. I'll be right back."

I snatch a brown quilt draped across the arm of the couch and spread it over Emma's chest. My hand comes to rest on her forehead. She's hot, *too* hot, her skin damp with sweat, her hair clumped in gluey strands above her eyebrows. And she's shivering . . . *has been* shivering since we set out this morning. I outline her cheek with my thumb, and she blinks up at me through a sheen of tears.

"Emma, baby. I'm right here. Daddy's right here."

Kayla squats next to me and takes her hand. "Me too, Ems. You're safe now. We're going to get you fixed up, okay?"

She manages to nod, streams of clear liquid trailing from the corners of her eyes.

"Here you are," the woman says, returning with a glass of water and some pills. I do the math. Two Advil last night, and two around 3 a.m., with one more this morning. Five in the last twenty-four hours, and this is Tylenol, so it should be okay. I take the pills and the cup and bring them to Emma's mouth. She whimpers and shakes her head, flings a hand at the glass.

I press it back to her lips. "Emma, it's medicine. It will make you feel better."

She moans and shakes her head again, her eyes clamping shut. Water sloshes and runs down her neck and onto her already damp shirt.

The woman crouches next to me and gestures for the glass. "Mind if I try?"

Do I? I'm not sure. But I have to do something . . .

In a daze, I pass her the water and pills. She takes my spot on the edge of the couch and leans toward Emma with a

70

soft smile. "Hello, sweetheart. I'm Clara. Your Daddy's right. This will help your leg feel so much better, but only if we can get this medicine in your tummy, okay?"

Emma stops squirming and cracks an eye open. She squints up at the woman, Clara, like maybe she recognizes her.

Lexi. She sees it, too.

"Can you take a big sip, honey, and hold the water in your mouth?"

Emma's brow furrows at the question, but she lips the glass and takes a drink, and then another. Relief pours through me as Clara guides the pills into her mouth.

"There you go. Show me a big swallow. That's it."

"Do you have a phone?" I ask. "I need to call an ambulance."

The glass twitches in Clara's hand. "An ambulance? I-I'm afraid that's not possible."

"What do you mean . . . 'not possible?'"

"The closest hospital is half a day's drive south. And that's in good weather."

"There's got to be something nearby. An urgent care or a doctor's office?"

What little color is left in her face drains. "No. No, I'm afraid not. I—"

"What about that truck out front? Can I borrow it? I'll take her myself."

"Well, yes, but" — her eyes dart toward the window — "with that storm, there's a good chance you'd get stuck along the way, or worse."

"I'll risk it. Please, I'll bring it back as soon as I can."

Kayla lays a hand on my arm and cuts me off. "Dad. She's right. Look."

I turn toward the broad square of glass planted in the far wall, and my throat glues shut. A river of silver and white flakes spatter the pane and whirl back out again to join a glittering, formless void. Peals of wind shriek and rake the

71

siding, rattling the eaves and gutters, the snow climbing the fence posts in heavy drifts.

No . . . It's all I can think. *No, no, no, no* . . .

Clara's voice comes in slow and steady like someone speaking through waves of speaker static. I glance toward her speechless, my lips numb.

"Sorry, what?"

"I said, I think I might be able to help."

* * *

We strip the cast together. I gently unwind my belt as Clara stacks the pine boughs next to the couch. Removing the T-shirt I used to cushion the break is worse. It comes off in a slow, agonizing pull that sets Emma to screeching, her fingers flexing open and shut like hungry little mouths. Kayla looks on with a face stripped of color, her forehead shining in a waxy, gray sheen. It's the same look she had in the forest before passing out.

"Try to keep your sister calm," I say, trying to distract her. "Talk to her."

She does her best, stroking Emma's sweat-crusted hair and whispering into her ear that it will be over soon, that we are being as gentle as we can. It's not enough. Emma whips her head back and forth in a series of shrieks that burrow into my ears until they ring. I slide a hand up to her chest and hold it there, feel her ribs quivering beneath her shirt.

"Emma, you have to stay still, okay?"

A tendon leaps across her neck in response, a wet, strangled cry rising up her throat.

Clara leans past me.

"Sweetheart, I know this hurts, but there are a lot of bad germs on your leg right now, and I need to clean them off so you can feel better again. It will sting a little, but you know what? I think you might be the toughest little girl I've ever seen."

Emma stills at the sound of her voice, looking at her with a pink slice of lip caught between her teeth.

"Do you think you can be tough for me for just a little bit longer?"

Emma breathes fast through her nose, her nostrils flexing, her cheeks streaked in clear strings of snot. Finally, she nods, the motion so subtle, I nearly miss it.

Clara's eyes flash to mine, her voice dropping a notch. "You'll have to hold her leg down. If she moves, she'll cause more damage."

The next few minutes drag past in a painful, endless smear. Clara fetches a bag filled with medical supplies and retrieves a large plastic syringe from within. She fills it with distilled water and irrigates the wound before soaking several cotton balls with hydrogen peroxide. She dabs Emma's ankle, and the solution mixes with the blood and foams over the damaged skin. Emma screeches and snaps her eyes wide. A fierce tremble breaks across her chest, and she sinks her fingernails into my arm so hard, I nearly release her leg. I tighten my grip. Tears cloud my eyes as she shrieks; each cry is a knife to the heart. Kayla chants for Emma to calm down next to me, to *breathe*.

"Breathe, Ems. *Breathe*."

"I need some newspaper to stabilize the splint," Clara says. "A couple rolls over there by the fireplace."

Kayla scrambles for them as Clara applies a thin coat of iodine with a cotton swab. Her movements are steady and crisp, her gaze focused. *She's done this before*. The thought is all that keeps me from falling apart. Clara strips a large bandage with her teeth and smooths it over the wound, followed by several layers of gauze. Kayla rushes back with the newspaper, and Clara snatches two rolls and sets them on either side of Emma's shin before securing them with a pack of bandage wrap. She winds the material around Emma's calf in a tight figure-eight pattern. "There. That should do it."

I barely hear her through Emma's purple-lipped howl, her eyes squelching shut as she claws at my arm in a frantic attempt to reach her leg. I slide my palms from her thigh and take her hands in mine. Her fingers are icicles, her skin damp against my own.

"It's over, love. It's over." I barely manage to choke the words out, Kayla sobbing next to me in a featureless blur with her shoulders jerking, her hands pressed to her mouth. I loop an arm around her and pull her close. I'm about to tell her Emma will be okay, that she'll be just fine, when Kayla stiffens and raises a trembling finger toward the hall. I follow her gaze, and my blood turns to lead. Standing there, pooled in shadow, is the biggest man I've ever seen in my life.

CHAPTER TWENTY

KAYLA

Please be okay, Emma. Please, please, please . . .

I'm scared she won't. Okay, more than scared. Beyond scared. I'm her big sister. I'm supposed to protect her, and what did I do instead? I ran off with Dad's phone. God, I'm so stupid. Mom would never forgive me for this, and if Emma doesn't heal, I'll never forgive myself.

The woman, Clara or whatever, finishes the splint and covers it with a blanket. I'm so glad we found her, and this place, even if it is a little weird. I think she's a hoarder or something. I've never seen so many boxes. They're stacked everywhere, piled next to the walls and pushed under tables, filled with things that don't make sense like toddler sneakers and gardening gloves and metal hangers twisted in knots. It's why I don't see the man sooner, the craziness of the place. I think he's a mannequin at first, that's how still he is, but then he moves, and I sink my fingers into Dad's arm and point.

"Billy . . . Billy, is that you?" Clara says, glaring into the hall. "What did I tell you about sneaking up on people?"

The man scratches his head. "Th-that . . . it's bad?"

"Yes. Now please, come on out here."

He limps into the room. He's huge and bald with a pair of cheeks that fall past his chin. His eyes remind me of a teddy bear's, small and black, and the way he looks at Clara, with his mouth twisted into a pout, makes me think he's more of a boy than a man. I can't really tell for sure, though, only that he's probably not a whole lot older than me. He sways in place in a pair of grease-splotched Carhartt overalls that look like they haven't been washed in years, his black rubber boots squeaking against the floor.

Clara smiles at me. "I'm so sorry. He can be a little shy sometimes around—"

"Blood! There's blood, blood, yucky blood!" Billy backs up and bangs off a glass-top coffee table. A mug tips off the corner and shatters on the floor, a stream of curdled milk running over the wood. "I don't like blood, Ma," he says, pointing at Dad's feet. "You know I don't. Make it stop!"

Dad blinks down at the cuff of his blood-soaked jeans like he forgot about his cut . . . which I'm pretty sure he did.

"Right," he mumbles, easing into a gray, suede arm-chair. "Sorry about that."

Clara scrabbles toward him. "Oh my, you're injured, too. Here, let me take a look."

Billy flaps his arms and buries his face in his hands, one of them covered with a tan leather glove. "Don't wanna look at it," he says, rocking back on his heels, "No, no, no . . ."

Ohh-kay, I think, pressing back into the couch. Emma stiffens in my lap. She's looking at Billy, too, her little face all wrinkled up like she's trying to figure him out. She's still crying, but not as hard, taking in these little whimpering breaths that break my heart.

"I'm right here," I whisper, smoothing her eyebrows with my thumb. "You're safe, I promise."

She looks up, and her lips buckle. I'm as scared as she is, but I can't show it. I need to be strong for her, be her big sister for once. I stroke her hair and look over at Dad, who's hissing as Clara dabs the gash on his leg with a fistful of gauze. It's pretty gnarly-looking and still bleeding some, but Clara seems to know what she's doing, so I'm not too worried.

"My word," she says. "How did you do this to yourself?"

Dad grimaces. "There was a bridge. It was slick."

"This needs stitches."

He pulls his leg back. "No. No stitches."

"Okay, okay," Clara says, easing his calf back into place. She applies a few butterfly strips. "These should work. Just take it easy and keep some pressure on it, and you should be fine." She strips another, larger bandage and presses it over the cut, then finishes it off with the same roll of bandage wrap she used on Emma. "The footbridge, right? It gets as slippery as a February morning in snow like this." She glances at Billy. "I'm done. You can look now."

He rocks in place. "Nuh-uh. No, no, no, no."

Clara stands, and I take her in for the first time. She has hair nearly as red as Mom's, falling in tangles over a ratty-looking blue sweater, the sleeves trimmed in lace. It's ugly, way too small, something I'm guessing she left in the dryer for too long. Her jeans are worse, though. *Way* worse. Total mom jeans, the fabric all scuffed and worn out at the knees. She's got them pulled up to her waist so high, I can see her ankles. Well, not her ankles so much as her socks, which are beyond ridiculous, stitched with all these little purple and green and orange crocodiles squirming up from a pair of fur-lined slippers. She blows at her bangs and flashes Dad a gummy smile, and I can't help but think she looks like she just fell out of a strip mall thrift store.

"So, now that you've met Billy and me, who might you all be?"

Dad grinds his thumbs into his temples. "Yeah, right. Sorry. I'm Chris. And these are my daughters, Kayla and Emma. This storm . . . it just came out of nowhere. If you hadn't have been here, I don't know what we would have done."

Clara waves him off like it's no big deal, like maybe she's used to total strangers crashing into her home from time to time. "Oh, don't you worry about it for a second. We're glad to help, aren't we, Billy?"

"I don't wanna look, Ma. Don't make me." His words are muffled and thick, trapped behind his hands, which are still smashed to his face.

Clara ignores him. "It's the earliest blizzard we've had in years. A Nor'easter down from Canada, I hear. It's supposed to snow like this for the next day or two."

My breath catches. "Wait? Another day or two?"

She nods. "That's what the news says."

"Can I use your phone?" Dad asks, suddenly looking pale. "I need to make a few calls."

"Yes, yes, of course. It's in the kitchen. Right this way. I'll make you all some food while you're at it. You must be famished."

"Yes, very," he says, rising from the chair with a groan.

I ease Emma's head onto a pillow and move to help him, but Clara beats me to it, looping an arm beneath his shoulders before he can stop her.

"I'm okay," he says.

Clara laughs and pats his chest. "Nonsense. I won't have you falling again. Not with what you've been through already. You just put your weight on me."

"I'll come with you," I say, anxious to get away from Billy, who's now sitting cross-legged and staring at Emma through a crack in his fingers.

Dad shakes his head. "No, stay with your sister. I'll be right back."

I nod and slump back onto the couch as they limp from the room, Clara's hand wrapped around his waist like she's known him her whole life instead of a few minutes. It's so bizarre — this house and this woman and her weird son, if that's even who he is. He could be an ax murderer for all I know. Either way, I decide, it's better than being stuck out in the storm freezing to death.

"Hi, I'm Billy," he says. "What's your name?"

I realize he's staring at me with his mouth open, his eyes popped wide like he's never seen a girl before. And it's a weird question since Dad just introduced us.

"Uh . . . yeah, I'm Kayla," I reply.

He gives me a big, yellow smile. "You're a stranger, huh? Ma says not to talk to strangers."

Emma grabs my fingers and squeezes. I tense and tell myself to calm down, but it's hard because there's something wrong with Billy's eyes. They're pressed way too close to his nose, and his lips are cracked and blistered. He scoots forward suddenly and comes up onto his knees. I'm hit with a sour cloud of B.O. as he fish-hooks two fingers into the corners of his mouth and stretches his lips into an insane clown smile. Then he's blowing into his palms.

"I did a fart. Whoops."

He burps a laugh, and I glance down at Emma, who, unbelievably, is smiling back at him. He does it again, blowing farts with his hands and laughing before thudding back onto his butt. He looks at Emma a moment longer before twisting his eyes in my direction. "Are you her ma? Can she be my friend?"

"Uh, no, I'm her sister. And yeah, sure, I guess."

He claps once, overly loud, and does it again. "Yay. A friend! I like friends." Then he's back to rocking in place, whooshing his hands over his overalls, rubbing away like a madman, with his yellow smile growing bigger and bigger. I stare back at him and wonder just what it is we've gotten ourselves into.

CHAPTER TWENTY-ONE

CLARA
1996

"I'm so sorry, Clara."
"Me, too."
Those words were all it took to bring them to tears, both of them crying and laughing as they fell into a hug. Sydney smelled the same, Clara thought, of lavender and mint. She made them margaritas and pulled Sydney out onto the porch, where she told Clara about the places she'd gone and the things she'd seen, places Clara had read about in books as a little girl and dreamed of someday seeing for herself. Sydney had studied abroad for a year, and Clara listened, rapt, as Sydney spoke about the men in Italy who were charming and beautiful, with dark olive skin and sand-colored eyes. France had coastlines that glowed for miles with houses perched above the Mediterranean, nestled in bunches along white sandstone cliffs.

But as she spoke, Clara noticed her words didn't match her appearance. Her hair was brittle and washed out, and her fingers twitched as she slid a pack of cigarettes from her purse and lit one. She pulled in a deep lungful of smoke, and her cheeks curved into little hollows that smoothed when she exhaled. Her eyes flicked and darted as she spoke, her toe tapping a steady beat on the porch, and Clara wondered what had happened to Sydney since she'd last seen her friend.

When Sydney asked about her life, Clara talked about her marriage and how she and John planned to buy a home closer to town, where he spent most of his days installing wiring and repairing old light fixtures. They were thinking about starting a family, Clara said; they had, in fact, already tried. With any luck, they would soon have a child of their own. It didn't take long for Sydney to spot the sorrow hiding behind Clara's smile, and she teased it out of her like she had all those years ago when they lay upon the loose planks of their forest shack.

"Are you sure you're okay?"

Clara's smile broke at the question, and she shook her head. She told Sydney about the miscarriages and how, most days, she struggled to get out of bed.

"John is so distant now."

Sydney listened as Clara wept through the rest of the story, edging closer to her on the porch swing.

"But is he still kind to you?"

"Yes, mostly," Clara replied, easing her tongue past her chipped tooth.

A crease formed between Sydney's eyebrows. "What's he done to you?"

"Nothing. I mean, he's lost his temper a few times. It's been hard on him, too."

Sydney's blue eyes flashed with anger, and Clara thought of the bobcat floating in the water all those years ago, of Mr. Oatman's tabby lying dead and broken in Sydney's lap, and their fight the last time they'd discussed John. She stiffened as Sydney opened her mouth to say something, but then her lips fell shut, and she laid a hand on Clara's arm with a gentle smile instead.

"It's okay. I'm here now."

Clara nodded and knew then she'd made a mistake letting Sydney walk out of her life. Besides John, she'd never been so close with anyone.

* * *

They spent every afternoon together after that, tucked inside the house or sitting out on the back porch, sipping tall glasses of iced tea until John came home from work. On the evenings he came home drunk, which, lately, was happening more often than Clara liked, she'd ask him if Sydney could stay a while longer. He'd give her a funny look at that, like he couldn't believe she actually had a friend of her own, but then mumble a "Sure, whatever," before stumbling off to bed.

On those nights, after Sydney shot John a cold glance, they talked as they used to, going on about the future and all the things they planned to do. Sydney said she wanted to move back to Meeker after veterinary school. She would start a practice downtown. There weren't many close by, after all, and the ranches needed more doctors to help with all the livestock and horses. Clara wondered if her career choice had anything to do with what she'd done to Mr. Oatman's cat all those years ago. A penance of sorts.

When Sydney asked Clara about her plans, she mumbled something about nursing, though she knew it was a lie; she'd enjoyed her studies, but the thought of touching another person made her shiver for some reason. Sydney said Clara could help manage the vet business when the time was right, and Clara agreed that that sounded like a wonderful idea.

Their time together brought Clara back to life, along with the house. She opened the windows and mopped the oak wood floors. She scrubbed the counters and polished their surfaces until they gleamed. She caught up on laundry and organized the pantry and refrigerator, throwing out old boxes of rice and spoiled containers of yogurt. It felt like she was cleaning herself out, and with each passing day, she thought about the miscarriages less and the future more. The pain inside her receded to a dull ache, and she grew happy again.

John noticed. They reconnected. He took her out for dinner, and they drove through the countryside as they once had, at sunset with the sky rimmed in pale pink above the mountains. She told him she was sorry for disappearing and promised it wouldn't happen again. They made love more often, and John seemed to see her again for the first time in a very long time.

She found out she was pregnant in March and hid it from him until May. Most mornings she threw up her breakfast, and her love for

82

sweet things faded, replaced by a craving for pickles. She napped hard and often, and when John asked what was wrong, she told him she was tired. He believed her. He had no reason not to. At twelve weeks, sure the pregnancy would take, Clara pulled his hand to her stomach and smiled.

"You're going to be a father."

"Wait, what? Are you serious?"

Clara nodded, and John swept her into his arms and laughed as he swung her in circles. Clara gave birth to a baby girl six months later. They named her Kinley, and she died before she took her first breath.

CHAPTER TWENTY-TWO

CHRIS

"Dispatch. What's your emergency?"

"My family and I — we got trapped outside in the blizzard. We—"

"Is everyone okay? Have you found shelter?"

"Yes, but my daughter is injured. She broke her leg. I need an ambulance right away."

"What's your name, sir? And your address?"

"Chris McKenna." I cover the phone and turn toward Clara, who is busy dicing an onion. "I need your address."

She swipes a pen and a stray bit of paper from the counter and scratches it out, slides it to me. I uncup my hand from the receiver.

"Okay, it's 4434 Station Dr—"

"—didn't catch that — Please . . . have . . . name again?"

"I said it's Chris. Chris McKenna."

" . . . "

"Are you there?"

"Sir . . . name?"

"What? Hello?"

" . . . "

"Hello?"

". . ."

"Dammit."

I slam the phone down hard enough to rattle the cradle. Clara flinches and looks up, sets the knife down and wipes her hands on a dishtowel.

"Did it go out?"

"Yeah, it's dead."

She slips past me and picks up the phone. Her nose crinkles as she presses it to her ear, her eyes narrowing. "Must be the storm. It happens from time to time up here. Especially in weather like this. Don't worry, they'll have it fixed soon enough."

I glance at my watch. It's 4 p.m. Lexi's parents will be nervous by now, anxious for my call, hoping to hear we made it back to the car safe and sound. If news of this storm has reached them, they'll be more than anxious. They'll be panicked. Hell, for all I know, they might be rounding up a search team already, making white-knuckled calls to the cops like the one I just made. I can picture it, the two of them looking at each other with the same question hanging in their eyes: *Surely, they're fine, right?*

"Can I borrow your cell phone?" I ask.

Clara rubs the back of her neck. "I . . . don't have one. I used to, but I'm, well, not really one for that type of thing."

I feel my chest tighten. *That type of thing? Basic technology?* "How about the Internet? Or email? I need to get ahold of some family and let them know we're okay."

"No, I'm afraid not. I'm sorry."

"I'll be right back."

My calf spits fire as I leave the kitchen and limp back into the living room. It's large, with high vaulted ceilings and a monstrosity of a chandelier dripping dirty, jaundice-yellow light over the wallpaper-coated walls. There are boxes everywhere, full of junk and scattered throughout, packed in between chairs and bookshelves and a bare antique china cabinet with no china. A worn breakfront leers at me from the corner with the doors hanging open, vomiting a sheaf of paper onto the floor. There's no sense of continuity to the room, everything a step below organized chaos. It's like they moved in years ago and forgot to unpack.

"Did you reach anyone?" Kayla asks as I stride past her for my windbreaker.

"No. The lines are down." My head throbs as I say it, a headache gathering steam at the base of my skull.

"Dad."

"Give me a minute." I dig through my jacket pockets. "Goddammit, where's my phone?"

"But, Dad, I—"

"*What*, Kayla?" I say, whirling on her.

Her lips part as if to say something, fall shut again.

"Sorry. I didn't mean to snap like that." I nod at Emma. "How's she doing?"

"She's . . . okay, she's—"

"Sleeping."

Billy's voice startles me. I forgot about him. He's seated cross-legged a few feet away, at the base of a blue recliner, staring at Emma with eyes that remind me of a trout's: dim and without substance, vacuous.

"She's sleeping," he says again, looking at me with a grin.

"Yes, she is."

I search his face in an effort to puzzle out what's wrong with him. He's mostly bald, his scalp peppered with sunspots, which makes him appear older than he is, a feature at odds with his full cheeks and a face devoid of wrinkles. He looks normal enough, doesn't have the facial characteristics of someone with Down's, no flattened nose or thin upper lip, but something about the way he moves, his hands rubbing his legs in jerky, hitching motions — it's odd, like he hasn't quite learned how to control his body yet. And the way he speaks, with his words thick and garbled, makes me wonder if he dropped out of elementary school somewhere around third grade.

Find your phone.

I turn back to the pack and tear it open.

. . . and stop.

A shot of ice water swims down my spine. *The bridge.* The phone won't be in the pack because it's in the goddamn creek. It slipped out of my pocket when I fell. I pull in a ragged breath, and my headache intensifies, creeping up my neck and bleeding into my skull like an electrical storm.

"Oh, Jesus," I mutter, sitting down hard.

"What's the matter?" Kayla asks. There's a slow-simmering panic to her tone, like she's hoping I'll say everything will be okay. That we're fine. But we're not. We're anything *but* fine. My calf pulses in response, tells me what I already know. We're stuck here for now.

Billy rubs his overalls and rocks in place. *Swish, swish, swish.* I glance out the window. The snow is blowing harder now, swallowing the light in a colorless wall of ash. The driveway is gone, the forest scrubbed from sight.

Swish, swish, swish.

Billy cocks his head and stares at Emma with those flat, black eyes shining. "She's sleeping." He plays the word out like a snake: *sssleeeping.*

I glance at her. She is, and, for now, I hope she doesn't wake up.

CHAPTER TWENTY-THREE

CHRIS

I didn't want kids. It was Lexi's thing, her maternal clock kicking in right after she'd turned thirty. We'd be at the park, a couple of mochas in hand, feeding the ducks, and she'd nudge me and point out a dad chasing after some wobbly-kneed toddler or smile at a mom pushing her kid on a swing set.

"Don't you want that someday?"

I'd nod and reply with something like, *"Sure . . . some-day,"* not really meaning it. I didn't bother to tell her the dad looked completely exhausted, and the mom had formula stains crusting the neck of her T-shirt. I didn't mention how utterly terrified I was every time she broached the subject of parenthood. I had no template to follow. My own father had abandoned me, and wasn't I his son? Wouldn't I do the same?

I'd been right to worry, though not about vanishing in the middle of the night like he did. Nothing so cold as that. No, I ran in different ways. At first, it was to work, where I had a semblance of control, a place of my own free from the chaos Kayla unleashed. The red-faced temper tantrums and endless bouts of crying. How she curled into a tight ball in my lap and shook her little fists with demands I didn't know how to meet.

I worked extra hours. I took on every project I could. On the weekends, I ran to the bar or the golf course. There were old friends to see and new ones to make. I took every chance I could to escape the house, with its incessant diaper changes and kitchen sink baths, the tables scabbed over in puddles of creamed spinach and spilled milk. And just my being there, at home, seemed to piss Lexi off. I didn't feed the baby the right way or organize the kitchen the way she liked. If I offered an extra hand, it was never fast enough. What had I been doing? Why hadn't I come sooner? It suffocated me, the overwhelming knowledge that my life wasn't my own anymore, that I was trapped. Kayla was the sun, and we were the planets; our orbit revolved around her. I remember thinking, *This is it, Chris. This is your life for the next twenty years. Enjoy it.*

And so, I ran.

And I'll never run again. The thought drills through my core as I drape another blanket over Emma and feel her forehead. It's hot, still pumping heat, but not as much, the Tylenol finally doing its thing. I lean close and smooth the hair from her eyes. Her lips twitch in response, her eyes pinching tight, and I want to reach into her chest and soak up her pain, rip it out and carry it myself.

"I'm so sorry, baby. I should have been there," I whisper.

Fingertips brush mine. I look up to Kayla standing next to me with her jaw clenched, fighting back tears. I cup the back of her head and pull her into a hug. She stiffens at my touch, and a hollow ache spills through my chest. "Kayla, I—"

Clara clears her throat from across the room. "I'm sorry, I don't mean to interrupt. Dinner is ready, if you two would like to join us."

Kayla squirms from my arms, and I hesitate long enough to swallow the lump in my throat before responding. "Thank you, but I'm not sure I should leave my daughter."

"She'll be fine by herself for a minute, Dad," Kayla says.

I let my gaze linger on Emma, on the shape of her shoulders rising and falling, so thin beneath the brown quilt.

"We'll bring her some food, okay? Let her sleep for now."

"Okay," I reply. "I'll meet you in there. There's something I need to do first."

* * *

A squelch of static pierces my eardrum, and I set the phone back in the cradle. Dread coats my esophagus. I *have* to reach someone, *have* to get Emma some real help, not just a few bandages and some Tylenol. If I don't, an infection might set in. Or worse. I can see it all so clearly: her ankle turned to a swollen marshmallow full of pus, a blood clot jammed somewhere deep in her thigh, the world-weary surgeon tapping his clipboard as he tells me we need to operate. *I'm sorry, Mr. McKenna, but we'll need to take her leg.*

I can't let it happen. And I won't. We'll leave in the morning, I decide. We'll wait for a break in the storm and then borrow Clara's truck and leave. We'll drive until we find a hospital or someone who can help.

It will all be okay, I tell myself. *You can still make this work.*

The thought provides little comfort. All I can do is pray the storm passes soon and hope my little girl can hold on until morning.

* * *

I slump into the dining room and take a seat next to Kayla. There are no windows, the mahogany-paneled walls soaking up what little light spills from the ancient crystal light fixture planted in the center of a popcorn ceiling. As is the case elsewhere in the house, the room is a cluttered mess. Faded oil paintings (all Monet prints, Clara tells me — "*Don't you just love them?*") hang above the wainscoting, centered over stacks of books and cardboard boxes tipped on their sides. One leaks a steady stream of porcelain figurines onto a stained blue carpet, several missing arms and legs. A doll lies headless beneath a fake fern, the plastic dimpled and scorched black at the elbow. Clara circles the table, ladling stew as Billy thumps down across from me, his joints cracking like a freshly felled tree.

"Chris, would you be kind enough to do us the honor?" she asks, easing into her chair.

"Sorry?"

"Grace."

I stiffen. "I . . ."

"Oh, what am I thinking? That's rude of me. A guest shouldn't be asked to say grace. Here." She offers a hand to Billy, then to me. Billy reaches for Kayla's.

"O-kay," Kayla hisses below her breath.

"Just do it," I whisper back.

She rolls her eyes and reaches across the table. Billy's hand swallows hers whole as I take Clara's. Her palm is hot, slick with sweat. She bows her head.

"Lord Almighty, you are our salvation in times of trouble, and we thank you for bringing Chris and his family safely out of danger and into our home. We ask that you provide Emma with a sense of peace and comfort until she can receive medical attention, and that her leg will heal once she does. Please bless this food you have so graciously provided, and thank you for the health and strength it will bestow. In your great name, we pray all of this and more, amen." She slips her hand from mine and surveys the table. "Please everyone, eat."

Kayla jerks next to me, does it again.

"Let go."

Billy still has hold of her hand, a dim grin plastered across his chin.

"I said—"

He lets go, and Kayla jerks back and nearly topples from her chair. She rubs her wrist and frowns. "Jerk."

"Kayla," I snap, glancing at Clara, whose eyebrows are knitted together in the direction of Billy.

"Billy, you will mind your manners at this table. Do you understand me?"

His cheeks flare, and he nods overly hard. "Uh, yes — yes, ma'am."

Her face smooths, and she laces her fingers and surveys the table with a smile. "Good. Now, please dig in before it gets cold."

I take a bite. It's delicious, the broth winding warm down my throat as my hunger flares, the heat soaking into my stomach.

"How is it?" Clara asks.

"Very good," I say.

"Mm-hmm," Kayla adds, testing hers.

"I'm glad you both like it. It's my mother's recipe. She always said, 'All you need to feel safe and warm on a cold wet night is a good stew.'"

"Does she live close by?" I ask.

Her eyes flatten. "No, Mother has been gone for a long time now."

"Grammy got kilt," Billy says. He laughs — three quick bursts in between bites of bread. "Grampa kilt her."

Kayla's spoon clanks to her bowl.

Clara glares at him. "Billy. That's quite enough."

He shrinks back, then straightens, looking hurt. "What? You told me so yourself. You said Gramps done it. He kilt her. And why we got to eat in here, anyway, Ma? We don't never eat in here. This room gives me the jeepers."

Clara steeples her fingers and presses them to her chin. "Because we have guests."

"I don't wanna eat in here. I wanna eat in the barn with Phillip! He's all lonesome out there by hisself."

"No. It's much too cold out for that. Now please—"

"No, no, no! I wanna go see Phillip!"

92

She pulls in a slow breath. "William Carver, you will mind your—"

He pounds his gloved fist into the table and rattles the dishes.

"Phillip! Phillip! Phillip!"

Clara's jaw bunches, her gaze darkening, and I half-expect her to leap for him, but instead, she flutters her fingers at the door with an exasperated sigh.

"Fine. Go on. Put on a coat first."

"Oh boy. Oh boy, oh boy, oh boy." He surges to his feet and grabs his stew, lurching from the room with half of it sloshing over his arm and slopping to the floor. Kayla watches him leave with wide eyes. I reach over and squeeze her knee, and she flashes me a *what the hell is going on here?* look.

"It's okay," I mouth with a nod toward her stew. "Eat."

Clara retrieves her napkin and dabs the corners of her lips. "I'm so sorry about that. He has trouble controlling his emotions at times. He can be . . . somewhat difficult."

"What's his prob . . . ?" Kayla starts, flushing. "I um, I mean, why is he . . . ?"

Clara smiles. "Why does he act the way he does?"

Kayla nods.

"He's adopted. He has certain special needs." She glances toward the living room. "He's twenty, but mentally he's closer to the age of your little sister in there, Kayla. He'll always be a child inside, no matter how old he gets."

As if on cue, Billy's voice booms from some distant corner of the house. "Phillip, here I come! I'm comin', lil' guy!" A door slams, and Kayla flinches. Clara reaches across the table and pats her hand.

"Oh, sweetie, don't let him worry you. He may be big, but he's as harmless as a housefly. Really. He's got a good heart."

I take a drink of water and place the glass back in the sweat ring on the table. "So, who's this Phillip?"

"Oh," Clara says with a laugh. "Our Appaloosa. He's in the stable out back. How do you think I knew how to splint your little one's leg? You don't grow up on a farm without mending a few breaks here and there." She gives me a tight smile, something off about the way she curves her lips, a sad weight to their shape. "You've managed to stumble onto the Carver family ranch, Chris. All thirty thousand acres of it. Number one supplier of sweet corn in the greater Grand Valley . . . or we used to be, anyway."

"Not anymore?"

She takes a bite and shakes her head. "No. Not for a long time now. It's just me and Billy here."

"Wow, so there's no one else around to help?" Kayla asks. "How do you run it by yourself?"

"Well, we don't . . . really. My father practically had an army of ranch hands back when I was a girl. He told me I'd have the same someday, but things haven't exactly turned out the way he'd hoped."

I shift forward. "Listen, Clara. I can't thank you enough for what you've done for us here. Truly. I don't know where we'd be without your help."

It's a lie. I know exactly where we'd be. Lost. Frozen. Worse . . .

She waves a hand. "Are you joking? I can't tell you how nice it is to have some company. I haven't had—"

A cry rips through the room and cuts her off. A shriek I'd know anywhere.

Emma.

CHAPTER TWENTY-FOUR

CLARA
1996

Clara moved back to the Carver ranch four months before she gave birth. Father had been hospitalized by a sudden stroke that left him in a constant state of drool, spouting nonsense until he collapsed in a pile on the kitchen floor. Mother called with the news. She spoke to John first. He sipped his coffee and stared out the kitchen window, nodding into a cold September drizzle.

"I'm so sorry to hear that, Mrs. Carver. Yes, yes, of course, we will. Right away."

When he told Clara what Mother had said, that she was needed back home, Clara nearly tipped from her chair. She'd never shared with John the things Mother had done to her, had never spoken of Father and the Black Place and the pain she'd left buried there. She feared John would view her differently if he knew — as something unclean, someone to be pitied rather than loved. She couldn't bear the thought of that; she wanted John's love for herself, unconditionally and without reservation.

He'd only asked her about them once, the morning after they'd arrived at John and Clara's rental unexpectedly with a housewarming present in hand, a pale-green table lamp that John set on a side table in the living room. It felt like poison to Clara, that lamp, like an intrusion, but she couldn't tell him that, especially in front of Mother and Father, so she excused herself to bed instead.

"What is it about them that bothers you, Clara?" he asked, the next morning when they woke. "You can tell me."

"There's nothing to tell," she said. "I was just tired. Really." It was all she could manage without breaking into tears.

When he left for work, Clara rose and threw the lamp into the garbage. She buried it deep, beneath a stack of moldy old towels, and then hauled it out to the curb for the dump truck to collect. John never asked where it went.

* * *

A week after Mother called, they moved into the guest room off the kitchen. It had a full-sized bed and a separate bathroom, with mauve walls trimmed in green olive-branch-patterned wallpaper that left Clara feeling dizzy if she looked at it too long. The carpet smelled of furnace dust and old tobacco, the ceiling scaled yellow with cigarette smoke, but the room was located on the opposite end of the house from Mother and Father, where, at times, Clara could breathe. She told Mother when they arrived, they would only stay until the baby was born.

"No, you'll stay for as long as your father and I need you," she replied.

Clara said nothing.

After that, it was like she'd never left. She tended to Father, wheeled him to and from his meals, and wiped the chicken soup from his chin when it dribbled over his lips in salty streams. She cleaned and swept and straightened, and told John everything was fine when he asked, despite her aching back and swollen stomach. It was a lie she was content to bear, because she could see how happy being back on the farm made him. Most nights he'd come in late from the fields, and Clara would flash back to the day she first saw him like that, covered in dirt and sweat with his fingernails lined in soil. For a moment, she'd lose herself in the memory. Then she'd recall where she was and scream in her head.

But for John, she bore it. He brought in the harvest in Father's place and managed the hands. He chatted with Father as he sat limp

96

and lifeless on the porch with strings of spit leaking from his lip. John told Clara how much better it felt to be out in the fresh air, rather than tearing through sheets of drywall in search of split wires and stranded cables. He smiled more, laughed more, and Clara wasn't surprised when he pulled her aside and told her he'd quit his job as an electrician.

"Why don't we make a go of this, huh? Just you and me and the little one." He set a hand on her belly, and Kinley kicked as if in agreement. "What do you say we make it permanent?"

Clara swallowed her despair, angry he hadn't talked with her before quitting, and told him she would think about it. Then she ran upstairs and threw up her breakfast.

* * *

She had to admit, it wasn't all bad on the farm.

Mother had grown old and frail, so Clara didn't scurry like she used to when Mother asked her to do things like, "Go check your father's oxygen," or, "Clean the washtub." She took her time. She sat longer and moved slower, holding Mother's gaze when she grew cross with her, smiling at her until she looked away. She gained a certain satisfaction from this. Mother no longer controlled her as she once had.

There were other things she enjoyed. She took long walks in the forest and let the fresh air fill her lungs. She thought of Sydney and all the times they'd run through the trees together, dreaming about their future and where they'd live when they were older, whom they would marry. She called Sydney, and they met at the cabin in the afternoons and talked like they used to until the air turned crisp, and the sky bled in ribbons of orange. When Clara mentioned John wanted to stay on the farm, Sydney looked at her like she'd lost her mind.

"You aren't seriously considering it, are you?"

"I don't know. Farming makes John so happy."

"But, Clara, the baby . . ."

The baby. She was all that kept Clara sane. She often imagined what Kinley would look like. A face shaped after hers, she thought, with John's brown eyes set above a bubble of a nose and ears tinged red at the lobes. She imagined her laugh — a sound like a waterfall, and her cry — sharp and needy. A cry that would never go unanswered because

Clara already loved her fiercely. She was determined to pour what was left of herself into her daughter. She would make sure Kinley grew up happy and strong, with parents who loved each other as much as they loved her. And if the farm is what it took for John to love her, Clara would bear it. She told Sydney a week later, and her face collapsed as she shook her head.

"No, no, no. Clara, no. It's not safe for you here."

"I'll be okay. John will keep me safe."

"He won't. You know he won't."

Clara felt a flash of rage at this, but she forced it into a hard ball she buried in the pit of her stomach as she said, "Come to dinner tomorrow and get to know him better. Please."

And Sydney agreed.

* * *

Clara spent the day baking. She made a creamy arborio rice and white bean soup with sautéed mushrooms and broccoli. She baked fresh bread and steamed two artichokes for an appetizer. Mother shuffled into the kitchen as Clara was preparing the salad and fixed her eyes on Clara's swollen stomach.

"He'll never love you the same when it comes, you know that, right?"

Clara ignored her, dicing a tomato into little squares, then dicing those further into pulp.

"And you'll ruin her, same as I ruined you."

She left, and Clara pressed the knife to her wrist and held it there, wondering if her skin would part as easy as the tomato's.

Sydney arrived a half-hour later, and Clara opened the door to her crushing a cigarette butt beneath the sole of her boot. She looked frazzled, with her lipstick smeared and her eyes stained red like she hadn't slept for a week. Clara didn't ask her what was wrong or why she smelled of liquor. There wasn't time. Instead, she quickly ushered her upstairs to wash up and prayed John wouldn't notice.

It wasn't five minutes later when she heard Mother's cry and found her lying at the bottom of the stairs with a broken neck, breathing in wet, ragged gasps. Clara took her hands and felt Sydney's gaze burning *down from the landing. She stared at Clara through a pair of swollen eyes and stumbled away a second before John rushed in from the dining room to ask what had happened.*

"She fell," Clara lied.

"Jesus, I'll call an ambulance."

But Mother was already dead, and Clara didn't feel a thing.

CHAPTER TWENTY-FIVE

KAYLA

Emma is sitting up on the sofa, going crazy like she used to when she was three, stiff from a night terror, with her fingers clawing at things only she can see. She's doing it now, flapping her hands like she's swatting at a hive of bees. She shrieks again, and Dad takes her by the wrists.

"Emma! Emma, I'm right here. You're fine, baby. It's just a dream."

She breaks from his grip and scratches his face. Then she's hitting his chest, pounding away until Clara plops down right next to Dad and grabs her shoulders.

"Shh, sweet girl. Shh. You're safe now."

Sweet girl. It's what Mom called her when Emma freaked out about a smashed finger or a bad dream. *"Shh, sweet girl, you're okay. I'm here."*

Emma's lower lip buckles into a pout, and she stills. Then she does something that blows my mind, something she hasn't done in almost a year. She *speaks*. It's a single word. One that, when I hear it, leaves me gawking at her open-mouthed with my heart hammering in place.

"Momma?"

Dad's hand rises to his chest and hovers there. He can't even talk. I'm as shocked as he is, neither of us able to move, both of us thinking maybe we misheard. But then Emma squints at Clara, and it comes again.

"M-momma?"

Clara doesn't say anything, just stares at Emma with this super intense gaze plastered across her face, like she's touched by Emma's screw-up or something. I don't know why, but it bothers me. I shove past her and take Emma's hand. "Ems . . . Ems, you *spoke*." I smile as I say it, tears I didn't realize were there clouding my vision. She looks right through me at Clara, like she actually thinks Clara is Mom. Like Clara has cast some sort of spell on her.

I try again. "Ems, can you say anything else?"

She rubs her eyes and blinks my way with her mouth trembling. I can tell it's hard work, whatever it is she's trying to say. For a moment I think that's it, that she'll never speak again, but then she does, her voice so soft, I have to lean closer to hear.

"Kayla . . . is th-that . . . Momma?"

I go dizzy at the question. Before I can tell her no, it's not, Dad gives me a quick shake of the head and reaches past me to thumb a tear from her cheek.

"Daddy?" Emma whispers.

His mouth splits wide, and he pulls her into a massive hug. "There's my girl. There she is." He's crying, his back shaking. I don't even know what to do. Say something? Join in on the hug? I can tell Clara feels the same way because she's got this *what did I do?* look splashed on her face with her fingers pressed to her lips and her eyes wrinkled at the corners, like maybe she's thinking about crying, too. Dad glances back at her and clears his throat.

"She hasn't said anything since her mother died last year."

"Oh . . ." Clara says. "Oh."

* * *

Clara brings Emma a glass of water along with a bowl of stew and a piece of bread. Emma nibbles at it, sitting propped up on a pillow with some color back in her face. She seems better off than she did when Dad hauled her in here a couple hours ago, looks more alert, but her eyes keep darting back to Clara every few bites like she's still thinking about it, still trying to make up her mind. I can practically hear her thoughts. *Is she Mom? Could she be?* I don't have the heart to tell her no, Clara isn't Mom. Not yet anyway. Dad was right. She needs a little hope after everything she's been through, even if it's false.

Even if it's dangerous.

And it *is* dangerous. There's a real chance once Emma figures it out, she'll stop talking again. The whole thing is so weird. I mean, sure, Clara looks a little like Mom, I guess, in some ways. She's got Mom's red hair, only it's lighter, and her almond-shaped eyes are more aqua than green. But Clara is taller by at least six inches, and she has way more wrinkles crowding her face. I'm pretty sure she's a few years older than Mom was when she died. Either way, it's more than enough to tell them apart.

"This is amazing," Dad says, beaming at Clara. "We've been waiting for her to speak for so long."

"She really hasn't said anything for that long?"

"No. Not a single word."

"Poor thing. I can't imagine the trauma she's been through." Clara wets a finger and smooths a strand of hair behind Emma's ear. The motion bugs me. It's too familiar, Clara smiling and blushing away like she's the reason Emma spoke — which, I guess, in a way, is true. But not in the way she thinks. It isn't something *she* did. It was Emma's dumb mistake, one she made because she's got a fever. And, even weirder, Clara hasn't once denied it, the whole Emma-calling-her-Mom thing, which she totally should have the minute Emma opened her mouth.

I keep thinking she will at some point, but then Dad starts filling Clara in on Mom and the cancer and a bunch of other stuff that isn't her business, and I know it's not going to happen. By the time Emma nods off, I'm almost asleep myself. Clara must notice because she plants a finger to her chin and says, "Silly me, I can tell you all are dying for some rest. Hmm, let me think about this. Where to put you? Oh, I know. Chris, you and Emma can stay down here in the guest suite, and Kayla, if you're okay with it, I'll take you up to the spare room on the second floor. There's a bed already made with fresh sheets and all. Or, if you like, you can stay with your father and sister, but I'm afraid you'd have to sleep on the floor."

It's an easy decision. There's no way I'm turning down a bed. Not after a week spent sleeping on dirt and rocks, and especially not after last night in the cave, with Emma kicking me awake every two seconds.

"Upstairs is great."

She pops to her feet with a smile. "Great. Right this way."

* * *

Clara shows Dad and Emma to the guest suite before taking me upstairs. There's more than a spare room, I realize when we reach the landing. There's a bunch of them, all these white doors with squares of frosted glass running down both sides of the hall. I can't see through a single one, and I don't want to. They're probably full of the same weird crap scattered downstairs. Boxes stuffed with old magazines and books, bags full of decapitated dolls like the one I spotted in the dining room at dinner.

Clara leads me to the end of the hall and stops in front of the second-to-last room. She reaches above the doorframe and snags a key she uses to unlock the door.

"I hope you don't think this is strange," she says, right as I'm thinking that exact thing, "but I have to keep everything locked up here. Billy tends to get into things from time to time if I'm not around."

103

I nod like it makes all the sense in the world, her locking all these doors to keep Billy out. Out from what? What, exactly, is in these rooms that she is afraid of him "getting into?" The thought makes me shiver, and I suddenly want to race back downstairs and sleep in Dad's room, even if it means crashing on the floor, but Clara flings the door open before I can and ushers me into a blinding sea of pink.

Wallpaper with roses in full bloom stretches toward the ceiling. Salmon-colored curtains cover the windows. All the furniture is antique and old-looking, most of it painted a gluey white. A rocking horse sporting a yellow yarn mane sits next to a desk and dresser set that looks like it belongs at a six-year-old's tea party. A plump-looking reading chair is pressed in the corner, buried beneath an ocean of perfectly arranged stuffed animals. And in the middle of it all, rising like a castle, is a four-poster bed peppered with decorative pillows and bright-pink throws. The only thing normal about the room is the floor, which is the same coffee-colored wood as downstairs, but up here it clashes with the walls in a way that makes me feel like I've stepped into a life-sized dollhouse.

"This was my room; can you believe it?" Clara says, smiling like we're both sharing the same trip down memory lane. She plants her hands on her hips and stares at the room. "This certainly brings back the memories. I'd sit right there beneath the window and color for hours when . . ."

I rub the back of my neck and stifle a yawn.

"Oh, where are my manners?" she says. "I should let you get some rest. Will this work?"

I give the room another glance, think about running again. "Um, yeah, It's . . . great. That bed looks super comfy."

She nods aggressively. "Oh, it is. You're just going to love it, Kayla. And I bet it will feel like floating on a cloud after that horrible, awful time you all had last night. I can't believe you slept out in the cold like that."

"Me neither." And I can't. The memory already feels like a nightmare. One I want to forget as soon as possible.

"So the bathroom is at the end of the hall," she continues. "Everything you need should be in there. Towels, soap, the works. Feel free to help yourself to anything at all. And don't forget to use plenty of lotion. Colorado is arid, and you don't want to dry out." She pauses, and I think she's about to leave, but then her lips bunch and she says, "Kayla, do you mind if I ask you a question?"

God, please don't. "Sure."

"Is Chris, your father — is he a good man?"

"He's . . . uh, fine, I guess."

She exhales long and slow as if what I've said has removed some great weight. "That's good. That's very, very good. Well, you have a wonderful night, darling. Sleep tight." And then she's gone, slipping out of the room with the glass panel rattling in place. I stand there and stare at the door for a long moment, consider following her out into the hall for a shower. Instead, I reach out . . . and lock the door.

CHAPTER TWENTY-SIX

CHRIS

I shut off the shower and grab a towel. My skin is a bright, stinging pink from water that, until a few minutes earlier, was brown with rust. I can still smell it on me. The tang of wet metal and the reek of old pipes. The scents of something forgotten, something abandoned.

I slip a pair of sweatpants from the pack and make my way into the bedroom. It's expansive, with a sloped ceiling and wallpaper drenched in a forest of chrysanthemums and marigolds, all of them twining together in a way that makes my eyes itch. Paintings speckle the walls: a framed print of pheasants bursting skyward from a cornfield. A family of foxes nestled beneath a dense curtain of roots. A rustic-looking barn planted in the middle of a wheat field, replete with rolling hills and a picturesque sky.

Nicotine percolates from the carpet as I trail across it toward the bed, the acrid scent invading my nostrils like an unwelcome ghost. I ease the comforter from Emma's leg and check the splint. It looks stable enough, better than my hand-iwork in the woods, but the skin above the bandage is littered with purple streaks, and her calf is swollen to about twice the size of her other leg. I gently raise her foot and place a few pillows beneath it to drain the fluid and relieve the pressure. Her eyelids flutter open with a whimper.

"Hi, baby, is your leg feeling any better?"

She gives me a slow shake of her head. "Uh-uh."

Heat stings my cheeks, the sound of those two syllables almost more than I can bear. I sit down and outline her chin with the pad of my thumb. "Listen, I'm going to get you to a doctor tomorrow, no matter what, okay? Someone who can make your leg all better. Can you hang in there just a little bit longer?"

She nods, trying to act brave, but the look on her face says she's as scared as I am, and still in a lot of pain. I lay a hand on her forehead. It's warm but not bleeding heat like earlier, the Tylenol she took before I showered working. I'd give her more if I could, but I can hear Lexi whispering in my ear, *"Chris, did you measure it? Did you check the dose?"*

She was always worried about things like that: Emma digging out fistfuls of kid vitamins, hungry for an accidental overdose, or leaving her alone with Kayla for too long, even when Kayla was more than old enough to watch her safely. *"She'll lose track of her, Chris. She doesn't pay attention."*

Neither do I, apparently.

"It hurts, Dadda."

Emma's voice washes through me like a rainstorm. My eyes blur. I wipe them and clear my throat. "I know, sweetheart. I know. Here, I have something that might make you feel better."

I trail back to the pack and dig into it, spot the gray snatch of fur I'm looking for buried beneath my sweater. I told Emma not to bring the rabbit, that she wouldn't want to lose him in the forest, but I knew by the way she clutched his leg, her fingers tightening, there was no leaving him behind. I snatch the stuffed animal — an overpriced thirty bucks from the hospital gift shop, which I'd gladly pay a thousand for, now — and limp back to the bed.

"Someone has sure missed you," I say, brushing the rabbit's love-worn ears over her forehead.

"Hops!"

She takes the rabbit with a squeal and crushes him to her chest. I can't help but smile as I flip off the lights and curl in next to her. The darkness is total, near-complete, save an alarm clock blinking zeros from the side table. I drape an arm over Emma's torso and draw close. She's so little, so fragile, her arms folded like popsicle sticks beneath mine. I press my nose to her hair and inhale her scent: campfire smoke and salt-crusted skin, dust and earth.

You came so close to losing her, Chris.

The thought burns through me like a lightning strike. A few feet higher, and the boulder would have crushed her stomach or her chest, vaporized her organs. If it had taken a different path, it might have landed on her neck . . . or her head. It would have cracked her skull like an eggshell.

Christ, you came so very close.

But it didn't happen, and she's still here . . . *right here . . .* and tomorrow, I'll get her the help she needs.

Outside, angry gusts of wind shriek against the window, pelting the glass with hard chips of ice. We'd be stuck out there if it weren't for this place, for Clara. No, not stuck. Dead. *And you'd never have a chance to fix things with Kayla.*

I roll onto my back and stare up toward the ceiling through the black pitch. I need to find a way to talk to her. *Really* talk to her this time. About all of it. About how her mother and I lost track of each other, and how sorry I am for what I did. It was a mistake. *She* was a mistake. Alicia. A cliché — the pretty, young analyst fresh from grad school, looking to climb the ladder, flirting with me, the dejected senior manager who was never quite good enough to make partner no matter how hard he worked. I pictured it all the time, what the other VPs said behind my back when promotions rolled around.

"He's more of a detail guy than a big-picture guy."

"He's not a dynamic-enough thinker, and you can't teach that sort of thing."

"Hmm, I don't know. I'm not sure Chris is VP material."

It picked at me, those thoughts. They deflated me, turned me into a balloon lying wilted in the grass. Then Alicia came along and blew me up again. I knew I was in trouble the first time I saw her: waves of glossy satin hair over olive-skinned shoulders. Long legs jutting from skirts more at home in a nightclub than an office. One look at her, and a thought hammered away inside my head: *This girl is trouble.*

I almost walked right into Bryce Gorman's office when he dubbed me her mentor. I knew it was a problem, spending too much time with a girl like that. But then there she was in my office, asking questions like, "You really landed the Callman deal? I heard the fees were massive on that one." and, "In your experience, what makes a good analyst great?" with a pen tucked adorably behind her ear.

I'd sit there and answer professionally, feeling my skin light up as she giggled at my jokes and pressed a knee to mine (*a mistake*, I told myself, *nothing more*). She actually seemed interested in what I did all day, brought me coffee and bagels, with her vanilla-scented perfume wafting ludicrously up my nose as she handed me my cup. Sometimes she'd brush the back of my hand with hers, and I'd think: *She can't seriously be interested in you, can she? This girl? No, surely not, right?*

But she was, and I ate it up, every second. I craved her attention.

There was so much more to it than that, though. The way she stared at me with those ridiculously intense brown eyes of hers . . . it made me feel important, *wanted*. Lexi hadn't looked at me like that in years, not since before Kayla was born. At home, I was the doofus husband, the guy who couldn't do anything right. I didn't brush Emma's teeth long enough. I didn't pick up the dog poop fast enough. I left urine stains on the toilet seat when I was in a hurry. I'd become the proverbial spouse-turned-roommate. The guy who paid the bills and did the dishes and carted the girls wherever they needed. By all accounts, I was a great guy, but completely dead on the inside — a caricature of myself. A corporate meat sack with his soul carved out.

And the thing is, I didn't even realize it. How pathetic is that? Not until Alicia brought me back to life, asking me what I did for fun when I wasn't grinding away at Gorman & Gorman; was I more than suits and spreadsheets and three mediocre cups of coffee a day? Yes, I was, dammit, and I made sure she knew it. I told her I played piano in college, was even in a band, dammit. *The Bangers*, a stupid name we'd settled on while swimming in bourbon at Slattery's, a bricked-in Irish pub on Boylston Street. I told her I'd originally wanted to go to art school, but had talked myself out of it because there wasn't enough of a career path. I told her I liked poker and darts and was semi-dangerous with a ping-pong paddle in hand. And, when I ran out of things to say, I talked about Lexi. Our trips together. Our failing marriage and our arguments and our crazy kids. I lobbed their names at Alicia like grenades, like a construction worker flashing a road sign: *Caution: Married Man Approaching!*

I expected her to run. I thought she'd slap the "closed" sign against the glass and disappear inside, but she didn't. She just sat there and listened, instead. I mean, *really* listened, bent forward at the waist and staring at me like I was the only thing that mattered. Being seen like that sucked the oxygen from my lungs. It made me feel alive for the first time in a very long time. So, one afternoon, when she begged me to play something for her on the baby grand in the office lobby, I didn't argue. When I keyed the first few notes of Chopin's *Nocturne in E-flat major*, she sucked in a dewy lip and looked at me in a way that made me melt. I knew right then and there I wanted her, all of her.

It happened that night after dinner. I told Lexi I'd be home late — a big meeting to prepare for (what can I say; I'm a cliché, too). I rented a room at the Eliot. I remember the sensation of floating above myself as I came, staring down at Alicia's glistening canvas of skin as her hips bucked and writhed, thinking, *You shouldn't be doing this, Chris. This is not who you are.* I said the same thing afterward, to myself in the bathroom, staring into the mirror with my hair plowed into messy rows by her fingers, the smell of her skin still fresh in my nose. *This is not who you are. You cannot take this back.* But I was. I was exactly that thing. A cheater. An adulterer. I'd crossed the line I swore I'd never cross. I'd become my father.

It lasted for a month, our affair. It felt so wrong. It felt so good. And then Kayla walked into my office that day, and I knew what it was I'd done. It was like watching a glacier crumble into the ocean, the way her face cracked, a sheet of ice dissolving in a dirty boil of foam and water. I pushed Alicia out of my office after Kayla fled, told her it was over. I swore I'd tell Lexi the same, that night, the minute I got home. I'd tell her everything and hope she'd allow me to do whatever it took to make things right. But then she got sick, and I lost my nerve, and I lost Kayla.

Overhead, the ventilation kicks on, spewing a fine layer of grit that settles between my teeth. I grind my jaw, disgusted with myself. It's all I can do, lie there, tense and angry, thinking, *you have to try and get her back, Chris. You have to find a way to fix it.*

"Daddy?" Emma's voice breaks through the thought, her voice so soft, I have to raise my head to hear it.

"Yes?"

"Dadda . . . I love you."

My chest swells. I want to tell her how much I've missed her voice, and how hearing it again, after nearly a year of silence, is like hearing an angel speak. But I can't get the words out. All I can say is, "I love you, too, Emma. So very much."

It's enough.

CHAPTER TWENTY-SEVEN

CLARA
1996

Kinley was delivered into Clara's arms on the twenty-second of December, blue and motionless. She held her for three hours, running her fingertips over Kinley's wispy head, soft as peach fuzz, crying at how beautiful she looked, so still like that, with the blood pooling behind her cherry-red lips. She had John's nose, Clara could tell, and her oval chin. She didn't know whose eyes Kinley had, though she wondered at the color. Her eyelids were glued together in thin, purple lines, and Clara couldn't bring herself to peel one open; it didn't seem right. When the nurse plucked the baby from her arms, Clara felt like the woman had cracked open her ribcage and removed her heart.

"You're still young," she said, with a nonchalant shake of her head. "You'll have another."

John brought her home the next day in silence, the only sound that of gravel spitting off the truck's undercarriage and the wind whistling through a cracked window. Clara heard none of it. Her breasts ached and leaked for Kinley, and she replayed the conversations with the doctors in her head. There weren't any obvious abnormalities, nothing to indicate why her beautiful girl never took that first gasping breath, but

Clara knew why. The universe was punishing her. She'd soaked up too much of her parents' evil to love Kinley the way a mother should.

When they got back to the ranch, John took her to bed and joined Father out on the porch. What they talked about, she didn't know or care. And besides, after the stroke, it would only be John doing the talking. She burrowed beneath the sheets and fell asleep and dreamed of Kinley, of her tightly curled fingers and the bubble of fat beneath her chin, of her legs and arms and budding eyelashes. She woke later, with her teeth chattering, and the padding between her legs clotted with blood. She pulled it free and flung it against the wall with a wet slap, and felt a sticky warmth ooze beneath her hip. She didn't care. She closed her eyes again and didn't move for a month.

* * *

John brought Clara her meals in bed, but he didn't talk or try to comfort her like before. He came and went and didn't say a word beyond "How are you feeling?" or, "Do you need anything else?" Clara didn't answer. She couldn't — the weight in her chest was wide and thick and dense, and it held her glued to the mattress with a force stronger than gravity.

There were times she would come awake in the middle of the night, and her eyes would flick over the room in lifeless jerks, open but not seeing, as her voice rose up her throat like a caged animal. John would rush to the kitchen for a cold glass of water and a bottle of painkillers, which Clara would take from him greedily, eager to remove the cap. The pills were a life raft in an ocean of pain, her only way to detach from reality.

A week after Kinley died, Sydney stopped by for a visit. She slid past John as he left the room without a nod or a glance and planted herself in an old wicker chair at the end of the bed. Her mascara pooled beneath her eyes in thin, black streams, and Clara knew she'd been crying. Sydney pressed a finger to her clavicle and opened her mouth to speak, but no sound escaped. Instead, she stood and pulled the chair closer and set her hand on Clara's arm and kept it there until the sun stained the blinds purple.

She came again, the next day, sitting in her wicker chair, looking like a scarecrow, thin and pale and silent. An image like a Polaroid developing rose from somewhere deep inside her mind: Sydney crouched at the top of the stairs, looking down on Mother's crumpled and broken form. Clara knew it had poisoned Sydney, this thing she'd done to Mother, and that Clara wasn't the only one hurting. But she couldn't bring herself to comfort Sydney, even though she wanted to. Even though she was grateful, in a way, for what Sydney had done. She simply didn't have the strength.

Sydney brought a plate of fresh chocolate chip cookies to her late the next afternoon. Clara tried one, not at all hungry, and the second it scraped across her tongue she threw up in the trash can John had placed next to the bed. Sydney took it and washed it in the bathroom, leaving the air tinged with the smell of soap and Clara's insides. She returned with a wet washcloth and mopped Clara's forehead, then cracked the window to a swirl of cold, bracing air. She brought Clara a change of clothes and cleaned and straightened the room, picking up Clara's bloodied bandages and plates crusted in old food. Before she left, Sydney kissed Clara's cheek, and she felt a sudden warmth bloom in her chest. At least Sydney still loved her, even if she didn't love herself.

The feeling didn't last. She'd think of Kinley, of those gray toes like pebbles, of her perfectly formed ears, and grief would run hot through her veins. Her world turned to a numb, insulating cocoon that she wanted to inhabit alone. She told Sydney to leave, to go home, or back to school, or wherever it was she belonged.

"No, Clara," is all she said. "I want to be here with you."

And so Clara let her move into the spare room upstairs, without asking John's permission, and Sydney sat with her day after day, week after week, reading passages from books like The Prince of Tides and A Grief Observed and The Color Purple. The words spoke to Clara in a way Sydney couldn't. They reminded her she wasn't alone, that others in this world endured suffering and somehow survived, and that life could still be beautiful if she let it.

And it came to her, in those soft, still moments, with Sydney reading next to her, that she couldn't heal here, entombed in this dark room surrounded by her past. She'd need to start fresh, and so would John. They needed to leave the farm, and this town. This godforsaken state. Clara decided she wanted to move to the coast and buy a little house on the beach and let it fill with the smell of ocean and salt and everything

114

clean. *And maybe, with enough time, she could forgive herself for failing to bring her baby girl safely into the world.*

Her hopes were dashed when Father died of a heart attack two weeks later, sitting on the porch with his hands still wrapped around a warm cup of tea. He left the ranch to John, and only to John, and Clara knew there would be no leaving after that.

CHAPTER TWENTY-EIGHT

CHRIS

Lexi. She looks at me with gleaming black mirrors for eyes and takes my hand in hers. Her veins are rivers of ice, her skin flaked in frost, so cold, it freezes my blood. "Run," she whispers, through blue-tinged lips. "Chris, you need to run."

* * *

I lurch awake with a gasp; a sudden, frantic gulp of air — the breath of a drowned man. The room is black and stale. Hot. A sound out of step with the storm clacks off the window-pane. It brings me back to life, blurry and unfocused. An irregular *tap, tap, scratch, tap,* like someone is out there in the blizzard, running a set of metal fingernails across the glass. *No,* I think, *not in this weather.* A tree branch perhaps, or the storm turning to sleet.

The thought fades, and I'm drifting off again . . .

* * *

Clink . . . clink. Clink . . . clink.

Clunk.

My eyes snap open.

Clunk . . . clink . . . clunk.

I pull myself from the bed in a daze, stumble to the light switch and flip it on. *What time is it? Where am I?* I rub my temples and search for something to anchor my disorientation, my head so thick with sleep, I can barely see. The room materializes in hazy chunks: the time-worn wallpaper and mint-green curtains. A stretch of blue shag carpet winding beneath a chest of drawers. Above me, the furnace burps through an aluminum vent in fits and starts, the storm still howling outside, gusts of wind throttling the glass and trying to claw their way in. And it's cold. *Way* too cold, Emma shivering now, one arm flung free of the sheets, her skin pebbled in goosebumps. I peel another blanket from the leather chest at the end of the bed and drape it over her, am about to curl back beneath the comforter when the sound comes again, only louder this time.

Clink. Clink . . . CLUNK!

It's like someone is taking a hammer to the pipes or tossing rocks into the ductwork by the handful. I slow my breath and listen. A groan runs through the house. The wood croaks and shifts, the joints settling. From the bathroom, the toilet gurgles and runs. *The sounds of an old home, Chris, nothing more.* Exhaustion tugs at my eyelids, the headache back, branching through my head in dull, throbbing waves. I so very badly want to go back to bed, but something keeps me glued in place, listening . . .

. . . and listening.

And listening . . .

Something draws me toward the door, where I plant my ear against the wood. Silence soaks the air. A heaviness deeper than silence. A crawling notion that someone is out there, standing on the other side of the door, listening back. My pulse thuds in my neck. My calf burns and aches. It's like the house is holding its breath, waiting to exhale.

A muffled patter rises down the hall and solidifies into footsteps. Fingernails rake the wood, and I spill backward with my heart racing. *What was that? Clara? Billy? Someone else?* Saliva floods my mouth, and my fear resolves into anger. Emma needs to sleep, to rest. We both do after what we've been through the last few days. This is beyond ridiculous. Whoever is out there, I decide, I'm not playing their game.

I force myself toward the door and out into the hall. My fingers scrape the wall and search for a light switch, find nothing but slivers of dust and old paint. It takes a moment for my eyes to adjust to the gloom, for me to spot the dim circle of light puddled across the floor, down the hall near the living room. There's a shadow there, a shape cutting over the shine . . . no, not a shape, a person, some*one* standing there . . . waiting . . .

A head slung to one side.

Hair dripping past a sharp set of shoulders.

Fingers thin and twisted by the light, hanging motionless like an arthritic pair of pitchforks.

Bolts of adrenaline spurt into my bloodstream, and I grind a fist into my eyes. My breath curls in fast through my nose and out again in thin streams. I'm seeing things. I have to be. A sudden wash of dizziness sets me to blinking, searching again for the shadow that's now gone, was never really there to begin with. A remnant of a dream — a faded afterimage burned into my fractured subconscious by stress and exhaustion.

But there *was* something there. And the way it stood without moving, the outline so black against the wood . . .

Leave it. Go back to your daughter.

Calf burning, I limp back into the room and shut the door, lock it.

You imagined it. No one was out there.

But there was.

No, it was a dream . . . nothing more.

I slide back into bed with Emma and stare through the window into the howling black outside. Despite my fatigue,

118

I can't bring myself to close my eyes. I don't fall asleep again for hours.

* * *

BAM!
BAM! BAM! BAM!
I sit up, heart pounding. Not a dream this time.
BAM!BAM!BAM!BAM!BAM!BAM!BAM!
I leap from the bed and scramble for the lights. Emma winces as they come on.
BAM . . . BA-BAM! BAM!
My heart crashes against my ribs, and I'm suddenly wide, wide awake, and very aware that someone is running up and down the hall, banging the walls and stomping around outside the room. Footsteps like thunder rattle the picture frames and shake the mirror on the dresser. A porcelain dog topples from the nightstand and thuds to the floor.
Find something. Protect yourself.
I take a quick look, and my gaze lands on a flimsy-looking broom near the bathroom. I snap it up and ease toward the door in a crouch, cocking it like a bat as the sounds from the hall suddenly die, the room now still and quiet. But there's something else in the silence, the same presence I felt earlier back, a noise whispering above my thumping pulse. Breathing. It's an erratic, huffing wheeze, someone out there, waiting . . . knocking now, smacking the wood, slamming against it over and over.
BAM! . . . BAM!BAM!BAM! . . . BAM!
I grip the doorknob and rip the door wide, ready to swing. My arm falls, and I release the broom. It's Billy, his face pooled in shadow, save his eyes, which flicker in time with the light from the ceiling fan spinning behind me. He's still in his overalls, and I suddenly wonder if he's been outside in the storm this entire time, from dinner until now, tapping on the window and peering through it, watching us like some

backcountry peeping tom. Puddles of melted snow shine up from the floor behind him in the shape of boot prints.

I stiffen. "Can I . . . uh, help you with something, Billy?"

He doesn't respond, just stands there clutching a wrinkled sheet of blue construction paper in his fist, which he presses into my hand. I stare down at a purple crayon drawing of a scarecrow man with a lopsided circle for a stomach and two X's for eyes. Next to him stands a stick-figure girl with acorn-brown hair and a peach shirt, the same color as Emma's. One of her legs is longer than the other, broken and twisted to the right. A stream of red crayon scribbles leaks from the break to pool beneath an oversized brown shoe.

"Can she play?" Billy's voice is mucous-thick, all vocal cords. He wipes a string of drool from his mouth and smiles. White balls of spit cling to the corners of his lips.

"Who, Emma?"

"I wanna play with her. She's my friend."

"No, she's sleeping right now. Maybe in the morning."

"I'm the magic man. I play lots at night. She can, too."

Waves of gooseflesh ripple down my arms. "She can't, Billy. Not now. She's hurt."

His brow furrows, and he hammers his gloved fist hard into the wall with a sharp crack. The wood splinters, and I step back as a cloud of dust spirals off the doorframe.

"We're gonna be good friends, so you can let her play."

He jams his hands into his pockets and rocks back and forth on the balls of his feet. I say nothing, his rubber-soled boots squealing in protest until I reach out and shut the door.

* * *

It continues all night, the incessant rattling and banging of doors. The hard *smack!-thud!-smack!* of boots on wood winding up the stairs and pounding back down again. The furnace screeches and groans through the vents, and I briefly consider going to the bathroom to stuff my ears with wads of toilet paper, only to kill the thought a second later. I need my hearing. I can't have Billy coming in to "play" with Emma. Or with Kayla, for that matter. I can imagine it, Billy knocking on her door and chewing his lip as he pleads for her to come out. Kayla refusing, trying to close the door. Billy turning violent . . .

I know I should go check on her, *need* to go check on her, but I won't leave Emma alone, not with Billy out there somewhere, lurking in the dark, waiting to snatch her up. And Kayla is fifteen. She can handle herself. She'll scream if she's in trouble. The thought gives me little comfort, the headache building, gathering strength. Pain booms and crashes against my temples like a distant squall. Emma moans and cries. I give her more Tylenol and rub her back until her breathing evens out, counting them to make sure they're regular and full before I return to my pillow. Fatigue leaks through my skull and drips into my eyelids, flooding them with exhaustion until they feel like thousand-pound weights.

I'm not exactly sure when I fall asleep, only that I do, accidentally and hard. When I wake, it's to a gentle spill of light through the drapes. I roll onto my side and reach for Emma, and my hand brushes empty sheets. I bolt upright, struggling to understand why she isn't there . . . because she's not. She's gone.

CHAPTER TWENTY-NINE

KAYLA
DAY THREE

I'm so beyond exhausted, it's not even funny. *What was all that last night?* The pounding footsteps and doors slamming? All the banging on the walls? It sounded like World War II. God, what a nightmare. I woke up a couple times convinced someone was standing right outside the room. I'm pretty sure it was Billy, based on the note I found slipped beneath the door this morning: a yellow piece of construction paper covered in a bunch of scrawled crayon.

I pick it up and glance at it again.

To, the gurl. I think yer supre purtty-n-nice!

Beneath the words is this rainbow and a smiley-face sun hanging over a girl with red hair. I think it's supposed to be me, but it's like a kindergartener drew it, or maybe even a preschooler, so it's hard to tell. *Ugh.* I crumple it up and toss it on the floor. I can't bear to look at it any longer. Or this room. It's even worse in the light, everything coated in Pepto Bismol pink. There's this jewelry box on the desk in the corner I keep staring at. It's one of the musical ones with a ballerina that pops out when you open the lid, only this one has half her leg snapped off. The whole room feels like that — snapped off and forgotten.

I blow my bangs and gaze at the ceiling. I wish Mimi were here. If she were, she'd find some way to help me forget about everything: the getting lost, and Emma's accident, and all the junk with Dad. That's the best thing about her. One minute you'll be focused on a stupid boy or some dumb drama at school and then she'll show up the next, and you'll forget all about it. She's the kind of grandma who's up for anything, just say it and you're there. A random trip to the beach, or a girls' night out on the town followed by ice cream and a double feature at the movies.

Sometimes, I wonder how Mom even came from her, with the way she worried about me all the time. No coming home later than nine o'clock. No parties or overnight camping trips or spending the night at Bree's house, because she has an older brother who might try to make out with me or something stupid like that. Never mind that her brother is a total jock and not at all my type. Mom didn't even let me get a phone until last year. It was mortifying. It felt like I was a ten-year-old pretending to be in high school.

But here's the thing: I totally used to worry like that, too. All the time about everything. My grades, and my hair, and my makeup, and what I ate, and where I should go to college, or what I should do afterward. All this stuff. I thought if I worried enough, it meant I had some control over my life. And then, out of the blue, Mom died. The person who I thought had everything under control, and I realized none of it meant anything — all the planning and worrying. The truth is, we're all just here one minute, walking around and pretending like we'll live forever, and gone the next. And nobody really knows when. Or cares. That's the scary part. It's why I don't want to worry anymore or get so angry all the time. I don't want to fight with Emma about every little thing or get so mad at Dad, even though I'll never forgive him for what he did. It doesn't help anything. All that matters is loving the people who deserve it and spending what little time you have doing what you want.

And right now, all I want is to be back home.

The thought is enough to force me from the bed and into the hall for a shower. After four days stuck in the woods, I'm aching for one. But more importantly, I want to be ready to go the second Dad says we can.

* * *

Hair wet and clinging to my neck, I make my way downstairs to the smell of frying bacon. I'm still in the same jeans as yesterday, the same shirt, both of them grimy-feeling against my skin. It's disgusting, another reason to get out of here as soon as possible: so I can find some clean clothes.

Clara is humming in the kitchen, her hair tied back in a French twist. She's wearing an apron over a white cashmere sweater, tapping out the beat with a pair of sharp-toed flats. Her mom jeans are gone, replaced by a green pencil skirt. She looks nothing like the wild-haired version from yesterday, the crazy cat lady with the mismatched socks. Today, she looks like she's ready for church.

I take a seat on the stool near the counter, and she whirls around with a hand pressed to her chest.

"Oh, my goodness, Kayla, you startled me."

"Sorry about that."

She gives me a pink lipstick smile and waves me off. "Don't fret, dear. I'm just jumpy. How did you sleep?"

"Okay," I lie. "Is my dad up yet?"

"No. Not yet. He must be exhausted. Your sister, too. I haven't heard a peep from them all morning. But I'm guessing they'll be up as soon as they smell this." She raises the frying pan and gives it a shake. "You can never underestimate the power of a good breakfast."

I squeeze out a nervous laugh. Like Clara, the entire kitchen has been made over, near sparkling compared to last night. It's the same as the living room now that I think about it, most of the boxes and clutter stacked against the walls or tucked behind the furniture. The transformation should make me feel better, but the difference is unsettling. It must have taken a lot of work, and I suddenly wonder if last night's racket was Clara bumping around downstairs instead of Billy, cleaning up like maybe she's expecting us to stay for a couple of weeks, instead of a few more hours.

"So, uh . . . where's Billy?" I ask, pulling a string from my sleeve.

Clara chirps out a laugh and looks at me like we're both in on the same joke, only I don't have a clue as to the punchline. "Oh, he won't be up for a few hours yet. I hope he didn't keep you up last night. He can be quite a pill when his imagination takes hold. I have a hard time dragging him out of bed before mid-afternoon most days, the lazy thing." She turns back to the counter and whisks some eggs, empties them sizzling into another skillet. "Kayla, I—" She clears her throat. "I hope I'm not intruding here, but it must have been so hard for you girls to lose your mother like that. It just breaks my heart."

I bury my face in my hands. *Please, not this. Anything but this.*

"I know how it feels to lose someone. I lost my mother when I was only a little older than — oh dear, I'm sorry, have I upset you? I have, haven't I?"

I raise my head an inch and realize she's staring at me with a flush creeping over her cheeks. I move to stand. "No, I'm okay. I just . . . I'm going to go see my dad."

"Wait. Please," she says. "I didn't mean to make you uncomfortable. It's just been so long since I've had company. Especially another woman." She crosses the kitchen and takes my hand. "Please . . . won't you stay and visit with me a bit? I promise not to put you off again."

I sigh. I probably shouldn't be rude to her. She did save our lives, after all.

I thump back onto the stool. "Yeah, sure. Okay."

"Ooh," she says, releasing my hand and scurrying back to the stove to stir the eggs. "So, your dad said you're from Boston? That must be such a fabulous place to live. Just fabulous. I've always dreamed of visiting the East Coast someday. Especially New York City. Have you seen it at night? It must be so divine. It's always been a dream of mine to go there."

"You've never been?"

"No. My ex-husband, John, was never one for travel. Our honeymoon was in Oklahoma City; can you believe that? At the Holiday Inn no less, the cheapskate. I'm afraid it's the nicest place I've ever been. I always swore I'd do more traveling, but then Billy came along, and . . . well, life just happens, I guess."

"You should visit sometime. It's amazing."

"Oh, I would so love that, Kayla . . . to see the ocean. Or even a beach, for goodness' sake. All that white sand and sun . . ." She waves an arm at the window. "Anything besides all this snow and ice." She glances back at me with a wink. "If I ever make it out there, promise you'll show me around?"

I nod, suddenly sorry for this lonely life of hers: Billy and the farm and whatever else it is she's had to endure. Life has sucked since Mom died, sure, but at least I'm not stuck living on an empty farm in the middle of nowhere like her. I think it's why the next question slips from my mouth before I can stop it. "You um . . . you said you lost your mom, too?"

She pauses. "Yes. She had a bad fall. It was . . . quite tragic. But we were never very close, so I managed okay, I suppose."

"We were . . . close," I mumble.

Clara turns and wipes her hands on the apron, her lips tugging into a sad smile. "You don't have to talk about her, Kayla. I shouldn't have put you on the spot like that. I have a way of putting my foot in my mouth sometimes."

"No, it's okay. I don't mind." And I'm not exactly sure why, but it's true. Something about the way she's hugging herself seems broken, like maybe she hasn't had a real conversation in years.

Her eyes soften. "So, you said you two were close?"

"Yeah. More so when I was younger. She used to take me on all these hikes. My favorite was Halibut Point. It's this trail right next to the Atlantic. You can see everything from there. The ocean and the birds and the coast. It's beautiful. Sometimes we'd take picnics, and Mom made us these sourdough sandwiches I hated. I remember eating a few bites and tossing them to the seagulls, just to see how many showed up. It was so funny. Mom would get mad at first, but then they'd start squawking away, and she'd laugh, and . . . are you okay?"

Clara is blinking hard, with a finger pressed to her throat. "Yes. I'm fine. Please, please. Go on. Where else did you go?"

"Yeah, okay. So, there's this other hike close to Boston called World's End we did a lot. There's a lot of wildflowers, and it's cool when the leaves change. On clear days, you can see the city across the harbor. It's not as pretty as it is out here, though. You and your mom must have gone on hikes all the time."

She looks away and shakes her head. "Not so much with Mother, but I had a friend who—"

A door bangs open down the hall, followed by Dad's voice. "Emma!"

Clara clutches her wrist and jerks toward the sound.

"Where is she?" Dad asks, blowing into the kitchen. "Where's Emma?" His face is a patchy, splotched red, his hair spitting off the side of his head in crazy angles. He blinks at me with baggy eyes, looking like he hasn't slept at all, his shirt rumpled. "Have you seen your sister?"

"No, I—"

"Have you?" he asks Clara.

"No. I thought she was with you?"

"Well, she's not. Where's Billy?"

"I don't know what that has to do with—"

"Where's his room, Clara?"

"In the basement, why?"

Dad doesn't answer. He's already gone.

CHAPTER THIRTY

CLARA
1997

John had Father cremated. He and Clara spread his ashes in the northernmost cornfield, next to the wall of quaking aspen where, as a child, Clara had sometimes spotted Father sitting perched on his tractor, deep in prayer. Clara didn't know what kind of god listened to a man like that, and if he did, it was one she didn't want to know.

The day was a cold one, hard bits of ice breaking loose from the branches as John emptied what remained of Father from the urn. The breeze caught it and swept a puff of his charred flesh over Clara's arm. She brushed it off with a shiver and then turned for home without saying a word. John followed with his boots crunching through the snow behind her, his breath steaming from his nose in white plumes.

Back in the kitchen, he made them coffee and handed a mug to Clara. He took off his tan sheepskin coat and settled into a chair with a sip before nodding at her to join him. Clara didn't want to. She didn't belong in this place, in this house with the broken shutters and rooms packed full of pain, bunched and stacked together like a rotting corpse, each one clotted with memories of Mother and Father that, like a mold infestation, only grew with time.

But still she sat, even though everything in her wanted to run screaming for her bed and the pills, to fall into that all-consuming void others called sleep. She pulled the mug to her mouth with a bitter swallow and thought of Father out in the fields poisoning the soil. She wondered if the corn would come in peppered in stalk rot as it drank him in next spring. John said something, but she wasn't listening. All she heard was the blood washing through her ears, and the wind scraping across the windows outside.

"Clara, I'm talking to you."

"Sorry, what?"

"I asked how you're doing. That couldn't have been easy."

She blinked and set the mug down, smoothed a wrinkle from the tablecloth with a deep breath.

"I want to move, John. I can't stay here."

"What?" The word shot out of his mouth like a bullet. He set his cup down, and Clara pretended not to notice the tremor in his hand.

"I hate it here. I hate everything about this wicked place, and I hate them."

"Who?"

"Mother and Father."

"Why would you say something like that?"

"Because it's true."

Fingertips brushed her hand, and she looked down at John's hand sliding over hers.

"Look, I know things have been hard for you lately. I understand that. But now isn't the time to talk about this. Not while you're still grieving Kinley and—"

She pulled her hand back, her eyes filling with heat. "They did things to me, John! They weren't good people. Especially Father."

John's jaw flexed at that, and he buried his mouth in his fist and cleared his throat. "It's because he left me the farm, isn't it?"

Clara flinched at his tone: gruff and stern, and that of a stranger.

"After all these years, you would take this from me? You would do that?"

"John," she said, her hand sliding for his this time, "it's not about that, I promise. It's simply that—"

And then his mug was flying into the wall, the porcelain shatter ringing through the kitchen as he stood with his finger outstretched and leveled at her.

"After everything I've done for you."

Clara didn't know what he was talking about, so she just sat there with her lips parted, feeling like everything was spinning out of control.

"I know you didn't finish nursing school. But I paid for it anyway. Do you have any idea how many extra hours I worked, Clara? Just so I wouldn't upset you?"

She shook her head.

"It's all I've ever done. Worked for you. Put up with your moods and the dirty house and you lying around in your pajamas all day like there wasn't anything you could do about it. Don't you know it hurt me, too? Losing our children? Don't you know it ripped me apart the same as you? No, you don't. You wouldn't, because you never asked. You never said a word. But I held it in for you, Clara. I had to be the strong one. I knew you couldn't handle it if I wasn't. And after all that, this is how you repay me? By taking the thing I most love?"

And it hit her then. His love that wasn't for her but the farm. It always had been. She knew that now. From the day she'd met him, he'd never loved her for her but what she gave him: a chance at his dream. Land of his own.

His charcoal hair hung over his eyebrows in wild chunks, and he smoothed it back and shoved the chair roughly against the table. He threw on his jacket and raised his lips in a snarl.

"Do what you want, Clara, but it will be without me. I'm not going anywhere."

It was then she spotted Sydney standing in the doorway behind him, holding something in her hand, a pink envelope creased at the corners. Her knuckles were white as she stared at John, her teeth clenched in a way that made Clara think she was about to rush forward and leap on his back. The room blurred, and Clara shook her head at Sydney. John was right. She had abandoned him as much as he'd abandoned her. Maybe more.

Sydney looked at her then, the rage in her eyes melting, turning to disbelief as Clara motioned for her to leave. Still, she stood there, her arms going slack, that envelope hanging as John stormed outside and

130

disappeared into the cold, gray air. Clara buried her face in her hands and sobbed until her chest ached and her nose burned. She cried for Kinley and for herself and for John and their fractured marriage. She cried because everything in her life was broken and ruined, and she'd been foolish to think it would ever be otherwise.

After an hour, she looked up again . . . and Sydney was gone.

CHAPTER THIRTY-ONE

CHRIS

This is not happening. This is not happening.

This is not happening . . . *again.*

But it is. Emma is gone.

Panic sheets through me, my entire body thrumming with it as I hit the stairs in a near run. Footsteps clack somewhere behind me, Clara telling me to slow down, Kayla shouting for me to calm down, neither of which I'll do, because my baby is *gone.*

But how? It doesn't make sense, not with her leg. She didn't simply wander off somewhere on her own, curious. No. She was taken, and I have a pretty damn good idea who did it.

Can she play?

"Billy!" I cry. "Billy, where are you?"

I tear down the stairs and bang through the basement door to a dank wall of rot. It's a putrid smell that worms its way into my nose like a container of mushrooms left to spoil on the counter. The stench of wet earth and decay. My eyes water as Clara eases past me and tugs a string dangling overhead. There's a click, and a cold wash of light spreads over the room.

It's so much worse than upstairs. There's junk everywhere, piles of it climbing from the floor to the ceiling: threadbare pieces of furniture with the stuffing foaming through blown-out seams; a stack of vinyl suitcases tottering over a heap of farm tools speckled in rust; boxes and garbage sacks jammed with God knows what, everything covered in concrete dust and mold. My gaze drifts to the far wall, which is lined in shelving units packed with glass jars. I can't tell what they house, only that whatever they once were — peaches, pears, tomatoes, green beans — have long turned to black, gelatinous blobs suspended in layers of viscous gel.

"Shit," I whisper, stunned.

"I'm sorry you have to see this," Clara mutters. "I've meant to de-clutter down here for years. It's just, well, Billy likes it this way. He pretends it's his fort."

"Where's his room?" I ask.

"This way."

She picks her way through the mayhem, squeezes past a massive bureau stuffed with books and dated issues of *Life*, and *Time*, and *Playboy*. A centerfold leers at me from the top of the stack as we pass, her mouth tied into a strawberry lipstick knot. We push past more junk — a urine-yellow crib and a leather trunk propped next to two ancient television sets, one with a splintered screen. A recliner with the seat cushion torn from the springs occupies the corner, next to a refrigerator tilted in a death throe, vomiting empty milk containers over the cement.

The hall beyond the room is worse. The smell of mildew is stronger, the mortar joints caked with mold, black veins of it running over the cinder block and toward the floor, spreading over the ceiling. My skin crawls at the thought that Emma might be down here with him, stuffed somewhere in his room. Maybe in the closet or tucked beneath his bed, maybe packed in a toy chest where I can't hear her scream.

I pull in a breath and tell myself to stop it, that if she's here, I'll find her.

Clara leads us toward a scuffed, metal door with no doorknob, a scarred sheet of tin that looks more at home in a slaughterhouse freezer than serving as the entrance to her son's room. She reaches out and gives it a polite rap. "Billy . . . Billy are you awake yet, honey? Billy?" Another tap, Clara knocking with all the force of a hotel concierge. *Room service, I have your breakfast.* I push past her and blow through the door.

"Emma?" I cry. "Emma!"

Clara slaps a switch, and the room comes to life in a shower of pale light. The ceiling is a checkerboard of drop-down tile with several pieces missing. Two-by-fours and yellow ribbons of insulation peer back at me through the yawning gaps. The walls are bare cinder block, every inch of which is covered in a forest of crayon scribblings and fin-ger-paint handprints. It's the handiwork of a five-year-old gone mad. Billy's clothes are strewn everywhere, scattered over the concrete in clumps, spilling from the closet. Empty soup bowls and peanut-butter-stained plates surround a spotty, sweat-stained mattress buried beneath a tangle of sheets. It's madness. I may as well be staring at the remains of a psychiatric unit — one Clara lets her son live in.

How does she let him stay in here like this?

"Where is he?" I ask.

"I-I don't know," Clara stutters. "He sleeps late most mornings. He should be here."

I whirl on her with my fingers balling into fists. "Where? Tell me now, or I swear I'll—"

She flinches back a step like she expects me to strike her, her hands coming up to cover her face.

"Dad! Jesus. Calm down. She doesn't know, okay?" Kayla's voice cuts through my panic. I blink at her and feel my jaw unclench. She's right. I need to keep my cool, go about this logically.

My fingers uncurl. "I'm sorry. I didn't mean to yell."

Clara drops her arms, her gaze still on my hands. "It's okay. You're scared. I understand."

"Please, Clara, where else would he go?"

She traces a finger across her collarbone and slides it beneath the pearl necklace draped around her neck. She's overdressed, her hair pulled back into a tight braid, her eyes smoky with eyeliner, her lips frosted a light pink. The combination is garish in the wan light, a look more befitting a back-alley hooker or a middle-aged cougar out prowling the bars than someone running a corn farm.

"Honestly, I'm not sure. This isn't like him."

"What about the rest of the house? Any place he might be hiding?"

"Maybe, but, Chris" — her gaze sharpens — "he wouldn't have taken your daughter. I'm sure of it. Billy is a good boy. He gets into his fair share of trouble from time to time, sure, as any child does, but he would never hurt someone."

"Billy's no child."

She pauses, chews the nub of a fingernail. "Are you sure Emma isn't still in your room? Perhaps you missed her? In the bathroom, maybe?"

I resist the impulse to strangle her. "No, I didn't *miss* her. She can't walk, remember?"

"Dad . . ." Something in Kayla's voice sends trails of ice racing down my spine. She's staring at Billy's bed with her finger outstretched and her nostrils flared wide. I turn and spot what she's looking at. It's a gray patch of fur. One I would recognize anywhere. Hops, Emma's rabbit, is lying half-buried beneath Billy's pillow.

CHAPTER THIRTY-TWO

CHRIS

I slam the phone down, still dead, the damn thing, nothing but static. Black spots dance through my vision, my breath coming in quick snatches. The clock on the kitchen wall reads 10 a.m. Outside, the storm has lightened some but not much, the wind gusting across the ground and dragging the snow with it, obscuring any view of the treeline from which we emerged yesterday. The driveway, if there ever was one, is long gone.

In September, I think again. *How?*

I dig my fingernails into my palm. None of this was supposed to happen. We weren't supposed to be here, trapped in this house with this woman and her linebacker of a son who could snap Emma in half on accident. We were supposed to be back in Boston by now, stitched together after a week in nature, ready for a new chapter and a fresh start. One where Emma talks, and Kayla doesn't despise me.

But we aren't; we're here, still fractured, and Emma is gone . . . *again.*

I have no doubt it's Billy who has her. Billy who slams doors in the middle of the night and stomps around the house with hunting boots that sound like they've been soled in lead. Billy with the dull eyes and sausage fingers I can so easily imagine running through Emma's hair, twirling strands between his knuckles before drifting lower toward her neck to squeeze, squeeze, squeeze. He could be doing anything to her right now. Snapping her fingers one by one. Pulling her arms out of socket just to hear them crackle and pop.

I glance at Clara, who is sitting at the counter next to Kayla with her fingers tap-dancing across the Formica countertop.

"Could he have gone outside?" I ask.

"No. I don't think so."

"How close did you say your neighbors were?"

"The Sharp farm is about ten miles down the road, but they aren't around much. There was a cantaloupe ranch closer, but the family moved several years back. No one bought the property after they left. There's not much left to it. It's a real shame. It was so beautiful once."

I stare at the snow whirling down outside the kitchen window, the wind shrieking and rattling the glass. Ten miles might as well be one hundred in this weather. And I can't . . . I *won't* leave Emma here alone.

If you can't find her soon, you won't have a choice.

A high-pitched ringing fills my ears. I grind my thumbs against my temples, the panic surging again, balling hard in my chest.

"Show me the rest of the house."

Clara nods.

* * *

We search the ground floor first, starting with what Clara tells us was her ex-husband John's office. Unlike the rest of the house, it's clean and airy, surprisingly functional with a high-back leather chair centered behind a dark walnut desk. Stacks of paper are squared neatly upon its surface set between a tower of manila files. An old Olympia typewriter rests on the corner. One look at it, and I want to throw it through the window. I want to rip it apart key by key, because it's not a computer. And that's all I want, something electronic, *anything*, in this goddamn house connected to the outside world.

Clara follows my gaze. "I've been meaning to sell that old thing. John wasn't really the office type. I told him to buy us a computer once, but he said we didn't need one out here on the farm. He didn't think there was much of a reason, I guess."

I press by her without a word.

The rooms are pure chaos after that, each room its own entity: a parlor crammed full of antique furniture, the walls spattered in dusty oil paintings set in between a pair of gold-studded mirrors. A mudroom overflows with mismatched shoes, the washbasin vomiting a stream of crusted washrags onto the laminate floor. A sitting room bathed in miles of ugly-kitsch wallpaper. There's no sense of unity or warmth. No theme, every room its own entity. It's like Clara is leading us through an M.C. Escher sketch: stairs that lead nowhere, with doors that open to brick walls.

Where are you, Emma?

I can taste my heart in my throat by the time we reach the back of the house. Clara leads us through a broken storm door and out onto an enclosed veranda. It's drafty with a broken ceiling fan hanging from the rafters with one of the blades gone. Oxidized windows frame a field of blurry, gray-white emptiness beyond the glass. I wipe a circle in the frost with my fist and stare outside. My breath crystallizes and branches across the pane, forming little white rivers that mirror the cold streams of panic cutting through my chest. *Don't be out there*, I think. *Anywhere but there.*

"How about we check upstairs," Clara says, already heading back inside.

I follow her inside. She's halfway up the stairs when Kayla stops and points at a door near the foyer. "Wait, what's that room?"

"Oh, that's just my bedroom," Clara says. "She wouldn't be in there."

I head for it.

"Wait. Chris, please. It's not presentable."

I tune her out and swing the door wide. Inside, it's dim, with a pair of heavy-patterned velour curtains blocking out most of the light, which is a good thing, because it looks like a bomb went off. Clothes litter the carpet and cover the furniture, the bed. Like Billy's, it's bare with a single blanket crumpled at the end of the mattress, twined with bras and underwear. A dresser rests against the wall with the drawers flung open, one missing entirely, socks and shirts climbing the base in multi-hued piles. A fuzzy pair of pink shorts dangle from the ceiling fan, swaying back and forth as it turns in a perpetual death spiral.

And on the walls . . . pictures. Pictures hung backward as if whatever images they contain are too horrible to behold. And not just on the walls. On the dresser and nightstands, picture frames turned face-down with the cardboard supports jutting up between a city of orange prescription bottles and mugs of old coffee.

"Oh, wow . . ." Kayla mutters next to me.

I grab one of the photos and turn it over to a man with intense, brown eyes and a square jaw covered in stubble. He has an arm wrapped around a younger version of Clara, her face colored with a shy smile as she stares up at him, her hair cut short in a way that suits her face. She looks lighter, freer. I snatch another photo and turn it over to the same man, a side-shot of him this time with a blade of yellow grass jutting from his mouth, his leg cocked on the trunk of a large birch. There's an emptiness hanging in his eyes, a deep contemplation, as though he's trapped in some memory without end.

"Please, they're just old pictures of my husband. Your daughter's not in there." Clara's voice comes out muffled, her hand cupping her mouth. Her eyes are downcast and broken. I can feel the shame radiating off her in waves.

"Emma," I shout. "Emma!"

There's no answer, no sound but the grating click of the fan as it turns. With a hard swallow, I lead Kayla from the room and close the door.

* * *

We head upstairs.

Clara stretches for a key resting on the casing above the first door. It adds to my thumping dread, the fact that she has the doors locked, waiting for her to grasp it and fit it in the doorknob, the seconds ticking past like minutes, like hours.

Thump. Find her.

Thump, thump. Find Emma.

"There we go," Clara says, finally sliding it into the lock.

The rooms are the same as downstairs, except with more disarray, each of them packed to the gills and colored with its own unique smell: glue and dust, stale air and nicotine, wood shavings and urine. More cheap crystal light fixtures drip from the ceilings, the glass pendants corroded and brown with age. One of the rooms sports a half-dozen fist-sized holes in the drywall, the trim missing in spots, as if someone had a go at them with a crowbar and then left. Probably one of Billy's night games. I can imagine it, Billy giving a *what the hell* shrug and swinging away like a redneck Barry Bonds, laughing and swinging again, cheering on the pointless destruction.

My nerves are singing by the time we reach the last door. Gauzy strips of light drip over the room, completely bare, with a thick plastic sewer line cutting from the floor to the ceiling. The floor, the walls, are nothing but plywood and two-by-fours, the entire space coated in sawdust like whoever built the house gave up right here and walked away. The wood is riddled with water damage, though I can't spot a water source, only spatters of black paint flung across the windows and supports. I stare at the congealed pigment with my mind spinning and blank with panic.

I edge back into the hall and step on something soft, a warm squish that brings my attention to my feet and the dead rat lying there, half-decayed, with its incisors showing through a tattered cheek, the flesh in ribbons.

"Is that an attic?" Kayla's voice brings me around, and I catch her staring up at a rectangular hatch tucked into the ceiling.

Clara glances up. "Well, yes, it is, but—"

"I want to check it," I say.

"No, I don't think that's necessary. No one has been up there in years."

"What about Billy?"

The way her eyes flick to the side a second after I ask the question is the only answer I need. I stretch for the release hook and lower the hatch, uncurl the ladder. Clara mumbles something about it being a waste of time, but I'm already climbing the steps and thrusting my head higher through a layer of yellow insulation. Unlike below, it's relatively clean with smooth, dust-worn boards running back toward a broad dormer window. There isn't much to the space — a few rolls of carpet stuffed near the joints, along with several plastic bins packed with scrapbooks and Christmas decorations. A wood-framed portrait of an old man with gray-and-white curls tilts against the wall near the window, his eyes sunken, his mouth hard, but it isn't what draws my attention. It's what lies next to it, scattered over the floor and placed along the windowsill. The hair on the back of my neck prickles. I spin on Clara as she ascends the ladder and steps into the attic.

"I thought you said it was just you and Billy here?"

She looks past me in a rapid blink, chewing on the inside of her cheek. I wait her out, stare daggers until she twists the ball of her foot into the floorboard and crosses her arms.

"Mostly it is, but not always."

CHAPTER THIRTY-THREE

CLARA
1997

Clara wasn't meant to be a mother, she knew this now, but she could still be a wife.

The thought came to her in April and stayed with her well into the summer. She clung to it like a life preserver when she woke at night slicked in sweat. In her dreams, Kinley crawled and cooed and grew like other children. She had lake-water eyes and pink, pudgy legs she kicked when Clara tickled her. Her laugh was high and bright and reminded Clara of summer wind chimes.

The dream always ended the same, with Kinley crying until Clara reached for her. The second Kinley's fingers brushed hers, they dissolved. It happened in bites: first her hands, then her arms. Her legs and waist and neck. And then it was her face raining down, falling away in tender flakes until all that remained of her sweet baby was a cloud of eyelashes hanging in the air. Clara would come awake with a scream lodged in her throat and that same thought bubbling up, distant through the grief.

You can still be a wife.

And so, she did. She rose from the bed for the first time in months, determined to fill the empty space Kinley left behind with movement and work, anything to keep her brain occupied and her heart numb. She cleaned and scrubbed and polished and vacuumed like she could blot out the pain . . . and in a way it worked. The ranch felt lighter as she erased Mother and Father one room at a time.

It took months. She started in the master suite, balling up Mother's favorite skirts and blouses with shaking hands before stuffing them into trash bags along with her precious art sets and oil paintings. She gathered all the World War II photo books Father had been so fond of and set them on fire in a big, blue oil drum behind the chicken coop. A thrill ran through her as the pages blistered and turned black. She imagined it was Father's face melting instead of the lonely-eyed soldiers staring up at her through the flames.

She cleaned the office and the kitchen and all of the rooms downstairs. A sense of freedom overtook Clara as she worked, a flicker of optimism she hadn't felt since she'd first heard Kinley's heartbeat all those months earlier. Father had never loved anything like he had loved the farm, and Clara could think of nothing more fitting than to scrub every memory of him from it, along with those of Mother.

Clara boxed and packed all of their things and took them to the county dump so they'd be buried with the rest of the trash no one wanted. She transformed the house and made it hers and John's — a place of love and light instead of one shrouded in darkness. She bought succulents for the living room along with floral votive candles, which she placed on the mantel and the coffee table in between vases of tulips. While in town one day, she purchased a fern with bright green fronds that she set near the bay window. The plant drank in the sunlight and grew and reminded her life could still go on if you let it. Maybe she could stay on the farm, after all, Clara thought; yes, she decided, if she couldn't bear John a child, she could at least bear him the ranch.

And then, on the afternoon of July fourth, she cleaned Sydney's room. There had been friction between them ever since Sydney had walked in on her and John fighting in the kitchen, but to her credit, Sydney hadn't said much besides, "I'm worried about you, Clara. I still don't think he deserves you." Clara told Sydney she was fine, but Clara knew Sydney didn't believe her by the way she averted her gaze and tightened her lips.

Spring melted into summer, and Sydney spent less and less time on the farm and more time elsewhere, doing whatever it was she did all day.

Clara didn't ask where she went, and Sydney didn't tell her. When at the farm, she lingered on the back porch, smoking cigarettes and sipping drinks that had turned mostly to vodka. Her arms had thinned, as had her cheeks, the skin caving into sallow hollows as she pulled in mouthfuls of smoke. Clara told her she could leave, that she and John were good now, and that Sydney had a life of her own to live. But she just stared at Clara, looking bedraggled with those bloodshot eyes of hers, and sighed.

"As soon as you're back on your feet."

Well, that was exactly what Clara intended to do when she cleaned Sydney's room — prove she was, in fact, back on her feet. That, and Sydney had never been one to prize tidiness, the guest room serving as a prime example. It was a mess. Clara wasn't looking for anything as she straightened and dusted. She only wanted to surprise Sydney with an organized space of her own, with a fresh change of sheets. But what she found instead, tucked out of sight beneath the desk, sent her into a tailspin.

It took half an hour to gather and arrange Sydney's things — a stack of veterinary textbooks, several pairs of shoes, two sets of head-phones, some scarfs, gloves and hats — and vacuum what lay beneath before turning her attention to the desktop. It lay cluttered and heavy with paperwork, old bills piled next to a manila folder full of graduate applications. The sight drove splinters of guilt into Clara's sternum. If it weren't for her, Sydney wouldn't have let them lapse. She'd be some-where else, living a different life, one free from the tremendous weight of Clara's problems, of her constant need for comfort and companionship, unable to give anything in return. Problems that Sydney no longer needed to shoulder.

It was with that feeling, that single, solitary thought — I will no longer be a burden — that she attacked the mess. She found an empty, green accordion file in John's office and brought it upstairs. She sorted through the documents, filing those that looked important and throwing out the rest. She took her time, made sure to smooth the papers and staple those that belonged together before placing them one by one into the alphabetical pockets. She'll appreciate this, Clara thought. It will make her smile.

She was near finished, the desk returning to form, when she knocked a pen off the desk's corner and knelt to retrieve it. There it

144

was, a pink snatch of paper lying among all the dust and boxes, a bit of color that seized her attention. She grabbed it absentmindedly, was in the process of throwing it away when the memory came back to her unbidden. Sydney in the kitchen, staring at John with all that hate boiling in her eyes, an envelope, this envelope, clutched tight in her hand.

Clara looked at it again. That's all it took, one look at the address stamped in the corner, the name — "Ashley Morgan" with a swirl of butterflies clouding the A — for her to lose her breath.

With tentative fingers, she pulled free the piece of paper inside and unfolded it. A picture fell onto her lap. She picked it up, and the image it bore tore through her like a chainsaw. It was of John kneeling in front of a woman with wide-set dimples and a pinched nose. The woman stood smiling, looking down on him as he pressed a sunburned ear to her belly . . . a belly swollen in the soft, undeniable curve Clara knew all too well.

The picture slid from her hand, along with the letter, and Clara's world turned black.

CHAPTER THIRTY-FOUR

KAYLA

"You're telling me there's been someone else here this entire time?" Dad says in a voice that's close to a full-on freak out. "Another woman?"

"Yes — I mean no, not at the moment. She's been gone for a few weeks."

Dad sinks his fingers into his hair and walks back to the mattress stuffed in the corner of the attic, stares at it, looking bewildered.

"Jesus Christ, what the hell is happening here?"

I'm asking myself the same question as I gaze at the mattress and the ashy ring of cigarette butts scattered around it like a bunch of dead flies. And it's not just cigarettes. There are beer cans, too, an army of them lying in between a bunch of glittering glass vodka bottles. It's like staring at the remains of a keg party for one. The most depressing keg party I've ever seen. And, even weirder, mixed in with all the cans and cigarettes is a tornado of crumpled paper. There are reams of it, all these pages flung about like we've walked into the middle of some mad author's office after a tantrum.

Dad digs one from the floor and uncrumples it, his eyes ticking over the words. He holds it up and shakes it in Clara's face. "What is this all about?"

She takes the paper gingerly between two fingers, like she's afraid if she grips it too hard, it might crumble. "I'm . . . honestly not sure," she says, reading it.

"Where is this woman? You said her name was Sydney, right? Where is this Sydney right now?"

"I don't know."

"You don't know? Or you won't tell me?"

"I'd tell you if I knew where she was."

"So she just comes and goes as she pleases, and makes herself at home up here in your attic in the meantime? Do you know how crazy that sounds?"

Clara's face sags, and she runs a hand over the back of her neck. "Yes, I suppose I do. It's why I didn't mention her earlier. But she's fine. I promise. She's an old friend of mine who's been going through a bit of a rough patch lately. It's temporary. I'm just helping her work through a few things."

Dad starts in on her again, asking more questions about the woman, really tearing into Clara about how insane it all is — and does she have Emma? Could she have taken her? Clara saying, no, no, she wouldn't, and I suddenly can't take it anymore. I slip past them and grab a piece of paper from the floor, smooth it against my jeans and then trail over to the window. The writing is harsh — all these angry-looking capital letters like whoever wrote them did so in a shout. It's the same sentence scrawled over and over: *I MUST PROTECT HER. I MUST PROTECT HER. I MUST PROTECT HER.* I grab another page. It's the same — more crazy block letters written so hard, the paper is torn in spots. *I MUST PROTECT HER.*

Protect who? From what?

The question gives me the creeps. I drop the page and glance outside. It isn't snowing anymore, the sky a patchy blue-gray with the sun shining through in spots, so that's one good thing, I guess. The first good thing I can think of since

Emma ran into the woods and started this whole nightmare. Maybe, with any luck, we can find her this morning and leave. The snow Is already melting, dripping in spots, water pattering off the icicles on the gutter and falling toward the base of the house to form little wet puddles in the snow . . . snow that's packed with tracks. My eyes widen. They're large, Billy large, and there are a lot of them.

"Dad," I say, over my shoulder.

He doesn't respond, still going at it with Clara interrogation-style, jabbing a finger in her face and pointing at the floor.

"Why would she do this? Write all this nonsense?"

"Dad," I repeat, louder. "I think I might know where Billy is."

That gets his attention. He rushes over and presses his forehead to the windowpane, his breath fogging the glass. "Where?"

"There," I say, pointing at the tracks winding away from the house toward a building that looks like a stable, with a slanted roof and a stack of hay bales piled near a blue, paneled door.

"Good eyes," he says, squeezing my arm and looking at me like he actually sees me for once, like he's actually proud of me. A sudden warmth spreads through my chest. It's a feeling like a candle lighting. He hasn't looked at me like that for a long time. Not since Mom died, and definitely not since I caught him in his office with his stupid girlfriend, or whoever she was. The thought is a cold wind, and just like that the candle goes out. Dad doesn't notice, because he's already heading back to the ladder with Clara.

"C'mon," he says, waving me after him. "Let's go find your sister."

I sigh and shuffle after him.

* * *

148

It's freezing outside, so much colder than yesterday despite the sun. The wind cuts against my face and neck in icy sheets as we push through the knee-high snow toward the stable. It scares me, the cold, not so much for myself but for Emma. There's no way she'd be okay out here in one of these rickety buildings, especially in her condition. Especially with Billy. He's so big. Bigger than Dad by at least a foot. My stomach clenches. It wouldn't take much for him to hurt her. The thought pushes me a little faster, and I catch up to Dad as he bangs into the stable with a shout.

"Emma! Emma, are you in here?"

His answer comes in the form of a snort, followed by a low chuff and a whinny. A long, spotted head eases over the lip of the nearest stall. Two dark globe eyes pressed into a vanilla-spotted face appraise me as we near. My stomach twists. The horse is so thin, his nostrils already out and nosing against my palm for food I don't have. His chestnut coat is dull and patched in spots, looking like a worn-out welcome mat. His ribs slice against his skin.

Poor thing, I think as I stroke his mane, which looks like it's made of straw. Behind him, in the corner of the stall, I spot Billy's half-eaten bowl of stew from last night, tipped over in between piles of manure. There's so much of it, the stall filled with it, on the floor, smeared on the walls. It's beyond disgusting, just like Billy's room.

I reach out and give the horse another pat on the cheek. "I'll try to get you some food, okay? And a clean place to sleep. Clara shouldn't be treating you like this."

And she shouldn't. The horse reminds me of one of those dogs you see chained outside in winter, the ones the TV people use for the animal abuse commercials with the dog making sad eyes for the camera. I'm shaking with anger as I march up to Clara and tug on the sleeve of her fur coat. It's ridiculous, huge and shaggy and way out of date, something the evil villainess would wear in an old-time Disney cartoon. She turns toward me, looking disoriented, like she might fall down at any moment.

"Yes, dear?"

"You need to feed your horse."

"I'm sorry, what?"

"I said you can't treat a horse like that. It's so cold in here. The water in his trough is half frozen. And I didn't see any hay. When is the last time he had something to eat?"

"He — well, Billy is supposed to make sure he has—"

"How is it Billy's fault? You're the one who said he has—"

Dad cuts me off. "Not now, Kayla." He shoots Clara a sharp look. "She's not in here. No one is. Where else?" He looks awful, sounds awful, his hair combed into wild rows from dragging his fingers through it over and over.

Clara tips her gaze to the floor and holds it there as if it will somehow give her an answer. "I-I don't know . . ."

"Think. We're running out of time here." There's an urgency in his voice that makes me shiver.

Clara digs a thumb into her wrist and sighs. "Well, there is one other place he might go."

"Show me," Dad orders. "Right now."

Her eyes flash, and for a second, it looks like she's the one about to lose her shit instead of Dad. She doesn't. Instead, she only collapses further into herself, her shoulders rolling forward as she nods. "Okay," she says. "Okay. Follow me."

CHAPTER THIRTY-FIVE

KAYLA

Clara's "other place" is a sheet-metal disaster full of rust and broken windows that she tells us is an old chicken coop, that Billy just loved playing out here when he was a kid. I can imagine it, Billy inside with the birds, running around, chasing them, wagging his arms and clucking away like some maniac chicken. I can picture him catching one, petting the terrified thing as it clucked and trilled in terror, flapping its wings before he broke its neck. He probably "just loved" doing that. He probably still does.

And now, he might be in there with Emma . . .

Fresh tears sting my eyes, and I struggle to hold them back. I can't fall apart right now, can't turn into a worthless ball of mush, panic-crying when I need to focus on finding Emma. God, I've been so shitty to her since Mom died, telling her to go away whenever she knocked on my door or pulled on my sweater with a book in hand. *Tug.* Will you read me this? *Tug. Tug.* Can you help me put this puzzle together? *No. Go away, Emma. Leave me alone.*

I think it was the voice thing that pissed me off the most. At first, I thought it was this needy cry for attention, a way to make Mom's death all about her. *Pay attention to me.* That's what it felt like, anyway. The Emma Show. I didn't want to pay attention to her. I didn't want to pay attention to anything. I just wanted to lock myself in my room and numb out. I wanted to pretend things were fine and that Mom was still downstairs making us dinner or folding laundry, or a few seconds away from screaming at me to take out the trash or put away the dishes.

There was no pretending, though. Emma made it impossible. Every time I asked her a question, she'd just stare back at me with those huge, unblinking eyes of hers, refusing to speak. Her silence was this constant reminder: *Hey, Kayla, guess what, Mom's dead. Hi, Kayla, don't forget how shitty our life is now.* It drove Dad nuts. Mimi and Papa, too. It became this thing. *The* thing. They were always whispering about Emma in the kitchen when they thought I couldn't hear, talking about what they could do to help her, how they could bring her voice back. The weekly therapist report was big news. Doctor Johnson said this, Doctor Johnson said that, and goodness, how very, very sad Emma must be to stay all bottled up like that. Blah, blah, blah.

It went on for months, them being all focused on Emma, worrying about her nonstop. So much so, no one noticed I was breaking, too. Not even Dad, not that I really expected him to. After The Incident (that's how I think of it), all he's been is fake nice, acting like he's interested in me, pretending that he cares about my feelings or whatever, when deep down, I know he's just pissed off he got caught.

I don't know if I'll ever forgive him for what he did to Mom. She died thinking he was this perfect guy who loved her completely. This wonderful husband who never made any mistakes and spent every moment doting on her. Correction, *I* let her die thinking that. She had the right to know. And I should have told her. It's just . . . I couldn't bear to crush her, and it *would* have crushed her with how sick she was. Just one more log on the fire.

But now, because of that choice, I'm stuck with Dad's dirty little secret forever. It's like this hole in my stomach I can't seem to patch, no matter how hard I try. And, trust me, I've tried *e-ver-y-thing*. I exercised my brains out when Mom first died. I ran around the school track until my legs turned to pasta. I went to church and even talked to Pastor Collins a few times, because that's what Mom would have wanted me to do. He told me I needed to turn it over to God, like it was as simple as that. Like if I prayed enough, God would magically reach down from heaven and make everything better.

Spoiler alert. He didn't.

After that, I dumped myself into whatever I could. School and friends and boys. I had sex with Ethan again. Twice. I thought if he loved me, maybe it would help me love myself again. He didn't, and it didn't, of course, so I tried other things. Stuff Dad has no clue about. Ecstasy and weed, and lots of the syrupy-tasting wine coolers Bree likes so much. Those at least made me feel better for a little while, made me forget everything for a few hours, but then I'd go to sleep and wake up right back where I started, feeling awful again, that hole in my stomach burning hotter, getting bigger, along with a nasty hangover.

Here's the funny thing about it all, Dad's secret: I used to look up to him. I thought he was Superman. He raised me to be honest and to work hard, to always do my best. He got all over me one time in seventh grade when he found out I stole this necklace from the grocery store, one of those stupid candy ones. He marched me right back inside and made me apologize to the blue-haired lady at the service desk. She frowned and snatched the necklace out of my hand with a lecture, told me girls who steal wind up working at gas stations and fast-food restaurants. She said it like the grocery store was an investment bank and she was the CEO. The people in line behind me heard every word. One of them even snickered. I'd never been so embarrassed. I sobbed the entire way home with Dad consoling me, patting my knee and telling me, "*Kayla, it takes a lifetime to build character, and a moment to destroy it. Promise me you'll do better from now on.*"

God, what a hypocrite. I mean, I know he loves me and all. I've never questioned that, but it doesn't change the fact that my skin crawls every time I look at him. It's like things are good one minute, I'm totally fine, and then Dad says something and — *Bam!* — I'm back to thinking about that dark-haired girl bobbing up and down on his lap.

I mean, who was she that Dad would go and betray Mom like that? I actually believed him when he said she was the love of his life. The love he sacrificed for what? Some airhead twenty-year-old? Some stupid college slut? I don't get it. Or I guess I do, when I think about it. It's the same thing Ethan wanted — to use me, to make me his toy for a while. His trophy to brag about with his friends. I just thought Dad was better than that. Wrong.

It's why I need to be better for Emma from now on. I can't change the stuff with Dad, but I can be the kind of sister to Emma who has time to listen, or hug, or play one of her silly restaurant waitress games. The kind of sister who doesn't let her wander off into the forest and break a leg. The kind of sister Mom would have wanted me to be. The thought fills me with a hot ache. I suddenly want her back. All of her. Even the annoying parts, because, after the last two days, I can't imagine my life without her in it.

Come back, Emma, and I promise I won't ever be mad at you again . . .

I carry the thought with me as Clara leads us inside the building where it's somehow colder, the wind shrieking through the broken windows like a pack of angry ghosts. There's trash scattered all over the place: all these old sandwich bags and soda cans and faded bottles of Clorox bleach, mixed in with other containers full of chemical names I don't recognize. Tires are stacked along the wall next to thick spools of chain and something else . . . chicken cages, or at least I think that's what they are, all these little gray-black

154

boxes covered in wire. They're so small, I can't imagine how they would ever hold a live bird.

I trail across the mostly gravel floor and ease close to one. A severed beak is shoved through the mesh screen. There are bones on the floor behind it, little ones, and a bunch of moldy white feathers stuck to the sides and glued to the wires in clumps. It looks like something left in the microwave for too long, the last few bits of a vaporized tomato. They're all like that, I realize as I look down the line, every single cage full of bones and feathers and piles of dried bird crap, like whoever took care of the birds gave up and left them to rot. It's disgusting, but not as disgusting as the smell: a mix of ammonia and vinegar so strong it makes my eyes water.

Dad strides toward a ring of crusted stones in the center of the coop that have been pulled together in the shape of a fire pit. Charred things fill the center, scorched Dole pineapple cans surrounded by shattered bits of glass and twisted mounds of plastic. A melted G.I. Joe peers up at me with one chalky, blue eye, the mouth burned away. Like Emma and her voice.

"What is this?" Dad asks Clara, waving at the fire. "Did you do this?"

She gives him the same deer-in-the-headlights look she had in the attic when Dad asked her about the woman, before mumbling a no.

"Who then? Billy? The crazy lady in your attic? Or is there someone else you haven't told me about? Do you have people living out here, too? A couple homeless guys, maybe?"

I don't wait for her to answer before wandering off. I know it's strange, the whole mattress-in-the-attic thing, the beer cans and the vodka bottles and the nutso letters, but the way Dad is grilling her like she's a child killer or something is embarrassing. I don't think she is. She's just lonely and confused. And it's not like anything about this farm makes any sense, anyway. The piles of junk and the crazy, ugly wallpaper and Clara's room with the backward pictures and her clothes strung out everywhere, like someone shoved a bomb

155

in her dresser. It's obvious she's a mess, and I don't think Dad's screaming at her is going to help us find Emma any faster.

I drown the thought and head toward the back of the building. The walls are covered in tools — all these pickaxes and shovels and a bunch of other stuff I can't name. Saws and hammers and some Grim Reaper-looking thing strapped to a length of chain-link fence, the blade old and covered in rust. Or is it blood from the chickens? I can't tell. I reach for it and trace a finger over the cold metal, imagine Billy swinging away with it, slicing the birds in half. What else would someone do with something like—

My toe hits something.

I glance down to a wooden lip in the floor, a square frame that looks like a cellar door. I can't tell for sure because it's buried beneath a stack of tires, but there is a handle near the edge and some hinges. I crouch and stare at the thin crack running alongside it. It's mostly black, but there's something else there as well, a shape darker than the rest. An outline I can't quite make out. I tilt my head and stare at it, the hair on the back of my neck rising. *What is that?*

With a jerk, it moves, and I scatter back.

"Where else, Clara? Where else could Billy possibly be? We've searched everywhere."

Dad's voice spins me around. He's squared off with her, pulling at his hair and spreading his hands.

"I . . . don't know. He's never disappeared like this before."

"You sure about that? He didn't have much of a problem storming out last night at dinner."

"Yes, but that's different. He was worried about Phillip. He and Billy have a special connection, and to be fair, Phillip does struggle in cold weather like this."

"You think I care about your horse right now? You have to be kidding me. I don't give a flying fuck about Phillip. We're talking about my daughter here, not some goddamn

156

horse. I'm done with this. We aren't getting anywhere on our own. Kayla, let's go!"

His eyes find mine a second before he turns and strides for the door. Clara grabs his arm, and he shakes free, her hand hanging frozen until she drops it and follows him outside. I glance back at the cellar door, the black through the gap even now. *It always was.* God, I'm so beyond fried at this point. Of course, no one was there. *You imagined it,* I tell myself. *You're just loopy.* For some reason, the thought doesn't make me feel any better.

CHAPTER THIRTY-SIX

CLARA
1997

It took over an hour to drive to Rifle, the blacktop a blurry, yellow-line smudge through Clara's tears. The taste of warm salt filled her mouth, and she struggled to keep the car pinned to the right side of the road, questions raining through her head like lightning strikes:

Would John really do this to her, after all they'd been through together?

Could he actually betray her so soon after Kinley? After the miscarriages?

Was he cruel enough to father a child with another woman . . . this Ashley Morgan? Had she married that kind of man?

No, she decided, that was not whom she'd married, the man with the soft smile and kind heart who'd pulled her from the wreckage of her life, where she'd been stuck drowning beneath the weight of Mother and Father's cruelty. The man whose very presence had once filled her like helium and sent her spinning for the stars.

He wouldn't . . . couldn't do something like that to her. It had to be a mistake, the photo, a picture of a friend, or a distant cousin, maybe an old co-worker who'd been overly excited to share the news of her pregnancy with anyone who'd listen.

Not John, she assured herself.
Never John.

* * *

The house was dark when she arrived, a bricked-over craftsman planted on a cheap, five-acre lot overrun with pockets of sagebrush and scrub oak. The front yard was more dirt than lawn with two cedar planter boxes near the porch full of weeds and a mailbox planted in the corner with the flag half-cocked like it couldn't decide if it held mail or not.

Clara saw none of it, her eyes grazing the property in search of one thing: John's truck. She breathed a sigh of relief when all she spotted was empty gravel and cracked cement, no F-150. She'd been paranoid, she decided, her mind still reeling from Kinley's death. John was no doubt down at Shooters, getting drunk with Steven Lewis and Bret Savage. He'd stumble home sometime after midnight like usual, Clara told herself, and fall into bed smelling of whiskey and ashtrays.

Feeling better now, she reached for the keys and was about to leave when something gave her pause. It took a moment to place exactly what it was. The front door, she realized. It was hanging wide open. A gaping mouth that gave view to a long, dark throat. There was something about the sight that hypnotized her, pulled at her, almost like she'd been here before, in this very moment. It was that feeling that caused her to draw a flashlight from the glove box and ease from the car and then across the street, up the spalling and cracked driveway, and toward the first few sun-cracked steps.

There she stood, unsure, blinking into the somehow-familiar home drenched in black, not a single light on in any room. In the distance, the first few fireworks crackled and hissed, painting the sky in blooms of pink and green and phosphorescent purple. Clara grew dimly aware that someone might spot her in their shine and hurried up the steps and onto the porch, where she paused. At her feet lay several oily-dark splotches spilled across the wood. A voice came to life in her head, sharp and pleading, when she realized they were boot prints. A man's boot prints. A large one.

Leave, Clara. Leave now.

159

And she would have if it weren't for the cry that followed. Piercing and frantic and in need. A desperate, lonely cry. A baby's cry. One Clara couldn't ignore.

She clicked on the flashlight and slid through the door, careful to avoid the slick, red prints soaking the carpet and splattered over the wood floor in the kitchen. The cry came again, so sharp and insistent it nearly broke her heart. She followed it down a short hall framed in pictures, vaguely aware that whoever had created the boot prints could still be in the house waiting for her. The thought crawled deeper into her brain, and the voice was back, screaming for her to go, go, go as she shined the flashlight into a room soaked in gore. The images popped and burned like camera flashes:

Half a face gone, buried beneath a bloody mat of hair.

A slim, pink flannel shirt peeled away in the shape of a shotgun blast.

A stomach left in tatters.

Behind the corpse, pressed to a row of crib slats, was a pair of apple-slice cheeks with a tiny mouth centered between them and bunched into a wailing cry. A cold line of sweat snaked down Clara's ribs. Her vision flickered in and out as she took in the child's deep, chocolate eyes and the prominent nose she knew so well. Her gaze trailed toward the picture tacked above the changing table, and her knees gave out. There was John with his arms curled around the woman from Sydney's picture, the woman looking down at the baby in her arms, this baby, in the same way Clara had so longed to look at Kinley.

I will do anything for you . . . I am your mother, and I am here, and I am yours.

Clara's heart dissolved and melted into her lungs. Her breath came in quick gasps. She glanced toward the glider perched next to the window and spotted John's Browning Gold propped against it, the barrel flickering blue and red with the fireworks. And then she was looking at the child again, staring into John's eyes pressed into this strange boy's face, mixed with features that were not her own. A wide chin and a square forehead, hair kinked in curls. Her lips peeled into a silent moan, and she tasted strings of bile on her tongue. The room spun, and she thought she might throw up.

After a moment, she found her feet and drifted toward the crib, tears burning in the corners of her eyes as she reached down and pulled the baby to her chest. He smelled like milk and sweat, and Clara inhaled deeply and imagined it was Kinley she held and not some other woman's child. The baby nuzzled into her neck, his hungry lips making quick, sucking motions against her collarbone until Clara raised her shirt and gave him her breast. The feel of his mouth on her nipple swam through her like a song, and she made a decision. It didn't take her long. She carried the baby right out of the house. She didn't give it a second thought.

CHAPTER THIRTY-SEVEN

CHRIS

I burst into the kitchen and head to the phone. *Work, you stupid thing . . . just fucking work.* I pick it up to a hiss of dead static and slam it down, pick it up to more of the same. *Work! Work! Work!* I don't realize I'm banging the phone on the counter in time with the thought until the earpiece cracks in half.

A hand grazes my shoulder. "Dad."

I whirl around. "What!"

Kayla's face brings me back to the moment, the way she's looking at me with real fear in her eyes, her fingertips hovering near my arm in a tremble, her face bright red and laced with cold. My anger dims. She's been through too much the last few days. We all have.

"Dad, where is she?"

"I don't know, Kit Kat. But we'll find her. We will."

"This is so unlike Billy. I just don't understand why he'd do this," Clara says, crouching to brush the snow from the fur lining of her boots. She looks ludicrous in her too-tight dress, her legs shooting awkwardly to the side. "He's never done anything like this before. He's usually so responsible."

162

"I need your keys."

Her eyes wrinkle. "What?"

"The keys to the truck. I have to get ahold of the police. We can't wait any longer."

Her fingernails sink into the top of her wrist, dig little half-moons into the skin. "I don't know if that's the best idea. Resources will be strained in a storm like this. The fire department is mostly volunteers. We do have one sheriff and a few police officers, but only for emergencies. They'll be busy helping with—"

"Clara, are you out of your mind? My kid is missing. And so is your son. Nobody knows where they are. We need the cops. I'd say this qualifies as an emergency, wouldn't you?"

"Yes. Yes, you're right, of course." She stands and digs through a wicker basket on the counter, pulls out a pair of mittens followed by a Broncos beanie and a set of coasters. "I know they're in here somewhere. Oh, here we go." Her hand comes out in a jingle. She tosses me the keys. "It does well enough in the snow if you drive slow. Meeker is the closest town, but it's a good way off from here. You should be able to flag someone down before you reach it and call for help."

"I'm coming with you," Kayla volunteers.

"No, I need you here in case Emma turns up."

"No way! You're not leaving me here by myself."

"Kayla. We can't both go."

She crosses her arms and looks away, her stance an echo from the past. Her as a toddler — jaw rammed forward, lips in a pout, bangs curled over her eyes. I take her chin and ease her gaze back to mine. "Look, think how scared your sister would be if she shows up and neither of us is around to take care of her. I'll be right back. I promise. You'll be fine."

"How do you know?"

"I just do."

I don't. I'm terrified things *won't* be fine, but I have to put on a brave face because, right now, it's all I've got. I glance at Clara. "Hey, keep an eye on her for me, will you?"

Kayla jerks back as if stung.

"Seriously? Dad. I don't need *her* to watch me. God, how old do you think I am? Ten? Whatever. Just go already. I don't care." Then she's gone, storming from the kitchen.

"Kayla, wait!"

I'm about to rush after her when Clara steps in my way and pats my shoulder. "Let her go. She's a teenager. It's what they do. Give her a few minutes and she'll be fine." She gives me a ghost of a smile and tucks a loose strand of hair behind her ear, and I think again of how much she resembles Lexi, that if I squint hard enough, it's easy to imagine Lexi talking to me instead of Clara.

"Head west after you hit the gate," she continues. "The plows are sure to be out by now. Oh, and fourth gear gets a bit sticky at times. You have to go easy on the clutch. You can drive a stick, right?" Her kind tone thaws me a little. The way she's put up with me shouting at her, ordering her around like this is my place instead of hers, is more than I would do if the tables were turned.

"Yeah. Listen, Clara, I didn't mean to bite your head off earlier. I'm just worried about my daughter."

"I know you are. I only wish . . ." She pinches the bridge of her nose and closes her eyes with a sigh before opening them again. "This thing with Billy . . . it's all my fault. I'm sorry. I only wanted to help."

"I know you did. I'll be back as soon as I can."

* * *

I push outside and head for the truck, cloaked in a pair of gloves and an old sheepskin coat Clara dug from the front closet a moment earlier. John's — all cracked leather and wool, something ripped from another decade, but it's much warmer than my windbreaker, with a stiff collar that blunts the breeze. I can picture him wearing it, working between the stalks, and cursing the early winter weather like I am now. It's grown even colder in the last few minutes, the mid-afternoon sun dipping toward a formless bank of clouds on the horizon. They look dark and hungry, ready to swallow the light. A reminder: *You are running out of time.*

My ankle throbs as I walk, blood seeping through what's left of Clara's bandage in a sticky bloom. Each step is like rubbing against broken glass, but I barely feel it, my mind gone, focused only on what comes next. Will the truck start? Is there enough gas? Will I get far enough to wave someone down or will I wind up in a ditch with the engine coughing in a death rattle until someone happens along, if they even do at all?

No, I tell myself. It won't happen. It can't. I have to find help, and then I have to find Emma because there's no one else.

I near the pile of snow that is the F-150, a dull-blue sliver buried beneath a heavy blanket of powder. The gloves do little to stunt the bitter cold as I scrape the snow to the ground in a series of steady *thwump-thwump-thwumps*. It's what I concentrate on — the sweeping and clearing, the sound of the snow falling — because it's better than giving in to the tendrils of panic squeezing my lungs, the gnawing exhaustion seeping behind my eyes, threatening to rob me of what little clarity I still possess.

The truck takes shape one swipe at a time. First the hood and windshield, then the cab and doors. I kneel and dig several compact trenches around the tires, careful to pack the snow at their base. They should provide enough traction if I ease the truck out slowly enough and make sure not to spin the tires. I've done it before, too many times, Kayla needling me on some gray winter morning from the backseat — *Hurry up, Dad, we're going to be late!* — me punching the gas, the tires whining, spinning away . . .

My back cracks as I stand and work the keys from the coat pocket and unlock the door. A burst of air rushes over me, colored with the smell of cold vinyl and plastic. The interior is nothing like the trucks I'm used to, wide bucket seats complete with warmers, every corner smooth and dripping in luxury, but it will more than do as long as it starts. And it *will* start, dammit.

I hold onto the thought like a promise, am about to slide in and wrap my hands around the hard rubber steering wheel when I hear the snow crunch behind me. I turn too late and catch the brilliant flash of metal arcing through my peripheral vision a second before it connects with my skull.

CHAPTER THIRTY-EIGHT

CHRIS

A voice leaks in, rough and full of grit.

"... him down in the cellar."

Cold. My head is thick and swimming with it.

Blood whoomps and crashes in my ears, pain lines branching and splitting across the backs of my eyelids in vivid streaks.

Hands dig under my armpits. Fingers seize my ankles.

The air turns warm around me. I am sliding ... my legs dragging across wood, thudding down stairs.

Concrete pulls at my shirt, scrapes my skin. The smell of raw earth invades my nostrils, my brain.

There's the squish of boots, the squeal of hinges and—

* * *

My eyelids twitch. I order them to work. Warmth bleeds down my neck. I grind my jaw, and the joints pop. Someone moans using my voice. A vague, suffocating sensation floods my lungs. I'm drowning, trapped somewhere within myself unable to draw a breath. Flashes of color leap through my

vision — burnt oranges and deep scarlet reds that scorch my
retinas like sunspots. A thought: I have to find something.
No, that's wrong. I need to find . . . some*one* — *the* most
important thing. But I can't summon her face . . . her voice.
Why? Who is she?

Find her, find her, find her.

She is gone, and I hate myself for it. She is gone, and I
am the reason.

* * *

". . . do with him now?"

"Whatever I say, whenever I say. Now go find that girl."

That girl?

What girl?

Emma . . . Kayla . . .

Crawling. I am on my knees now, my kneecaps scraping across stone and cement. My bones ache as I pull myself
toward a weak stream of light coming from . . . from somewhere. There's a hard circle around my shin, something
metal sinking its teeth into my ankle. It won't let go.

Don't you touch her. Don't you—

* * *

I wake in a lukewarm puddle of drool. My tongue tastes like
copper, like rust. There's a heartbeat throbbing somewhere
near my ear, a mound of soft flesh the consistency of a hard-
boiled egg rising beneath a clotted clump of hair. There is
blood on my neck, blood soaking my shirt. A low groan rises
up my throat as my thoughts wash in and out like a tide,
there one second, gone the next.

Where am I?

It's dark. So dark.

How did I get here?

I take a sip of cold, damp air. The smell of concrete dust
and rotten wood fills my nose and coats my gums. A weak

rectangle of light bleeds across the floor from the ceiling. There's a door there — no, a hatch. I push onto my hands and knees and crawl for it, those teeth biting again, seizing my ankle. I jerk against them, and a river of pain rolls up my leg and saturates my stomach. I have a sudden, powerful urge to vomit, to push the pain up my throat and spew it from my mouth. I feel down my jeans to thick links of chain and a metal clasp strapped to my ankle, a cold padlock holding it in place.

Why? Why am I—

It comes back to me in flashes.

The storm.

Emma's leg pinned beneath the boulder, her cries muffled by the thrashing rain.

The cave and the storm and the house rising through the snow.

Emma speaking, whispering to me, and then gone again.

The snow outside as I cleared the truck. That burst of light when I tried to get in, and then . . . nothing.

I finger the wound again. It's a painful wet mess, scabbed over and crusted along with the fringe of hair matted to my neck. I pull in a deep breath, and a wave of dizziness sends me crashing back to the floor, everything spinning, the room tilting like I'm inside a washing machine. I lay my head back, and my eyelids become lead weights. I need to close them for a few minutes and—

No. Don't. Find a way out.

But from where?

A name surfaces: Clara. I'm in her . . . basement. I recognize its smell — that damp-wood rot scent mixed with the moldy laundry air. I pat the concrete and try to gain a sense of my surroundings. My fingers crawl down my leg to my ankle and then up over the chain to a length of smooth powder-coated metal. I recognize its shape and the heat bleeding from it into my fingertips. A radiator — I'm chained to a radiator.

Gouts of pain wash down my neck, and I pull back in a wince. It's hard to think, my brain swimming in a sluggish parade of thoughts: I'm sick. I need a drink of water. I have to pee. My head hurts. The thoughts are like a nest of ants: hard to pin down, there one second, skittering away the next. My skull is on fire, the room back to spinning again in crazy tilt-a-whirls. The nausea hits hard and fast, and I retch violently to the side. A fountain of vomit splashes off the floor somewhere to my right. The smell of gastric juice floods the air, of stomach acid and bile.

I have a concussion . . .

Another worthless thought. Another fact that won't help me escape this place.

Get out of here . . . get out of here . . . get out of here . . .

Sounds filter down through an overhead vent, muted and tinny, spilling faintly through the ductwork. I can't make them out, only that they're words. Some belong to a woman. One I don't recognize, her inflection harsh and guttural. The others are a man's. *Billy's.* The pace is right. The slow drawl of it, as though each word is work.

". . . can't . . . find her . . ."

I strain to hear them. It's futile, and soon they die away and turn to footsteps. Doors thunk open and shut in a volley of collisions that vibrate the walls. More muted voices trickle down, then a crash that sends a blanket of dust spiraling from the ceiling and into my eyes. Someone shouts — more yelling, the woman at it again with that guttural voice.

"Where is she!"

Objects crash to the floor. The sounds reverberate around me, so heavy they can only be pieces of furniture toppling over. They continue, the booms and thuds filling the small space in bumps and rattles. And then it comes — a voice I recognize cutting through the clatter, a high-pitched shriek raining down through the vents. *Kayla.*

I take the chain in my hands and pull with everything I can. Lights spark and wheel through my vision. Deep cuts of vertigo threaten to swamp me, swallow me whole. I fight them off and thrash until there's a tearing sensation, something ripping near my calf as a fresh wave of blood runs down my ankle. I ignore the pain, my hands gripping and pulling. Yanking. And I'm screaming. Screaming, screaming, screaming. Shouting like someone can hear me.

CHAPTER THIRTY-NINE

CLARA
1997

Don't do this, Clara. You can't do this.

The thought echoed through her head as she drove, the baby crying and squirming in her lap until his neck gave out and his head wobbled back against her chest. There she held him with one hand cupped over his ear, his cries fading, growing lighter, until he fell asleep nestled between her breasts.

The car seemed to drive itself, angling over the familiar county roads until Clara sat once more in her driveway with the window down, the air sweet with the scent of lilac from the bushes flowering near the porch. She remained there for a long time, tracing her fingertips over the baby's face, brushing the tops of his ears and wondering if they looked more like John's or the woman he killed. Other questions surfaced. Would he someday have John's deep groove beneath his nose, the same laugh lines etched near the corners of his mouth when he smiled?

An hour passed before she eased from the car and carried the boy inside safely clutched in her arms. His warmth bled through her chest all the way to her heart, and something deep within her clicked into place — an empty space filling in. He felt so right nuzzled against the crook of her elbow, his little mouth working in and out, his eyes moving rapidly against his lids as he dreamed. In a way, he already felt like hers, but she knew she couldn't keep the baby here at the farm. Not after what John had done to his mistress. She thought of her then, of Ashley Morgan with the frosted tips and light-brown eyes turned to pulp in the spray of John's shotgun blast.

"He'll hurt you the same as your daddy."

Sydney had been right. All these years later, and she'd been right; Clara had married a man like her father. No, someone worse — a murderer. A man who'd killed the mother of his child in as savage a fashion as she could imagine. And what would he do to Clara if he found out she'd brought that very child back home to the ranch? His ranch. Clara knew she didn't want to find out; she had to call the police.

She'd barely lifted the phone from the cradle when she heard the door bang open down the hall. She knew it was John the second he slid into the kitchen behind her. She could smell him in the air, the scent of whiskey and tobacco leaching from his clothes, growing stronger with each step. His voice came out in a slur, and she knew he'd been drinking.

"Whadd're you still doin' up?"

Clara froze, unsure what to say. Her mouth ran dry, and her hands trembled. She'd never felt fear like she did in that moment. Not the times her door would creak open to Father's shadow dripping across her bed before he took her to the Black Place. Not when Mother dragged her into the cellar by the hair for misbehaving and made her scrub the grease stains from the cement floors. No, this was a different kind of fear. A feel-it-in-your-bones kind of fear that had her quaking in place, every muscle in her body tensed, afraid to turn around and face him.

She set the phone down and curled her shoulders forward over the baby, praying John would lose interest, if she didn't answer, and slip off to bed. He didn't. He moved closer instead, his hot breath falling rank across her neck, standing there with her bones rigid and her cells swimming in fear until she finally turned around. The baby squirmed in her arms with a single milky grunt, and John's bloodshot eyes cracked wider and went cold. His jaw flexed, and he breathed hard through his nose, beads of sweat shining beneath his hairline.

"Give him to me, Clara," he said, taking a step forward.

"Leave me alone, John."

"Give him to me. I won't ask again."

His fingers worked open and then curled into a fist. A vein throbbed hard beneath his chin. Clara wondered if it was the look Ashley saw right before he killed her — the same rage she saw now, simmering just beneath the surface, waiting to boil over.

"Clara . . ."

She glanced over his shoulder and spotted the bedroom door hanging open down the hall. Lock him out, she thought. Run.

And she ran.

John was on her with a speed that betrayed his size. A hand seized her wrist, another grasping at the child, trying to wrest him from her grip as she shrieked and twisted away. Her arms wrapped tighter around the boy, the baby waking, coming to life with a single shrill cry. John caught him by the thigh. Clara jerked him free and edged back, back, back, thinking you will not have him, you will not have him, you will not have him. *And then her calves met with something she hadn't expected, a shape hard and square, and she lost her balance.*

It all felt so slow. The fall. The baby slipping from her grip, hanging mid-air in a tangle of arms and legs as she reached for him. The thunk of his head off the open dishwasher door, and the warm squish of his skull. She heard it as much as she felt it, a thought rolling through her mind as it happened — he's broken now . . . and you broke him.

It didn't last long. John brought his hands down and wrapped them around her neck with a seething snarl. She tried to buck him off, but her legs had lost their strength and her vision was already smoking and curling in at the edges. She screamed and all that came out was a gurgle as John squeezed harder, pressing his thumbs into her Adam's apple in an attempt to collapse her windpipe. To her right, she glimpsed the baby, a wrinkled lump of pink flesh blurring away. The thought hit again, sliding loose and formless somewhere near the back of her skull, soaking the coils and twists of her brain. He's broken now. He's broken just like you. *And Clara knew it was the truth.*

CHAPTER FORTY

SYDNEY
1997

Deep breath in. Long breath out. Take a drink, let the vodka do its thing. *Get ahold of yourself, Sydney. Clear your mind.* I keep repeating it, this mantra — *clear your mind* — as if it will somehow stop my hands from shaking, that if I can just breathe deep enough, or long enough, it will slow my pounding heart. It hasn't worked yet, but with a few more drinks, it will.

    Clear your mind.

* * *

Things weren't supposed to turn out this way. All Clara had to do was look at the picture. One single goddamn look was all I needed. One look to see the John I've seen all along: a liar and a manipulator. A dumb country clod who'd somehow wormed his way into Clara's head because he knew how desperate she was for a man's approval, especially for *his* approval.

Look, I'm no man-hater. I'm not some raging feminist bent on emasculating every football-watching, beer-drinking, NASCAR-loving Neanderthal that crosses my path. I try to judge everyone based on their own merit. You like hunting and crushing twelve-packs of Bud Light with the boys on the weekend? Fine. Good for you. You prefer chugging bottles of Jack Daniels and tossing your wife down the stairs when she lips off a bit? Yeah, we're going to have a problem.

But that's the issue with John Gibson — his anger isn't the obvious kind. It can't be seen in black eyes and missing teeth (though there was the whole chipped-tooth thing). His violence is more clever than that. A stray comment here (*You don't really need that last cookie, do you? Aren't you trying to lose some weight?*), some gas-lighting there (*That was never my intention, Clara. Stop being so emotional.*) And if that's all John was, the average, shitty husband (*Hey honey, grab me a beer, will you?*), I suppose I would let it pass. But he's not. He's so much worse than that. His abuse is a slow kind of poison, the proverbial frog-in-the-pot kind where you don't know you're boiling until it's too late.

And for Clara, it's too late.

I knew he wanted the farm for himself the minute I met him. It was all so obvious in the way he cozied up to Clara's parents, especially her old man, kissing his ass all the time, acting like he had so much to teach him. "*Please, Mr. Carver, tell me more,*" and, "*I consider you a mentor, I really do.*" I stomached it, I didn't complain to Clara, because I knew how happy John made her. Happier even than I could make her, despite the fact that all I've ever done is try to make her happy. Yes, it hurt, I'll admit, the way she clung to him, the way he became her sun and she hung in his orbit, her moods rising and setting with his. But I put up with it for her. *Always* for her. I was fine with it, until Ashley Morgan came along.

Do you want to know how I caught them? It was the post office, of all things. I'd been following John for a while by then, convinced something wasn't right. I didn't know what it was, exactly; it was more of a feeling than anything.

Something is wrong here. It was like he wasn't there most nights, his eyes distant as he mumbled something to Clara about feeding the cows or what tractor they needed to buy next. He seemed, I don't know . . . *off*, like an actor stumbling through life reciting lines. So I wasn't exactly surprised when the answer came to me early one morning, the thing I couldn't shake, no matter how hard I tried.

It's the post office, Sydney! Every other Monday, he goes to the post office. Why? The Carvers have a mailbox.

I don't know why I didn't think of it before. I suppose it never struck me as all that odd. Everyone goes to the post office from time to time. There are presents to mail and stamps to purchase, addresses to change and packages to collect. Except John never came out with a package, did he? He hardly went in with one, either. But there *were* letters. Neatly pressed envelopes he carried a little too close to his chest, his glances a bit too furtive as he hurried for his truck. (*Nothing to see here.*) He even smelled the envelope once. I think that's what did it, what hung with me for so long, the image of him sniffing that envelope like a bloodhound.

I have to admit it was smart, him going analog like that, keeping their relationship offline. No emails, no calls. Shrewd bastard. I didn't think he had the discipline. He picked up the next letter a few days later, a tacky, pale-pink envelope he quickly stuffed into his back pocket. I followed him to the feed store on the outskirts of Meeker and snatched it from his truck when he went inside. It took all of fifteen seconds. No one saw. No one so much as blinked. And then I returned to my car . . . and read it.

I get wet just thinking of you. I can't stand writing like this anymore. I need you here. Now. Inside of me.

There was no way I could have shown it to Clara. Carving her heart out with a butter knife would be less painful. And, knowing her, she'd just deny it, say I'd made it all up. *You've never liked him, Sydney. You don't know him like I do. John would never do something like that.* I knew I'd need some real evidence first, and this slut — Ashley Morgan: 4468 Bay

Bridge Road — was dumb enough to use custom stationery with her address stamped in looping print in the corner. Who does that?

So, I went to her house and saw what I saw, and I took the picture, and Clara never looked at it once.

* * *

I planned it meticulously, honed the details over and over and over for weeks. How? John's favorite shotgun, obviously. The Browning Gold pump action Clara bought him for pheasant season a couple of years ago. The one he used to bring down a pair of yellow-billed mallards near Green River last week. She had his name engraved in the stock, along with her initials. How sweet. I remember her showing me the gun with a look of nervous anticipation.

"Do you think he'll like it?"

Sure, he'll like it.

It was easy enough to slip from the gun case on my way out. Clara didn't notice. She hasn't paid much attention to anything except her grief since losing Kinley.

Where? The easy part. Ashley Morgan's house. The same place I first spotted John cupping her ass and pawing at her shirt. The house I've studied for weeks now, hidden away parked beneath a thicket of cedar and pine. John never saw me, but I could sure see him . . .

When? A harder question, but not so hard when you consider a town that simply loves its fireworks nice and loud with all those pretty colors booming across the sky, everyone crowded into the park with greasy buckets of fried chicken and cold cans of beer. And, I'll admit, there's something cosmic about the date — something fitting about destroying John's life on the anniversary of his proposal. It's about as perfect a night to kill someone as you could ask for.

It all went pretty much as planned, John heading off in a jingle of truck keys to drink himself stupid with his friends (after fucking Ashley, of course). Me heading into her house right after, decked out in John's camo hunting jacket and his rubber rain boots, the Browning loaded and ready in my hands. Granted, I'm not as tall as John, but tall enough that someone could mistake me for him if spotted from a distance, not that any of the neighbors were home. I'd checked. All of them had gone to town with the rest of the gawkers, save the Smiths down the street, who were both in their eighties with bad hearing and a penchant for falling asleep, heavy and hard, in front of *Jeopardy!*

I'll admit, I wasn't exactly thrilled with where I had to kill her. I'd envisioned shotgunning her in their bed. A smooth pull of the trigger followed by a nice, firm kick. I planned to savor it, to watch the sheets soak up her blood until they were as red as her insides. It would have been appropriate. Instead, I found Ashley in the child's room, perched over his crib in a lullaby, her face hidden behind a trashy drape of bottle-blonde hair. I cried as the baby cooed up at her the way Kinley should have cooed at Clara. I wiped my eyes on the sleeve of John's coat.

I waited as she kissed the child's head and lowered her lips to his ear in a whisper; waited, without moving a muscle, without taking a breath, as she eased from the crib and retreated back toward the hall; watched as her eyes widened when she spotted me draped in shadow beyond the door: John returned, his baseball cap cocked low on his head.

"Hey love, I thought you were—"

I pulled the trigger. The shot took off most of her skull in a warm whoosh of sound and smoke. I stood there, ears ringing, my heart thudding at the sight of all that blood and glistening bone. The baby's cries sounded distant, like something heard through a television turned down low. I saw it all so clearly in that moment. John's arrest. The media circus. His trial and conviction. The years stretching out from there in an endless loop, John trapped in some barren prison cell, staring through his barred window at miles of razor-tipped wall. The sheet with which he'd eventually hang himself. A tattered, stained thing he'd have to double-knot so it would

179

hold his weight. The guards finding him the next morning and shaking their heads. *Looks like we have another one . . .*

If only it had been so easy.

I'd just turned out the lights and headed back to the car, had everything packed away nice and neat when *she* showed up. Of all nights, Clara had to pick *this* night to piece things together, with me watching silently from the shadows, pleading for her to *go, go, go go!*

But she didn't. She eased into the house instead. Her cry was so loud, it nearly shattered my eardrums. I thought for sure I'd spot Mr. Smith shuffling down the street on his cane, with a string of red-and-blue lights bubbling behind him. I pictured a beer-bellied cop dragging Clara from the house in handcuffs as she sobbed and pleaded for him to let her go, that she didn't do it. That she loved him. She loved him oh so much.

I imagined John free and settled into a comfortable life on the ranch with his freshly minted wife, twenty-two and doe-eyed with a nice set of tits, their three perfect boys wrestling with each other in the living room. The sounds of joy. The life in the house. I heard her voice in his ear as they drifted off to sleep — *I cannot believe you actually married that woman, John. Clara Carver, of all people. A murderer. My god, what did you ever see in her?*

Stop it, I told myself. *Think. You can still figure this out.*

And maybe I could have, but nothing prepared me for what happened next, the thing I could have never in a million years predicted.

Clara left the house . . .

With.

The.

Baby.

A clump of gore-spattered human wrapped in a blue-and-pink footie blanket. She clutched him in both arms, John's bastard squalling loud enough to raise the dead. I prayed for him to shut up, to *Please, God, just shut the fuck up.* He wouldn't. His little mouth only stretched wider with each

180

scream, with each piercing cry. Worse, Clara took her time about it, pausing on the porch to shoosh the boy, patting his back and *there-there*-ing him like she was his mother and this was her house instead of John's whore, who was inside, lying on the carpet in pieces, at this very moment.

And, *Jesus*, Clara was crying too, *sobbing*, her eyes a swollen mess as she scurried for the street. It rattled me, how tender she looked. How lost and broken. I didn't know what to do. So I froze and did nothing. And then she was in her car, driving off, and I knew she had just undone *everything*.

CHAPTER FORTY-ONE

KAYLA

I run upstairs to the stupid pink room with the stupid pink wallpaper and the stupid furniture and throw myself onto the stupid bed with tears spilling down my cheeks. I *cannot* believe Dad is leaving me here alone after all the weird shit we've seen today. It's like he doesn't care about me. It's only Emma he's worried about. I mean, I get it, I'm worried about her, too. I am. Okay, I'm terrified. It's only . . . I don't want to be here anymore. Especially not by myself, even if Clara seems mostly harmless, I guess. It's just, I don't know, nothing about this house feels normal . . . or safe. I bury my face in the pillow and scream.

I wish I could close my eyes and be back in Boston and—

A door bangs open downstairs to a voice I don't recognize. It's a woman's voice, angry and hard, one that sounds like it's spent years swimming in cigarette smoke. I wipe my eyes and ease from the bed, creep into the hall, and pad toward the stairs.

"Grab his arms."

I peer over the banister, and my legs go boneless. A pair of boots drag beneath the landing.

Dad's boots.

I clamp my hands over my mouth. I can't move, can't think, as the woman, whoever she is, barks more orders in her old-lady voice. And there's someone else with her — someone large, based on all the thudding footsteps.

"Let's take him downstairs and chain him up, then we'll come back for the girl."

The girl. Me. *Oh, God.*

"Okay, Miss Sydney. Whatever you say." *Billy.* I wait until his voice fades into the basement, along with the woman's, and then slip downstairs and rush for the door . . . stop.

Chain him up . . .

Dad. I can't leave him here alone . . . or Emma. There's no way Dad would ever leave me in a situation like this, but I can't stay here. Not with him hurt like that. And he *has* to be hurt if they were dragging him. I wouldn't stand a chance against Billy and whoever it is he has with him. I need help, and so does Dad, so I have to run, now, *right now*, before Billy and the whack job come back upstairs to find me. It's the only thought that makes sense — *RUN!* — so I scramble for the foyer and tug on my still-frozen shoes, my fingers fumbling at the laces until they're tied into clumsy knots. And then I'm up and jerking on the doorknob, yanking on the front door like a lunatic, the door . . . Which. Won't. Open.

That's when I notice the locks. There are so *many*, all these deadbolts and chains latched into place. At least seven. Maybe more.

". . . need to get her before she finds out about this."

The voice burns down my spine. Fingers shaking, I turn the locks, one after another, the chains falling off, the deadbolts clicking open — *clack, clack, clack* — until all that's left is a big, black, metal knob that won't budge no matter how hard I twist it. A sob works up my throat. *Open!*

"We ain't gunna hurt her, are we, Miss Sydney?" Billy's voice is close now, nearing the living room.

Hide.

The thought is all that saves me. I dash from the door and into the kitchen a second before a low, hacking cough slides through the air. "Not if she behaves. Go see if she's still upstairs."

Billy clomps away, and I press back against the wall and work my way toward the pantry. I'm hyperventilating, breathing so hard through my nose, it sounds like a freight train.

"Come on out, Kit Kat," the voice calls. "I just want to talk for a minute. No one's going to hurt you."

I go limp at my nickname on her lips, whoever the hell she is. How does she know to call me — It hits me. The mattress and the cigarettes and empty vodka bottles Oh my God . . . it's the woman from the attic. It has to be. She's been listening to us. She's been listening this entire time. How else would she know?

Fingers shaking, I ease the pantry open and slip inside. Pale rectangles of light fall through the wooden slats and paint my feet in pale stripes. I'm trembling so hard, I feel like I'm about to collapse.

"You don't want to make me mad, sweetheart. Really, I just want to talk."

Everything goes silent and still. I squeeze my eyes shut. *Go away, just go away . . .*

Glass explodes somewhere behind the wall. I fight to muffle the cry that leaps off my tongue. Furniture crashes down heavy and hard, tables and chairs being overturned in the living room, the hall, the woman shouting for me to show myself. *Thunk, thunk, smack!*

Footsteps scrape into the kitchen and draw closer. Cupboards slam open, one after another, the drawers rattling in response.

"I'm getting angry now, Kayla!"

My stomach twines into knots.

She nears the pantry, and my bladder jerks. I see a hand drift for the knob through the slats—

I bite my tongue. *Oh, God, please no.*

The fingers pause as Billy pounds into the room. "I-I dunno where she gone off to, Miss Sydney. Please don't be mad at me. I looked real good. She ain't upstairs."

"Oh Billy, I'm not mad at you. It's your momma I'm worried about. You know that. She can't handle this. It's up to us to make sure we get that girl before your momma finds out and worries herself sick. Do you think you can do that for me? Be my big helper?"

Clara. I suddenly wonder where she is, if she's locked up downstairs somewhere with Dad, unconscious or worse.

"Yes'm, Miss Sydney."

"Good. Then let's find that little *bitch.*"

A fist bangs against the pantry door, and I skitter backward, bumping against a shelf full of canned beans with a series of loud clinks.

"What was that?" the voice snaps. A cold pebble of fear settles into my stomach.

"What was what, Miss Sydney?"

"That sound. Behind you. Oh, for Chrissake, not there. Look in the pantry, you dumbass."

The knob turns, and Billy's eyes shoot wide as I bolt past him. He grabs for my shoulder, but I twist from his grip and burst for the dining room, pulling chairs down behind me, sprinting for the back door.

"Get her!" the voice cries.

I'm halfway down the hall when something bangs off my kneecap. I teeter and wheel for balance. Slam down. My forehead cracks off the wood. Sparks shoot through my vision.

Go, go, go! I scramble back to my feet and crash down again, fingers seizing my ankle, ripping me backward. I kick out and connect with something soft. There's a low crunch, and Billy howls. The fingers slide away, and I'm bursting for the door once more. I can't breathe, can't think. A blur of motion sweeps in from the side in a collision that tears the air from my lungs. I catch a glimpse of matted hair and a pair of flat, glittering eyes. Fingernails rake across my cheek and neck. I spin away and claw for the doorknob, swing the door open and—

Billy tackles me.

The force is so strong, it steals my breath. We topple together. My shoulder strikes a glass-top table, the glass splintering, shattering, hands yanking at my shirt, fingers tearing into my hair. I thrash and scratch and claw. Billy flops on top of me with a grunt. I bite into his palm, taste dirt and sweat and blood. He roars and rears back, something sharp digging into my neck, holding me there. It's a knife, the woman's arm wrapped around my throat, her breath sour in my ear.

"Shh. Shh. Relax, Kayla. Relax. We're not going to hurt you. You're a part of this family now, after all."

CHAPTER FORTY-TWO

SYDNEY
1997

She took the baby.

Why, oh, why did she have to take the baby?

I knew the moment Clara carried him from the house, things had changed. The child would bring trouble, would make things more difficult than they needed to be, both for her and for me. I just didn't know it would happen the minute I arrived at the ranch.

I had barely slipped into the kitchen, was lost in thought, trying to figure some way out of the mess Clara had made when I saw John on his knees, bent over her, wearing this awful purple-face-death-look. John with the veins in his forearms popping, his hands sinking into the soft flesh that was Clara's neck. John, who'd taken everything from her — the farm and her heart, her ability to trust and to *love*, her dignity and self-respect, all of it — about to take the only thing she had left: her life. I knew right then he'd kill her if I didn't do something.

It only took a second for me to spot the handle of the butcher knife protruding from the open dishwasher. I pulled it from the dish rack slowly, quietly, wrapped my fingers around the hilt and buried it in the side of his neck with a quick, upward looping strike. His eyes popped and went wide with one of those *this-isn't-happening* looks, one of those *what-the-fuck-just-happened* looks: his eyebrows stretching for his hairline, his mouth for his neck.

He stood and clawed at the knife, spun a circle with a bright waterfall of blood splashing onto his shirt. It was comical in a way, his stumbling, his gurgling. It was like he was playing the role of the town drunk clowning around a few too many drinks (*Sorry, Johnny, no more for you. I think it's time you head on home*). A wet moan rolled around his mouth when he spotted me, a flicker of rage coming back into his eyes. He seized the hilt, and he pulled the blade out with a moist *Plop!* He took a step toward me with one palm out and reaching, his lifeline creased in blood. Another step, his eyes blinking hard, losing focus and lighting again, the hate driving him forward, the knife slipping, falling . . .

It's too late, Johnny boy, I thought, *you're already dead.*

Clara groaned as he toppled, coming back to life with a heaving lungful of air, coughing and hacking, grasping at her throat. It worried me, yes, but not as much as the baby. I nearly came undone at the sight of him lying crumpled next to the dishwasher like that with one chubby arm trapped beneath his stomach and the other flung above his pale, milk-colored head.

My stomach roiled with acid. I picked him up and carried him into Clara's bedroom and set him gently on one of her blue satin pillows. There was an indentation in his skull the consistency of an egg cracked but not yet broken, the yolk bulging out against the shell. I pressed two fingers to his neck, sure he was dead. A small cry rolled off my tongue when I felt his pulse flutter beneath the skin. I brought my hand to his mouth in a prayer, and it was answered with a warm puff of heat, his breath coating the pads of my fingers. He was still breathing, still somehow . . . *alive.*

I looked at him with grief flooding my veins. It never had to happen, this awful thing. My plan was so perfect, all the evidence pointing straight back to John. I'd laid it out in a simple paint-by-number pattern, drawn it in such a way a child could figure it out. John's boot prints. His gun. The journal I concealed in his drawer documenting how very difficult Ashley had made things since the pregnancy. And there were his own contributions, of course. The semen he'd spilled all over their bedsheets for months, his DNA spattered everywhere throughout the house. And now here he was, back at the farm, taking the easy way out, already dead, the bastard.

I wrapped the baby in a striped Afghan blanket and forced myself back into the kitchen. John watched me enter with a glassy-eyed stare. Blood wept from his neck in strings. Pink pockets of foam peppered the corners of his mouth, and a dark circle soaked his groin from where he'd pissed himself. I crouched next to him with my stomach in a clench, the smell of whiskey and bile stinging my nose, and cursed Clara again. All she had to do was nothing, absolutely nothing, and everything would have been just fine. But she had to go and complicate things, and now, like always, it was up to me to clean up her mess.

They'll still think he did it if you can make him disappear.

But where?

It came to me then, the only place I knew of deep enough and dark enough. And I figured if I wrapped him just right, tied him to his truck in such a way he could never float up, up, up to bob in pieces on the surface . . . *well, yes*, I thought, *it should do*.

CHAPTER FORTY-THREE

CHRIS

I wake slumped against a frigid, cinder-block wall. Memories spill through my head in fragments: trudging through the snow toward the truck. Brushing it from beneath the tires. Standing to grasp the frosted metal door handle. The sense of something — of *someone* — rising behind me. The hiss of iron slicing through the air as I look back. My vision exploding and turning black. Snippets from there. Dragging across the floor. Hands on my ankles and arms. A bitter voice in my ears, barking orders, the words a vague collection of unintelligible sounds smearing together into nothing.

A cloud of decay fills my nose, and I blow it out and listen because that's all I can do. Feel and listen. Listen and feel. It's silent, the darkness total, save a weak, vertical slash of light in the ceiling at the far end of whatever space I'm locked in. The air is cold and rank, smelling of sulfur and vomit, the floor beneath my legs nothing more than hard-packed dirt. It's a crawlspace or a cellar, another room hidden somewhere in Clara's basement.

Insect legs scurry across the back of my hand. Water drips to the soil in a slow *plip, plip, plip* that mirrors the warm trickle of blood near my ear. My lungs ratchet tighter as a parade of thoughts marches through my head.

Who did this?

And why?

Who made Kayla scream, because that wasn't Clara I heard upstairs.

The thought sets me to yanking on the chain again. A circle of fire rips through my ankle and snakes higher into my shin. I roar and pull harder. It's useless. The chain is thick and heavy, wrapped around my calf in a series of tight loops that won't give no matter how hard I try to free myself. Unless I can get my hands on a hacksaw and cut off my foot, I'm not going anywhere.

I lean back and rest my head against the wall. My heart is hammering so hard, it feels like it will shatter my ribs. I picture Emma's face, her deep, brown eyes and her sweet smile. I think of Kayla and how she's still growing, not quite a woman yet, beautiful like her mother but breaking apart on the inside. Breaking because of me. I whisper a prayer. *God, rescue me, and I promise I'll be the father she needs from now on.*

The thought sends me spiraling, my eyes watering as another sludgy nausea attack rolls up my esophagus. I dry-heave to the side, my diaphragm jerking painfully, seizing painfully until at last, it subsides. I wipe a rope of bile from my lips and listen. There's a sound. A sudden scraping coming from overhead. The squeal of hinges and the protest of ancient metal. A dagger of light slashes across the ceiling, and I squint against it as the door opens.

There's someone there, standing at the top of a crumbling set of concrete steps, framed against the light. No, not someone . . . people. Two of them, their voices ringing out in an argument. I recognize one of them as Clara's.

". . . no, please don't. He doesn't deserve this."

"He does. I've seen how he talks to you. He's no different than the rest."

I cringe. It's the voice from earlier, the same one that soaked through the ceiling right before Kayla screamed.

Hollow. Full of grit. I stand and cup a hand to my forehead, hoping to see more, but all I can make out are a thin pair of legs stuffed into worn leather boots.

"But he is," Clara pleads. "He was just worried about his little girl."

"Who's up there?" I shout. "Let me out of here!"

"Like John was worried about yours? He left, remember? They all leave. Just like this one nearly did."

"He's different, Sydney. I know you think all men are—"

"No, he's not! When will you learn? They will *always* hurt you in the end, Clara. Always. When has it ever been any different?"

A pause, feet shuffling. "Never . . ." Clara's voice floats down the stairs soft and sullen. The voice of a little girl acknowledging her fault.

"That's right. Now go. I can handle him."

She can't leave. The thought is like an alarm blaring in my head, red lights flashing. It spurs me into a shout: "Clara! Clara, please, don't leave! I need to find Emma. Clara! C'mon, I know you don't want to do this. Don't leave me here! Please!" My voice echoes and is swallowed by the room, the only response that of a lighter flicking followed by a long, burning inhalation.

"Clara!" I say again.

"Clara's gone."

The words are cold. Brusque. The voice is a register deeper than Clara's, a woman's but barely. I'm suddenly certain it belongs to whoever has been living in the attic, the same presence I felt when I stepped into the hall and saw that twisted shadow flung across the floor.

"Who are you?" I ask.

Another pull of air. More smoke. "A friend."

"Then let me out."

"A friend of Clara's. Not yours."

The legs descend the steps in a hitch and lose their form in the dark pool of shadow at the bottom of the stairs. The cigarette burns a dim orange ring as she sucks in another lungful of smoke. I can taste it on my tongue, my gums, can feel her gaze crawling from my legs toward my chest and settling on my face. She tilts her head, and I recognize something familiar in the motion, in the shape. Her eyes become orange pinpricks as she plants the cigarette to her lips and grasps for something in the dark. There's a click as a naked bulb blares to life, coating the room in a dirty, yellow light. And I see her . . .

The ground falls out from beneath my feet.

It's Clara.

* * *

I rise to my feet in a mix of fear and rage — fear for what she's done to my daughters, rage that she's tricked me. She's lied this entire time.

Because it was her.

It was always Clara.

And I'm going to rip her apart.

* * *

I narrow my eyes as she draws closer, carrying a scuffed, blue bucket along with an empty trash bag. I don't move a muscle. I stand there stiff and seething, my vision bleached by the light, my muscles rigid. I'm coiled and ready to strike. Waiting. *Come closer, Clara. Just a couple more steps.*

She does, and I lunge for her.

My fingers scrape her throat as the chain snaps taut. She stares at me without moving, one of her eyelids lower than the other, the skin twitching in place.

I grab for her again and miss. "Let me out of here, you bitch!"

"Sit down." Her voice is alien, the tone like something run through a meat grinder.

"No."

She nods at the floor. "Your girls would want you to sit."

The threat is like a fist to the gut, all the air gone. I back up and slide down the wall, suddenly sick again.

"Clara, why are you doing this?"

"Clara hasn't done anything."

"What the hell are you talking about, I—"

"Clara's not here. I'm Sydney."

I blink, and for a dizzy moment, I wonder if she's right, that the woman in front of me isn't Clara. I could almost believe it in a way, a deranged older sister or a distant third cousin in town for a visit. Her hair is undone, no longer twisted into a braid. Greasy strands of it spill over her forehead and past her cheeks. And there's this putty-like droop to the left side of her face. It's nearly slack compared to the right. But it *is* Clara. Of that, I'm certain.

She's wearing the same green dress from earlier, the same blush and lipstick, only the lipstick is now smeared halfway across her cheek, and the rouge is a patchy, salmon-colored smudge. Her eyes, though, hold none of the warmth I remember from earlier. They're harder. Colder. And the way she's looking at me, like I'm a science project she's about to dissect, has me on edge.

That lazy eyelid twitches again.

"Where are my girls?" I say, grinding my teeth.

"They're around."

"If you've touched them, if you've done anything to them . . ."

She drops the sack and bucket, then crouches with her knees spread apart. Her underwear flashes in a dull-pink strip between her thighs. She sucks on the cigarette and stares at me, blows another cloud of smoke into my face.

"You done?"

"What do you want?"

She stands and kicks the bucket toward me. A wave of suds sloshes over the top and darkens the clay near my knees. "Here's what's going to happen. You're going to clean up that mess of a face and all the blood. The vomit, too. I won't have you sitting down here in that nasty filth. Then" — she nods at the bag and smiles — "you'll get dressed. Billy will be down to get you when dinner is ready."

She takes another drag and lets the smoke bleed through her nostrils.

"Chris, I need you to listen to me. You're going to behave down here. You're going to behave when you come upstairs. You're going to act like the perfect gentlemen because there are two girls depending on you to do just that." Her smile slashes wider. "It would be such a shame if anything . . . unfortunate were to happen to them because their father can't control himself, don't you think?"

I sit there stunned, wordless — *What in the actual fuck?*

"Do we understand each other?"

All I can manage is a weak nod.

She flicks the cigarette to the floor. "Good. Now get to it. Dinner will be ready in an hour."

* * *

The dress shirt is too big, a cream-colored button-up with cuffs that swallow my hands. It smells old, the collar greased in someone else's sweat. The faded navy slacks are no better, several inches too large, as is the tweed sport coat. I pull it on and slowly knot the paisley tie, the sensation like a noose. John's noose. Clara's ex-husband, wherever he is. I can picture him: John telling her he's leaving, that he's done with her. Clara's face collapsing into that of Sydney's. The leering scowl as she pulls a rifle from the wall and pumps the action. John turning at the sound too late, his head exploding in a shower of watermelon pulp a second later.

I massage my temples, the last thing she said before she disappeared upstairs bouncing through my skull over and over again.

"*Remember, Chris, I'm always watching . . . and Clara doesn't know where Emma is.*"

CHAPTER FORTY-FOUR

BILLY
2003–2011

To Billy, the world was the farm, and there was no better place.

It was full of all sorts of animals. Cows and pigs and goats and chickens, and Billy loved them all. Ma spent her days caring for them, and Billy often tagged along as she made sure the chickens had enough grain to eat and that the pigs hadn't dug beneath the pen again. They stopped most mornings to watch Brownie the milk cow nurse her two calves, Willow and Buttercup, in the alfalfa field beyond the grain silo. Ma would tell Billy what a good mom Brownie was to feed her babies like that, and Billy would think of how Ma fed him the same way, but only with cereal or pancakes or eggs instead of milk, and that she was a good mom, too.

Before they finished their rounds, they would stop by the stable to feed the horses, and for Billy, it was the best part of the day. He loved to run his hand along their soft, velvet muzzles and feel their wet nostrils pressing into his palm for a treat. He laughed as they shook their manes and whinnied in excitement when they saw him coming with a handful of carrots. There were four horses in all — two stallions, Shadow and Thunder, and a sweet Appaloosa named Millie . . . but the horse Billy loved most was Millie's colt, Phillip.

196

He was born small with a scatter of vanilla circles stamped into his coat that reminded Billy of clouds. Like Billy, he had a hard time walking in a straight line and bumped into things if he didn't pay attention. Sometimes he ground his teeth and flattened his tail in anxious fits and often left his pail of oats untouched. He lost weight and grew too thin. Ma said he wouldn't live long, that he'd likely die before he turned four, but Billy knew different. He'd heard Ma pray the same things about him when he was little. Things like how worried she was about his legs and how his hands didn't seem to work like other children's. She said he'd never learn to speak or to feed himself. But he'd lived, right? So Billy figured he'd pray for Phillip like Ma had prayed for him, and the horse grew stronger every day.

Sometimes, if he was lucky, Ma would let him stay out in the stable with Phillip while she finished up with her chores. Billy filled those lazy mornings brushing Phillip's coat and telling him about his adventures around the ranch. Billy loved exploring the endless cornfields and jumping in the big mud puddles left behind by the summer rainstorms. He told Phillip about the wall of green trees that skirted the property and how the hayfield had grown so thick and tall, Ma wouldn't let him go in it anymore because she was afraid he'd get lost. Phillip would whinny like he understood, and Billy would laugh and jump in circles and then tell him another story, and another, until Ma yelled for him to come inside for lunch and a nap. For Billy, life was pretty much perfect. Except for the days Miss Sydney came.

* * *

It usually happened when someone stopped by for a surprise visit. Ma would see a car coming down the road or hear the doorbell or a knock, and her eyes would get that weird, faraway look that made Billy shiver. Her voice would drop, and her face would shift, and Billy knew not to call her Ma anymore, because she wasn't Ma, even though she kind of looked like her. She was to be called Miss Sydney, she said as she hustled him into the basement. He must keep very quiet and not make a peep. Strangers were bad, bad, bad, and if anyone heard him or found out he was here, they'd call the men in blue uniforms to take him away. If that happened, Miss Sydney said he'd never see Ma again. He'd be put into the "system" with the other kids no one wanted. And no one would want Billy, Miss Sydney assured him. No one but Ma would ever want him. Not with his problems.

That scared Billy more than anything . . . more than Miss Sydney's scary voice or the way one side of her face got all saggy when she talked. More than the way she walked funny or grabbed his arm so hard it left pink marks on his skin. He couldn't imagine anything worse than losing Ma. She made him yummy meals and gave him big hugs when he had his fits. She told him he was her whole world, even though Miss Sydney said he wasn't. She said Ma had wanted a baby girl more than anything in the world. She said Billy was just an accident from the mean man she used to live with. He didn't know what any of that meant, but he knew it made him sad.

Sometimes, if Miss Sydney knew someone was coming over or she had to go somewhere, she'd take him to a special place deep in the ground and leave him there for a while. It smelled funny, like wet earth and old wood, but Billy didn't mind. It meant going down into the tunnels, and he loved the tunnels. There were so many, and he wanted to explore them all. Each and every one! He imagined they led to the faraway places he sometimes saw in his picture books. Places like the ocean or one of the big, shiny cities that Ma talked about with the buildings that stretched to the sky. Maybe they led to the mountains or to outer space or even to a castle in another country!

But Billy never found out, because they only ever went down one tunnel. It was long and wide, an empty tunnel that led to the special door in the floor that squealed when it opened. The sound made Billy laugh because it reminded him of a donkey's bray. Even better, the room below provided the perfect place to play his war games. He hid his toy soldiers in the wires on the walls and beneath the empty stack of egg crates that climbed to the ceiling. He hid them in the couch cushions and pretended to shoot the bad soldiers dead. He played with them for hours.

When he grew bored of his games, he'd draw animals in the black dust on the floor, lions and eagles, and the polar bears Ma said they kept at the zoo. Mostly they came out as scribbles, but to Billy, they looked like the real thing. If he was left for too long, he'd pretend aliens had invaded Earth, and this room, his Hideaway Box, was the only *safe place left in the world. And even if that wasn't true, being in the Hideaway Box meant he didn't have to be around Miss Sydney.*

* * *

Billy grew, and Miss Sydney came more often. Sometimes she spent entire days bossing Billy around, making him do the chores Ma used to do, like mucking out the stables and cleaning the coop. He tried to do a good job, but it was difficult because focusing was hard for Billy, and his hands were clumsy. He'd gather eggs from the chickens, and his fingers would come away wet and yellow with yolk. He'd feed the cows but forget to feed the goats, and they'd bleat until Miss Sydney stormed out to do it herself. He'd weed the garden and pull up most of the vegetables instead. Nothing he did seemed to turn out right, and Miss Sydney let him know it with sharp swats to the back of his neck.

In time, the farm fell apart, and Sydney said it was because of Billy. She said Ma wanted to hire men to help with the work, but she couldn't with him there. Billy's Pa had done something bad to Ma, and so Miss Sydney had done something even worse to him in return. She said if anyone found out about it, the bad thing she did, or found out about Billy, Ma would go to jail, and he'd never see her again. So Billy did as best he could to help. He raked and hoed and swept until his palms blistered and his fingers bled. He baled hay and carried bags of feed until his eyelids turned to lead weights and his back muscles went as stiff as planks.

But no matter how hard he worked, it wasn't enough. Every year, more crops died. Every year they had less to feed the animals. Billy dragged those that died to the shed behind the coop, where Ma dissolved them in a stainless-steel vat, mixing water and lye before bringing the entire thing to a rolling boil that turned the carcasses to a thick, brownish sludge. Those that lived were sold off one by one, all except Phillip, and Ma spent what little money they brought in on food and clothes. It was a struggle, she said, to keep up with Billy's changing wardrobe. She said that he seemed to grow an inch every month.

In the end, Ma simply quit trying. She spent her days in the rocking chair on the back porch, looking about as sad as Billy had ever seen her. He'd try to cheer her up with funny stories about Phillip or

199

by giving her a big hug and a wet kiss on the cheek. He did his best impressions of the chickens and cows, mooing and clucking around the porch, acting like a goof. Sometimes he'd make her smile, but mostly, the sadness won, and Ma would sigh and say, "I'm tired, Billy. Go play, and let your Ma get some rest."

Billy knew why she was tired. It was Miss Sydney. She was the reason Ma never slept. How could she with her and Miss Sydney fighting all the time? At night their voices rang through the walls as they argued about the farm, or about the bills and crops and all the work piling up. Sometimes, and more frequently of late, they argued about Billy.

"He doesn't belong here, and you know it."

"Don't say that! He's my son."

"But he's not, Clara. He's John's, and you'll never heal with him here."

Billy didn't know why but hearing the bad man's name made his heart hurt. It hurt Ma worse. She'd cry for hours after Sydney brought him up. She'd wake up red-eyed and sometimes let out a burpy sob while scrambling the eggs. It made Billy cry, too, hearing her do that. It made him hate the man and hate Miss Sydney even more. So much so, he finally decided to do something about it.

CHAPTER FORTY-FIVE

EMMA

I wish I knew where I was. I wish I knew if it was day or night or if Dad was coming soon. But I don't. All I know is I'm stuck on this couch in a room that reminds me of our shed in the backyard. The one with all the spiderwebs and bugs with the pinchers on their butts. I hate the shed. It's full of gas and oil and dead grass.

This room is worse. It smells like rotten eggs. And I can't see outside. There aren't any windows. Just a bunch of brick walls and a ceiling covered in wires that look like snakes. In the middle is this bright light bulb that stings my eyes if I look at it too long. It never goes out, and even though I hate it, I don't want it to. The dark would be worse.

I turn on my side and pray that Kayla and Dad will find me soon. I yelled for them when I first woke up. I shouted and screamed and cried. It didn't help. My voice bounced right off the walls, which just made me cry harder. And then my voice got all scratchy, and I knew, wherever they were, Dad and Kayla couldn't hear me. If they did, they would have come by now.

I don't know when, but at some point, the lady I thought was Momma came in and sat down next to me on the couch. At first, I was happy to see her, but her lips were puckered like she'd just taken a big bite out of a lemon, and she kept blinking her eye all weird. I wondered if she maybe got some dirt in it. I don't know why I ever thought she looked like Momma. And her voice — it was so freaky. It sounded like a cartoon witch. She kept shaking her head and saying all this crazy stuff, almost like she was talking to herself instead of me.

"Why do you do this to me, Clara? Why?"

"This is going to bring more trouble. I hope she's worth it . . ."

"You'd better take good care of her this time. Better than the last one."

I had no idea what she meant by "the last one." It didn't make sense. It just made me wish she would leave. But of course, she didn't. Instead, she patted my leg and ran her fingers through my hair. Her fingertips felt like dried-out raisins, all cold and rough. Momma's fingers never felt like that. They were always so soft. She finally left when I pretended to fall asleep. Then I cried some more and went to sleep for real. When I woke up again, it was to the big man sitting in the corner, rubbing his palms over his legs real fast. *Whoosh, whoosh, whoosh.*

I think his name is Billy. He's sitting on the stool in the corner right now, staring at me. At least I think he is. I can't tell for sure, because his eyes look like someone just gave his head a hard shake. He has baby cheeks. I don't want to pinch them, though. Not like how I like to pinch my baby cousin Maribelle's to make her giggle. Hers are *so* cute. His are all splotchy and pink and hang off his face like pancakes that jiggle when he talks. And he won't stop talking, talking, talking . . .

"So, do you got a cat? Or a dog? I gots me a horse. His name is Phillip. He's a funny guy. Funny and nice. You wanna meet him?

"Do you like candy? I do. Oh, boy, it's good. Mm, mm. 'Specially licorice. It's so super-duper good. It's my favorite, but sometimes it gets stuck in my teeth, you know? Does it get stuck in yours?

"What got your leg all messed up like that? Ma fixed my broke leg once when I was five. Oh man, it hurt. I fell off a wall. Well, Miss Sydney done it. She pushed me. Now my leg don't work as good no more, but it's okay. I was being bad."

The way he speaks makes me think he might not be a man after all but more of a boy. I mean, some parts of him look like a man's. Like his hair. It's thin. Enough so that I can see all the pink-and-brown spots tucked beneath. He likes to scratch them. He does it all the time, scratching his head while telling me stories about Phillip. There was this one time he ran away to the field, but Billy tricked him into coming back to the barn with some carrots and sugar cubes. It took him a whole day. Another time he tried riding Phillip, but the saddle came undone and Billy fell into the mud. "It made my butt look poopy!" he says with a laugh.

I almost laugh, too, thinking about how funny that must have been, but then my leg hurts, and I don't feel like laughing anymore.

Billy tells me he and his momma used to have cows and goats and chickens on the farm, but they died 'cause Sydney (whoever that is) didn't feed them enough. He says he misses them a lot. They were his friends. He tells me more stories, all kinds of stories, but it's hard to listen with how cold I'm getting. I shiver harder and harder, and Billy must see me do it, because he suddenly stands and digs a blanket out of the basket in the corner and lays it on me. It's blue and red and smells worse than the sheet, but it's heavy and warm, so I don't mind. I even stop shivering a little.

"You don't wanna get those bad ol' flu germs. Germs is bad," Billy says, looking down at me with a big smile. His teeth are so yellow, I wonder if he's ever brushed them. He claps his hands together, and I notice one of them is stuck in a brown glove.

"You feeling toasty yet?" he asks.

I nod, scared at how big he is this close. But I'm not as scared as I was with the lady for some reason. I think it's something about his eyes. They don't look as mean as hers do. In fact, they don't really look mean at all.

"I always get cold down here in the Hideaway Box," he says. "But I don't mind, since Ma don't let me play down here all that much. Sometimes Sydney does, though, but only a little."

"Th-the what box?" My voice comes out wobbly and soft. I'm still getting used to it, and I'm scared that if I talk too much, I'll lose it.

"The Hideaway Box." He spreads his hands wide. "It's fun, but" — he puts a finger to his lips — "shhh, you can't never tell no one about it. It's a *secret*." He laughs and jumps up and down in a circle, making dust clouds with his boots. "Isn't it cool? It's the coolest!"

It is? I don't think it's too cool, but I don't tell him that.

"Billy, could you, um . . . ? Could you please go get my dad for me?" I ask, suddenly remembering how bad I miss him.

"No way, Jose. Uh-uh. Sydney won't let no one down here but us."

"Why not?"

He shrugs. "Dunno, it's just the rule."

"Who is Sydney?" I ask.

"Sydney's the boss. You got to be *real* good for her, okay? Not like the last girl. She always misbehaved around Sydney and never did what she said. She done lotsa bad stuff, and Sydney . . ." He chews a lip and looks away. "No, it's too bad to tell."

"She . . . had another girl down here?"

His face droops, and he stuffs his hands under his arm-pits. "Yeah. Her name was Lillypad. Sydney said she weren't a nice girl, with how much she misbehaved and all, but I don't believe her on that. Lillypad played good with me. We did all sortsa fun stuff together! I miss her a lot."

I don't know why, but hearing the girl's name makes me scared all over again. I stop talking after that. Whatever happened to Lilly, I don't want to know.

CHAPTER FORTY-SIX

KAYLA

She calls herself Sydney, and her monster voice won't stop scraping through my head on repeat:

"You are to behave like a lady at dinner. Pleases and thank-yous only."

"I won't have any attitude, do you understand? None whatsoever.

"Don't be a glutton. A girl your size doesn't need to overeat."

Like I could eat anything right now, chained to the dining room table in one of Clara's hideous farm dresses with my hair spun up in a bun and my eyelashes dripping her mascara. I caught a glimpse of myself in the mirror before she dragged me downstairs. I looked like a little girl playing dress-up, a toy doll with hot-pink lipstick and circles of rose-colored blush stamped on my cheeks. I barely recognized my own face.

"Stop your crying! You'll ruin your makeup."

My face still stings from where she slapped me, her eye twitching away with half her face looking like melted plastic. And, God, the way her voice sounds, so rough and broken . . .

Do I understand? Will I behave?

Yes, ma'am, I do, and yes, I will.

And I will behave, because I have never been more terrified in my entire life than I am right now with Clara or this . . . Sydney, or whatever she calls herself, telling me what a brat I was to hide from her and Billy like that. What a little bitch. That if it were to happen again, me hiding or running or misbehaving, I won't be the only one to pay the price. It will be Dad and Emma, too. *"There are a lot of fingers and toes to work with, after all."* That threat scares me the most because I think she'd totally do it, cut off our toes with a pair of garden shears or a butcher knife or something.

I'm still thinking about it when Billy yanks Dad in by the arm. He looks terrible. His skin is all waxy, and he has the same glassy-eyed look he had when Mom died — the one that left him drooling on the couch for a week. Like me, he's got a big chain wrapped around his ankle, the bad one, and his limp is worse. He winces with each step, dragging his foot in a painful shuffle that almost makes me feel sorry for him. Almost. And also like with me, Clara has him dressed up in a bunch of weird clothes: an old blazer with scuffed elbow patches and a tie that looks like it was cut from one of the curtains in the living room.

Billy disappears beneath the table to secure his chain, and Dad leans in and takes my hand. "Are you okay? Did they hurt you?"

Did they? I've been too busy freaking the hell out to notice.

"No, I don't think so. I'm—"

There's a loud bang, and Billy jerks from under the tablecloth with a finger smashed to his lips. "*Shhh*, be quiet! You don't wanna wake up Miss Sydney!"

Before I can respond, Clara waltzes into the room in a zipper-back, cream-colored dress with a strand of pearls wound tight around her neck. Her hair is pulled into a loose French braid, and she's humming, flitting around the table with a platter of chicken parmesan and a bowl of salad. She sets them on the table and uncorks a bottle of white wine, filling her glass first, then Dad's. She hums as she does it, like keeping us tied up in chains at dinner is the most normal thing in the world. Dad watches her through slivered eyes, probably trying to decide the same thing as me: Which version is this? Crazy Clara or normal Clara? Normal Clara, I decide . . . if there even is such a thing, which, at this point, I'm pretty sure there's not.

She pours a splash of wine into my glass with a pitchy giggle, her perfume tickling my nose. "Oh, I'm sorry, Kayla. What am I thinking? You aren't old enough, are you?" She gives me a quick *hey-we're-cool-right?* wink and lowers her voice as though Dad isn't sitting right next to me. "But a little won't hurt."

"Ma. Let's eat. I'm starving," Billy says, thumping down across the table.

"Be patient, Billy," she says, taking her seat. "There's plenty of food for everyone." She smiles at him, then us. "Well, isn't this just lovely? A real family dinner for once." Her gaze shifts to the empty chair next to her, and her smile broadens like there's actually someone sitting there smiling back. That's when I notice the plate in front of the chair and the neatly folded napkin resting beneath the silverware. The glass of water and the bowl full of salad. A shudder spills through me when I realize what . . . or rather *who* it's for. She laces her fingers together and leans in. "Billy, will you please say the blessing?"

"Okay, Ma." Billy bows his head. "Bless the meat, damn the skin. Open your kisser and cram it in." He snorts out a laugh and pounds the table. Glasses rattle, and my fork skips onto my plate. Clara snaps up her wineglass before it tips.

"Billy, I will not have that type of language at the dinner table. Apologize this instant."

He glances up, sheepish, looking like a four-year-old caught raiding the cookie jar. "I-I'm sorry, Ma."

"Please mind your manners or I'll — what's that?" She turns to the empty chair and shakes her head. "No . . . no, I don't think that will be necessary. He'll be a good boy." She fixes her gaze on Billy. "Isn't that right?"

He nods, only he isn't staring at her. He's blinking at the empty chair instead, his head tipping up and down like an out-of-control bobblehead. His face is two shades paler than it was a second ago, and he's breathing through his nose in these quick, little bursts that make me want to be anywhere else but here. *Anywhere* else.

Clara spreads her arms. "Well, dig in, everyone. I didn't slave away in the kitchen all afternoon for nothing."

Billy dives in first, grabbing the platter of chicken. He slops two pieces onto his plate, along with a fist-sized chunk of bread, and passes the chicken my way. I take the smallest piece and hand it to Dad, who does the same, neither of us touching our food.

Clara sets her fork down. "What's the matter, Kayla? Not hungry?"

"Not really," I mutter.

"I know you've been through a lot lately, but you need to eat something in order to keep your strength up. You need the calories. And a good meal will help lift your spirits." I take a bite, and she rests her chin on the back of her fingers, tilting her head slightly. "You look so pretty in that dress, Kayla. Really. It certainly brings out the color of your eyes." She leans closer, and I wilt beneath her gaze. "Has anyone told you how beautiful they are? All that green. I would certainly guess the boys have."

My cheeks burn, the chicken going dry in my mouth. "No. Not really."

"Well, they will, let me tell you. You're absolutely gorgeous. Don't you think so, Billy?"

"Mm-hmm. She's super-duper purdy," Billy blurts out, spraying a quarter-sized chunk of meat onto the tablecloth.

I glance at my plate with my stomach churning. I want to run. I want to get out of this house and as far away from these psycho nut-jobs as possible. Especially Clara. And I would if I could. But I can't. Not without Emma. She's all I can think about. Is she safe? Is she okay? I want to ask Clara, but there's no way I can risk it. It's one of Sydney's rules.

No talking about Emma. "*Clara doesn't know what happened to her . . .*"

"*. . . is it?*"

I realize Clara is still talking to Dad.

"Sorry, what?" he says mid-bite.

"The chicken parm, you silly goose. How is it? It's my grandmother's recipe."

Dad chokes and wipes his mouth, takes a long sip of water, and sets the glass back on the table. "It's very good. Thank you."

"My, my," she says, staring at him. "You certainly do cut a striking figure in that suit. That was John's favorite sport coat, you know."

Dad forks another bite of chicken into his mouth with a grunt. Clara gasps and clamps a hand to her mouth.

"Oh my, Chris, you're bleeding."

Dad tenses and drops his fork, stares at her. He is, a trail of blood seeping down his neck toward his shirt collar.

"Here, let me help." She dabs her napkin in her water glass and leans in to wipe the cut. "How in the world did this happen?"

He seizes her wrist. "You did it. Just like you did this." He shakes his leg, the chain rattling against the floor. "Don't act like you don't know what—"

Billy pounds the table. "No, Miss Sydney! No! No! No!" He does it again, pounding his fists into the wood over and over until my glass topples. "No! No! No! No!" He bangs harder still, and the salad bowl vibrates off the table and shatters. A glass joins it, and then another, silverware raining down, everything breaking at once.

"Billy . . . Billy, stop that!" Clara says, standing and working out of Dad's grip to move around the table.

"No! No! No! No!"

She cups his cheeks and gives his head a quick shake. "Billy!"

"No! No! No—"

She shakes again, and this time he falls silent. His eyes clear and he looks at Clara. "M-Ma?"

She glances back at us. "I'm sorry about this. He acts this way sometimes. But don't worry. It's just one of his fits. They always pass."

"I . . . I'm sorry, Ma. I just got scared is all. I — it was the b-blood on his neck. I don't like blood. It's yucky."

"I know, sweetheart," she says, pulling him into a hug. "I know." They stay like that for an awkward moment, Billy crying into Clara's shoulder, and Dad looking on with his jaw clenched like he's about to have an aneurysm. Finally, Clara pulls back and plants her hands on her hips. "I think I know what will make you feel better, mister. How about some Scattergories?"

"Yay, for reals?" Billy says, straightening with a clap.

Clara smooths her dress. "Yes, for real. I think it's a great idea." She glances at us. "How about you two?"

Dad manages a nod.

"Kayla, what do you say?"

"Um, yeah, sure."

"Scattergories! Scattergories!" Billy chants.

"Scattergories it is, then," Clara says cheerfully. And with that she's gone, clearing the plates and heading into the kitchen like nothing has happened.

CHAPTER FORTY-SEVEN

BILLY
2011

Billy had never run away before, and he didn't want Ma to worry, so he gathered a piece of paper and a brown crayon and left her a note on the table.

Ma — ima runaway to git u help for Mis Sydney. Be bac soon. I luv u.

Frum: billy

The screen door banged closed behind him as he slipped out of the house, and his heart thumped so hard at the sound, he was worried Ma might hear it and chase after him. Her or Miss Sydney, even though both were still fast asleep in their bed and wouldn't be up for some time yet. Still, the thought gave him little comfort, and his stomach boiled like he'd swallowed a mouthful of fire ants as he crossed the yard and stumbled into the corn.

The stalks were brittle and thick with rot, and try as he might, he couldn't creep through them without rattling the husks or snapping the sheaths. With each crack, he imagined Miss Sydney's cheesegrater voice echoing somewhere behind him — "Get back here, Billy, you naughty boy! You get back here!" — and soon he was running, barreling forward through the tassels with the razor-edged leaves slicing into his arms and legs like a thousand paper cuts at once.

Finally, after what felt like a lifetime, he burst from the corn near the forest line and tried to remember where he'd planned to go. To town? Or was it the road? A neighbor's house? It was useless. He was stupid, just like Miss Sydney said. He hated how his thoughts were there one second and gone the next, buzzing through his head like a cloud of flies. He glanced back at the farmhouse, now a blurry, white thumbprint on the horizon, and told himself to hurry up because he didn't have long.

You dumb thing, *he told himself*. You dumb, dumb thing.

The flies buzzed louder, and he thought he might faint, but then he remembered the nice farmer from beyond the pond, and he was running once more.

* * *

The house was robin-egg blue with a lush, green front yard and a ginnala maple that turned red in the fall. Unlike Ma's house, the paint wasn't spider-webbed with cracks and there was a flowered full of columbines and geraniums and poppies resting beneath the porch railing. He'd never been this close before, had never crossed the fence that bordered Ma's property because she'd said it was off-limits, as was the pond. He might fall in and drown, she said. He might be snatched by the mean old man who lived beyond it. But at age ten, Billy decided he was old enough to go exploring despite what Ma said, and that's exactly what he'd been doing, exploring, tossing rocks into the pond, when he heard the man speak.

"Hello there, young lad. And who might you be?"

The voice was like a fist to the gut. Billy startled and looked up to see a man staring at him from across the fence, chewing on a long piece of straw. Billy wanted to run. He wanted to jump in the water and sink into the mud. But no matter how he ordered them to, his knees wouldn't bend, and his legs wouldn't move. All he could do was stare wordlessly as the man's light, blue-gray eyes sparkled in a way that Ma's had not in a very long time.

"Do you like butterscotch?" he said suddenly, rooting around in his pocket. Billy didn't know. He'd never had butterscotch. When the man offered him a piece, Billy nodded and snapped one from his palm.

212

He unwrapped the gold foil and placed the yellow disc in his mouth, marveling at the sweet flavor that spread over his tongue like a spoonful of pancake syrup.

"Mmm," he said. "Mm-mmm."

The man smiled, and Billy suddenly wondered why Ma thought he was mean. He seemed nice to Billy. "Want another?" the man asked, and Billy opened his mouth to say yes, but he heard Ma crying for him in the distance, and he ran home as fast as he could.

That night Ma found the gold foil in his pocket and told him to never, ever go near the pond again, because that's how strangers took you, by tricking you with candy and sweets. She cried and shook him, and Billy promised he wouldn't, scared at how close he'd come to being abducted. But as the years passed, Billy often thought of that kind old man's face, and wondered if maybe he'd know how to fix Ma, because even Billy was smart enough to know there was something wrong with her.

So it was with watery legs that Billy climbed onto the old man's front porch and knocked on the snow-colored door. The wooden welcome sign rattled hard when he did, sounding louder than he'd expected, and Billy wondered if maybe Ma was right. Maybe this was all a trick, the man only acting nice so he could snatch Billy up and cut out his insides. But nothing happened, and Billy stood there a few minutes before knocking again, louder. Still nothing, and Billy's blood fizzed with panic. Ma and Miss Sydney would be up soon — at any moment! — and one of them would surely find his note and go looking for him.

That prickling fear was why he reached out and swung the storm door open and shouted a weak "Hello!" No response met him but that of a smell — a sweet smell that reminded him of spoiled meat and rotten cabbage. Pink spots danced through his vision as he pushed inside. The home was nothing like his with warm, eggshell walls covered in family photos and a living room in perfect order with the furniture neatly arranged near the fireplace. He called out again, and when no one answered, he turned to leave . . .

. . . and stopped.

On the floor, hidden behind the bench of an old Wurlitzer piano, were a pair of legs and two bare feet. Billy rushed over and found the nice man sprawled on his back, staring at the ceiling with dull, lifeless

213

eyes. He had one hand curled into a claw at his side, his fingers sunk deep into the carpet, and the other clutching his chest in the shape of a fist. Billy dropped to his knees and ran his hand along the man's arm and let out a blubbering moan. He'd never seen a dead person before, and the sight of that, of the man who'd smiled so kindly at him near the fence decaying on the floor, made Billy's eyes burn and his nose run. He knew then the man had not been bad, and if he'd come sooner, maybe he could have saved him. He didn't have long to linger on the thought before a voice drifted up behind him, slow and coarse.

"My, my, you have been a very, very bad boy, Billy."

He jerked away from the body and looked toward the door where Miss Sydney stood, outlined against the crisp fall sky. Her elbows were cocked off her hips, thrusting outward like knife points, and her head was lowered in a way Billy could only make out the whites of her eyes. He tried to mumble something, an apology or an explanation, but all that slid past his lips was another worthless moan.

Miss Sydney strode forward and grasped him hard by the wrist. "I told your ma you'd be nothing but trouble. I told her over and over again, but she's never listened when it comes to you." She jerked him to his feet and pushed him toward the open door, through it. "She's protected you for too long now, Billy, and it's time I do something about it."

214

CHAPTER FORTY-EIGHT

CHRIS

Billy is terrible at Scattergories. Beyond awful. We play for an hour before we finish the first game. Clara gives Billy extra time as he scrawls out his answers, chewing his lip like writing is the most difficult thing he's ever attempted. I can hardly read his handwriting, it's pure chicken-scratch, more scribbles than words.

"Okay, time's up. Pencils down," Clara announces.

"Not fair!" Billy mutters, slapping the table. "That's too fast."

"I'll give you ten more seconds."

I watch her, trying to make sense of what, or *who*, I'm seeing. Dissociative Identity Disorder. Multiple Personality Disorder. Whatever it's called. Lexi was fascinated by strange diseases of the mind. Schizophrenia. Munchausen. Multiple personalities.

"Chris, sometimes life is stranger than fiction . . ."

It's what I'm thinking now, staring at Clara, at how she moves and acts and speaks. Her mannerisms are so different than a few hours ago — both eyes wide open, the stroke-victim droop to her mouth gone. *Stranger than fiction.* I watch her roll the dice and click the timer, laughing and shifting in her chair like nothing strange is going on, like Kayla and I aren't chained to the table right now, waiting for the other woman to erupt if we happen to say the wrong thing or do the wrong thing. And the way Billy talked about Sydney before dinner, with real fear flooding his eyes. *Don't wake her up.* It's almost enough to make me think he's as scared of her as the rest of us.

"Hammer," Billy spouts, scratching his ear.

Clara gives a girlish giggle. "A hammer's not a toy, you goofball."

"Is so, is so!" Billy replies. "I play with Gramps's all the time out in the coop!"

Clara smirks, chews on her pencil. "Okay, I suppose I'll give it to you. But just this once. No more funny business, though." She takes a sip of wine and eyes Kayla. "How about you, darling? What's your answer?"

"Hula hoop." Kayla keeps her gaze on her answer sheet. Her hair is pulled back into a glossy bun, her dress hemmed in ribbons of frilly white lace. The makeup Clara applied, a smear of pink lipstick set beneath two wet rows of eyeliner, somehow makes her look younger rather than older. One of those childhood beauty pageant contestants soaking up body image issues.

"Oooh, good one!" Clara says. "Nice alliteration. Double points. You see, Billy, that's a real toy. Not a hammer."

His lower lip curls into a pout. "*Is* so."

"And you, Chris?" Clara asks, turning my way.

"Harmonica," I mutter.

"Mmm, I don't know . . . I guess that works, though it's more of a musical instrument. But, yes, okay. I suppose I've seen children play with them from time to time." She licks the tip of her pencil and marks the score. "Harmonica it is. My turn. How about a horse?"

"Phillip ain't a toy, Ma!" Billy cries.

"I'm not talking about Phillip, Billy. There are toy horses, you know. I had one growing up. I named her Eloise and . . ."

I stare at Clara as she tells Billy all about her toy horse, watching her lips move without hearing a sound. I want to leap across the table and ram the game board down her throat. I want to tighten the cheap string of pearls around her neck until her face purples over and she tells me where Emma is, but I can't. Billy has at least a hundred pounds on me, and he's a good twelve inches taller, full of clumsy bull strength. The kind of guy who accidentally crushes a baby bird to death while helping it back into its nest, his hand coming away covered in guts. *Whoops.*

I'd never be able to overpower him on my own, especially not with this damn chain choking my ankle, cutting deeper by the second, tearing through the scabs on my calf. And, despite the rage coursing through my bloodstream, the murder boiling there, I need to be smart about this. Violence isn't the answer. Not yet anyway. Not when something I do might end up hurting Kayla or Emma.

My fingers float to the bruise above my ear, and I wonder again who clubbed me outside. Was it Clara or Billy? I realize I still have no idea, not that it matters. All that *does* matter is finding a way to reach the cops. Using the phone that . . .

Doesn't.

Fucking.

Work.

"Well, would you look at that? I believe I just won," Clara chirps. "Why yes . . . yes I did. I never win. Oh, lucky me!"

Billy sweeps his board to the floor and crosses his arms, his forehead crumpling into a row of dark, purple lines. "Not fair. That's cheating. I wanna win!"

Clara frowns at him. "William John Carver, that is no way to act. I did *not* raise a poor sport. Now you will clean up that mess this instant, do you hear me?" She glances toward the empty chair and nods, her eyes going distant a second before she looks back again. "There is to be no more of that awful behavior. Is that understood?"

Billy's lips quiver and he melts beneath her gaze. "Y-yes ma'am." He slides from his chair and picks up the board, his scratchpad and pencil.

"Right, then," Clara says, standing and clapping her hands together. "Who would like some dessert?"

"Me, me!" Billy says, waving his arms from the floor. "I do!"

* * *

Dessert is brownies and ice cream along with a glass of port, *None for me, thank you,* Clara pouring it anyway, *No, I insist. It's a Noval. I've been saving it for a special occasion. You wouldn't want to spoil that, would you?* Me drinking it, *No, no I wouldn't.* Her refilling my glass, *Please have another,* my stomach twisting with every sip, the wine doing its thing, putting a sick glow on the room, turning the light buttery along with my thoughts.

Emma. I have to find Emma.

Have to escape . . .

Billy . . . I need to get him alone, force him to tell me where she is.

He crams another brownie into his mouth, his third, and burps. His lips are muddy with crumbs and powdered sugar. "Mmm, mmm, mmm. So good! Brownies is my favorite special treat!"

Kayla picks at hers and watches Billy like he might explode from his chair at any moment. He finishes and eyes her plate. "You want yours?"

She pushes her saucer his way, and he packs it into his mouth in a single bite.

"What do you say, Billy?" Clara asks.

He gives Kayla a chocolate-paste smile. "Fank you."

"That's better." She eases back from the table, finishes her wine and sets the glass down with a flourish. "Well, that was simply a delightful evening. Just delightful. Billy, dear, will you please show Kayla to her room? She looks pooped. I think a good night's rest will do her well."

Kayla's eyes go saucer-wide as they find mine. I know what she's thinking: *Should I run?*

I give her a subtle shake of my head. *No. Not yet.*

But soon.

CHAPTER FORTY-NINE

CHRIS

Billy takes Kayla upstairs then returns for me, his mouth still ringed in brownie paste and sugar. He ducks beneath the table with a set of keys and unlocks the chain, smacking his head against the wood as he backs out and stands. "C'mon, let's go," he says, jerking me to my feet.

I limp after him into the living room. Fire burns down my calf with each step, a stream of blood seeping from what's left of Clara's bandage to pool in the heel of John's worn Oxford. Billy leads me to the same couch I laid Emma on yesterday, forces me down onto the cushions with a hard shove.

"You be good so's I can tie you up."

"Leave it off."

Horror spikes through me. That *voice* . . .

Clara moves toward us in a hitch, her face blank, a void there like the dark of space. A black hole thirsty to consume the sun, and the stars, and all their light. It's a look that turns my blood cold because I don't know how to reason with this woman, what to say to this *stranger*, whoever she is. *Whatever* she is.

"Really? I dunno, Miss Sydney," Billy replies. "I don't want Ma to—"

"You heard me. Go on upstairs and watch over the girl." Her gaze tilts my way. "He'll behave. If he doesn't, well, you know what to do to her. But I don't think that will be necessary, will it, Chris?"

I nod slowly, my head so thick with fear I can barely swallow.

"Uh, okay. If you say so," Billy says, dropping the chain. He lumbers away, thundering up the stairs and down the hall, his footsteps fading until I can no longer hear them. My chest ratchets tighter. It wouldn't take much for him to hurt Kayla or for her to piss him off somehow. I can see it, Kayla making some smart-ass comment (*screw off, jerk*) and Billy losing his temper, like he did when he punched the wall last night, or a moment ago when he flung his board game from the table. He could so easily do the same to Kayla, knock her to the floor like an annoying board game — a toy he's bored with. A toy with a lot of bones to break.

"Be gentle with her, Chris." Sydney's voice boils in my ears, and I turn her way and watch Clara's face slip into form once more, that blank look receding, a tide pulling back to reveal a strip of freshly scrubbed sand. She straightens and floats over to a wooden cubby in the wall, flitting through a shelf of records one by one, delicate about it, using her thumb and forefinger as though she's turning the pages of an ancient tome. She glances over her shoulder with a wink, and my brain-vapor locks.

This can't be real . . .

"What would you like to listen to? Some Elvis, maybe? Or how about The Stones? I've always loved Mick. Or Creedence? John has every album. He was a huge fan of Fogerty." Her voice is smooth again, normal. "Ooh, here we are," she trills, pulling a record from its jacket.

She sets it on a vintage-looking record player, the track skipping a few times before settling into the fluttery-smooth voice of Stevie Nicks: "*Rhiannon rings like a bell through the night and wouldn't you love to love her . . .*"

Clara sways in place for a moment, lost in the song as she reaches up to undo her French braid. She shakes her head, and her hair washes over her shoulders in strawberry waves. She eases back to the couch and plops down next to me, propping an elbow on the cushion and looking my way. The weight of her gaze pins me in place. Or perhaps it isn't *her* gaze but the one behind it, the other *her*. The woman watching and waiting, the one judging my answers and assessing every move, every posture, looking for a reason to surface. A shark circling beneath the waves. A shark with a lot of teeth.

Tread carefully here.

"You remind me of John," she says after a sip of wine. "You have his profile, I think, and his nose. He would sit right there where you are most evenings, smoking a cigar. I never could quite tell what he was thinking. Isn't that just the strangest thing? We can spend our whole lives with someone and not have a clue as to who they truly are. Sometimes, I wonder if those closest to us are the real strangers."

My tongue turns to sandpaper.

"Anyway, it was a game we played, him sitting there, me trying to figure out what was on his mind. I'd get three guesses before he'd tell me. Usually, it was some business to do with the farm. That, or money. He was always so concerned with bills and things breaking down. There's a lot of equipment on a farm, as you probably know. A lot of moving parts. Something is always breaking around here. Oh, and of course sports. He just loved the Broncos. Anything to do with football, really. Anything he could pair with a beer." She pauses, laughs. "Isn't that a man for you? Sports, beer and money."

She falls silent, and the room presses down around me, a sudden weight to the air. "So, you two, uh, never really . . ." *Say something, you idiot.* "You never talked about anything else?"

Her eyes dim, that empty look rippling across her face again. "Mostly. He was never one to go too deep, but sometimes we'd talk about . . . other things."

"Like what?"

"Nothing. Things that are just bad memories now." She clinks a silver ring against her wineglass and circles the rim with her finger. The glass hums. Her eyelids flutter, and she's looking at me again with that awful weight bearing down once more. "But enough about me. Tell me about your wife. What was she like?"

Eyes like seafoam. That tender, barely-there smile. Fingertips that knew when to graze mine or pull away when I needed some space. The way we spoke to each other in looks, a language developed over a decade-and-a-half of marriage, hidden in a quirk of an eyebrow or a quick tip of the head. The way she just slid into my arms after a rough day without me having to say a word. Her familiar warmth bleeding into my chest as she listened . . . *I know you, Chris. I get you.*

And I threw it all away.

I clear my throat. "She was . . . a good woman. It's hard to talk about."

Clara nods. "I haven't told you this, but I lost John, too. I know how much it hurts."

I can tell she does, by the sudden tremor sliding through her hand, the pained look slashing across her face.

Use it. Connect with her. Make her think you care.

"Cancer, too?"

She shakes her head. "No. He had an accident." Her eyes unfocus, and I know she's thinking of him, this man whose presence I can sense permeating this house, whose stinking, moth-balled clothes I'm wearing right now, the feel of them almost like I'm wearing his skin.

"What kind of accident?"

"It was . . ." She trails off, and the water ripples again, her breath spilling out slowly through her nose. *Too close. Change the subject.*

"I imagine it can get lonely out here without him around."

"Oh, yes. At times. A place like this, it can swallow you. But it's mine. It's all I have."

"And you really run it all by yourself, just you and Billy?" *Please tell me you don't. Please tell me there's someone else who can hear my screams.*

"For the most part. Sydney pitches in here and there when she's around, but she's got a life of her own to worry about."

My heart freezes. *She believes it . . . she actually believes it.* I ask the question I've been holding back, lob it out like a grenade and suck in my breath.

"So, how long have you known her?"

She brings a finger to her chin. "I'm not exactly sure. I don't know, but since we were both little, maybe five or six? I didn't have the easiest childhood. My parents were . . . difficult at times, to say the least. Sydney was always there for me. Someone to talk to when I needed to talk. Someone to listen. It's funny, she's always been there for me. Even when I lost John. Even when I lost myself." Her voice wobbles, and I think she's about to crumble, but she sips her wine and continues. "Most people would have run by now, if they'd seen the things she has."

"She sounds like—" I swallow hard, force myself to play along. "Like a good friend."

"The best. I don't know what I'd do without her, honestly." Her gaze finds mine. "Listen, Chris, I'm sorry I didn't tell you about her earlier. I haven't been up in the attic in a while, and, well, I'll admit she has some issues. But she's working on them. After all she's done for me, the least I can do is give her a place to stay. And I didn't even think to mention her, with how much she's been traveling lately. I hope you can forgive me."

"Clara . . ." *Don't do it.* "Clara, are you sure she wouldn't take Emma?"

224

Her expression hardens, a blind snapping shut.

"No. Why would you say that?"

"I'm sorry, I-I'm just worried about my daughter is all."

She drains what's left of her wine and sets the glass on the side table. "You're a good father, Chris. I can tell you love your girls. I wish my father had been more like you." A sudden heat slides over my knee, and I glance down to her hand lying there, her fingers cupping my kneecap. "He never worried about me. He never cared at all."

I shift my knee away and tug at my collar. "I . . . I'm sorry, Clara. Everyone should be able to depend on their parents. My father wasn't the best man, either. He left when I was young. I've never stopped hating him for that."

"We're not so different, are we?"

Like night and day. I shake my head.

She lets the statement hang there for a moment before bringing her hand to rest on my knee again. "Chris, I don't mean to be forward, but will you . . ." She drops her gaze to her lap as if thinking it over, whatever it is she's about to ask. Her eyes click back to mine. "Will you dance with me?"

Dance with me? A nest of scorpions skitters down my neck. The thought of touching her, of *dancing* with her, leaves me feeling queasy and shaken. Ill.

"I — um." I cough. "With Lexi and everything that's happened recently, I don't think that would be a good idea."

Her eyes drift to the floor and then come back to mine, two lanterns glowing a soft, liquid green. "Please . . . I would very much like to dance with you right now."

The track changes as if on cue: "*I took my love, I took it down. Climbed a mountain and I turned around . . .*"

I stare at her, unable to move. *Christ.* It's what Lexi and I would do when it was just the two of us without the kids for a night. We'd dance. Dance until I pulled her upstairs for another glass of wine, the two of us laughing and fumbling at our clothes, falling into bed naked.

Falling into each other.

"Please," Clara whispers, her voice soft. Pitiful. A breeze rustling grass.

225

A dull ache blooms through my chest. I have to find a way to reach her, have to find Emma.

I'm sorry, Lexi . . .

With a deep breath, I rise and take her hand, my other coming to rest on the small of her back. Her body feels foreign against mine, her hips wider than Lexi's, her breasts larger, softer. Her perfume fills my nose — an overpowering floral scent so very strange compared to the smell of Lexi's fresh-soap skin. She hated perfume, refused to wear it. She said it gave her headaches. I bought her a bottle of Vera Wang for our first anniversary. I'd been hunting for a receipt when I found it stuffed in the bathroom trash two days later, hidden beneath a pile of paper towels. It was endearing, in a way, how she spared my feelings, how she told me she loved it. It became this thing only I knew about her. That she didn't need perfume or jewelry. She didn't need anything other than my love. She was her own, and she was perfect.

The thought lingers as Clara moves to the music, and I with her, everything about the moment so foreign and wrong. I haven't touched another woman since Lexi died, haven't so much as thought about it since Kayla caught me with my penis glistening on my slacks, staring at me like I'd stared at pictures of my father when I was her age. Thinking the same things. *What a traitor. What a coward and a liar.*

I knew then, right then, I had to fix things, that I'd never again touch another woman besides Lexi. That I'd make it all right. With Kayla. With Lexi. I swore it to myself. I gave my word, and yet here I am dancing with this *creature*, this *thing* that has promised to visit violence upon my daughters if I don't play by her rules, a liar once more.

"This is so nice," she says, staring up at me with half-lidded eyes.

Make it stop. You have to make it stop.

She pulls closer and lays her head on my chest, nuzzling against it like we've known each other for years instead of a few days. I can feel her warmth soaking through my shirt all the way to my ribs.

226

"Clara. I have to find my daughter. Will you please tell me where she is? I know you don't want to hurt her."

She looks up and traces a finger over my chin, then guides it along the ridge of my jaw and up to my ear. Her fingertip brushes my earlobe, and my neck prickles. I want to — *need* to — pull away from her, to free myself from her grip, from this endless, agonizing moment.

"Please don't worry so much. We'll find her, I promise."

"*. . . and the landslide brought me down.*"

Then she's leaning in, her lips parting, nearing mine . . .

"Dad?" Kayla's voice is like a glass of cold water. I jerk up to see her staring down at me from the banister, breathing hard, her cheeks flushed and her face in pieces. I gaze at her unable to speak, choking on the words as they tumble out.

"Kayla, I — it's not what you—"

Billy crashes down the hall behind her and sinks his hand into her hair, yanking her back so hard, I'm afraid her neck will snap. She crashes to the floor with one foot dangling past the railing and the other pressed against it. She squeals and flails at his arm with all the force of a two-year-old. An over-tired toddler throwing a fit.

"Let go, you asshole!"

"Sorry, Miss Sydney," Billy blares over the banister, ignoring her. "She tricked me and got away for a sec. But I gots her. I'll get her locked up again."

I jerk into action, shove past Clara and stumble for the stairs, my ankle lighting up, the joint screaming like it's packed full of razorblades. It's pure anguish, but I don't care. All I can think about is reaching Billy and pounding my fist into his face, over and over, until it turns into a pile of wet meat.

"Let her go, Billy, you sonofa—"

A hard length of metal slams into my back and sends me tumbling to the floor. I roll over to Clara . . . no . . . Sydney, staring down at me with her mouth twisted into a snarl and her fingers wrapped around a wicked-looking fire poker. "*Don't.*"

It's all she says before glancing up at Billy. "Get her to her room, you moron, and *do* not let her out again! Break her arm if she tries anything!"

He gives a robotic nod and yanks Kayla down the hall. She doesn't fight this time, doesn't cry or speak, her eyes still on mine . . . eyes that are empty and broken. Lifeless.

Sydney brings the poker down again, this time across my shin in a bright splash of pain. I skitter backward and raise a hand. "Please . . . Clara, I mean Sydney, don't. No more. Please." I barely recognize my voice as my own. The anguish there, the fear. *You fucking coward.*

She smacks the poker against her palm. "Downstairs. Now." It's an order she issues through clenched teeth, her gums flashing pink.

I steady my voice and try again. "Please, Clara, John wouldn't want you to—"

Another strike, this one landing on my kneecap. Lightning rips through my quad. Black spots cloud my vision.

"I said, now!"

I scramble to my feet and lurch toward the stairs. It's agonizing, my leg blazing with pain, screaming for me to stop, to collapse and beg for mercy. *Please, just leave me here.* My mind spins. It's all I can do to keep my feet moving forward. The record skips as I near the landing, the poker jabbing into my back, into my kidney.

"Move it."

I stumble down the stairs. Somewhere behind me, Stevie Nicks's feathery voice chases me into the dark.

The landslide, the landslide, the landslide . . .

CHAPTER FIFTY

BILLY
2011

Miss Sydney took Billy to his room in the basement, along with a rusty set of garden shears, and sat him on the bed. She stood in front of him, her face beet red and streaming sweat from the march back home. Her hair clung to her forehead in damp chunks, and she huffed hard through her nose as she stared at him. Billy had never seen her so mad before. Not the time he broke the blue ornamental lamp in her bedroom, or even the time he snuck into the truck and dislodged the gears, sending the truck rolling through the wire cattle fence beyond the driveway. No, he knew by the way her hands were shaking and had gone white at the knuckles that this time was different.

Finally, she spoke.

"What are the two most important rules, Billy?"

"I-I dunno."

"Yes, you do. Tell me."

"Don't say nothin' to strange people."

"That's one. And the other?"

"That I can't go from the farm?"

She nodded. "That's right. No running away. There are only two rules, Billy. Two. And how many of those rules did you break?"

"Only one, Miss Sydney. I just runned away. I didn't talk to no one."

A tremor ran through her jaw. "Yes, but you have to look at the intention behind your decision. Do you know what that means?"

Billy didn't, so he scrunched up his face and shrugged.

Miss Sydney sighed. "It means what you planned to do. What were you planning to do with Mr. Oatman just now, Billy? Were you going to talk to him?"

"I — well, I . . ." Billy trailed off. Miss Sydney always knew when he was lying, so he figured he should tell the truth. "Yes'm."

"Then I'll ask again. How many rules did you break?"

Billy's gaze dropped. "Both of 'em, I guess. I been bad. I'm sorry, Miss Sydney."

"You've been very bad," she echoed. "And now we have to do something about it. Give me your hand."

Billy obeyed, wondering what she was about to do. Miss Sydney had him lie down on the concrete, and then she knelt squarely upon his right elbow with all her weight. She looked at him, and he was surprised to see a tear running down her cheek. She shook her head, and Billy heard Ma's voice crack through.

"No, you can't do this. It's too much."

Her face snapped firm. "I have to. He has to learn."

"But he won't do it again, will you, Billy?" And there she was, Ma, staring at him with wide, unblinking eyes, waiting for his response.

He shook his head. "No, nuh-uh. Cross my heart." He wouldn't. He'd never leave again, never talk to another stranger so long as he lived. Never, ever, ever. But Ma's eyes hardened as he spoke, and she was gone.

"He might not. For a while. But at some point, he'll forget, and he has to remember, Clara. I have to keep you safe, both of you." Miss Sydney's lips curled into a soft smile, and she looked about as sad as Ma had a moment earlier, which surprised Billy because Miss Sydney wasn't sad very often. "I'm sorry, too, Billy," she said in her ragged voice. "I really am." And then she grabbed the shears and placed Billy's pinkie and ring fingers between the cold metal blades.

Billy realized then what it was she planned to do. A liquid terror filled his veins, but it was too late. There came a violent snap, followed by heat like a blowtorch. He screamed, and the pressure on his elbow *released. He brought his hand up to a hot stream of gore that pulsed and sprayed his face, the wall. A bolt of blazing, white pain crackled from his knuckles all the way up his arm, and he nearly bit through his tongue.*

And then he saw them, his two severed fingers lying on the cement in a pool of arterial red. There was so much blood. Blood spurting everywhere. On his shirt, his jeans, welling up over the white bits of bone and severed ligaments where his pinkie and ring fingers had been, fingers now turned to nubs.

Purple splotches flooded his vision as a hand grabbed his wrist. Miss Sydney pressed a towel to his stubs, and the heat in his knuckles blazed hotter. He jerked and thrashed, and somewhere Ma, or Sydney, he couldn't tell which, begged him to calm down, told him to pull the air in through his nose and push it out through his mouth. He was fine, the voice said, just fine. But he wasn't fine, and the splotches kept growing and growing until he couldn't see anything else.

* * *

Billy stayed in bed for three weeks, crying and clutching his newly mis-shapen hand. He remembered feeding Phillip with that hand, his good one, and he wondered if he'd ever be able to do the same with his left. It didn't work as well as the right, and it often disobeyed him when he ordered it to complete the simplest of tasks. Grasping an apple or a baseball was difficult at times, all of his fingers moving at once and in different directions. Would he be able to pet Phillip properly? Would he be able to scratch him behind his ears the way he liked? It felt like a death of sorts, his injury, and Billy didn't think he'd ever be happy again.

Ma noticed this and was extra kind to him. She brought him his meals on trays and made sure to include plenty of grilled-cheese sandwiches with potato chips and tomato soup (his favorite meal). It didn't matter. Billy wasn't hungry most days. He barely touched the sandwiches, and his soup grew cold in the bowl. Ma said he needed to eat so his tummy could handle the little white pills she fed him with cold sips of ice water. She said he needed them to fight the nasty germs trying to get in through his scabs, or to calm the pain in his bandaged fingers, but they made him sick, and he frequently threw them up, and the pain went on and on . . .

When she wasn't trying to feed him or change his bandages, Ma would sit on the edge of the bed and read him Grimm's Fairy Tales *in a soothing voice: Hansel and Gretel, and Rumpelstiltskin, and The Frog Prince. His favorite was Rapunzel, because she lived with a witch who did terrible things to her until she escaped. Billy wanted to escape. He was pretty sure Miss Sydney was a witch, too.*

But unlike Rapunzel, there was no prince in shining armor to help him, and even if there were, he didn't want to leave Ma alone with Miss Sydney. So Billy lay there with his finger stubs pulsing and throbbing and did nothing but stare at the ceiling for days on end. Ma grew worried. She checked his temperature regularly. She brought him hot chamomile tea with milk and ran her fingers through his sweat-crusted hair. She told him story after story, and Miss Sydney was nowhere to be seen.

One day, Ma had to run into town for some groceries. She said she'd be right back and told Billy to try and get some rest while she was out. Billy nodded and fell asleep the second his head hit the pillow. He dreamed of a safe place, of an ivory castle nestled in the clouds with dozens of brightly colored rooms for him to explore. They were full of toys and games, and Billy played with them all without once thinking someone might take his fingers.

When he woke, Ma still wasn't back, and Billy grew worried. She never stayed away long, and Billy thought about running down the road after her to make sure she was safe. But the pain in his nubs throbbed, and he knew he would never leave the farm again. So he lay in the bed instead, worried, clutching his ruined hand and mumbling to himself until he fell back to sleep. The next time he opened his eyes, Miss Sydney was standing in the doorway. He could tell it was her by the way her shoulders curved in toward her chest and her head hung motionless to the side. Billy wondered how long she'd been staring at him like that. It made him uncomfortable. It made him shiver. And then she turned on the lights, and Billy sucked in a breath.

Standing next to her was a girl. A real, live girl! He'd never seen one in person before. She had big, blue eyes and hair the same color as the fall corn. She came to Miss Sydney's hip, and her lips were sealed shut with a gray square of tape. Twin trails of clear liquid dripped

232

*down her face, and her nostrils pulsed with each breath. Billy thought
she looked scared. He didn't know why. He wasn't scared. He was
excited! He pushed himself upright in the bed and the girl scattered
back, yanking on Miss Sydney's dress until Miss Sydney frowned and
thrust her roughly back into the room.*

    "Billy," she said, looking at the girl. "This is Lilly."

    *He couldn't believe it — her name rhymed with his! Lilly! — and
for the first time in nearly a month, Billy smiled.*

CHAPTER FIFTY-ONE

EMMA

The Hideaway Box is so cold, all I can do is shiver no matter how hard I rub my arms to stay warm. I wish there were a window in here. I don't know if it's day or night. All I have is the light in the ceiling, the one that never goes off. I don't know how long I've been trapped in here, but it feels like forever. Forever and ever. It's not even scary anymore. It's just boring, which wouldn't be too bad, except for how much my shin aches. I need more medicine. But that means seeing the scary woman, and I don't want to see her. Nope. Not with how she talks with that scrabbly witch voice of hers and does the weird eye-blinking thing. I can't stand—

Croaaak.

The door in the ceiling opens. It sounds like a frog. That's how I think of it, a big metal frog croaking above me. It means someone is coming. I know it's Billy because his footsteps are so loud. *Bump, bump, bump.* The lady is super quiet. Like, so quiet I didn't even hear her the last time she came in. She woke me up with a cup of soup and some bread. I told her I wasn't hungry, but she frowned and said I'd better not be any trouble, so I ate it. Boy, was it gross. The soup was cold and tasted like glue. The bread was so hard, it hurt my teeth. After a few bites, I asked her about Dad and Kayla, and she said I couldn't see them until they realized we were all "one big family." I don't know what she meant by that, but I didn't like the sound of it. I don't want to be in a family with her.

Billy comes down the steps, grabs a stool and plops right down next to me. "Hiya, Emma. I'm s'posed to check on you. Are you good?"

"I'm still cold. Can I have another blanket?"

"Yeppers." He goes over to the crate and pulls out a blanket that looks like a giant checkerboard — big and black with all these gray-and-white squares. I like checkers. Me and Kayla played it a lot before Mom died. Kayla mostly beat me, but sometimes when she was being nice, she'd let me win. I hope we get to play again.

"It's Phillip's," Billy says, laying it over me. "We don't got no more in here. Phillip needs the rest 'cause of how thin he is, okay?"

I nod. The blanket is the itchiest one yet, but I don't care. I just want to be warm. "Where's my dad and sister?"

Billy sits and plants his chin in his hands. "Your pa and sissy got in trouble with Sydney. They got grounded to their rooms for being bad."

I feel my brow scrunch up. "For being '*bad*'? What'd they do?"

He shrugs. "Dunno, but they made Miss Sydney mad. She had to teach your pa a lesson. Hey, you wanna play a game? You like cards?"

"Sorta," I say. "What did she do to my dad?"

"I think he tried to run away, so she hit him with something."

My heart stops. "Is he hurt bad?"

"No, but you can't run away. It's one of Miss Sydney's rules. *The* most important rule. I don't like her rules." He frowns, and I know thinking about it is making him sad.

"You okay?"

235

He squints. "Huh?"

"You look sad. My dad says if you're sad, it's not good to keep your feelings boxed up inside."

"Well," he says, chewing on a fingernail, "Sydney don't like me to talk about my feelings too much. When I do, I sometimes cry, and if I cry, she calls me stupid and tells me to zip my lip."

"That's not nice," I say, thinking how mad I'd get if Dad told me that. "Does that make you mad?"

He scratches his head. "She makes me mad lots of times. She's always bossin' me around and telling me to do all these things I don't wanna do. But if I don't do 'em, she teaches me her lessons. I hate her lessons. They hurt."

"They do? You can tell me about them if you want. I won't say anything, I promise."

Billy blows a raspberry through his lips. "You for real wanna know?"

I nod.

"You can't tell no one, though. 'Specially not Sydney. You gots to promise it." He holds out his pinkie finger. I won't tell. No way. I can tell it's important. I wrap my pinkie around his and give it a squeeze.

"Okay, um . . . there's this secret right here." He rolls up his sleeve and shows me a pink, shiny mark on his arm, a scar.

"Ouch." It's all I can think to say.

"Yeah. It's what happens from Miss Sydney if I don't be good. Look, I gots even more." He pulls his sleeve higher, and I gasp. There are so many, all these spots in his skin that look like melted plastic.

"She shouldn't do that."

He chews his lip. "That's not even the worst of it. She did this other thing once, but only because I was real, real bad. She . . . um . . ." He shakes his head. "No. I shouldn't tell about that one. It's too scary."

I'm scared already, but I decide to be brave. "I won't be scared. It's okay."

He stares at me with tears filling his eyes, and for a minute, I think he's about to tell me no, but he grabs his glove instead and pulls it off. I go shaky when he shows me his hand. Two of his fingers are *gone*. Or mostly gone, that is. There's only a little bit of them left right below his knuckles. He looks at his lap while he shows me. He's probably wondering if I think his hand looks gross or something, which I do, a little, but mostly I just feel bad for him. I reach out and touch one of the nubs to show him it's okay.

"How bad did it hurt?" I ask.

"So, so bad." His mouth twists. "Super bad. I don't never want it to happen again."

"Your mom did this?"

His nostrils go big, and he shakes his head. "Nuh-uh. Ma didn't do it. Ma wouldn't never do that. It was Miss Sydney. I tried to run once too, like your pa did. She says it's so I can remember not to do it again."

It makes me want to cry. I decide right then and there I hate Miss Sydney. I *hate* her. And even though I'm feeling dizzy again, and a little sick, I think I know how I can help Billy so he doesn't get hurt anymore. He sits real still while I tell him my plan.

CHAPTER FIFTY-TWO

KAYLA
DAY FOUR

I'm in a new room — the ugly, unfinished one, chained to the black drainpipe. The ceiling looks like Swiss cheese. There are holes everywhere with chunks of drywall crumbled all around me. The walls are just as bad, stripped to the studs in spots, with patches of yellow insulation fluttering with the air from the heat vents — the vents that did nothing to keep me from freezing my ass off in Clara's stupid maxi dress last night.

I spent most of it shivering. Shivering and sawing. Sawing for hours. Cutting into the black PVC with the dinner knife I slipped into the pocket of my dress last night as Clara cleared the table. The dinner knife that's left my hands blistered and raw. At first, I tried to find some weak point in the pipe, some way to just slip free or break it, but it was impossible. It doesn't look sturdy at all. It looks like it's made out of plastic and would break right away, but I couldn't even get it to bend, no matter how hard I pulled or jerked on the stupid thing. All it did was rattle in place.

Rattle. Rattle. Rattle.

So I began cutting. And sawing. And crying. Crying as my fingers ached and spasmed. Crying as the pipe wore away what little teeth the knife had. Crying as my hands cramped and blistered, then bled, which they're doing right now — bleeding. Bleeding so bad, I can barely grip the knife as I saw back and forth. But, I'm nearly three-quarters of the way through now, and I'm not about to stop until I break out of this fucked-up room, and this fucked-up house, and get as far away from psycho Clara as possible.

I heave again on the chain, and the pipe creaks. *Good.* Getting closer. I can't wait to get the chain off. Billy wrapped it so tight around my ankle it feels like it's rubbing bone every time I move.

"Sorry, but Sydney says it gots to be super-duper tight this time, cause you runned."

"You don't have to do what she says, Billy. I know you don't like her. Help me find my sister, and I promise we'll help you get out of here."

"Oh, no, no, no. That would be bad of me. Sydney don't want no one knowin' about the Hideaway Box."

It's still blaring through my head even now, hours later. *The Hideaway Box.* It's where Emma is, I'm sure of it. It scares me, that name. Like, why would something like that even exist? How many children has Clara abducted besides Emma? One? Two? More? I can't stop thinking about it. Some dirty room with Emma chained to the wall like me, screaming for help, crying and staring at the bodies of the kids who came before her, piled neatly in the corner.

My eyes swim with tears, and I stand and drift over to the window. It's the only thing I can reach before the chain pulls taut. It's mostly blacked-out save for a small patch of glass at the bottom I can see through. This little square that fogs over every time I breathe. It looks like a Hallmark movie outside, a clear blue sky hanging over puffy blankets of snow, the kind where some fake family sits around a fire talking about how great everything is, fresh from patching up whatever stupid drama unfolded a few minutes earlier. I think, in some sick way, it's what Clara wants. To make us her family. *"Well, isn't this lovely, a real family dinner for once."* A river of pinpricks spills down my arm. It's *so* messed up. Almost as messed up as what I saw with Dad last night.

What was that about, anyway? The two of them dancing all close like that? The almost-kiss? I know he isn't into her, *can't* be into her, is probably trying to turn the tables and get into her head or something, but whatever. She can stuff *him* in the Hideaway Box for all I care. It doesn't matter. All that matters is getting out of here and finding help before something bad happens to Emma.

If it hasn't already . . .

I stare up the snow-covered driveway. It's where I need to go. Up the driveway to the road and then take it wherever it leads me. There has to be someone out there who can help. A neighbor or a plow truck or—

An SUV. *Oh, my God.*

My heart explodes as I catch the flash of silver turning onto the driveway near the gate.

I slap my hands against the window and push up.

It doesn't budge.

Why? I search the glass, and my eyes narrow on the lock above the window rail. I fumble at it, pry it open, and try again, shoving up, up, up . . . but it still won't move! *Why won't it move?* I see it then, the seam of paint gluing the window to the frame. *Shit!* The Styrofoam crunch of tires on snow sends my nerves into overdrive as I attack the paint with a fingernail, scratching maniacally until a splinter breaks loose and slices beneath the cuticle. I jerk my finger back with a hiss and suck at the dark button of blood beading on my fingertip. Outside, brakes squeal, and a car door thunks open. The sound rips through my head like a tornado siren: *Go!*

I try again, scratching and raking the paint. More splinters, but I don't care. I have to get it open!

Footsteps now, drawing closer: *Crunch, squeak, crunch.*

I peer through the glass and catch a man in a brown work jacket, carrying a clipboard, trudging toward the porch. His breath clouds his face as he works through the powder, his fist pressed to his mouth in a cough. Seeing someone else, *finally* someone else, besides Clara and Billy, makes me dizzy with panic.

I bang on the window. "Hey! Up here! Up here!"

He stops and glances over his shoulder with a black fringe of curls sprouting from beneath a green ball cap, a pair of aviators swinging upward, the sun catching and reflecting my way as he—

"Can I help you?"

The man adjusts his cap and heads toward the porch with a wave, his voice muffled and friendly through the window.

"Hello, ma'am . . . from . . . utility company. We're working on . . . phone lines, and—"

I search the window again, spot a nail wedged into the corner of the windowsill.

Use it!

I grip the head and spin the nail in a circle, yank it up and down, up and down, pulling as hard as I can, the nail screeching and whining, giving an inch, another. It comes free in my hand . . .

And falls.

Clinks off the heat vent and—

I snatch it before it falls through.

Go! Go! Go!

I rake the nail point over the seam. The paint flakes, and the wood appears in dim stripes. I saw harder, and the seam splits. It's enough. It *has* to be. I try the window again, shove upward and . . .

It. Still. Won't. Open.

Why, why, why?

Think, Kayla . . . quick!

Break it.

I whip my gaze left and right in search of something I can use. A board, or a brick, or—

The chain! Use the chain!

The chain that won't reach the glass. Not unless I free it from the pipe.

With my heart pounding, I squat and wrap it around both hands and then pull. Pull with everything I have; pull for Emma and all the life she still has left to live. Pull for Mom, because I know she's inside of me, yelling that I can do this, that I'm strong enough. Pulling for myself, as I ignore the agony in my hands because—

I. Will. Not. Die. Here.

The drain pipe bends, cracks, and with a sharp *snap!* breaks. I thump down onto my butt, in shock that I did it — *I actually did it* — before scrambling back to my feet. Then I'm looping the chain around my knuckles—

". . . have a good day, ma'am."

—and slamming my hand straight through the glass.

The pane explodes, the sound a bright, stinging shatter as I yell at the man to—

"Help me! *Please, God,* you have to help me!"

He turns and raises his sunglasses, one eyebrow popping *as he sees me.*

"Call the police!" I screech, pointing wildly at the porch. "Quick! The lady inside is crazy! She's got us trapped in here! My dad and my sister and me! All of us! Please, hurry! She's a psycho! She'll kill us if you don't!"

"Sorry? What's that?" He cups his hand to the brim of his hat and works back through the snow. "You're . . . trapped?"

"Yes!" I clear the glass with my chain-wrapped fist, dumping shards onto the roof. I have to get out. I have to get out *now.*

"Hey, whoa! What are you doing?"

But I'm not listening. I'm squeezing through the frame, slivers of glass cutting into my arms, slicing my back. And I don't care. I just need *out.*

"Be careful!"

Even as he says it, I'm already sliding. Tumbling and rolling down the steep pitch of the roof, toward the gutter and over it — flying into empty air. My stomach knots as I fall. I try to right myself, the ground rushing for me, giving me alternating snatches of sky and snow — blue, white, blue, white, blue.

I land on the man. Or rather, he catches me — or tries to, both of us coming down into the powder together. The air rushes out of me like a punch to the gut, but I'm already scrambling back to my feet and yanking him up with me. His eyes drift to the chain still wrapped around my fist, widen at the blood there, dripping through the links, and then widen further as he sees the padlock attached to the chain around my ankle.

"Okay," he says, with a quick glance at the house. "Okay, come on. I'll get you help."

I want to cry. I want to scream with relief. *Help*. He's going to get me to *help*.

He loops his arm in mine — "Don't worry. You're okay now. I've got you." — and helps me through the snow and into his SUV. It's still running, the heater dumping hot air on my bare legs. My gaze remains on the house, looking for any sign of movement, as the man works around the hood toward the driver's side and opens the door.

He lingers there, a wet *thunk* sounding as his eyes wobble and then roll higher, up into his head. He sways in place for a moment, then crumples forward onto the seat. Clara stands behind him, gripping a tire iron — one she brings down in a hard arc, right into the back of the man's skull. A sound like an egg breaking. A downward curl of her lips, her face doing that strange droop thing — not Clara, I realize — Sydney. Her lips move: "*You did this.*" Then, before I can look away, she raises the tire iron over her head and drives the point straight down through the back of the man's neck.

I run. I slide out of the SUV, *and I run*.

Cold air drenches my throat. Tears I didn't know were there leak down my cheeks. Blood rushes to my face. My naked feet punch into the snow and go numb — needles of ice lancing up my calves. I don't care. I'll run until they fall off. I'll run until I can't take another step.

Toward the house.

Through the glittering snow.

Around the corner — and right into Billy's arms.

Billy, who wraps me in a lung-crushing grip that glues my arms to my sides. I shriek and wriggle and try to break free. "Let go of me, Billy! Let go!"

He doesn't. He only squeezes harder as I wail, his dim, country monotone voice filling my ears. "There's no runnin' off now. Sydney says so. It's the number-one rule. Sydney says you gots to stay. Kayla's gots to stay, stay, stay."

CHAPTER FIFTY-THREE

CHRIS

My hands shake as the images of last night tumble through my head in pops and flashes: Clara asking me to dance. How broken she seemed as she set her hand on my knee. The dark cloud of despair that swept across her face when I refused. Her keeping at it, begging me until I finally gave in. The creeping revulsion I felt at her touch, my gorge rising when she tried to kiss me . . .

All night they've haunted me, these images, sleep coming in thin slivers. Billy thundering up behind Kayla. Kayla staring at me as he dragged her down the hall, looking at me like I was Hitler or the devil incarnate. The fire poker swinging away, forcing me back, back, back, toward the stairs. Clara wearing her Sydney mask again, her eyes turned into two smoldering bits of charcoal.

I slam my head back against the cinder-block wall and groan. Whatever it was that broke Clara, that splintered her in two, it had something to do with John. I'm certain of it. It's a feeling I can't shake, reinforced by the backward pictures of him hanging in her room and the overturned photos on the nightstand. *I hereby sentence you to a life of darkness,*

John. *An eternity of night without parole.* It's an act of hatred. But there's love there, too, or why not just trash the photos? Why not burn them in the fireplace, in the time-honored, fuck-you fashion? Why keep a dozen reminders of your dead husband lying around when you can't bear to look upon his image?

Because she can't let him go.

I've seen the way her face turns to putty every time she mentions his name. How her eyes go soft at the corners. It's like he's still alive, imprisoned in some dark recess of her mind. A twisted, unstable mind full of pits and bogs and marshes from which he'll never escape. But even that doesn't make sense, does it? People fight all of the time. They get married and divorced and come out the other side mostly intact. Was Clara in a marriage so cruel, and with so much ill intent, that she halved herself to escape? Did John do something so unspeakably atrocious to cause her to split into two distinct personas, each aware of the other with no idea they inhabit the same body?

It seems unlikely, especially as an adult. Isn't that what Lexi's book said? That things like this mostly occur during childhood? So what else happened to her? What is it that am I missing? *Who hurt you, Clara? Who did this to you? Your parents? A stray uncle with too much time on his hands? Some overly friendly stranger lurking near the neighborhood park?*

Whatever it was, I have to figure it out. I have to find a way to break through to Clara and convince her she knows where Emma is, that she is Sydney, and that Sydney isn't safe for her or for anyone. It's either that or violence. A violence I can feel rising, can suddenly see so very clearly — my hands wrapped in her hair, ripping out the roots as I slam her head into a nearby hutch or through the frame of one of her precious oil paintings. The dark rivulets of blood the impact will create and how she'll beg for me to stop with trembling hands. (*Don't . . . please. No more. I'll take you to her, okay? I'll take you to Emma.*)

But as much as I want to unleash my anger on Clara, to break every bone in her face, something tells me it's the wrong choice. She might shut down completely, might turn into some impenetrable vault I'll never be able to unlock again. Not to mention how something like that would trigger Billy. Billy with his short fuse and brute strength. I have no doubt he would rip Kayla to pieces if I hurt his "ma." He loves her; of that much, I'm sure. I've seen it in the way he looks at her, the affection on his face when she speaks. The fear. It's like he's four and she holds the keys to the cookie jar.

No, I can't hurt her . . . yet.

Still, I need to do *something*, and I need to do it fast. It's been too long since I've seen Emma, an entire day gone without assessing her leg or checking her temperature. Twenty-four hours in which an infection could take hold or worse. A cold sheet of panic spirals through my chest: Is she okay? Does she think I abandoned her? That I let this happen? Is she even still alive?

It's a thought quickly severed by a distant cry. Kayla's cry. Dim and muffled, as though bubbling down through twelve feet of water. For a moment, I wonder if I've imagined it, if my mind has fractured like Clara's. But then it comes again, another trembling, piercing shriek, and I'm back on my feet and shouting for Clara to let me out, to leave my daughter alone. I stand there, crying out, clenching and unclenching my fists, until my voice shreds and I can no longer scream.

They come for me.

The cellar door creaks open to a shape. A woman in a dress. Clara . . . or is it Sydney? *Because I have to think of her that way. As two separate people.* A lighter sparks, and she limps down the steps with the eyes of a cobra. Cold. Calculating. Ready to strike. Sydney. Definitely Sydney. And it's no longer a dress she's wearing but rather a trench coat and a sweater with jeans tucked into a sturdy pair of rubber galoshes. Behind her, framed against the light spilling from the hall, is Billy.

247

He stands with his arms crossed, immobile. A hulking statue planted at the top of the stairs.

"We've got a problem," Sydney says, blowing a cloud of smoke my way. "And you're going to help clean it up."

Billy leads me upstairs by the chain, yanking faster than I can walk, telling me to hurry. It's agonizing, my knee grinding and crunching with each step, clicking in and out of place. The pain is enough to make me wonder if Sydney fractured it last night with the fire poker. That, or it's deeply bruised. Either way, there's no use thinking about it, or how much my back hurts, my calf. My entire body is on fire at this point. I'm nothing but a slab of muscle stitched together with thread.

Billy pulls me outside, where I'm forced into a squint. The sky hangs overhead in a cold, blue arc pierced by a white sun, the snow a blinding sheet of light. I can barely see anything, my pupils on fire. The chain bites into my ankle as he drags me off the porch, the steel ridges of the shackle further stripping the ruined, aching flesh from my calf as we drift toward a Jeep I don't recognize. Next to it, lying crumpled a few feet away, is a man.

My stomach twists. There's blood *everywhere* — in the snow, drenching his jacket. The back of the guy's skull is caved-in, a length of powder-coated metal lying next to him. *It's a tire iron*, I realize dully. *She killed him with a tire iron. Oh, Jesus. Oh fuck.*

My pulse ignites. I look to Sydney in a daze. "What have you done?"

"What have *I* done? Me?" She jabs her cigarette at the house, where Kayla is sitting against the wall, chained to a downspout, her face as white as ice. Sydney glances higher toward a shattered window on the second floor. "Your daughter did this, not me. She killed him the minute she broke that glass." She takes another drag from the cigarette and flicks it at the man. The butt skips off his back and hisses out in the snow.

"Sydney . . ."

"Listen, Chris, Clara speaks highly of you and your family. You all seem wonderful. You truly do. She says you love your kids and that you're a good, good father. She especially adores your little one, but you've probably guessed that already."

Heat stings my cheeks. I'm vaguely aware of Billy hulking next to me, his hands still holding fast to the chain.

"Unfortunately, Clara's also a bit of a soft touch. She has this way of only seeing the best in a person. Their bright side, if you will. Don't get me wrong. It's an admirable quality, but it can lead to certain . . . well, lapses in judgment at times."

My eyes dart toward the corpse and then come back to her. "Just tell me what you want from us."

"I don't *want* anything from you."

"Then why are we here?"

Her brow buckles like I'm a fat-lipped toddler gumming nonsense at his mother, like she's trying to translate my words into something meaningful. "Haven't you figured it out, yet? This is for Clara, of course. This is all for Clara." She spreads her arms. "Do you think I want this life? *Any* of it?"

"So go, then. Let me talk to Clara."

"Talk to her about what? Letting you leave? Don't you think I've tried? I've begged her to leave for as long as I can remember. And now you, a man she's known for all of two days, are going to convince her of something different? Don't you know she stays here because the pain won't let her leave?" She waves at the house. "You have no idea how much misery and hate live in those walls."

I don't care what Clara's lost or how she feels. I don't care about anything except that a man is lying dead in the snow with his brains seeping through his eye socket, and Kayla saw it happen. "We all have problems, Sydney. It doesn't mean you get to kill someone."

A storm cloud rolls across her face, the sky cracking open. Eyes dark. Lips flat. Ears red. "Did your father rape you in a hole in the ground most nights? Did you feel his stinking breath on your neck or taste his sweat as he moaned behind you? Did he pepper your arms in acid if you spoke back to him? Did your mother watch? Did she *let* it happen?" Her voice drops to a growl, a barely-there hiss. "Did you wake up every . . . single . . . morning, scared to death of the two people God put on this earth to protect you?"

I swallow my tongue, unable to speak.

She dips her head, and her gaze renders me motionless, her eyes pale green slivers. "Well, did you!"

The blood drains from my face. I shake my head.

"No, I thought not." She folds her arms across her chest. "You're just like John." She says his name like it burns her tongue, like it's a poison she can't hold in her mouth for more than a second. "The man who was supposed to fix *everything*."

"I don't understand."

"Don't you, though? Clara's broken. She's a puzzle missing her pieces. She's always needed to be filled in. I thought all of that had stopped after she lost Kinley. After she lost John. I thought we were past all of this nonsense, that we were finally, *finally* good. But then here you come, you and your happy little family, and it's like nothing's changed." She clucks her tongue and snickers. It's a sound like a whale surfacing, a long, steady hiss of air, followed by pockets of phlegm rattling in her lungs. She reaches into the coat and comes out with a gun, a nine-millimeter like the one I have locked away on the top shelf of my closet back home. "You're her fix now, Chris. You and your girls. *Especially* your girls. None of you will ever leave this place."

CHAPTER FIFTY-FOUR

KAYLA

I stagger after Billy with the wind knifing through Clara's dress like I'm not even wearing it. My skin is numb, my face tingling. Snow ices over my boot collars and melts down my ankles. I'm shivering, beyond cold, as we trudge toward the chicken coop, and then past it, everything a blur through my tears. They leak between my lashes and freeze on my cheeks. I don't bother to wipe them. I don't care. I'm not even here right now. I'm still sitting in the SUV watching Sydney bash that poor man with the tire iron.

I can't get his face out of my brain, or the horrible moment when she first hit him. It keeps replaying in my mind like a series of camera flashes. *Pop!* The man hesitating near the open door, squinting at me. *Pop!* Him stumbling forward, looking drunk, trying to keep his balance, falling onto the seat. The metal coming down again. His skull crunching. *Pop! Pop!* Sydney staring right at me—

"*You did this.*"

—before driving the tire iron straight into his neck.

After Mom, I didn't think death would bug me anymore. It felt like I was dying, seeing her like that, all wrinkled up like a grape left on the sidewalk for too long. It hurt so much, I didn't think anything could ever hurt worse. I was wrong. This is worse. This is *so* much worse. He probably had *kids*. A *wife*. If I'd kept my mouth shut, If I hadn't broken that window and yelled for help, he'd still be here. He'd probably be walking into his house right now, with some cute little boy dropping his toys and toddle-running toward him for a hug. "*Daddy!*"

But he's not. He's dead. He's dead because of me.

I moan and drop to my knees. Snow spins around me, whirling sideways off the ground. My nose is running, the snot icing over above my lips. I don't bother to wipe it. I don't care. I can't feel my thighs anymore, or my feet. The chain snaps taut and jerks me onto my back. Billy trudges forward, dragging me through the frigid crust like I'm his stuffed animal. I lie there and let him. I'll probably get frostbite soon. If I'm lucky, maybe even freeze to death.

I don't care, I don't care, I don't care . . .

A shadow falls across the sun. "You gots to get up! Quick! Do it before she sees!"

"Go away," I murmur. "Leave me alone."

"C'mon, hurry." He yanks the chain, and my foot rises with it, falls.

"No."

Everything goes quiet for a moment. Still. All I can hear are the wind in my ears and my heart beating somewhere in my neck. My adrenaline is gone. I'm tired and cold and I don't care about anything anymore. I just want to lie here and close my eyes and never wake up.

Billy won't let me. Something warm covers my chest. It's his coat, I realize, as he curls a hand beneath my shoulders and another under my knees. And then he's carrying me. I'm like a child in his arms, weightless. I crack my eyes and see his cheeks puffing in and out, his breath turning into clouds of frost. The sky is a cheery blue above him, not a cloud in sight. For a moment, I can almost imagine I'm back in Boston with Mimi, staring up at it with a couple of cups of hot tea, talking about my day or what movie to watch or where I should go to college. Maybe Wheaton, because it's so close. Maybe UCLA, because it isn't, and it has a good biology program. Decisions that don't matter now.

Nothing does.

I close my eyes and sink into Billy's arms. It's better than walking, I decide. At least he's warm.

"Where are you taking me?" I ask.

"The vat."

"What's that?"

"It's a bad place. A bad, bad place."

And just like that, I'm freezing again, wishing he'd put me right back into the snow.

* * *

We wind past the coop and toward some sort of industrial-looking shed. I'm surprised I didn't spot it when we were out here yesterday. It's huge with three garage doors, painted white and in the same shape as everything else around here, dented and old and broken. Billy sets me down beside a door missing its doorknob, a hole in its place punched through the chipped wood. He leans close in a whisper, his spit flecking my cheek.

"Your sissy says you could—"

"Billy! Billy, is that you? Get in here."

I startle as the door swings open to Sydney. I can almost believe she really is two different people with the way her gaze keeps twitching, her mascara streaked and smudged at the corners, her eyes a filmy pink. She's a mess, dressed in a faded, leather trench coat and a coffee-stained sweater. She gestures for Billy to bring me inside.

"Hurry up. Move it." My bladder clenches at the sound of her ripped-paper voice, and I'm suddenly afraid I'll pee my pants.

Billy takes the lead, and we shuffle through the shed in a line. It's gross and run-down, tools everywhere I look, stuffed in between seed bags and stacks of fertilizer reeking of manure. We pass a tractor with a horizontal cylinder attached to the front, bristling with rows of curved spikes. Billy slows, and for a minute, I'm worried Sydney is going to get in and run me over with it. It's all I can think about as Billy continues forward, that she's going to kill us — me, Dad, and Emma. That she'll murder us like she did the man, one by one, and stuff our remains into the manure sacks, turn us into fertilizer to feed the corn in the spring.

It's a terrible thought, one swallowed by the sight of the man's SUV parked in the corner. The hatch is open, a dark-red stripe staining the trunk, the cement. We follow it up a ramp toward a raised metal platform surrounded by a steel railing. There's a wrist chained to it, an arm. *Dad.*

He stands as we near, and I suck in my breath. I don't want to feel sorry for him, I still hate him, *so much*, but he looks awful. His skin is ashen, and his hair is thinner than usual, greasy, with strips of scalp peeking through. A pile of wrinkles branch across his forehead, and his hands won't stop squeezing open and shut as we draw closer. He seems older, as old as I've ever seen him, like he's aged ten years in a day. He looks like someone split open his chest and pulled out his soul.

I don't realize I've stopped until Sydney jams her gun into my kidney. "Go on."

I stumble up the ramp toward the familiar sound of boiling water. Centered in the middle of the platform is a giant vat about three times the size of a hot tub, the surface nothing but rolling bubbles kicking off fat tails of steam. The fumes sting my nose and burn my eyes. It's why I don't see the man sooner, all the steam. He's crumpled against the railing next to Dad, with his head slumped forward onto his chest. His jacket is covered in blood, a white patch showing through all the red. It's a name tag, I realize. I can read his name: Scott Wilkins. His name was Scott Wilkins.

Sydney's voice crawls through the air behind me.

"Well, what are you waiting for?"

I turn. She's standing a foot away, with her mouth doing that droopy thing again, holding the gun so it's pointing straight at my stomach. My mouth fills with peanut butter. I don't know what she wants me to do or what to say, so I just stand there looking back at her with my arms shaking.

She glances at the man, back to me. "You're the one who made this mess, aren't you?"

My head moves, but it's like someone else is nodding. It's like I'm a puppet with strings wound through my cheeks. Strings someone else is pulling.

"I'm glad you agree," she says, expressionless. "And what should someone do when they make a mess?"

"Clean it up?"

"Very good." She waves at the man's corpse and then at the boiling pool of water behind me. "So, clean it up."

CHAPTER FIFTY-FIVE

CHRIS

My anger is a river frothing through my bloodstream. My breath comes in hard through my nose and out through my mouth in quick, hitching expulsions. I am rage and bile and all things hateful, a mass of coiled tendon and grinding teeth as Sydney shoves Kayla up the ramp — the ramp over which I dragged the man Sydney turned into a corpse a few minutes earlier — the man who had a life, which she stole in the most savage way possible. All while my daughter *watched*.

She'll never be able to un-see these things.

She'll never be the same after this.

Sydney is talking to her, telling her this is all her fault, the words coming out muted and indistinct, like she's speaking through a pillow or a mile of cotton. I'm not listening. I'm watching Billy, the one thing in this world Clara seems to care about. He has his back turned to me, not far away now, only a couple feet, edging closer while watching Sydney lay into Kayla.

It's close enough.

I move fast, snatch a length of my chain from the ground and loop it around his neck. The muscles in his shoulders flex as I yank back, his hands clutching the links, his fingers trying to dig beneath them. I tighten my grip. I won't allow him the space. He groans and slams me into the railing with his tremendous bulk. Something in my midsection cracks. All the wind rushes from my lungs. Still, I pull. *I will not let go*.

Spit flies from his mouth. He sputters and chokes. His fingers find mine and twist. Currents of pain spike across my knuckles, my vision turning white. I yank harder, and they fall away. I can smell his sweat, taste his salty stink. My arms scream for me to stop, that I can't keep this up much longer. Billy is too big. *Too strong*. But just as I think it, his right knee unlocks and buckles. His left. We thud down together, my biceps churning with lactic acid as I struggle to hold on, heaving on the chain until his neck turns purple.

"Let her go!" I snarl at Sydney, over his shoulder. "Or I swear I'll kill him."

I expect her to panic, to beg for his release. I expect her to drop the gun. She doesn't. She stands there appraising me coolly instead, her head cocked slightly to the side, the gun still pressed into Kayla's back.

"Go ahead."

Billy gives a rumbling cough, and his head tilts forward onto his chest.

"I'm serious," I say through clenched teeth. "Give me the gun and let her go."

Her lips carve into something resembling a smile. "Oh Chris, I thought you were smarter than this. I don't need Billy to make Clara happy. Or you, for that matter. Not now. After Kinley, all Clara's ever really wanted is a girl of her own. And now she has two. That is, unless you keep this up." She raises the gun and plants it against Kayla's temple. "The little one is all that truly matters."

Bits of static rain through my vision. "You're wrong, Sydney. It will hurt Clara if I do this. I know she loves Billy." I try to sound strong, resolute, but already the strength is dripping from my fingers and flagging in my arms. My voice is brittle-sounding and weaker than I'd like.

"Maybe," Sydney replies, "but not as much as she loves Emma."

Kayla's Adam's apple quivers as a dark stain soaks the material around her crotch. "Dad, p-please stop."

My fingers release their grip and Billy topples forward, choking and gagging, gasping for oxygen with wet, lurching breaths. I settle onto the gridded metal behind him, and a tidal wave of despair swamps my chest. What little leverage I thought I'd gained is gone . . . was never really there to begin with.

We're going to die here. She's going to kill us all.

After a moment, Billy works back to his feet with a ragged gasp. He gives me a wary look and coughs, his eyes watering. "That—" He hacks, spits. "That weren't nice. I dinn't do nuthin to you."

"He's right, you know," Sydney says, still staring at me, before turning to Billy. "And you need to be more careful around him." She shoves Kayla hard into his arms and nods at the body. "Now help her get him in the tank before he starts to stink."

"*At altitude, water boils at approximately one-hundred-ninety-four degrees.*"

The memory spreads through my mind like a sheen of oil, filmy and ill-formed, the four of us on Yellowstone's Fountain Paint Pot trail, a pimple-faced park ranger waving casually at a natural hot spring a few feet away. It was deadly, he said. A man had died at this very pool in the eighties attempting to rescue his dog. When he got out, his flesh came off in strips. He passed the next day, his entire body canvased in third-degree burns. The story surprised me. Water like that? It was stunning: a piercing, turquoise blue I couldn't imagine so thoroughly melting someone.

I don't have to imagine this.

Billy hefts the man by the torso, Kayla, by his legs. She looks like she's about to faint, her forehead pulsing sweat, her face pallid and gaunt. The water fizzles and pops as they set him near the edge, and for a sick moment, I expect her to fall in. She coughs and covers her mouth, glances my way. There's something broken in the look, all the light gone. And something else as well. A slash of doubt. *Should I do this thing? Should I destroy what is left of him?*

Sydney flutters her fingers at Kayla and then the roiling water. "Well, what are you waiting for?"

I hold Kayla's gaze and force everything I have into the look. All my sorrow and regret and shame. All my love. I want her to know that this is my decision. My burden to carry. Not hers. I nod and, together, they roll him in.

The man's hair unkinks first, the curls turning gelatinous before dissolving outward in a hazy brown cloud. His face whitens next, chunks of his neck peeling free and sloughing into the water. They look like the remains of undercooked fish meat flaked onto a fork. Bubbles of cheek fat render and break loose, pods of grease popping and hissing at the surface. His remaining eye liquefies and dissolves, followed by his nose and lips and ears. A blanched pocket of bone appears through all the viscera, the muscle shrinking back, turning sinewy and gray. My gorge rises, and I glance away.

Just end already. Please, God, just end this.

It doesn't. Even though I'm no longer looking, I can smell him disintegrating. It's a cloying, sweet stench that sticks to the root of my tongue and clogs the back of my throat. Saliva swells and floods my mouth, running over my lips in strings. The burning haze shifts my way and claws its way up my nose to eat away at my sinuses. I cover my mouth and try to pull in a clean mouthful of air, the mist in my lungs now, in my stomach. I gag and choke back my vomit. I won't give Sydney the satisfaction. Kayla isn't so lucky. I hear what little is left in her stomach splash off the concrete beneath the platform in between a series of jagged sobs.

Sydney looks on impassively, her arms crossed. "We usually seal it before turning on the broilers. It's not safe this way. Too many fumes. But unfortunately, we don't have that kind of time. It won't be long until they're out looking for him."

"What—" I cough. "What is it?"

She keeps her gaze on the vat. "Sodium hydroxide. Or lye. It's not all that hard to make, really. You'd be surprised at how effective it is. Digests a dead bull or horse in, oh, I don't know, about a day or so. A lot less time for someone his size. There won't be much left of him in a couple of hours. Maybe a few bone chips and hulls. But those can be cleaned up easily enough. His vehicle is another matter, but I know a place."

"Let us go, Sydney . . . please. We won't tell anyone about any of this. No one. I promise." My plea is weak, a splash of baby vomit she easily wipes off.

"You know I can't do that, Chris." She holsters the gun and kneels next to Kayla, who is still on her knees, dry-heaving through the grates. "I'd like to, but I can't. Not now. Unfortunately, Kayla has forced my hand." She strokes Kayla's hair with the back of her knuckles. "To discipline a child is the greatest act of love, for, in it, we punish ourselves."

Kayla skitters back, wiping the drool from her mouth. "Leave me alone!"

Sydney ignores her, lost in a memory. "Clara's father used to say that every time he dragged her to the Black Place. It took me a long time to understand what he meant. When Clara had Kinley, it finally made sense." Her eyes find mine. "A child isn't just a child. They're a piece of your soul. Something you can never recover once it's gone. You love them more than you love yourself, and the thought of punishing them, of hurting them in any way, shape, or form, is something a parent never wants to do. Chris, I'm sorry for this. Truly, I am. But it's the only way." She reaches into her coat pocket and retrieves a glass vial, tilts it toward the mesh-covered window beyond the vat so that the fluid inside catches the sunlight.

"Wait a minute, just wait. What are you going to do?" My words come out fast and choppy, soaked in panic. "Please, whatever it is, don't."

"Kayla has to be disciplined, Chris. Something like this . . ." She glances at the vat, at what remains of the man. "It can't ever happen again. Get her arms, Billy. Hold her down."

He rubs his head, stands there. "Miss Sydney, I don't think she needs no lesson. I think she learned it already."

"I wish that were true, Billy. But she hasn't. Remember what it took to teach you?"

His mouth sags into a frown. "Yes'm."

"And did you misbehave after that?"

"No, nuh-uh. Never."

"Then you know why I have to do this. Now grab her arms."

It's more growl than order, but Billy bends over all the same, taking Kayla by the wrists and stretching her arms over her head until her back is pressed flat against the grating. She fights him the entire way, screeching and spitting, trying to bite his hands, his neck.

"Leave me alone! Stop it, stop it, stop it!"

Sydney crawls on top of her, centering her bulk on Kayla's stomach as she twists and flails.

"Be careful, now," she says, unscrewing the vial to reveal a dropper. "You don't want me spilling this."

"Wh-what is that?" Kayla asks, suddenly going still.

Sydney tilts her head toward the metal tub. "Same as what's in there, but I bet you've guessed that already, haven't you? You're a smart girl, Kayla. And curious. A little too curious for your own good. I know you thought what you did this morning was right. Breaking the window and yelling at that poor man. But look what happened to him, because of you. What will his family think when he doesn't come home tonight? It's tragic, really. Especially for his children. You wouldn't want something like that to happen again, would you?"

Kayla shakes her head. "It won't. I promise. I swear. It will never happen again. Ever."

Sydney clucks her tongue and sighs. "Clara is a good woman, Kayla. She's got a good heart, a lot like you, I think. You'll learn to love her, and my hope is that someday you can come to see her as a mother of sorts. Of course, I don't mean to say she'll replace yours, but hopefully she'll hold a special place in your heart." She smiles. "You'd like that, wouldn't you? A new mother? Someone you can talk to and share your feelings with?"

Kayla nods. "Yes. But . . . but only if you stop. Please stop."

"I promise, you'll be happy here in time. But that's exactly what it will take, Kayla: time. Until then, we have to learn to trust each other, and clearly, I can't have you screaming from the windows whenever someone swings by for a visit."

"I won't. You can trust me. You can!"

"I wish I could. Truly I do, but I can't. Unfortunately, there's only one way I'll be able to trust you now." She reaches out and thumbs Kayla's eyelid, peels it higher. It hits me then, what she means to do to my daughter. She's going to blind her.

Kayla's eyes turn into those of a rabbit's, two glittering globes of fear whipping my way.

"No. No, no, no, no. Please, Dad, help me. Please!"

Sydney grabs a fistful of her hair and rips her head back to center. "Hold still now. Be a good girl for me."

Kayla squeals and closes her eyes. Tears snake down her cheeks. The dropper lowers, hovering over the bridge of her nose. "If you don't open them, I'll burn away your eyelids. And trust me. It won't take much. Then I'll keep going until your eyes are gone. Is that what you want, Kayla? Two nasty holes in your face instead of a few easy little drops?"

A cry escapes her lips, something inhuman and primal — pure fear. I see it then, all the way down into the future Sydney has planned for my daughter. A life stripped of color, spent shuffling through the bowels of her house, dressed in chains, pretending to love Clara. Smiling and calling her mother for fear Sydney will return and burn more of her away if she doesn't. I can't allow it to happen. I *won't* allow it to happen. Not after all Kayla's been through. Not after what I've done to hurt her myself.

I know what I have to do.

CHAPTER FIFTY-SIX

KAYLA

I sob and buck against Sydney, trying to gulp air, but it burns, and I think again of the man, of *Scott*, and how his face melted right before the acidic water turned his eye into a hard-boiled egg. It's what she wants to do to me. Dump that stuff into my eyes and turn them into the shiny plastic beads I sometimes see pressed into the faces of the blind people shuffling around downtown Boston asking for change. The thought swirls through my stomach, how much it will hurt, and I'm suddenly sick again, about to throw up, but there's nothing left, and Sydney is shifting her weight forward, planting her knees on either side of my head with her thumb and finger attacking my eyelid, trying to peel it open, telling me let's just get this over with, that it won't hurt *that* bad, Billy holding my wrists, me doing all I can to keep my eye closed, but I can't because Sydney's fingers are too strong, her face appearing as she slivers it open, everything around her blazing orange and pink, that's how hard she's pressing down, the dropper descending, the fluid inside bubbling toward the tip, dripping lower and lower.

"No, no, no, please," I beg. "Don't do this."

"Keep it open. Last chance, or I spray it all over your face."

I feel the wetness between my legs spread.

"No! Stop! Do it to me instead!"

Dad's voice comes in tinny and wild, and I think I'm imagining it, the dropper pulling back an inch as Sydney speaks.

"That's not the way it works."

"Yes, it is. She doesn't deserve this. I do."

An acid teardrop appears, clinging to the end of the dropper directly over my eye.

Ohmygod, ohmygod, ohmygod.

It falls.

I press hard into her thigh and jerk my head left. The liquid skims the side of my neck in a trail of fire. I lock the pain deep in my lungs and hold it there. I can't let it out. I won't. Not while Dad has her distracted. *Keep it in, keep it in. Do not let it out.*

"Children must be punished for their actions. You know that. They have to learn right and wrong."

"I *have* punished her! I've nearly destroyed her!"

The flame turns to molten lava, and the scream rockets up my throat before I can stop it. I shake my head and strain against Billy's grip, but he won't let go. My jaw is wide, wide open, every part of me pulsing and shaking. I'm crying so hard, I can't see anything but a dark smudge where Sydney used to be. I want her off me. I want air and space and a handful of cold snow on my skin, and—

"Jesus Christ! Calm down already! See what you made me do?" Sydney wipes my neck with her coat sleeve and rubs the fire deeper.

"I-I'm sorry," I blubber, still shaking. "It just . . . it hurts. It hurts so bad. Please let me up. I won't misbehave anymore."

"I know it does, sweetheart. I know." She sighs. "Now stop moving."

265

Her fingers drift for my eyelid again. My back arches and spasms as the dropper descends. *Nooooo . . .*

"I cheated on my wife, Sydney. I betrayed my wife, goddammit. I cheated on Lexi, and Kayla saw it. She saw everything, you *bitch!*"

A ripple runs through Sydney's legs, her muscles clenching. The dropper rises.

"I never told Lexi," Dad continues. "Not one single word the entire time she was dying. Kayla wanted to. She begged me to, but I wouldn't let her. I told her I would do it. I'm a liar and an adulterer and a coward, and I can't believe something as good as my daughter came from something as bad as me. So you take your goddamn hands off of her and you punish me instead, because she's been through enough already!"

A moan rolls out of Sydney's mouth and turns into a croak. It's low and coarse, like she's crunching on rocks. But it's worse than that, because I can see a dribble of blood leaking off her lip. She's biting it, I realize. She's chewing her lip apart.

"Billy, let her go."

She stands, and weight on my stomach releases. Billy follows suit, and I can breathe again, rubbing my wrists as I scuttle into a sitting position. Sydney crouches in front of Dad, and Billy joins her.

"Hold his eye open," she says.

"Okay, Miss Sydney, if you says so."

"That's right," Dad says, looking at Billy. "Do it to me." And then he glances my way with a whisper, the words sinking all the way down to my heart, to its very center, the place I never thought he'd reach again.

"*I. Love. You.*"

And then, before I can say it back, Billy has Dad's head tipped back against the railing ready to stretch his eyelid wide, but he doesn't need to because Dad already has it all the way open. Sydney brings the dropper down—

"That's right. You punish me. You leave my daughter out of this."

—and squeezes.

A cry like I've never heard explodes from his mouth. It's all pain, the sound of every nerve in his eye frying, burning away to nothing.

Goosebumps cover my arms, and I'm screaming with him, back on my feet and straining against the chain. I *have* to get to him, *have* to make this stop, make *her* stop. But I can't make it stop. I *can't*, no matter how hard I try. All I can do is cry and shout and slap my hands against Sydney's back like a maniac, sobbing as I do, crying so hard I'm choking, my voice breaking apart. Still, I attack her, grabbing her coat and pulling her away from him, trying to reach her hair so I can rip it out of her stupid head and—

The backhand comes hard and fast. I thump down with sparks shooting through my vision. Sydney's face twists into a snarl. "Get her back to the house, Billy. Lock her up tight and do *not* let her go this time" — she shakes the dropper — "or this happens to you, too."

Billy moves, his hands on my chain, reaching down for the padlock, his keys out, turning, a lock clicking. And then I'm free, and he's jerking me away from Dad. Dad, who I can't leave. Not after he gave his eye for something *I* did. *Not* him. But I'm not strong enough, and all I can see is him clawing at his face. All I can hear are his sobs as he convulses with tears streaming through his fingers and over the backs of his hands. And I have to get to him. I *have* to.

I raise my foot and am about to slam it down onto Billy's when a flash of silver stops me. The keys, *his* keys, are there, hanging off the lip of his pocket. I slap at them with a shriek, throw my weight into his torso as they fall and clatter onto a square of metal grating near Dad's hip. And then I'm wailing and twisting, fighting against Billy with everything I have because all that matters is getting his attention and Sydney's, distracting them long enough so they don't spot the keys.

"I hate you!" I shout at Sydney. "You'll never be my mother! Never!"

Her eyes cut to mine, hard and clear, so much hate there, and she doesn't see the keys. She only sees me.

"I hate you!" I screech. "I hate you, I hate you!"

I shout it over and over as Billy wraps his arm around my neck and drags me from the platform, down the steps, and across the concrete, my feet sliding in between rows of shelving units and past nameless pieces of farm equipment, all of it a blur, until I'm back outside in the biting cold with Dad's cries fading away.

CHAPTER FIFTY-SEVEN

CHRIS

Voices.

She did it. Jesus Christ, she actually *did it*.

Of course she did, you moron. After what you said, how could she not?

My God, it hurts. Make it stop . . . please make it stop. MAKE. IT. STOP.

I can't. You did this to yourself. You went and pissed her off and now look at you, you dumb bastard. You deserve it. You deserve every last drop.

No, not this. Never this . . .

* * *

Fingers.

Grasping and pulling. Prying.

Don't let them in. Don't you dare let them!

Raking and jerking, hungry to eat my other eye.

No! No, you will not give them what they want. They will not take what's left.

But they will. You know they will.

Pain.

Pain beyond pain.

Agony and misery. Torment and ache.

There are no words sufficient to describe the feeling of my sclera dissolving, of the acid burning deeper through the cornea and lens toward the delicate layer of vitreous fluid hidden beneath. It has color, the pain. A brilliant vermilion cut with searing webs of light. An electrical storm of suffering consuming what's left of my vision. I can taste the pain on my tongue, smell it in my nose. Ammonia and cat piss. Rust and metal.

And the fingers keep digging . . .

. . . and clawing.

And scratching.

The voice back now, a cockroach burrowing into my ears and pushing deeper toward my tender inner parts, each word a thrust of the head, a shift of the thorax, those hungry little legs skittering for the dark folds of my brain.

"Stop fighting, Chris. I'll be fast. Just a few more drops and it will be over with.

"Behave, goddamn you! Don't squirm!

"I'll still take her eye if you don't open up. It's your choice. Will it be you or her? Make up your mind."

The threat is enough.

* * *

My hand slides from what's left of my eye while the other blinks itself back to a blurry sort of life. Sydney appears in snatches through the agony. At first, she's a vague outline, a snatch of hair and teeth followed by an aimless impression of a face. She pulls closer, with eyes that are dark and feature-less and of infinite depth as the dropper descends, the glass materializing through the knife-slit space carved between my upper and lower eyelid. It's the last millimeter of color and light I will ever see. I know what I will become. A walking corpse with two pitted hollows for eyes. A gaunt-faced stranger casting about with a cane, the man the children point at while tugging on their mother's shirt.

Mommy, what's wrong with that man?

The acid beads, and I force my eye wider because it's worth it. For Kayla, it's worth everything.

The sound of hands on glass filters through the haze, the slapping muted and indistinct, faint, followed by a voice I recognize. Its tone and cadence, someone shouting through the window. The weight on my chest shifts, and Sydney goes rigid. Alert. She's looking at something. No, not at something. At *someone*.

Kayla.

Before I can register the movement, Sydney is gone, muttering to herself and spitting, striding down the platform steps and over the long stretch of cement toward the door that leads outside into the snow. There's a force to her steps, a violent intention, and I know, then, that she'll catch Kayla, and Billy. And that, when she does, the woman I know as Sydney will do something worse to my daughter than what she's already done to me.

Unless you stop her.

I focus on the thought, force it to the front of my mind and hold onto it like a life preserver as the searing blaze in my eye swells and courses through my head, dissolving my retina now, the optic nerve. I order my hands to move, and they do, searching, feeling, crawling down my leg toward the chain, all the way to the padlock and shackle. It's solid and immobile, a steel circle swallowing my ruined ankle from which there's no release, no space through which to slide my foot. There is only panic, a tangible, living dread thrumming in my chest, telling me I'll never escape and that Kayla is already dead.

No . . . No! Keep fighting.

I do, following the chain back to the iron railing, and then lower over the grate. It's hard to see, my good eye

271

blurring in sympathy for my weeping socket. My fingertips brush something out of place. A ring dripping with iron teeth. A shape I recognize. Billy's keys. But how?

It doesn't matter! Move!

I snap them up and, with shaking fingers, jam one key after another into the padlock, nothing fitting, the ends jamming again and again, until, with beautiful precision, one clicks.

CHAPTER FIFTY-EIGHT

KAYLA

The door bangs shut, and all I want to do is crash right back inside and get to Dad. He doesn't deserve what Sydney is doing to him, no matter what he's done. And he did it for *me*. The thought is a knife to the heart, and I twist against Billy and swing my heel back into his shin as hard as I can. It connects, but it's nothing to him. He doesn't even move. I'm like a mosquito trying to sneak a few drinks of his blood before he gets annoyed and slaps me away. "Let me go!" I scream, trying to jerk out of his grip, twisting in his arms until he spins me around with a finger smashed to his lips.

"*Shhh.* Your sissy's tummy's hurt. We gots to help her."

I don't know why he's telling me this unless he plans to — I go still, my anger clearing in an instant. "Where is she, Billy?"

Dad's cries echo through the shed, and Billy glances at the door with his eyes shining like headlights. "Shhh, be quiet. You gotta whisper. And you gots to make a promise to me before I can show you where she is." He looks back again, leans close. "Your sissy said your pa could help make Sydney go away with a doctor. Is that true?"

A doctor? I feel unsteady. I have no clue what he's talking about, but I nod anyway. I'll promise him anything if it means he'll take me to Emma.

"You have to swear it. That he's gonna help Ma get better." He raises his right hand and yanks off his leather glove, the one I've never seen him without. My mouth falls open as a slow puff of air shivers past my lips. Two of his fingers are gone, turned to white-pink nubs at the knuckles. The skin above the joints is scarred and knotted.

"She did that?" I mumble.

He nods, staring at me with his face tight and his eyes pleading. "Yep, and Miss Sydney'll cut off more if she finds out I'm being bad. She'll cut off yours, too. You gotta swear on it. Cross your heart and hope to die." He nods hard, bobbing his head up and down like it will help me do the same. I slide my hand over his, suddenly and blindingly aware that my father and I aren't the only hostages here.

"I promise, Billy."

"Okay," he says, handing me my chain. "Okay, let's go."

He barrels toward the stable at a full run. I follow, stopping after a few feet to glance back at the shed. Billy slows and waves me on. "C'mon! C'mon!"

"I'm sorry, Billy. I can't let her do this to him."

I turn and pound back through the snow toward the window. I can barely make out Sydney through the layer of dust on the glass. She's a blur on top of Dad, who's curled against the railing, fighting to pry his hands from his face. I make a fist and batter the window, banging on it until Sydney whips her head in my direction.

"Leave him alone, you bitch! Why don't you come and get me instead!"

Her eyes narrow to two black holes, and for a moment I can't move. All I can do is stare back with my stomach churning, unable to look away.

"She knows! She knows! We gots to run!"

Billy's voice cuts through the haze, and I back away, slowly at first, then faster, running toward the stable, pumping my legs until I can no longer feel the ground beneath my boots. Billy waits for me, yanking me forward by the arm as soon as I reach him, pulling so hard I nearly trip.

"Why'd you do that?" he gasps. "Why, why, why?"

He doesn't wait for my answer, and it's all I can do to keep up with him as he jerks and heaves through the frozen crust, running like the snow is a marsh sucking at his feet and about to pull him under. We reach the stable together and bowl inside in a headlong rush. I go snow-blind, blinking hard as we pass Phillip's stall, Billy pulling me toward a stack of hay bales piled high in the corner. My heart lurches when I see them, because there's nothing else there. No window. No door. Just a bunch of hay and wood sitting in a puddle of muddy light. It's a dead end.

"Billy! Billy, you get back here this instant!"

Sydney's voice is distant but feels like a gunshot, one that sets Billy to attacking the haystack, picking up the bales and flinging them aside like they're nothing more than pillows. He tosses the last one, and I'm left staring at a rusted storm door stamped into the floor like the one I spotted in the chicken coop yesterday. It's just as thick and heavy-looking, and I'm suddenly panicked Billy won't be able to lift it.

"Billy!"

"Hurry," he says, bending and yanking on the handle, heaving the door up. The hinges squeal, and we scramble down the steps together, the wood spongy beneath my boots, my hands out and feeling through the empty, black pool in front of me. Billy stops, and I slam into him. He slaps at the wall, muttering to himself, searching for something I can't see.

"Billy . . . you have been a naughty, *naughty* boy!"

Sydney's voice scrapes across my eardrums like a fork on metal. She's somewhere above us now and coming closer, her steps clacking off the boards, sending clouds of dust spiraling down into my eyes.

"Go, Billy," I hiss.

He doesn't, still searching the wall, smacking away until something clicks. A small cry erupts from his mouth as a string of light bulbs blazes to life overhead, illuminating a long, empty corridor with walls of black earth framed in wooden slats.

"Billy, you bring that little slut back this instant, and you won't be in trouble! I know she tricked you into doing this! It's not your fault, it's hers!"

"Go," I say, shoving Billy. "Go! Go! Go!"

He does, his elbows churning hard, his breath chugging in and out in fast gasps the same as mine, both of us pushing ahead together farther into the dark.

CHAPTER FIFTY-NINE

EMMA

My stomach hurts, and my eyes sting, and I can't breathe. It feels like someone is sitting on my chest. It keeps whooshing in and out, in and out like it does after I finish a big race. And my leg burns worse than ever. Like someone dunked it in a hot pot of water. And itches. I want to scratch it, but every time I do, all this green stuff comes out from under the bandage. Worse, it smells. I begged Billy for more medicine, but he said he didn't have any, that only Sydney did. But she was gone somewhere, and he didn't know when she'd be back, so he ran off to try to find some himself. That was forever ago, and I'm worried if he doesn't come back soon, I'll pass out. That, or maybe even die. I don't want to die. I just want Kayla or Dad to find me.

Why haven't they? Did Sydney do something bad to them, too? Did she lock them in a room somewhere like she did me? If so, maybe they're waiting on *me* to *find* them? I hope not. There's no way I can walk with my puffed-up leg.

Plus, I'm so tired. Beyond tired. Even with how bad everything hurts, I just want to go to sleep. I can't, though. If I do, I might not wake up again. I don't know how I know it. I just do. It's like I can hear Mom whispering to me, *Don't go to sleep, sweet girl. Not yet. Hang in there.*

I shiver and pull the blankets up to my neck and struggle not to close my eyes. The only thing that helps is thinking about Mimi and Papa and how excited they'll be to know I got my voice back. Mimi will smile and give me one of her big grandma hugs. The ones where she scoops me up so tight, I can smell her flower perfume and kiss her neck. Papa will get all teary and say something like, *Well, will you look at that,* and then take me out for ice cream to celebrate.

It's what I'm thinking about, taking a big bite of cookie-dough Blizzard from Dairy Queen, when I hear the noise. At first, I think maybe I'm dreaming, that I really *did* fall asleep after all — but nope, it's the frog door squeaking again.

". . . is she?"

It's a woman's voice, and even with how cold I am, I start sweating. And shaking. I don't want to see Sydney right now. I don't want to see her *ever* again. I just want to go home and play with Bernie and Hops and watch cartoons on the couch and have Dad feed me soup until I'm better.

I squeeze my eyes shut and pretend to be asleep as the footsteps come down the stairs.

"Ems? Ems, you down here?"

When I hear the voice, I sit up right away because — *Oh, my gosh* — it's Kayla!

I squeal her name and it comes out as a whisper. Her mouth falls open when she sees me, and she rushes over and pulls me into a big hug so tight, I can barely breathe. I've never been happier in my whole life! I start crying, saying her name over and over and over, not really believing she's here.

But she *is.*

She finally lets go and puts her hands on my cheeks. She's crying the same big crocodile tears as me.

Billy hops up and down. "We gots to go! Fast. She's coming!"

I know right away he means Sydney. I don't even have to ask.

"Oh my God, Ems. What has she done to you?" Kayla says, picking me up and feeling my head. "You're so hot."

"C'mon, hurry." Billy shakes his hands, looking *way* more scared than I've ever seen him before, which makes me scared, too. "Let's go, let's go!"

"Billy!"

The voice is distant, but I recognize it right away. Sydney.

Kayla's eyes go wide, and just like that, she's carrying me up the steps after Billy, going so fast, my foot bangs hard against her hip. Fireworks explode behind my eyes, and I nearly bite my tongue in half. I want to scream, but all I can do is whimper, because Sydney would hear. And she can't know about this.

She *can't*.

We run down tunnel after tunnel. The walls have boards and big sheets of plastic on them. It's dark, with only a few light bulbs here and there, which makes me worried Kayla will trip. She keeps stopping to readjust how she's carrying me, shrugging me upward so I can rest my chin on her shoulder. It hurts every time she does it, but I don't say a word.

The egg smell gets worse, and my belly does flip-flops. I'm afraid if we don't stop soon, I might throw up. Cobwebs hang from the ceiling and stick to my face. I brush them off and hope no spiders got in my hair. I hate spiders. One bit me once when I was little, and I had to go to the doctor for a shot. I was sick for a week. I hate shots, but not as much as I hate spiders.

We reach an old wooden ladder, and Billy climbs up toward a metal door in the ceiling. He pushes on it with both hands, and I expect it to open because he's so strong, but it doesn't even move an inch. He grunts and shoves again, and this time it squeaks a little before he gives up.

Kayla makes a panicked sound. "Billy, where are we?"

He looks down, and I can tell he's terrified by how high his eyebrows have climbed up his forehead. "The coop. This door gets us up to the chickens."

Kayla shakes her head. "Oh my God, Billy, it's locked! We have to go back. Tell me there's another way out of here!"

"Th-there is. I know a tunnel that goes to the fields — but we have to hurry or Miss—"

"You aren't going anywhere."

Sydney's voice ties my tongue into a slippery knot. Billy climbs down, and I see Sydney walking toward us all hunched over, looking like one of the zombies from the horror shows Kayla likes so much. My heart *whoomp, whoomps* in my chest as she gets closer. She's even scarier-looking in the shadows, like a Halloween skeleton. But that's not even the worst part. The worst part is what she's got in her hand. I've seen them on TV shows and in cartoons but never in real life before. It's a gun. One she raises and points right at me.

CHAPTER SIXTY

CHRIS

I keep pressure on my destroyed eye with one hand, the other out and fighting for balance as I push through the snow toward the stable. My stomach is wrapped so tight around my esophagus, I can hardly draw air, let alone think. My brain struggles to compensate for my newly misaligned vision, my eye muscles quivering, dragging me farther right with every step. It's disorienting. A slow, queasy march with the sun slicing off the white macadam in bright shards that make it impossible to see. I stumble, and my palm slides down my face and back up again, the sticky circle of napalm still burning through my head like radioactive fallout. My eye socket is all fluid and fire, blood seeping hot over my cheek and running into my mouth. The world around me flickers and pops. Tears course down my face in frozen streams. I totter and nearly collapse.

Lie down. Just lie down.

No — keep going . . . Don't stop. You can't stop.

It's like someone else is speaking, this stranger in my head begging for me to surrender, telling me to give in to the pain and fatigue. That I've *done enough* . . . But I haven't.

After this, after the hell Sydney has inflicted on my girls, on *me*, it will never be enough.

I groan and shove onward. Every step is a battle, every foot gained a victory. Images appear as though in duplicate, the stable splitting into two and breaking apart, the corners and edges blending together and melting down the walls in gluey colors. Trees blur and shift, form skeletal shadows on the horizon. The snow is an empty white sheet stretching for miles, a frozen wasteland impossible to cross.

The pain shifts and intensifies, blooming outward through my skull with an ache I can feel in my intestines. Sweat threads over my neck and cuts down my spine. All of me hurts; every single inch of my body is a fire waiting to be put out. I tell myself to *breathe*.

Breathe.

In, out, in.

Now move, goddammit. Save them.

I lurch into the stable and float down the aisle in pictures: Phillip and a pair of wet ring nostrils pushed over a stall door. A shovel crusted in manure propped against a support beam. A snatch of sheet metal roof caught in the rising wind. It's empty and desolate: a building without secrets, without hope.

I round the corner and curse myself. It was there. It was there all along, hidden beneath the stack of hay bales now flung to the side, the staircase I know will lead me to Emma. To Kayla. It was there and I missed it.

I move for it with a fresh wave of anger spitting through my blood. *You will not take them from me.* The thought blazes and churns, burning itself into my brain, my very DNA — *You will not take them* — as I descend the stairs and disappear into the dim wash of light below.

* * *

The smell hits me first — a vile miasma of sour air and rotten mud. The scent of sulfur is so strong I can taste it. I spit it out and force myself down the tunnel. It's long and black, framed in a patchwork collection of two-by-fours and timber posts riddled with wood rot. A string of light bulbs blinks above me, the bulbs running ahead into the dark with a faint trail of color. I move more by feel than sight, my feet clacking against squares of plywood and wet patches of earth that suck at my boots and threaten to pull them off. I keep my palm pressed to my eye, the blood dripping in between my fingers like oil, like warm streams of wax. The pain is blowtorch bright, a million fiberglass splinters working through my skull at once.

I try to focus on something else and think of Clara and her red shock of hair as she welcomed us into her home. The green-ocean eyes and wary gaze as I laid Emma upon her couch, Emma staring up at her later as Clara cupped a hand to her cheek and told her everything would be okay. "*Shh, sweet girl. Shh.*"

Sydney now, with a cigarette smoldering between her lips and that broken engine voice leaking out, her posture so different than that of the woman who met us at the door, a stranger with scarecrow limbs.

Run, Chris. Focus and run.

I do, flying, tamping down the fire, locking it somewhere deep. Forcing my feet to go faster . . . and faster yet. The bulbs flashing past: light. Shadow. Light. Shadow. Images of wood and grime. Walls carved from black earth. That smell of sour eggs and burning metal stinging my nose, my tongue, my ankle feeling as though it will implode.

Run, Chris. Run.

* * *

I hear Kayla first, her voice winding down the tunnel distant in a plea that punches me in the heart.

"No, please . . ."

I slow and catch my breath. Waves of vertigo crash against my temples and threaten to send me spinning to the ground. I stop and gather myself, then press closer toward the voices. They hang in the air like ghosts, beckoning me forward and to the right, down a long, empty expanse and through a rancid column of air flavored like old pennies. Left now, listening, listening, following the words as they grow louder, stronger. A final right, my vision fluttering again, my equilibrium shot, feeling as though I'm walking through yards of ankle-deep mud until I finally reach them.

Sydney stands illuminated beneath a flickering bulb at the far end of the tunnel, the gun raised toward Kayla. Kayla, who has something clutched to her chest, a girl with matted hair spilling over a skeletal pair of shoulders. Familiar shoulders. *My God. Emma.* Billy stands stiffly next to them with his hands up, his face bunched and tight with fear. "I-I won't let you hurt 'em, Miss Sydney. Not this time. Not like you made me do to Lillypad. You has to hurt me first."

He steps in front of Kayla, shielding both her and Emma with his broad torso, and my heart splinters.

Sydney tightens her grip on the gun. "And to think your ma thought you'd be a blessing when she stole you away all those years ago."

I slip silently around the corner.

"Go away!" Billy shouts. "Go away and leave us alone!"

Sparks swirl, a fresh bout of nausea welling from somewhere behind my diaphragm. Warm liquid drips from my eye and splatters on my wrist. *Get to Sydney. Reach her.*

"You got your daddy killed, Billy. Did you know that?"

"No, I dinn't. Pa runned away from us. Ma's told me so a hunerd times."

"Your ma *lied* to you, you stupid boy. She's not even your real mother! Your father was a bad, bad man, Billy. He cheated on your ma with some little slut he met down in Rifle. You belong to her, not your mother. You're a bastard, Billy. One she should have left behind years ago."

Billy shakes his head. "No . . . no . . . no . . . no . . ."

284

"Oh, it's true. Clara stole you right out of your crib. Then she brought you back here because she couldn't bear the thought of being alone, even though she was *never* alone."

He covers his ears and shakes his head. "Stop it! Shut up! Shut up!"

I reach the bank of shadow near the far wall, slide into it and ease toward Sydney in a low crouch.

"She stole you from your daddy, Billy, and he tried to get you back. Clara should have let him take you, but she didn't, and that made him mad. So mad, I had to kill him before he killed her. I knew — I *knew* — you'd be the death of her, Billy. And now you will be." She spits to the side. "After what you've done today, I'll never let you see your ma again."

"No!"

Everything happens at once: Billy roaring and rushing her with his face tied into a snarl. The clap of the gun, and the blast reverberating down the tunnel in a heaving groan. Billy stopping like there's a chain tied around his waist, thumping to the ground ass-first. Kayla crouching to cover Emma as Sydney raises the gun to shoot again. Me charging her before she does.

Kayla's gaze cuts my way. Sydney sees it and whirls, the barrel rising like an empty black eye.

I skid to a stop and bring a hand up. "Sydney, don't."

The gun trembles. Spirals of dust clog the air. She swings the nine-millimeter toward the girls and then brings it back to me. It wavers as she coughs in a long, wet hack. A cough that isn't a cough, I realize, but a laugh. Jesus, she's laughing, the sound crawling up her throat from somewhere deep inside her chest and worming into my ears.

"Look, girls," she says, leering at me. "Daddy's here. Isn't that sweet? Now we can finish this like we should: as one big happy family."

CHAPTER SIXTY-ONE

SYDNEY

No one speaks, the only sound that of Billy fish-gulping air as he clutches his stomach. A grim circle of blood darkens his beige overalls. He stares at it, then looks up. "Wh-why, Miss Sydney?"

I had to. For Clara, I had to.

I wave at the wound as if it's nothing more than a scratch. "You'll be fine. You've had worse."

"We need to get him to a hospital," Chris croaks.

"No. We aren't going anywhere."

Emma moans and dissolves into a full-body cry. Her sobs lodge in my brain. Shrill icepicks. I can't think with all the racket, can't process what to do next. Kayla pleads for her to stop, but she won't, writhing and clutching her leg, screaming for Chris, and I'm suddenly shouting at her: "Shut up! Shut up! Shut! Up!"

Her cries fade and turn to snuffling whimpers. After a moment, Kayla glances toward Billy. "He's bleeding. We have to help him."

"No! No one is leaving," I snap. "You're going to listen to what I have to say. All of you."

And they are because it's what Clara wants. I can feel her whispering to me, telling me I can trust them with the truth, even now after everything they've done to her. To *us*. Kayla breaking the window to yell at the man. How *dare* she put Clara in danger again after all these years! How *dare* she.

And Chris with his mind games, his lies and deceit. He acts like he cares about Clara, but he doesn't. He's like every other man who only tells her what she wants to hear. Like John, as he feeds it to her in sweet, bite-sized spoonfuls. "*My father wasn't the best man, either.*" It's all so obvious. Why can't Clara see him for who he is? Why does she still think anyone will love her like I love her? Or go to the same lengths I will — and have — to protect her?

Because you allowed it to happen.

I have. So many times, even after swearing I never would again. John. Billy. Lillian.

An image of the girl leaps to mind. Lilly, with her spiteful pout and red-faced tantrums — the way she bit and hit and scratched whenever Clara tried to take her into her arms and hold her. To comfort her. How she rejected Clara's love with her '*I Hate Yous!*' How she trampled on it with her shrill, snot-nose cries to '*Get away from me! You're not my mom!*' until Clara broke all over again . . .

With Emma, it was different. There wasn't the same fear. Or hate. The way she looked at Clara . . . it was like Emma needed *her*, like Clara was all that mattered. And the way Clara stared back, I knew she needed Emma just as much. I hadn't seen her look at anyone in that way since Kinley. It was like Emma filled all the hollow space Kinley had carved from behind her ribs.

She made Clara . . . *happy*.

So I took the girl. I thought I could control things, like I always do, and it fell apart, like it always does. And now I have to hurt them. I have to make sure Clara never wants something like this again.

But first, they'll listen.

I wave at the ceiling. "Believe it or not, this entire farm was under water before they dammed the river. Clara's grandfather thought there was gold down here. The fool went broke digging for it, nothing to show for his work but all these godless tunnels and a place to tie his noose.

"After a while, most folks forgot about the mine, but not Clara's daddy. No, he made sure to put it to good use. He said it was for his special time. That's what he called it. 'Let's go see if we can rustle up some gold and have us some special time, Clare Bear. Just you and me.' And Clara always thought if she did what he wanted, maybe someday he'd love her the same way she loved him. She never learned there was no pleasing that man. Still, she always had this *hope*.

"Her mother was worse. She could have stopped it. Anytime she could have stopped it. But she never did. She just sat there and *watched*. Imagine that, Chris, your mother watching your father do things like that to you? Violate you. Penetrate you. It's unfathomable."

My voice cracks on the last word, and I think of Clara stuffed in the Black Place all those years ago when I first met her, her face splattered in dirt and ash, so alone. So broken. Anger swells dark in my chest.

"But still, Clara hoped. She never *stopped* hoping. Her mother used that against her. She'd fill Clara up with a kind word here, a hug there, only to suck her dry a moment later. She was a vampire, that woman. Her neck snapped easy enough on those stairs, though. Even easier than I'd expected." I shrug. "See, Clara? It's not so hard to stand up for yourself. All it takes is a little accident."

Chris raises a hand, looking unsteady, half his face covered in a waterfall of blood. "Sydney, please lower the gun. We can talk without it."

"Stay where you are," I hiss, leveling the gun at his chest. "I'm not done yet, and I'll be damned if I'm letting you anywhere near me after what you did to Billy." I risk a quick glance his way and know I need to hurry. He's breathing too hard, his chest moving too fast. Clara can't see him like this.

I bring my gaze back to Chris. "Anyway, where was I? Oh yes, Clara's old man fell apart after that bitch died. I made sure to let him suffer her loss for as long as I could before I finished him off. It was far more painful than anything I could inflict."

"You s-said—" Billy coughs, blood flecking over his lips. "You said G-Gramps k-kilt her."

I shoot him a withering look. "Don't interrupt me, Billy. And I never said that. That was your momma's lie."

His face buckles. "Momma w-would never lie!"

I snicker. "Oh, she would, and she did. All the time, in fact. She'd say whatever it took if it meant she didn't have to deal with something difficult. But not me. You should have seen your grandpa's face when I told him the truth about what happened to your grandma. 'That's right,' I told him. 'It was no accident. I pushed her. I shoved her as hard as I could.' I said it right after he finished his oleander tea."

I arch an eyebrow at Chris. "It's such a pretty plant, oleander. Have you seen it? No? It's amazing what those delicate pink petals will do to someone's insides. It makes it look just like a heart attack." I twist my lips and clutch my chest, mime a gagging sound. "You should have seen the way he choked. It was the funniest thing, almost like he'd bitten into a lemon." I smile at the memory — one of my favorites.

"Clara, I—"

I wag the gun at him, and he falls silent. "Don't interrupt me." My smile fades. "Here's the thing, Chris. Clara fought me even then. Can you believe that? She still wanted to protect him, after all the horror he'd inflicted on her. Just thinking about it makes me sick. *Sick.*" I shake my head, disgusted. "Clara's always been so weak for love, even though all love's ever had for her was ruin. And she'd finally come to accept that, was doing just fine on her own, until you all came along."

"Ma. Please," Billy chokes. "Don't h-hurt'm. They ain't done nothin' wrong."

My lips pinch, and I turn on him. "How many times do I have to tell you not to call me that?"

Billy lifts his head from the hard-packed dirt. His cheek is caked in ash, and his lips tremble as he speaks. "I don't care what you say, Ma. I don't care. I'll call you it 'cause I love you. Even when you're Miss Sydney, I love you. Even when you hurt me. If you has to hurt them, you do it to me instead. I won't be mad. You can hurt me all you want. Just don't hurt no one else no more."

I stare at him, suddenly at a loss for words. I'm not his mother. I've never *been* his mother, this broken creature John left behind for Clara to raise. This burden I've helped her carry for two decades. I've told him a thousand times, *a million*, but something about the way he's looking at me right now *hurts*.

"Clara, don't you see?" Chris says, wheezing hard. "If that's not love, I don't know what is."

"No. No more of your tricks," I snarl.

He glances at Billy and shakes his head. "I could never fake something like that. Jesus, Clara, he loves you. He loves you enough to give up his *life*. You want a family? Well, it's right there waiting for you. You have to fight for him, Clara. You need to fight!"

My arms twitch, and a hard shiver breaks across my skin. The gun grows heavy in my hand, as heavy as a brick. As heavy as my heart. It's always been my love for Clara that has kept me from doing the thing I now must do. I never wanted this for her. Not *this*. But it's that exact same love spilling down my finger as it wraps around the trigger and swings the gun from Chris toward his girls, and then higher, until the barrel comes to rest in a cold circle against my head.

"I love you, Clara," I whisper. "I love you so goddamn much."

And I mean it.

CHAPTER SIXTY-TWO

CLARA

I'm floating over layers of white marshmallow crust toward the stable, the sun sparkling off the slanting roof, turning the snow to ice, and the ice to a frozen slush that drips from the eaves and hangs from the gutters in the shape of icicles. Sydney leads, and I drift after her, watching her anger rise like steam from her shoulders. Her steps are forceful, her pace hurried, and a sense of doom spreads through me, a scream lodging somewhere behind my sternum. We reach the stable door, and she glances back and tells me to wait for her here.

"I'll be back soon. Don't follow me."

Okay, I lie. *Okay.*

I trail behind her, walking silent down the steps and into the mine where a creeping darkness folds in around me and blurs the edges of my vision until I can no longer see. Sydney moves ahead with a speed I struggle to match, the darkness hungry to consume her.

"Sydney," I call. "Sydney!"

There's no answer save for the encroaching black.

I walk for what feels like hours with my hands trailing over the plastic-sheeted walls and my feet shuffling across soft beds of coal and splintered plywood. Time slips and spins. Cries come in low and distant like voices carrying across a smooth body of water. There's something . . . wrong here. Something . . . *off*.

Panic creeps down my spine. I want to, *need* to, find Sydney, but I'm lost in this place — a bad place with air that has texture and taste, a mouthful of spoiled eggs peppered with metal and rust. I realize it's all around me, the reek. Filling my nose. Saturating my taste buds. Curling in through my sinuses and sliding down the back of my throat. The panic blooms from my spine and leaches into my bloodstream.

Whatswrongwhatswrongwhatswrong?

And with it, words . . .

". . . it hurts so bad. Help me, Ma!"

Billy's voice slices through the fog, and I can suddenly see again. See *him*. He's on the ground, curled on his side with his hands clutching his stomach, his fingers red and dripping.

Why are they red? What could possibly make them so red?

But then I spot Sydney with the gun, and I *know*.

She gives me a look, and in that look is a sadness heavier than any I've ever seen her carry. It covers her like grease, running from her forehead and into her eyes, dripping down the creases and folds of her face, pooling in the corners of her mouth.

"I'm sorry, Clara," she says.

And then she's raising the gun, the black steel barrel climbing higher before coming to rest against her skull. Billy shouts, and the girls wail, and Chris pleads for her to stop, but it's my voice that keeps her from doing the thing she can never take back.

"Sydney, no!"

Her finger twitches but doesn't jerk.

"What are you doing?"

"It's the only way." Her voice is wounded and fluttering — an animal dying on the side of the road.

"I don't understand."

"To heal, Clara. You have to heal. *We* have to heal."

Behind her, Chris is saying something, his mouth open, his face weeping blood. It slicks over his cheek, saturates his neck and shirt. So much blood. *Why is he bleeding? What did Sydney do to him?*

The gun wavers and falls, then rises again in a swift arc toward Chris as Sydney shrieks for him to "*Shut up, shut up, shut up!*"

He's still talking, though, words rolling off his tongue in waves that don't make sense as he calls her *Clara*. Says that I am her and she is me and we need to give him the gun.

"Just give me the gun, Clara."

His words rip into me, *through* me, punch holes in my lungs until there's not enough light and air in the universe left to fill them.

Then I hear it . . . a voice leaking through the madness, soft and broken.

"I love you, Ma. Don't let me die."

And it's that voice, *Billy's* voice, that pulls me forward and fills me like a river.

I'm nine again, suffocating in the Black Place, pushing against the hatch like I have for so very long. Pushing until my legs burn and my elbows pop, knowing it doesn't matter, that the hatch never opens — it *never, ever* opens — until it does. The latch breaks, and I see her for the first time, Sydney, with her black hair shining and her hand brushing mine. My sweet Sydney, looking down with that smile, and I love that smile. Oh, how I love it, and oh, how I love her.

"Would you like to come out?"

Cool air rushes over my skin. I'm in our forest skipping across a bed of pine needles. The smell of sap and earth hangs rich in the air, and I see her racing in front of me, her feet kicking hard for our cabin. The sun drips warm honey, and we are free, and we are alive, and we are together, and we are whole. And for the first time in my life, I am happy.

Inside now, the air warm as a blanket. Sydney is there too, with Mr. Oatman's cat lying so still in her lap. Her tears patter onto his soft, orange fur and she pets him and prays that he'll open his eyes because she didn't mean to hurt him, she *never* meant to hurt him, not like this, but he doesn't, and we bury him outside in the deep loam beneath the bur oak as Sydney promises to never, ever do it again.

Time spins and drifts and, *oh God*, I'm in the woman's house now, *her* house, watching Sydney pull the trigger of John's shotgun. There's a kick, followed by the moist reply of bone shards and pulp splattering over the wallpaper. A sob bubbles up from somewhere, a moist gurgle.

A piercing *mwah! Mwah! Mwah!* Chases us down the hall and out of the house into the cool night air, where we can breathe again. Where we can think. Sydney tries to leave, but I can still hear the cries, can feel them sink into my heart and tug me back through the open door, where I see it all with fresh eyes. The blood tracked everywhere, through the living room and down the hall. The hair and gristle and wet ruin of the woman's face splattered over the bedroom floor.

It's too much, the sight of her, and I'm about to run, but the cries hold there, pulling me ever closer to the crib. And there he is — my sweet Billy. Billy with his tiny, clenching fingers and his round, cupcake cheeks. Billy with his mouth opening and closing like a bird abandoned to the nest, waiting for a mother that will never return. It's then I know that, without me, he'll die. He'll shrivel and fade away into nothing. So I take him, and I flee.

They pulse faster, the memories. Holding Billy in the kitchen as John lunges for me. How fresh and pink Billy's skin looks as he spins, helpless, from my arms. How strong John's hands are around my neck as we fall with him. John's fingers squeezing, forming an iron fetter above my collarbone. The knife as it glitters at me from the dishwasher, and how I bury it deep in his neck. The taste of his blood fills my mouth, and his weight squeezes the air from my lungs. So much weight . . .

294

The years drift from there. The farm blooms and dies, and there is nothing I can do, because Billy is all that matters now, and no one can know. No one must *ever* know. They will take him, the severe-faced men who visit and question John's disappearance, who rigorously search the house and tear through the woods with their dogs. They will snatch him away, and I'll never see him again. But they won't because he is hidden, and I am not a suspect. I am a tragedy, a cliché they've seen far too many times. The philandering husband. The wife betrayed and abandoned, left to fend for herself with no means to do so. I'm no murderer. John is. He killed his mistress. He took his bastard and ran.

The story is splashed across newspaper and magazine racks, featured on talk shows and newscasts in all its salacious glory. Pictures of John smiling (*Have you seen this man?*), of *her* smiling, the woman who stole my husband, who lived the life I was meant to live. She has a family, this woman. Ashley is her name. Ashley with the gray-haired parents who are desperate to find her, and the two siblings who weep and dab appropriately at the corners of their eyes with handfuls of tissue as they talk about how much they miss her. Oh, how they want her back, back, back. They haunt me, these images, these words, so I rip the television from the wall and break the computer, and all of the noise and fear and doubt seeps away.

All of it except for Billy.

Billy. Something about him is . . . wrong. Off. He's difficult and needy, and his body doesn't work like the other boys I sometimes see in town, bopping down the sidewalk next to mothers who ignore the miracle of their easy movement, who shoo and hush them and tell them to run off and play so they can have a few precious moments to themselves. Women who don't love them the way I would love them, if they were mine.

But they're not mine. Only Billy is, and he's broken, and Sydney breaks him further when he runs. She does the unspeakable thing in the basement, and it nearly destroys me.

I find myself on a bridge of blue iron, staring down at a river running angry and loose with rapids that look like storm waves. The water is green and dense, and it wouldn't take much to slip beneath it, to join its ceaseless march to the ocean. To slip into its beautiful, black nothingness. The wind scrubs my hair and tickles my skin, and I know it's right to take that last step when Sydney appears.

Sydney who says nothing, simply stares across the water at the girl on the swing set dressed in a blue lace skirt and rainbow shirt with a comet of butter-yellow hair arcing out behind her. She tells me she knows how to fix it, this dark mood I'm going through. A way to ease my suffering and breathe life into me once more. She'll heal Billy, she tells me. This girl will glue him back together again.

She does. He smiles for the first time since Sydney took his fingers. He comes to life in a way I never thought possible. She plays his games, and laughs at all of his jokes, and holds his hands. But it comes at a cost. Both Sydney and I are monsters in her eyes. The girl cries and scratches and spits whenever one of us comes near. It doesn't matter who, and finally, Sydney can take no more . . .

We bury her in the cornfield along with the tattered bear of Billy's she clung to all those hard nights, and I think about Mr. Oatman's cat and how Sydney promised to never do it again, something like this. She promises it once more: never again. And I can tell by the way her voice splits down the middle, she means it.

Never again lasts for years. We isolate. We bury ourselves in each other — Sydney, and Billy, and I. The three of us are life and love and all the family we will ever need. But then comes the knock and the cinnamon-haired girl cradled in her father's arms. It's dangerous to invite them in — so very dangerous that it's like walking out onto a thin sheet of ice. Still, the girl is injured, and I can't leave her and her family to freeze on the porch, so I do what I must.

The ice holds. It's fine, *we* are fine, until the girl utters the word that sends me crashing into those frigid depths.

Mama. Suddenly, I am right back in that dry-lit hospital room, holding Kinley, pressing her head against my chest. I taste warm salt and I know my heart will never beat again—

Mama.

—unless it beats for this girl.

So I take her . . . and *I make her mine.*

CHAPTER SIXTY-THREE

CHRIS

"I-I took her, didn't I?" Clara's voice. The gun falls from her temple. Her face is sunken and bleeding mascara. It coats the hollows beneath her eyes and paints thin, black trails down her cheeks. "It was me. It's always been . . . *me*."

"Yes," I say, edging toward her. It's impossible to tell how close I am. Maybe a few feet. Maybe a dozen. My depth perception is ruined, obscured by the acid rotating further into my skull with each step, unleashing molten needles of fire that splinter and burst in my brain. "Let me help you, Clara."

A tremor runs down her arm. "No. I'm not . . . safe for you." She glances at Billy, at the girls. "For any of you."

My lips peel apart to tell her it's why she needs to give me the gun, but all that comes out is a long, slow puff of air as her posture stiffens and the voice returns, the one that sounds like she's talking with a throat full of weeping scabs. *Sydney*.

"All I've ever wanted was for you to be happy, Clara. To be loved. I'm the only reason you survived Father's cruelty. Mother's and John's."

A sob — Clara again: "I know. You taught me how to survive. I learned from you. But you have to let me go, Sydney."

My mouth is numb, my face a wet sheet of blood. "Clara, I—"

"Don't." The gun climbs in a smooth arc, her eyes dulling into Sydney's asphalt glare. "You *can't* have her. I won't *let* you."

My breath catches in my chest, my entire existence narrowing to this moment. "Is that what Clara wants?"

Tears curl down her face. She's in pain, in agony, her face twisting into a terrible coil of tension. "It doesn't matter *what* she wants."

"Doesn't it, though? Isn't that all that's ever really mattered?"

The gun sways and erupts. White fire blazes from the barrel. Dirt rains from the tunnel ceiling. My ears burst and ring. I grow aware of Emma shrieking, of Kayla crying and begging for Emma to calm down and to be quiet.

"Shh, Emma. *Please*."

"Clara . . ." I can barely hear myself speak through the ringing in my ears, turning my words to cotton. "I know you don't want to hurt us anymore. I know you're a good person. Which is why you have to let us go."

The mask of pain tightens, then breaks. "Oh god, oh god, oh god . . . what's wrong with me?" Clara tears at her hair, pulls out a fistful by the roots. The barrel ticks back and forth dangerously. And then she's looking at me with tears snaking past her nose and outlining her lips. "*Go! Go now!* Take your girls and go. I don't know how long I can hold her back."

"Daddy!" Emma cries, and I'm moving, limping toward them, forcing my legs to work, ignoring the agony ripping through my head in waves — a dark riptide of pain threatening to drown me, to pull me under before I can get us outside, get us away.

And then . . .

299

And then.

My hands are running over Emma's face — *my Emma, who is still alive, who is too hot and thin and fragile in my arms* — and cupping the back of her head. I'm crying, pulling her close and asking if she's okay, telling her we need to go. Telling Kayla we need to *run*.

Another flare of white light erupts behind us. A sharp, thunderous clap that sends a cloud of dust shivering down around us. Emma screams. Kayla skitters back. With a heavy swallow, I turn and step in front of them. Sydney stares at me with her eyes in slits, the gun steady in her hand and aimed at my forehead. Sydney, whom I can barely see through the fountain of flame still burning into my eye socket, and the blood weeping, weeping, weeping down my face.

"You can't have them. They're *mine*," she says.

"No, they aren't," I reply. "They never were. They're mine, and they've always been mine. And I'll gladly trade what's left of my life for theirs."

A shiver rakes her body. A cold, drumming wind. I brace for the bullet. For the hot metal that is about to punch through my skull and send me howling into the void. Instead, an awful keening wail fills the air. A gurgling cry.

"Ma! Don't do it!"

Billy.

He writhes in a tight ball, clutching his stomach, from which leaks a dark gutter of blood. A sob rolls up Sydney's throat, and she tilts her head back and screams. And then she's rushing forward, toward me, then past me, to kneel at Billy's side.

"Ma? Ma, is that you?" he chokes.

The gun stutters and falls from her hand. "Yes, baby, it's me. I'm here. I'm not going anywhere." She looks up at me, eyes bright with panic, Clara staring back once more. "Hurry, Chris! Please. Get help. I don't know how much longer he has left."

I nod, tears burning down my face in hot streams as I take Emma into my arms and help Kayla to her feet. Her hand is cold against mine, clammy and wet. I tighten my grip, and we limp away from Clara's crumpled, weeping form. Her voice filters after us, low and soft — a final whisper uttered in the dark: "Stay with me, Billy. Stay with me, and I promise I'll never leave you again."

CHAPTER SIXTY-FOUR

EMMA
TEN YEARS LATER

The building isn't much to look at: a beige, brick rectangle coated in cherry-red trim, stamped in between two equally dreary apartment complexes. It's one of those places you pass without much thought, and if you were to give it any, you'd probably think, *Hey, now there's a place I wouldn't want to live.* You'd think, based on the crispy, yellow lawn and all the cracked asphalt, that it's full of people who are stuck. People who dream of a house with a backyard and some space to move around but can't afford it. That's exactly what you'd think as you drive past, wiping the place from your mind a moment later.

But you'd be wrong.

Valley Acres is nothing like that. Especially on the inside, where it's bright and full of light. There are these big, rectangular skylights carved right into the ceiling that the residents love to stare through as they sip their tea. They sometimes make a game of it and point out shapes in the clouds only they can see: mountains and windmills and daisies.

Sometimes they even paint them. I've seen their work, and it's great.

That's the thing, the residents here, well, they're full of light, too. That's what I love about them. Everyone here likes visitors. They go out of their way to talk to you and to smile and wave. They really *see* you, unlike in Boston, where most people would rather be wherever it is they're going than where they are. That, or glued to a cell phone. But this place, it's different. And there's one person in particular here I miss almost as much as I miss Mom sometimes, even though we write letters and talk on the phone most weeks. I only wish Kayla were here with us, like she normally is, but she has a new baby named Olivia with a head full of chocolate curls who giggles like crazy when you tickle her. She's the cutest thing I've ever seen. Kayla says she'll come with us next year, when Olivia is old enough.

"You ready?" Dad asks, squeezing my knee.

"Yup," I say.

"Let's do it, then," he says, opening his car door with a smile.

* * *

Inside is buzzing. Probably because it's Thanksgiving. A pack of blond-haired boys dressed in wrinkled suits weave around the furniture like miniature fighter jets. The youngest, a toddler clutching a sippy cup, follows behind them blowing raspberries. A woman with cherry-red lipstick snatches him up and tells him, "This isn't the place for roughhousing, Ian." He squirms and laughs, and she can't help but smile at him. Neither can I.

"Reminds me of you and Kayla when you were younger," Dad says, watching them with a bemused grin. "You two were pretty crazy sometimes."

"Really?" I ask.

One of the boys slams into a side table and sends it crashing to the floor, along with a pile of wooden coasters and a china set. The woman issues a small cry and darts after him.

Dad laughs. "Well, maybe not that crazy, but close. Wait here. I'll be right back."

He goes to check us in, and I find an empty chair in the corner and make sure my present is still in one piece, which, of course, it is. I've only checked it about a thousand times. *He's going to love it*, I think as I re-tie the bag. It took forever to pick out. It's glittery blue with a herd of white horses caught in full gallop, racing toward a setting sun.

A palm slips over my shoulder, and I look up to see Dad nodding toward the dining room with a wink. "He's waiting for us."

I take his hand and stand, notice the slight wince in his cheek as he pulls me to my feet. Most people wouldn't even see it, but I know cold weather hurts what's left beneath his eye patch, which isn't much. When people ask him what happened, he mostly laughs it off and says something like, "*I tripped*," unlike the old days when he wouldn't say anything at all. It took a long time for that to change. He kept us close for years, scared whenever Kayla and I even mentioned going somewhere without him.

Not that I can blame him. It wasn't easy. We were big news for a while. You wouldn't believe how many crazy reporters followed us everywhere we went. Or maybe you would. I was too young at the time to know that was a thing — how much people loved to watch other people suffer. There was even a *Dateline* special on us a couple of years after the investigation wrapped, and a Lifetime movie we never watched. Dad did whatever he could to shield us from the media and all the attention, which was a lot. Too much for anyone, really.

It went into hyper-drive after they found the remains of Lillian Roberts, Clara's first experiment at a daughter. She'd been missing for more than a decade. Her mom turned up on the news a few times, this small woman with thinning hair and a nose like a bird's beak. She choked up whenever she talked about Lilly and how she disappeared from the park near their house early one summer morning. "*I lost my little girl that day. I lost my life.*"

Hearing her say that hurt my heart. It still gives me chills to think that could have been me. Or Kayla. I guess that was one good thing that came out of our time with Clara: Kayla seemed to love Dad again. I don't remember a lot from when I lost my voice, but I do remember how pissed off Kayla was all the time, especially at him. Oh man, she was so pissed. She never told me why until a few years ago. We were sitting at a picnic table near Houghton's Pond one lazy July afternoon after taking a hike, and it just spilled out of her. I didn't even ask. I was disappointed in Dad for a while. But you know what? It helped me realize everyone makes mistakes from time to time. Even Dad. It helped me learn that it isn't the mistake that matters so much as what you do afterward to make up for it. And Dad made up for it big-time with Kayla, even though it took him a while. They have lunch together every Tuesday, and I don't think Kayla has missed it once in the last ten years.

As for me, well, I still miss Mom, even if I can't really picture her face like I used to. I know Dad does, too. Sometimes, I catch him staring at her paintings when he thinks no one's around. There's this one in particular he loves of him and Mom before Kayla and I were born. They have their arms wrapped around each other, in Maine somewhere, staring across this lake with all these red-and-yellow trees crowding the bank. Dad is looking at her with the biggest smile you've ever seen. It's great, but my favorite part is Mom's hair. It's the color of a newly ripened strawberry, and when I stare at it, I can sometimes hear her laugh again. My hair will never be as pretty as that, but I don't mind. Dad tells me I got her heart. He says that's what really counts, how you treat people, not what you look like. I learned that from Billy, too.

* * *

We trail into the dining room, and I'm the first to spot him. He's sitting in the corner with his back to us, talking to himself and straightening the tablecloth like it's out of place, which, of course, it isn't. I sneak up behind him and slip my hands over his eyes with a laugh.

"Guess who?"

He whirls around and his face splits into a massive grin. "Ems!"

He leaps to his feet so fast his chair tips over. He pulls me into a bone-crushing hug, and I hug him back just as hard, until Dad claps him on the shoulder.

"How you been, Billy?"

"Hiya, Chris," he says letting go of me. He pulls back and waves at the room "Did you guys see all this great food? It's the best meal there is all year! I love Thanksgiving. You gotta try it!"

"It looks wonderful," Dad says with a laugh, taking a seat.

"Guess what?" Billy asks, his eyebrows popping.

I can't help but smile. "What?"

"I'm resident of the month! Me!" He jabs a finger at the wall where, sure enough, there's a framed picture of him with his cheeks shining like freshly waxed apples.

"That's great, Billy," Dad says, chuckling. "Really great."

"It means I gets to choose my own seat in here all month. I get a extra cookie, and they read all about me and how good I been. They do it all month."

He tells us the other perks. There's ice cream in the afternoon and his choice of what to watch on movie night. He has the first pick of any board game he wants to play, whenever he wants to play it. While he talks, I notice the gray streak running through his beard. It makes me sad to think he's getting older, his baby face fading away. Not his eyes, though. They're still bright and full of warmth. They weren't always like that. Especially in the early days. The doctors said the bullet missed his liver by an inch. Any closer and Clara would have killed him. They say it's a miracle she didn't.

He doesn't talk about her as much anymore, but when he does, it's like watching a sail deflate. He still misses her, I can tell. He says she misses him too, and I believe him. I don't remember much about the day she nearly shot us, except this look coming over her face, like someone had pulled the shades up and she could finally see again. Billy says she calls him once a month and that, with good behavior, she might be able to visit him in a few years. For his sake, I hope she's right.

The conversation drifts as it always does. Stories about Billy's friends and how much he loves Jango, the house tabby cat. ("*They even let him sleep in my room sometimes!*") Dad fills him in on Kayla and baby Olivia and how sad Kayla was to miss this trip. I tell him about how I want to be a vet someday and help animals like Jango when they get sick. He smiles and claps his hands. He tells me how happy that makes him and how much he misses Phillip, that Phillip was the very best friend he ever had, outside of me, of course.

"Oh," I sputter, remembering the gift bag at my feet. "I have something for you, Billy."

"Really? What is it?"

I reach below the table and snag the bag and hand it to him.

He stares at it, his eyes widening. "Wow, I never seen such a pretty bag before."

I laugh. "Well, look inside, silly. That's the real present."

He tears into it and lets out a slow breath when he sees what's at the bottom. He gently slides the horse figurine free and cups it in his hands.

"Oh, wow, wow, wow."

I know what he's thinking. Phillip. It's the reason I bought it. It's a hand-painted Appaloosa with rich, cream circles painted over the hip. The eyes are coffee-colored and reflect the light in two perfect, gleaming beads. The second I spotted it on the shelf in the gift shop near Public Park, I knew Billy had to have it.

His mouth trembles, and he looks up with his eyes stained pink. "It's him. Oh my gosh, it really is. It's Phillip." He strokes the horse's back with a finger and sucks in his lower lip. "*Phillip* . . ."

I scoot next to him and lay my hand on his. "Oh, Billy, don't cry." My throat tightens, and I know I'm close to tears myself.

He sniffs. "It's just — it's the nicest present I ever got. Ever." He sets it on the table and then pulls me into a hug. His tears form little circles on my shoulder. When he pulls back, he's smiling and wiping his eyes, and so am I. Dad looks on swallowing hard, nodding at both of us like maybe he's about to cry, too.

"It's for when you get lonely," I say, patting Billy's arm.

"Thanks, Ems. But I don't get too lonely no more. Not since I met you guys. And I gots lotsa friends here. They're real nice to me."

"That's good, Billy."

His jaw tightens, his eyes creasing at the corners. "Make me a promise, okay, Ems?"

"What's that?" I ask.

"Promise that no matter what, you's and I will always be friends."

A wave of heat floods my chest. It's ironic. All Clara wanted was someone to love who would love her back. And she had that with Billy. He *was* her family; she just couldn't see it until it was too late. And now, after everything that's happened, he's become a part of ours. I reach out and take his hand tight in mine and smile. "I promise, Billy. No matter what."

And I mean it. It's a promise I can keep.

THE END

THE JOFFE BOOKS STORY

We began in 2014 when Jasper agreed to publish his mum's much-rejected romance novel and it became a bestseller.

Since then we've grown into the largest independent publisher in the UK. We're extremely proud to publish some of the very best writers in the world, including Joy Ellis, Faith Martin, Caro Ramsay, Helen Forrester, Simon Brett and Robert Goddard. Everyone at Joffe Books loves reading and we never forget that it all begins with the magic of an author telling a story.

We are proud to publish talented first-time authors, as well as established writers whose books we love introducing to a new generation of readers.

We have been shortlisted for Independent Publisher of the Year at the British Book Awards three times, in 2020, 2021 and 2022, and for the Diversity and Inclusivity Award at the Independent Publishing Awards in 2022.

We built this company with your help, and we love to hear from you, so please email us about absolutely anything bookish at feedback@joffebooks.com

If you want to receive free books every Friday and hear about all our new releases, join our mailing list: www.joffebooks.com/contact

And when you tell your friends about us, just remember: it's pronounced Joffe as in coffee or toffee!

CPSIA information can be obtained
at www.ICGtesting.com
Printed in the USA
LVHW100816030723
751369LV00006B/585